THE JURY SERIES

THE JURY SERIES

ALL FOUR COMPLETE NOVELS

JUDGMENT
ADJOURNED
PAYBACK
GUILTY

LEE GOLDBERG

Originally published in paperback as *.357 Vigilante #1* under the pen name "Ian Ludlow" by Pinnacle Books, March 1985

Special thanks to Jerone Ten Berge for the cover art and Eileen Chetti for proofreading.

TABLE OF CONTENTS

JUDGMENT

BY LEE GOLDBERG

For Linda and Tod, who know better.

PROLOGUE

Esther Radcliff was trying to pull a fast one on Father Time, Mother Nature, and the human eye. And was failing.

One morning five months ago Esther looked in the mirror and saw a wrinkled, gray-haired, sixty-eight-year-old widow with age spots staring back at her. That day she declared war. She enrolled in the Beverly Hills Nautilus, saw a doctor about her aging breasts and age-beaten face, and spent $4,293.37 on shiny, satin polyester jumpsuits, Head sportswear, leg warmers, Chic jeans, Fila sweat suits, Izod polo shirts, Nike tennis shoes, and three pairs of high-heeled leather boots.

She bought herself a twenty-two-year-old bisexual, blond-haired struggling actor to sleep with and be seen with, read Harold Robbins and Judith Krantz and Sidney Sheldon, discussed orgasm and California politics at the Hard Rock Cafe and Ma Maison, and roamed the streets of nearby Westwood on weekends to soak up the college scene.

She signed up for aerobics, trying to work off decades of scrambled eggs drowning in butter every morning, traded in her Cadillac Seville for a BMW 633, and even went to an X concert. Yet, she could still hear Father Time laughing at her. Laughing hard.

Esther's skin was now golden brown, her face stretched tight, her breasts firm, full, and high, her body covered with the right names, and she thought and talked about all the right things. But one aspect of Esther Radcliff hadn't changed—she still walked her dog, Samuel, every morning, rain or shine, good or unhealthy air quality.

It was 11:15 Thursday morning and already 101 degrees. The brutal Santa Ana winds seemed to sweep down on the city from some giant, unseen '67 Chevy's exhaust pipe. Esther coaxed Samuel from his Tudor doghouse, fitted his bony legs into blue doggie leg warmers, clipped on his leash, and led him to the street.

She put on her headphones and flicked on her belt-clipped Walkman, luxuriating in the few moments of silent tape before the latest from Oingo Boingo blared in her head.

Her Samuel seemed to get slower every morning. She tried to instill in Samuel the same youth she had acquired but it didn't seem to work. He just refused to get excited about his doggie designer jeans, rhinestone collars, and private beautician. He just kept on growing old. And sick. And that made Esther very uneasy.

For now, though, she was content just to get him walking and get through her morning ritual. Somehow listening to Oingo Boingo and all the other new music seemed easier if she did it while walking Samuel. Sometimes she would imagine she was listening to Ol'Blue Eyes singing "Fly Me to the Moon" and she wouldn't hear Oingo Boingo, wouldn't notice the street, wouldn't care about her problems, and wouldn't come out of it until Samuel whined and she discovered she had been dragging the poor thing for blocks.

Esther was falling into one of those trances again this morning. Sammy Davis was singing "That Old Black Magic" to her, and her body was naturally slim and sleek—the tan came from San Monique and her smile came from genuine self-satisfaction. She didn't notice the metallic blue Monte Carlo slide around the corner behind her, low and growling.

Samuel stopped and whipped his head around. The passenger-side window rolled down slowly. A round, smooth face smiled behind the descending glass. Esther pulled Samuel down the sidewalk, his nails scratching white marks in the cement. That old black magic had Esther in its spell…

The round-faced boy laughed with the others in the car and aimed his Saturday night special at the label on Esther's gray jumpsuit. Right on her surgically refined ass.

Esther hardly noticed that first, sudden gunshot until the slug slammed into her and lifted her off her feet.

The car was alongside her when the second bullet exploded "That Old Black Magic" and blazed a trail of fire through her stomach and into her neck. She saw the beautiful red rose blossom on her chest and heard Frank Sinatra call her from the bottomless black pit. She swan dived into the blackness and waited to feel his arms around her.

Samuel scampered down the street, his leash drawing a thin red trail on the sidewalk.

The boys were delirious with laughter. The gunner closed one eye and looked down the barrel of the Saturday night special with the other.

"This is for ten points, man," someone said in the backseat, snickering.

He fired at the dog and missed, raising a divot on someone's front lawn. Samuel yelped and kept running.

"Fuck!" The boy aimed again. "The goddamn son of a bitch ..." He pulled the trigger just as Samuel dashed around the corner. The bullet ricocheted off the pavement.

"Shit!" The boy slammed his palm against the driver's head. "Faster, asshole."

The Monte Carlo screeched around the corner, fishtailed, and then roared down the road after Samuel. The dog looked back and the boy fired, tearing off Samuel's head just above the rhinestone collar. The four leg warmers strutted to the edge of the sidewalk and then buckled under what was left of the tiny body.

The Monte Carlo jumped the sidewalk, crushed the headless torso, and skidded off down the street, leaving a trail of blood, rubber, and laughter in its wake.

⚜ ⚜ ⚜

Two days after Esther Radcliff settled her bets with Father Time and Mother Nature, Oscar Lee was blowing kisses to Lady Luck—for once his friends and family weren't the only ones having dinner at his restaurant. He didn't know how, but finally the Bit of Italy had been noticed. And in a big way. There were actually people waiting to be seated.

Oscar knew it would happen, eventually. After all, the restaurant wasn't exactly new. It used to be Vito Sorrento's Bit of Italy, a buffet that featured pizza, spaghetti, ravioli, minestrone soup, salad, and a low price. It sat just on the edge of Chinatown and did a good business. The picture on the sign, of a fat Italian eating an oversize wedge of combination pizza, was practically a neighborhood landmark. So when Oscar bought old Sorrento out, he kept the name, kept the sign, and kept the Italian cuisine. But the only bit of Italian in his buffet was some thin sausage-and-cheese pizza wedges squeezed between the *chashu* and Mandarin beef.

Oscar didn't kid himself: there was frozen pizza that tasted better than his. The Chinese cuisine, however, was top-notch for the greasy-spoon trade. He had his mother and wife in the kitchen supervising the cooking. They were experts.

Oscar smiled at the waiting patrons. He could actually smell the money in their pockets. He looked at his customers stuffing themselves on overflowing plates resting on "Great Sights of Italy" place mats. If Lady Luck walked into the Bit of Italy, he'd escort her to a table and then make savage love to her on one of those place mats.

At the table of honor (or as he called it, the "Big Spenders Table"), the big table under the gondola-shaped chandelier, were four three-piece-suit-clad executives. Young, clean shaven, well paid. He liked them because they were talking a lot, eating little, and ordering lots of booze. At the worst table, the one in the corner near the kitchen door, sat an overweight family of seven who

Oscar was certain were stuffing food in their pockets, purses, and cleavage when his back was turned.

The "pizza wheel" buffet table beside Oscar was filled with steaming entrees in wedge-shaped trays, and people were waiting two-deep to get at it. Oscar smiled again. They were even eating the pizza.

For a moment Oscar let himself drown in the pleasant clanking of silverware, animated discussion, and people milling around the cash register.

A scream rose above the comforting sounds of success. It was the unmistakable voice of agony.

A deep silence fell like a shroud over the dining room. Oscar's bowels rolled. He looked at the obese family, frozen like propped-up mannequins in their seats. A glass broke in the kitchen. Then there was a loud crash, a cry, pots and pans clanking against one another to the floor.

Lady Luck blew a kiss to Oscar and kicked him in the cojones.

As Oscar stepped forward, eight grinning youths, eyes alight with malevolent joy, burst through the kitchen doors and began firing into the crowd. A waterfall of bullets swept through the room, upending tables, riddling the walls, splattering glass, and twisting people across the floor in obscene, blood-splashing dances.

Two bullets tore into Oscar's chest, spinning him around like a top and bouncing him off the buffet table. Oscar, feeling little pain, grieved for himself as he lay on his side and felt the hot flush of his fleeting mortality.

The slugs caught the four executives and slammed them against the wall. They slid slowly to the floor, covering the wall with bloody self-portraits of violent death.

The storm passed for a second. The boys, in their sleeveless T-shirts and faded jeans, hard faces and grim smiles, took in the scene with a breath. Sweat glistened on their faces and dampened their chests.

Lady Luck, in a red nightgown, lay down beside Oscar and pressed herself against him.

"Fuck, JD, that goofball in the White House is tryin' to kill me. I swear t' God he's got a picture of me on the wall he tosses darts at." Moe, sitting on a stool in front of Saul's tiny hot-dog stand, slurped down his Coke and scratched his belly, which hung over his belt and hid his Pacific Railroad buckle. Every so often Moe would lift the flab and show whomever was occupying the stool next to him the silver buckle he got after working the rails for twenty-five years.

It didn't look like it was worth twenty-five years. Then again, neither did the silver star on JD Macklin's hard, rigid chest. The big cop, sitting beside Moe, rested his elbows on the counter and rested his head on his hands. Macklin shared a weary grin with Saul Rosencranz, whose grin always seemed weary.

"Between that nut and the railroad it's a miracle I'm still alive today. I'm lucky I got twelve cents in my pocket. Damn lucky." Moe tilted the glass until a mound of crushed ice slid into his mouth. Moe, short and cherubic in a Munsingwear cardigan and double-knit, green polyester slacks, practically lived at Saul's hot-dog stand. Day or night, Moe was there dishing out his own brand of political commentary. "The president should stop pussyfooting around and just line up all us poor old folks, all the niggers, all them pregnant girls, all them Mexican fruit pickers, and just gun us all down. Bang, bang, bang! That's what he'd like to do—bang, bang, bang!"

Macklin's stomach growled loudly, which was good, because Saul's food tasted good to him only when he was ravenously hungry. Saul, his pants buckled just under his pigeon chest, handed Macklin a chili dog and leaned forward on his elbows. "Isn't this a beautiful night, JD?"

The searing Santa Ana winds had pushed the thick smog out of the Los Angeles basin, leaving a soothing, clear pocket of air over the city. The stars shone brightly and the city was framed by mountains usually hidden by the brownish haze. Macklin felt warm, the sort of soothing warmth he felt while nestled in bed on a cool morning.

"Sure is, Saul." Macklin took a bite out of his hot dog, catching the chili dribbling down his chin with a napkin. "Why don't you close up early and walk with me?"

Saul smiled. "And who'll guard your patrol car while you're gone?"

"Moe." Macklin grinned, knowing Saul would have another excuse. He always did.

"And who will keep him company while he's guarding your car?" They laughed the easy laughter of long friendship.

Saul looked beyond Macklin to the peaks of downtown Los Angeles, the dark monoliths against the moonlit clouds.

Towering in front of them all was the Silver Tabernacle, which reflected the night skies and the city lights in its stories of shimmering mirrored glass. Looking at it made Saul feel old, insignificant, and weary. Always weary.

"How much you think that fella Simon spent on that Silver Tabernacle?" Saul asked.

"Shit, it's not what *he* spent—it's what those suckers who watch him on TV spent," Moe said, chewing ice. "I heard the guy is gay. A fairy, you know?"

Macklin grinned. "The guy is smooth—you have to give him that. Real smooth. That TV preacher has style."

"Style, shmyle. That guy doesn't impress me. I agree with Moe. That mission of his down the street is nothing but a den of thieves. I wish that schmuck would stay in his silver tower and keep his missions out of our neighborhood."

"C'mon, Saul, there isn't anything I can do about that mission. They haven't committed any crimes. Christ, I'd rather see a dozen of those missions than one bar like the Pistol Dawn or one Nat's Pawn Shop, you know."

"If he said, 'Simon says cut off your wang,' three million people would drop their pants and reach for a meat cleaver. Ain't that criminal?" Moe said. "The way he talks, you'd think God was a fuckin' bank."

Macklin reached deep into his pocket and pulled out a crumpled bill and some change. "Say, Saul, gimme another one of those chili dogs, will you? I'm in the health-food mood tonight."

Saul swept the money into his hand, joking, "JD here is gonna put me through college."

They laughed again and Moe asked for a second helping of ice. When the chili dog was ready, Macklin scooped it up and ate it as he walked down the street. Monday was winding down. Shopkeepers were drawing their barred curtains across the outside of their windows and padlocking them. Waving to Macklin as he passed.

Emil the shoe shiner gave Macklin his nightly nod. "How ya doin', JD?"

"Real good, Emil. How was business today?" The tall black man wore a flowered shirt over his hunched torso and had wisps of gray in his hair.

"I'm gonna eat," Emil laughed. "Some days, that's enough." He turned and shuffled away. Macklin kept walking, munching on the chili dog.

He paused outside the Pistol Dawn and peered through the window. Fat Tommy smiled from behind the bar and motioned Macklin inside with broad arcs of his arm. A large group of guys huddled under the television set watching football. Macklin smiled his thanks and moved on. Tommy shrugged his shoulders. Cops made him nervous anyway.

A couple of kids on the street skirted Macklin as if he were a great white, not wanting him to chide them about being on the streets this late. Macklin grinned. He and the neighborhood were one and the same, and he liked it. No, he *loved* it, especially at night, when they looked at him with that familiarity, that respect, that security. That look, more than the gun strapped to his waist or the badge on his chest, gave him the strength he needed to maintain a semblance of law and order on the streets.

He had long since given up the idea of ever getting ahead of the crime. It was just a matter of keeping things reasonably in check. But lately, Macklin realized, things were getting bad. Rumors of gang violence kept getting back to him, and each story he heard was worse than the last. He resolved to get to the bottom of it, at least the part of it that happened on his beat.

Macklin still believed that being a police officer meant something, that it was a social responsibility accepted with pride and honor. He didn't see any reason why Sergeant Joe Friday or those fine boys riding around in *Adam-12* couldn't exist. It was a stereotype he embraced.

He could have been a detective by now, a desk boy, a gray four-door Plymouth Fury kind of guy if he had wanted it. He didn't. Above all else, police work always meant the streets to him, a blue uniform and a gun holstered securely against your side. The few guys still around who had attended the academy with him made a point of ignoring him, not wanting to associate with some nut who willingly flattens pavement when he could let his fingers do the walking from the fifteenth floor of Parker Center.

"Hey, Joe."

The voice was almost a whisper but broke through Macklin's thoughts like a scream. He broke his stride and stopped, listening for another sound.

"JD?" The voice implored from the alley Macklin had just passed, "C'mere, I gotta talk with you."

Macklin sighed, turning back and walking to the alley's mouth. He recognized the squeamish tentativeness behind the words. It was Enrico Esteban, the Bounty Hunters gang's nervous errand boy. Every now and then someone would put a scare into Esteban and he'd go running to Macklin for help. In return, Macklin pumped Esteban for information on gang activities. Lately, Macklin had been using Esteban to ferret out the truth behind the rumors the cop was hearing on the streets.

Esteban's constant nervousness made Macklin uneasy. The cop tried to keep their meetings as short, and infrequent, as possible.

Macklin peered into the darkness. "Where the hell are you, kid?"

"Back here, man." Esteban was scared, Macklin realized. So what else was new?

"All right, I'm coming." Macklin reluctantly swallowed the remainder of his chili dog and stepped into the shadows. The moon cast a narrow beam on Esteban's pockmarked cheeks and large, frantic brown eyes. The kid had a fleeting, uncomfortable smile on his face.

"What's your problem, Esteban?"

"I got no problems, JD." The smile jittered. "But you do."

Macklin's internal alarm went off too late. As he reached for his gun, someone grabbed his arm from behind, wrenching it back until his tendons screamed. Before Macklin could react defensively, two guys sprang on him from the darkness and spun him around.

He saw the alley closing in on him and then felt his nose smash apart like an egg, bursting with blood and cartilage. Intense pain bore deep into his head like a screw, leaving him limp and disoriented in his captors' grip. The alley walls whirled past him and he found himself facing a dark-complexioned youth, just over five feet tall, a tight sneer underscoring his pencil-thin mustache. His hands were behind his back and he shifted his weight anxiously.

Macklin recognized him immediately: Primo Manriquez, leader of the Bounty Hunters gang.

Esteban, his smile gone, slipped quietly into the darkness behind Primo. "Howdy, Officer." Primo's sneer grew into a sadistic smile as he approached Macklin. "How are you doin'?"

Macklin swallowed, his mouth thick with the sour taste of blood. "You're making a big mistake," Macklin said quietly.

"Really?" Primo laughed. "Shit, man, you *are* a mess. What you need is a bath."

Primo nodded and Macklin was forced to his knees.

Macklin, breathing hoarsely through his mouth, glared into Primo's gray eyes and strained against his captors.

Primo smiled down at him. "Time to wash up." He brought a rusted gasoline can out from behind his back and tipped it over Macklin's head. Macklin felt the gasoline splashing over him, soaking his wound with a sharp, stinging pain that brought tears to his eyes. The heavy fumes churned his stomach. Macklin closed his eyes tightly, trying to choke back the rising bile and overcome the pain.

"Pick him up," Primo said with disgust. Macklin was pulled to his feet and pushed back against the wall.

Through the blur of gasoline and tears, Macklin saw Primo strike a match. The flame was sharp and cast a glow that flickered on the youth's face. "I'm gonna barbeque a pig."

Primo met Macklin's gaze, searching for a trace of fear, and found none. It unnerved Primo, and Macklin knew it. A small, final victory.

Macklin spit into Primo's face. "Fuck you, shorty."

Bertrum Gruber sucked gently on the chalky antacid tablet as he leaned forward and cranked the steering wheel, twisting the groaning bus through the empty intersection.

The bus smoked and coughed its way down the street while Bertrum thought about his favorite *Honeymooners* episodes. He was trying to take his mind off the Hoagie Steak sandwich that crouched in his stomach like a brick. The next time he took a shit he figured he'd have to bring along some dynamite to clear the pipe afterwards.

Ralph Kramden, as immortalized by Jackie Gleason, was the only hero Bertrum could identify with. Bertrum had a nagging wife and a shithole apartment and drove a bus full of noisy punks and smelly winos just like hapless Ralph. He never missed an episode, rushing home for the two a.m. rerun on the UHF channel that *never* came in clearly. Under his driver's seat he kept a ninety-eight-page handwritten script for the ultimate *Honeymooners* episode. Should a Hollywood producer ever step on the bus, Bertrum planned to convince him that the world was waiting to see Ralph and Norton become folk singers. Bertrum had even written the songs.

The acid bubbled in Bertrum's stomach as he wrestled the bus around the next corner. A light of flame burst out of an alley, screaming across his path like a crackling fuse. He knew his eyes were playing tricks on him again; it looked like a human being at the center of the flaming torch.

Bertrum gasped, choking on the tablet and wrenching the wheel hard to the left. The back end fishtailed and swatted the burning body into a row of parked cars. The bus started to roll, hesitated on two wheels, and then slowly regained its equilibrium.

Bertrum lay across his huge steering wheel, gurgling for air, the right side of his head pressed on the horn, filling the darkness with a wailing bellow.

A speeding Camaro screeched within inches of the bus before Bertrum saw it veer away, plowing through the window of the Pistol Dawn. The customers fled as the car splintered the bar apart and smashed into the wall just under the TV set.

An instant later he saw another car closing in on the bus. He closed his eyes.

POW! ZOOM! To the moon, Alice!

Bertrum was knocked to the floor by the impact. An explosion rocked the bus, lifting the tail end up like a teeter-totter.

The customers stumbling out of the Pistol Dawn cowered against the searing heat of the flames that enveloped the bus. Arms of fire seemed to reach out to the adjoining buildings, wrapping around the structures and spiraling upwards. The customers scrambled down the street and could hear glass shattering like firecrackers in the inferno behind them.

The flames were licking the night sky when the local precinct desk sergeant, eating from a bag of corn chips, got the first call. The woman wanted to report an earthquake.

CHAPTER ONE

Now, this is a fucking car.

Long, sleek, and black, the body arced forward like a wave. The shiny front grillwork, sharp and mean, tapered back to a pair of sharp fins that sliced the air so bad you could swear it whined.

Now, this is a fucking car.

"What are you doing, Brett, waxing the car or making love to it? Shit, I can read your mind. It's written all over your face. 'What a car.' It's another dinosaur, that's what it is. I'll keep my Chevette, thanks."

Brett straightened up and wiped his brow with the back of his hand. "It's more than a car, Mort. It's an experience."

Mort groaned. "Wait, wait, I know the next golden words that are gonna come out of your mouth. 'You haven't driven a car until you've slid down the road in a fifty-nine Caddy.' Gimme a break, will you?"

Brett grinned, damp with sweat in his UCLA jersey and dirty jeans. "You're a real asshole, you know that, Mort?" He bent over the trunk of the car, rubbing a rag across the black finish. "Turn on the set."

Mort finished his Tab, crinkled the can, and shuffled across Brett's garage to the cluttered workbench, flicking on the black-and-white portable and tossing his can amidst the tools and auto parts.

A great gray fuzzstorm filled the screen.

"Smack it, Mort."

Mort slapped the side of the set, kicking up dust, and Elias Simon filled the screen, heading full throttle towards the end of his evening sermon.

"Simon says it's time to give some WORTHSHIP, to give to the Lord and show Him the VALUE of His work, to give the money that can keep this ministry and Jesus alive in our sin-ridden city."

"I love this guy," Brett said."Best comedy on television." He caressed a Caddy fin with his rag.

"So, lemme tell you about my date last night." Mort popped open another Tab and adjusted himself on three weeks' worth of the *Los Angeles Times.*

"Shoot."

"... *Simon says give; Simon says HE must know the value of your faith* ..."

"First I took her to McGinty's for a drink. Course, I had a club soda."

"Yeah, I bet."

Mort Suderson had been an LAPD copter pilot until one night, while blind drunk, he flew over downtown Los Angeles and dropped wine bottles full of piss on city hall, superior court, Mel's Meat Burgers, and a sleeping derelict.

The derelict, who took a shower for the first time in seven years and needed thirty-seven stitches to patch up his wounds, filed a $3.2 million lawsuit against the city.

Mort was promptly fired.

Brett hired the boozing pilot, on the recommendation of Brett's friends in the department, and brought him to work as a mechanic at his Blue Yonder Airways hangar at the Santa Monica Airport. Once Mort dried out, Brett used him as a pilot on a limited basis.

Although he was sober most of the time, Macklin suspected Mort still courted the bottle.

"Hey, I don't get bad drunk, you know that." Mort swished the gulp of Tab between his cheeks like mouthwash and then swallowed it. "Only thing that happens to me when I'm drunk is that I think as fast as I talk."

Brett glanced at the set. Simon, trim and crisp in his blue suit, his eyes sparkling, moved along the stage like a cat on a fence.

The television audience applauded and Simon soaked it all in with a broad grin. "*What are you saving your money for? Material things? A new Mercedes? These things won't bring you closer to HIM...*"

"She had blond hair and dark eyebrows," Mort said. "I couldn't help thinking what color her pubes were, ya know? It was a sick thought but I couldn't help it."

"*... use your money in a way that will make HIM proud. Come Judgment Day the Almighty doesn't want to see your Mercedes. He wants to know you helped His ministries, that you helped bring JEEESSSSUUUUSSSSS to others.*"

"Her boyfriend is a urologist. He's in Boston now. She's good people. She's interesting." Mort looked at Brett, who was rubbing down the driver's side of the car and shooting glances at the set. "Hey, are you listening to me?"

"Yes, yes. She's good people. So, what happened?"

"Nothing happened. We went to her place, she talked about her boyfriend, and I left. I'm seeing her again tonight."

"Uh-huh."

"I think she wants me, Brett."

Brett groaned. "C'mon, Mort. It's always the same story. You always say they do and they don't."

"No, I can feel it. I saw it in her eyes: *I want you, Mort Suderson.* It was right there." Mort finished his TAB and winced. "I just gotta get over this premature ejaculation thing. I don't mind it, but they always do."

Brett grinned. "What's the workload like this week?"

"Not too heavy. I'm flying some exec types to Fort Lauderdale in the morning, and some movie crew wants to take the chopper on a spin over the valley. The rest of the week looks pretty light. I dunno."

"So we'll be spending some time in town, then?"

"Yep."

Brett straightened up and stretched. "Finished. How's she look, Mort? Beautiful?"

"It's just an old Caddy. Just like the three others on the front lawn."

"Maybe to you." He caressed the hood. "But this is a fuckin' car."

The phone rang.

"Gotta go, Brett." Mort waved and headed for the side door as Brett dashed inside the house to answer the phone.

"Hello?"

"Hi, it's me." It was Ronny Shaw, Brett's oldest and closest friend. They'd met in the first grade when Ronny, a quiet black boy with few friends, came to Brett's aid when he was attacked by three third graders after his lunch money. They later went to UCLA together, Brett on a track scholarship and Ronny on a minority fellowship. Brett graduated with a degree in aeronautical engineering, while Ronny, a philosophy major, drifted among nowhere jobs before becoming a police officer and eventually a homicide detective.

"How's your Caddy running, Ron?" Macklin had given Shaw one of his completely restored classics, a '55.

"Great. Are you ever going to sell one of those heaps or are you just going to keep giving them away to everyone you know?"

Shaw's lightness seemed unnaturally forced.

Brett's heartbeat inexplicably quickened. "I'm going to sell 'em, really, all of 'em except the Batmobile. I was just working on it when you called."

"Listen, ah, I've got some bad news. Jesus, I wish I didn't have to tell you this."

Score one for instinct. Brett Macklin's chest suddenly felt hard and tight.

"What happened to Dad?"

"He was killed, Mack."

"How?"

There was a silence.

"How?"

"Ah, Jesus. Listen, it looks like some kids ... ah ... set him on fire."

Macklin winced, didn't know if he could breathe. Suddenly a wave of images, a high-speed slide show of his experiences with his father, flooded his thoughts. And then they disappeared. A deep, profound emptiness washed them away. He wanted to cry, he *needed* to cry, but anger held back his tears and made his head throb.

"Where?" Macklin finally coughed. "Where and when did it happen?"

"An hour ago in the neighborhood. There was ... ah ... also a bad accident with a bus. A bunch of people are hurt. Two others are dead."

"You there now?"

"Uh-huh."

"I'm coming down."

"Mack—"

Macklin hung up. Elias Simon smiled. *"Children of God, rejoice in His name!"*

Brett Macklin was flying.

Somehow he hoped the freedom of flight would make the deep ache disappear, that he could soar above the hurt and anger and take refuge in the skies that had always soothed him in the past.

This time he just couldn't soar high enough. There was no refuge. His father was dead, a lump of charred flesh smoldering on the pavement.

He had seen what fire does to a body. If you fly long enough, you eventually see the aftermath of a crash. Macklin remembered the featureless black corpses and the acrid, stomach-wrenching odor.

A cruel, twisted image tortured Macklin, his father's body, skinless and hairless, sizzling and crackling on the street among uncaring, smiling onlookers.

Macklin brought the helicopter down in a clockwise arc towards South Central Los Angeles, towards the insignificant little patch of lights his father had devoted his life to for two decades.

If Macklin had a bomb, he would have dropped it with no regrets. He would have reveled in the fireball consuming the neighborhood, scorching the land the way they had scorched his father's flesh.

The press copters buzzed over the neighborhood like flies to a rotting corpse. Macklin dove in the path of one copter, causing the "Channel 7 News Spotter" to veer left suddenly, nearly dropping the cockpit cameraman into the night.

Lighting the street was a fountain of flame. The fire roared amidst a pulsing circle of water. Macklin swooped low over the scene, arced sharply upwards and to the right, and then dived down over the street again through the laser-beam-like crisscross of flashing red lights.

The ground below Macklin looked like a scene from a grade B war movie. World War II. London. The Luftwaffe had leveled streets into ash piles.

Cinders glowed where buildings and life had been. This was no movie. But to Macklin, it was very much a war zone.

Macklin landed the copter in a parking lot, forcing a throng of reporters, gawkers, and police away from his path. He jumped out of the copter and strode past the angered crowd, stepped over the police barricade, and moved towards the fire-engulfed bus.

"Just who the fuck do you think you are?" A plainclothes cop grabbed Macklin by the shoulder and spun him around. Macklin punched the man in the mouth, sending him sprawling, and continued walking.

"Hold it, fucker, or I'll blow your goddamned head off!"

Macklin stopped. He turned around slowly.

Behind Macklin, legs spread and gun pointed at him, stood a mustached man in a beige polyester knit suit. The man's lips were thin, so tight and narrow you couldn't shove a Nabisco vanilla wafer through them, and drawn into a satisfied smile.

The man stormed up to Macklin and pointed the gun right in his face. Macklin was motionless, eyeing the man with cool reserve. "Do you want to get out of my way," Macklin whispered, "or do I have to walk over you?"

"So you're a comedian." He stepped aside, lowering his gun. "Sure I'll move. Excuse me. My mistake."

As Macklin passed him, the man raised the gun like a club and brought it down towards Macklin's head. Macklin caught the motion out of the corner of his eye, sidestepped the blow, grabbed the man's wrist, and pinned his arm behind his back. The gun clattered to the ground.

"Let him go, Mack." Macklin felt a reassuring hand on his shoulder. "Let him go."

Macklin released the man with a push, nearly knocking him down.

"Jesus, Mack." Shaw sighed.

The man picked up his gun and pulled a pair of handcuffs from inside his pocket. "You're under arrest, hotshot."

"Relax, Sliran. No one's getting arrested." Shaw stared at his flustered partner on the homicide detail. "Put the cuffs away. This is JD Macklin's son, Brett. He's a little agitated."

"A little agitated," Sliran said. "Jesus fucking Christ, Shaw, your agitated friend came real close to sharing a slab with his daddy tonight. Tell your agitated friend that next time he'd better pray you're around to save his neck."

The cop adjusted his glasses, holstered his gun, and walked away. "I'm sorry, Ron," Macklin said tonelessly. "Fill me in."

Shaw put his arm around Macklin and led him towards the flames. "It looks like your father was walking his beat and was crossing that alley over there when some kids... ah... must've jumped him and dumped gasoline on him."

Shaw and Macklin stopped just beside the firemen, who had nearly succeeded in drowning the flames.

"How did this happen?"

Shaw looked into Macklin's eyes. All he saw there were the flames. "Ah, your dad ran into the street. The bus tried to avoid him, and, well, there was an accident."

An ambulance screeched away from a nearby curb and screamed down the street. From within a huddle of men surrounding a row of cars, a black body bag was carried by two officers and hefted into the back of the coroner's wagon.

"What have you got?" Macklin said, barely audible.

"A few leads. We'll have more tomorrow." Shaw tightened his grip on Macklin's shoulder. "Mack, there's nothing more you can do here. Go home."

Macklin sighed. "I want the people who did this Ron."

"Mack, I'll get 'em. I promise. Now, go home, please."

The headlights of the coroner's wagon flashed in Macklin's eyes, momentarily blinding him. "I want a call tomorrow."

Shaw nodded as Macklin turned and headed back to the copter, its blades still spinning.

"Goddamn it!" Shaw growled, looking into the bus's smoking, gutted hold and then at the receding lights of the coroner's wagon as it took away the best cop he ever knew. "I hate this fucking job."

CHAPTER TWO

"... James Douglas Macklin was a humanitarian, devoting his life to the protection and care of others. He was more than just a police officer doing his job. JD was a trusted friend to the people he dealt with on the streets and among those he worked with on the force. Officer Macklin was a role model for all young officers to aspire to, a man who ..."

Brett Macklin, his arm around his daughter's shoulders, wasn't listening to LAPD Chief Jed Stocker's praise-laden eulogy. It was an empty charade for the press and made Macklin feel nauseous. Stocker had hated JD Macklin.

Stocker and JD had gone to the academy together, and while Stocker desk-hopped to the top, JD preferred to remain on the streets. Although technically JD was a peon, he freely (and frequently) criticized Stocker to his face. To JD, Stocker wasn't a policeman but a glorified publicist, an armchair general who had no idea what the urban battleground was like. To Stocker, JD was an obnoxious, disrespectful, old-fashioned, simpleminded, bigmouthed pain in the ass.

"How are you doing, kiddo?" Macklin whispered to Corinne, his eight-year-old daughter. Her blond hair was cut in what her classmates called "Olivia Newton-John style," and she wore a white sweater over her black dress. Her eyes were red, her puffy cheeks tear stained.

"Okay, I guess," she whispered, blinking back tears.

Macklin looked past Corinne to Brooke, his ex-wife. She caught his glance and smiled thinly. Stocker's an asshole, their eyes agreed. It was one of the few things they had agreed on for some time.

For a moment, it was easy for Macklin to see in Brooke the woman he had married. She still had the youthful face, the dark skin, and the slim, athletic body that had caught his attention a decade ago when they were in college. That wasn't it now, though. It was a sparkle, an almost guilty flash of sly cleverness and childish mischief, that flickered in her eyes for just a second.

In that instant, he felt his need for her again, the desperate ache in his chest. Then it passed, and the years and the barrier between Brooke and Brett fell between them like a shroud.

It was a different Brooke who had said "I do"—not the Brooke he had loved.

The magic was gone. The air between them never seemed to be clear of the debris from some argument or other. The fact that they stayed together for three years was a testament to their love for Corinne.

Macklin tightened his grip on Corinne's tiny shoulder. She leaned against him and sniffed. He scanned the faces in the crowd, ignoring Stocker's litany. There were several cops. Among them was Shaw, who stood solemnly with his live-in lover, Sunshine, her white gauze dress standing out like a flashing neon sign amongst all the black-clothed mourners.

Sunshine played nervously with her long hair or fingered the tassels at her neck, casting speculative glances at her sheepdog, Guess, who was panting happily inside their orange Volkswagen Bug parked fifty yards away. She always felt uncomfortable away from Guess.

Sunshine tried, as least superficially, to embody the flower children of Berkeley, circa 1967 (she bought Bob Dylan's last album out of respect and then broke it into pieces in a teary tirade when she discovered he'd "sold out to Jesus, goddamn it"). She seemed quite happy in this self-made time warp but managed to irritate the hell out of Macklin, who often wondered if she slept with Shaw just to be sixties hip.

Shaw, for his part, grudgingly put up with it out of love, loneliness, and a casual ambivalence. He even put up with his mother's frequent tirades about him "living in sin—with a *white* woman, no less!" She prayed he'd someday "stop playing cops 'n' robbers and sleeping with crazy white women" and help run his parents' fish market. After growing up around fish all his life, just thinking about the smell made him nauseous. When Shaw heard in junior high from Petey McGrew that pussy tasted like anchovy pizzas, he groaned, "Just my damn luck..."

Shaw met Macklin's gaze and smiled awkwardly, trying to be reassuring.

Macklin didn't seem to see him, his eyes searching the faces in the crowd.

The look in Macklin's eyes disturbed Shaw. It was as if Macklin was a cobra waiting to strike.

Macklin was seeking those faces he didn't recognize, those faces from the neighborhood his father had protected for so long. He looked at the short man with the basset-hound face, his yarmulke-capped head hung low. He looked at the fragile Mexican woman with the deep-set brown eyes and rock-hard face. He looked at the man shifting his weight, his hands plunged into the pockets of his wrinkled slacks. Macklin looked at each face, one by one. Behind one of those faces Macklin believed was the trail to his father's killer.

Stocker finished his remarks and glanced at Macklin with a sympathetic expression he'd picked up from Chad Everett in *Medical Center.*

Macklin didn't even notice.

Stocker stepped back among the mourners, sliding past a big bear of a man whose appearance caused a rustle in the press corps huddled a few yards away on the access road.

Lucas Breen was unmistakable. There wasn't a face anywhere like his.

His thick, blond eyebrows, sideburns, mustache, and beard were one, nearly hiding his bright, beady eyes and full-lipped mouth. At times, under a certain light, all you could see of his face was this mass of hair with a long, narrow piece of flesh sticking out of the middle. It was no wonder every reporter and underpaid city worker in town called him Prickface.

Breen had stepped out of his lair to pay his respects to a slain officer of the law. It was an expression of his deepest feelings, feelings he shared with his gubernatorial campaign manager, who figured a graveside appearance and some sympathetic words to the barbecued cop's family were good for a few headlines in the *Los Angeles Times*. If Breen brought along his starlet squeeze, the one whose acting abilities rested in her 38D cups, maybe a second or two on *Entertainment Tonight*.

California's regional golden bear flashed his famous smile, though a bit restrained under the circumstances, to the mourners and the Nikons. "The cruelty of the human soul knows no bounds." Breen's voice had a natural echo, rising deep out of a neck seemingly carved out of granite. "Sometimes it makes one wonder whether there is any goodness left..."

Macklin tightened up, unknowingly squeezing his daughter's shoulder until her aggravated squirming snapped him out of it.

"...JD Macklin was a good man, an honest man, a man devoted to the happiness and well-being of his fellow man. JD Macklin made you *believe* in the power of goodwill and neighborly respect. The insidious disease which claimed his life..."

Insidious disease? Shaw groaned. He stole a glance at Macklin, the pilot's face an expressionless mask to everyone but the black detective, who knew Macklin well enough to see the anger struggling to break free.

Shaw wouldn't have been surprised if a hairline crack split the side of Macklin's head and a fanged, bloody dragon clawed its way out.

"... can still be beaten. We need more men like JD, men with foresight and courage, men with a heart and vision. We need them on the streets and in the highest positions in the land. It's a battle JD Macklin fought every day, a battle that he dedicated his life to. If JD Macklin's death is to mean anything, we must carry on. *We must win!*"

Breen stared at the flag-draped coffin and then cast his face to the sky. "JD, we'll fight. And like you, we'll fight with everything we've got." Macklin saw tears stream down many of the faces he didn't recognize. Suddenly, all he wanted to do was vomit. Breen ambled aside for the reverend, who said a few words while two officers folded up the flag into a neat triangle and handed it to Corinne, who took the flag uncertainly, as if it held her grandfather's spirit.

Brooke stroked Corinne's hair and glanced at Macklin. He smiled reassuringly as the gunshot salute rang out behind them. The coffin slowly descended into the ground.

The mourners stood awkwardly around the grave, the echoes from the gunshots slowly fading. Then, in groups of two and three, the mourners began to dribble away towards the access road, where the press waited, hungry for quotes.

Stocker approached Macklin, reaching for his hand, "Your father was a damn good officer, Brett. We're going to feel the loss."

Macklin wanted to wrap his hands around Stocker's neck and squeeze it until the chief's eyes popped out. The funeral was a show and Macklin was being forced to play along, an unwilling actor in a mediocre melodrama staged to boost Stocker's image and Breen's gubernatorial chances. Stocker missed Brett's father like he missed contracting AIDS.

"Thanks," Macklin said, shaking Stocker's hand. Their eyes met, just long enough to establish contact and short enough to avoid acknowledging their insincerity.

Stocker shuffled away and Breen stomped up to Macklin. All the Nikons in the area were trained on him.

"You should be proud of your father, Mr. Macklin. He was a credit to the badge." Breen wrapped his paw around Macklin's hand. "If I can be of any help, just let me know."

He clapped Macklin on the shoulder and made a beeline for the press.

Macklin watched him, saw Breen feign avoidance, and then plunge right in.

Brooke stepped up behind Macklin and slid her arm around his waist. It felt warm. "Are you coming home with us?"

Macklin spotted Shaw and Sunshine striding towards their Bug. "No, I don't think so. I've had enough of this for one day."

"Will we see you tonight, Dad?" Corinne asked, bravely fighting back the tears she'd felt all afternoon.

"Sure." He bent down and kissed the top of Corinne's head. Brooke looked at him, and meeting her gaze, he kissed her cheek. "I'll see you later, about eight."

Macklin lingered for a moment, smiled, and then headed toward the orange Bug.

Guess was running excitedly around the car, his big tongue lolling out as he bounded. For the first time all day, Sunshine didn't look fatally anemic.

"Ronny, could I talk to you a sec?" Macklin asked.

Sunshine came over to Macklin and touched his arm tenderly. "How are you feeling, Mac?"

Guess leaped up on Macklin, puffing and drooling all over his suit. "I'm doing fine, thanks." Macklin tried to push Guess away, looking to Shaw for help.

"C'mere, Guess, give Mac a break." Shaw pulled Guess away and followed Macklin down the access road away from everyone.

"Okay, Ronny, just how close are you to nailing the bastards who killed Dad?"

"We've got some leads and I've—"

"Oh, stop giving me this shit, Ronny. Just who the hell do you think you're talking to? C'mon, spare me the bullshit and give me the bottom line."

Shaw stopped and faced Macklin. "It's probably the Bounty Hunters. They were in the area that night and JD had some run-ins with them before."

"So what's stopping you? Why aren't these guys in cages?"

"No one will talk, Mac."

"Run that by me again."

Shaw signed. "No one will talk. Everyone on the street has suddenly developed laryngitis."

Macklin stared past Shaw to row after row of tombstones. "Well, Ronny, you'd better make them talk."

Shaw didn't like the sound of Macklin's voice. It was cold and distant, not the Brett Macklin he had grown up with.

"We're doing our best. "

"Just make them talk," barked Macklin, turning and walking away.

"Tell me, Mac, should I use a rubber hose or shove bamboo shoots under their fingernails?" Shaw yelled. Macklin kept walking. Guess bounded toward him but was stopped cold by Macklin's face, a gaze that even Guess knew meant "get near me and I'll rip your tongue out and strangle you with it."

Jacob Zimmer of the *Herald Examiner* wasn't as smart as Guess. A self-proclaimed asshole's asshole, he prided himself on his ability to out-son-of-a-bitch anybody with a press pass and a reporter's notebook. He wore his customary blue corduroy ensemble, his dirty canvas tennis shoes, and his have-I-got-a-Chevy-for-you smile.

Zimmer grabbed Macklin's forearm. "Can I have a word with you, Mr. Macklin?"

Macklin yanked his arm away without breaking his stride. "No."

"How do you feel about your father's death?" Zimmer chewed on his Wrigley's spearmint. He bought the stuff by the case.

Macklin turned. "Disappear, buddy. " He walked toward his black '59 Caddy.

"Has this shaken your faith in the law? In society? In your fellow man?"

Zimmer skirted around and headed off Macklin. "How is your daughter dealing with the killing?"

Macklin grabbed Zimmer by the neck and slammed him against the Caddy's dorsal fin.

"If you don't shut up and get out of my way, you're going to get an exclusive interview with my father." Zimmer gurgled on his gum wad. "End quote, got it?"

He pushed Zimmer away and left him gagging on the sidewalk. Macklin walked around the Batmobile, unlocked the door, and got in.

Zimmer pulled himself off the ground and pressed his face against the passenger window. "You'd feel a whole lot better if you talked with me, Macklin."

The car roared to life. Macklin shifted into drive, pressed the pedal to the floor, and left Zimmer to interview exhaust fumes.

CHAPTER THREE

The *TV Guide* crossword puzzle was only half-finished. It lay there beside JD's recliner, still missing 14 across (David Banner's 5-letter problem), 23 down (Book 'em, __________), 51 across (Napoleon Solo's boss), 3 down (Where Batman lived on his day off), and the corker, 27 across (It was Don Rickles last series).

Macklin picked it up and dropped it gently on the chair. The warm, three-room apartment still felt and smelled like his father. The nightly cigar. The leaking, whining, busted old Mr. Coffee. Cold Schlitz. The radio tuned to KNXT News radio. Georgia Montgomery's gourmet frozen dinners, the 11:45 p.m. fart (JD called it "The Big Gasser"), his buddy Jimbo and his Marlboros, Mennen antiperspirant.

The pain Macklin felt as he looked around his father's apartment was tangible, a dull, throbbing ache in his stomach and sickly, foul taste in his mouth.

Dad is dead.

Pictures of Macklin, his mother, Corinne, and JD crowded the dusty TV top. Macklin fingered them. There was the twelve-year-old picture of Macklin in his graduation attire, one of those self-assured jock smiles on his tan face. There was Corinne, sitting in JD's lap with a big grin on her face, wearing his LAPD hat and nearly disappearing inside of it. There was an old black-and-white shot of his mother, slender, pale, bright brown eyes flashing. She died slowly of bone cancer between Macklin's fifth and sixth birthdays.

There was a picture of Brett and Shaw in Macklin's shiny new Corvair. It was the summer before Brett headed to UCLA on a track scholarship. Both Shaw and Brett had been tall, gangly, and thin. Awkward and horny and ready to conquer the world.

Macklin remembered the picture well. That night Shaw and his girlfriend, Georgette, who was trying hard to be Diana Ross, and Brett and his girlfriend, Stacy, a dentist's daughter with the world's straightest teeth, went to the drive-in to see a horror double feature.

Shaw and Georgette left to get popcorn at intermission and never came back. Macklin and Stacy left in the middle of the second show. Driving up to Mulholland Drive to fog up the windows. Macklin desperately hoped to celebrate getting his new car by convincing Stacy to let their hands wander below the belt. He kissed her with big expectations.

When Stacy, in the midst of their fervent groping, unzipped his pants without coercion and dropped her head between his legs, Macklin almost fainted with surprise and anxiety. He had never expected her to do *that*, not in his wildest fantasies. When he opened his eyes afterwards, he expected to see powder burns on Stacy's face, a hole in the Corvair's ceiling, and a contrail in the night sky.

Brett Macklin grinned at the memory. Stacy now weighed 347 pounds and was married to a guy with a chain of Culver City Laundromats. Georgette, last he heard, was a backup singer for Diana Ross. Then suddenly his grin disappeared. His father was dead and all his mind wanted to do was think of almost anything else in the world. It made him feel guilty.

Macklin put the picture down and walked into JD's bedroom. The bed was neatly made, the sheets tucked in tight. Everything was crisp and clean, like a bunk at Camp Pendleton. Brett resisted the urge to toss a quarter on the cover to see how high it would bounce. Macklin never understood his father's compulsion for orderly, clean bedrooms and his tolerance of casually sloppy kitchens and living rooms. It was strange. But then, so was being a cop, so was being JD Macklin.

There were two pictures on the nightstand beside JD's bed. One was a picture of JD and his wife with their newborn son. JD was a big man even then, but his physical threat was tempered by a gentle, childlike face that the years would turn hard, lined, and rough. His mother had a fragility and innocence that was unabashedly sensual and eyes that said she knew more than she was telling.

Macklin never remembered his mother the way she became when the cancer began gnawing on her bones, only the way she was then, in that picture, before he ever really knew her.

The other picture was taken on Brett Macklin's wedding day. He stood beside Brooke, both of them smiling the happy, naive smiles of two people who see nothing but love songs, dances, sunshine, and sweet candy in their future. Two people who are looking at life as one long honeymoon in the same neighborhood with the Cleavers and the Nelsons.

Shit, he wished it could have been that way.

He sighed, touched the picture frame gently, and then knelt beside his father's bed, reaching under the mattress until his cheek pressed against the bedspread. His hand found what it was seeking and pulled it out.

His father's insurance: a short-barrel, Colt Python .357 Magnum. It was cold and heavy in Macklin's hand. Black and mean, it was the Cadillac of handguns.

Macklin shoved the gun under his waistband, pulled his jacket over it, and walked out.

It was dark by the time Brett Macklin pulled up outside Brooke's apartment building, a new three-story brick structure designed to look like a colonial townhouse and located just two blocks south of the posh, multimillion-dollar condominiums that made up the Wilshire corridor.

Macklin sat in the car for a moment, letting the engine hum, and glanced up at Brooke's window with mixed emotions. As much as he wanted to see Corinne, he hated having to face Brooke to do it. He always left the apartment feeling empty, mentally torturing himself with dreams of what might have been and could never be, the family life he craved but didn't have.

However, his need to be with people right now, to avoid the loneliness that would only stoke his grief, outweighed his trepidation. He switched off the ignition and stepped out, walking around the car and across the street with long, easy strides. Macklin's brisk stride was a source of irritation to his friends, most of whom found it hard to keep up and assumed the former track star was running some personal marathon.

Macklin quickly picked up the door key and let himself in, crossing the small, mailbox-lined lobby to the elevator in two steps. He slapped the button, surprising himself with the loud smack his hand made against the steel.

Relax, Macklin told himself, his hand stinging just enough to let him know he'd hit the button too hard. He took a deep breath and stepped inside the elevator, gently pressing the third-floor button with his index finger.

That's better.

The doors slid shut and Macklin held his breath to avoid being assaulted by the cloud of Grey Flannel cologne that filled the elevator. It seemed to Macklin that every man in the place bathed in the stuff. The scent was so strong that whenever Corinne came to visit him she inevitably brought the odor with her.

The elevator stopped with a lurch at the third floor. Macklin exhaled and walked down the narrow, dimly lit hallway to Brooke's apartment: 312. He paused outside her door for a moment, shifted his weight, and then reached out his hand to knock. The movement made him aware of the coldness against his stomach, and he stiffened, jerking his hand back as if electrocuted by some invisible force field.

The gun. He had forgotten about the gun.

Macklin turned abruptly and dashed to the stairwell, taking the steps down two at a time. *Fuckface!* The thought of bringing the firearm, a tool of violence, inadvertently into the home where his daughter lived seemed vile to him.

He had taken it from his father's apartment on impulse and wasn't even sure why.

Macklin burst out of the stairwell. He slammed open the door and startled a young couple in matching sweat suits as they came through the lobby doors.

He ignored them, bumping the man's shoulder as he slid past him to the street.

What if Corinne had seen it? What would I have told her?

Macklin unlocked the passenger door of the Cadillac and opened the glove compartment. *What would I have told myself?* Shit, what a stupid fucking thing to do. He opened the glove compartment, put the gun inside, and shoved it closed, vowing to leave the damn gun there until he could take it back to his father's place. Where it belonged.

Macklin locked up the car and went back upstairs. When Brooke opened the door, Macklin felt the familiar longing. She wore the yellow bathrobe he had bought her for Christmas early in their marriage. He knew the moment she unwrapped it that she hated it. She pretended to like it, though, steadfastly refusing to return it or buy a new one even after they were divorced.

"Corinne's getting ready for bed," Brooke said. It was her idea of a greeting. She moved aside to let Macklin in.

Macklin stepped past her and immediately noticed Lyle Richter, a stocky real estate agent with a fondness for turtleneck sweaters, sitting at the butcher-block table and cupping a glass of white wine in both hands.

"Hey, Mack, I'm sorry about your father. Really." Lyle drew his tanned face into a sorrowful frown.

"Thanks," Macklin said flatly, turning to Brooke as she closed the door. "I'll just go in and say good night to her. I won't keep her up long."

Brooke nodded. "Fine. You're welcome to join us for some wine if you want, you know."

Macklin glanced at Richter. The guy worked hard at the eligible-bachelor-on-the-go look, and, worst of all, he used Grey Flannel cologne. Of the several men Brooke saw on a regular basis, Macklin liked Richter the least.

"Maybe," Macklin mumbled, meaning *no*, and went down the hallway to Corinne's room.

Blinker, the magic elf, and Tommy, the ten-year-old boy who had no friends, sailed over the Candyland in the flying top hat. They weren't paying attention to where they were going. The top hat flew right into a cotton candy cloud and tipped just a bit. Tommy fell from the hat, screaming *"Help! Help!"*

Tommy bounced off the Jell-O Lake and landed right in front of the Big Sucker, who gave him a chocolate kiss…

Brett Macklin closed *Tommy's Sweet Adventure* and saw that Corinne was sleeping, her head almost buried under the blankets. Corinne didn't want to talk to Brett about JD's death. She wanted a story.

Macklin put down the book, pulled the blankets away from her head, and kissed her on the forehead.

"I love you," Macklin whispered hoarsely.

He slipped quietly out of the room and gently closed the door. The water was running in the kitchen and he could hear the clatter of dishes and Brooke's absent humming.

As he stepped into the kitchen, he saw Lyle's glass on the table, but Lyle was gone.

"Is Cory asleep?" Brooke asked, her back to Macklin.

"Like a rock." Macklin stood near the front door.

Brooke turned off the faucet and grabbed a towel, drying her hands as she turned to face Macklin.

"Lyle left a while ago." She set the towel on the counter and put her hands in her bathrobe pockets. "Would you like to stay and talk?"

Macklin looked into her eyes and felt himself sag inside. He wanted to talk, he wanted to cry, he wanted to hold someone for the rest of the night.

"No, Brooke. I think I need to be alone tonight," Macklin said. Staying would cost too much emotionally later. His grief was all he could deal with right now.

"Are you sure?"

Macklin smiled. "Yes, I'm sure." He opened the front door and lingered for a moment, fighting the desire to go to her. She seemed so vulnerable, so true, so comforting to him then.

"Sweet dreams," Macklin said softly, closing the door behind him as he walked out.

CHAPTER FOUR

The neighborhood seemed gray and rougher to Shaw in the bright sunlight. There was nothing glossy or fresh here, nothing that could take the scrutiny of a clear day or the punishment of sweltering heat.

Shaw and Sliran, working on his second pack of cigarettes since beginning the shift, cruised slowly down the street, the windows of their four-door Plymouth rolled down in a vain attempt to create a cooling breeze.

No matter what color the buildings were, it seemed to Shaw that the neighborhood dulled them. These streets were color-blind. The buildings appeared flat, without character. Their merchants' signs, regardless of how much neon or plywood or paint was put on them or how recently, fell quickly into decay from age, vandalism, or lack of care.

Shaw saw the neighborhood as a concrete reflection of its people—tired, forgotten, beaten, and yet, resilient and enduring. On hot days the people appeared to Shaw to be even more downtrodden than usual, wearily seeking the cool air offered by shadows and doorways. Crime would be up today, Shaw groaned to himself, the heavy hot air prodding the already anxious and frustrated people into violent acts of rebellion or sheer boredom or both.

Shaw steered the car around the corner and the gray street turned suddenly black.

No one had bothered to clean up after the fire. There was no point. The scorched streetlights twisted like vines towards the blackened skeletons of buildings claimed by the flames. Shaw drove past the rubble and slowed to a stop outside the alley where JD Macklin was set aflame.

"What are we doing *here*?" Sliran whined, his eyes hidden by the ever-present pair of dark sunglasses. "I thought we were going to get a burger."

"I want to look around."

"What are you going to do, collect some charcoal? We've been over every inch of this street. Let's go. I'm starving."

"Just stay here. I'll be back in a few minutes. You can gnaw on the dashboard until I get back."

Shaw stepped out and disappeared into the alley.

"Asshole," Sliran hissed, lighting another Marlboro.

Shaw walked in measured steps. *Can't appear too eager.* The kid would be at the end of the T-shaped alley, shitting bricks. Shaw could feel his squeeze play coming together. One by one he had faced the Bounty Hunters, looking for the weakest link. He found it in lanky Tomas Cruz. Made to order. His two doped-out sisters liked to whore, like their mother, who also ran numbers and sold a few 'ludes to boot. An inner-city Brady Bunch. After JD's death Shaw began arresting the Terrible Trio every time they stepped out of the house. They couldn't breathe without being read their rights.

Then he shadowed Cruz. Everywhere Cruz turned, there was Shaw, popping up like some supernatural specter. Shaw made it very clear. Talk, or your momma and sisters are finished, one way or another, either starving on the streets or feeding the dykes in the state pen. It was up to the kid. The hard way or the easy way? Tomas was sixteen, the youngest and newest member of the gang. Not as mean as he looked or liked to believe he was. Day by day, Shaw tightened the screws.

Shaw had never come down this hard before. He didn't like to do it. But he didn't like his friends getting *fried* either.

"Lay off my momma."

A tall, muscular boy in a white T-shirt stepped into the narrow beam of sunlight.

"C'mon, Cruz, I didn't come down here to play games."

"Shit, man, I *can't*."

"Bye." Shaw turned.

"Wait."

Shaw stopped.

"You'll lay off my momma and my sisters. You'll talk to the Man, make it easy on me."

"Talk."

The boy began pacing, shooting angry glances at Shaw. He wanted to kick in Shaw's face until it looked like applesauce.

"Okay, we did it."

"Did what?"

"Torched the cop. We torched the damn cop."

"Who's we?"

The boy paced. *How would you like to wear your nuts, nigger?*

Shaw sighed. "The women at the state pen are gonna love your mother. Close your eyes, Tomas. Think of the bulldykes with their fingers all over your mother's body. Inside her body. Think of it. And your sisters, well, ever see what happens to someone who gives up smack straight? Not pretty."

He turned and walked away.

Tomas picked up a garbage can and tossed it against a wall. "Stop, you mother-fucking son of a bitch!"

Shaw continued to walk casually down the alley.

"Wait!" Tomas kicked the can. "I said wait!"

Mucus rolled out of Tomas' nose. "Esteban, Primo, Mario, Gomez, Baldo, and Jesse." Tomas fell against the wall and slid to the ground, defeated. "I didn't know they were gonna torch the cop, I didn't. I just thought we were gonna beat him up a bit, you know, cram his badge up his ass. Esteban got him to come in and Baldo, Mario, and Jesse pinned him."

Shaw looked at Tomas. "You and Gomez were lookouts."

"You lay off my momma now, okay? You lay off. Let my sisters and my momma alone."

"Let's go." Shaw said.

"Wait! Listen, man, two hours. You gotta give me two hours to settle with my family."

Shaw looked him in the eyes. The boy was broken.

"Please," the boy whispered.

Shaw stood silently for a moment. "Two hours. Any longer and ..."

"Save it. I'll be home. Two hours."

"Okay, give it to me again," Shaw pulled out a tape recorder. Ten minutes later Shaw walked away, leaving the boy in the darkness.

Sliran was leaning against the hood when Shaw emerged from the alley.

"Let's go." Shaw got in and started the car up.

Sliran snubbed out his Marlboro and smiled. "Yes, *sir.*"

⚜ ⚜ ⚜

The man stood bloody in the middle of the street, his legs spread wide apart, his arms dangling loosely at his sides, watching with studied weariness the car speeding crazily towards him.

The car barreled down the hot asphalt, the driver's gleeful howling making the battered Grand Prix seem like a wailing banshee just escaped from hell.

The howl was still echoing down the street when the man slowly raised his right arm, gun in hand, aimed, and fired. The windshield shattered, and the car veered and spun in front of the man, who stepped aside as the car rolled end over end beside him and then erupted in flame.

Wisps of fire reached for the man's emotionless face. He ran the back of his hand across his brow and walked down the street, the fire raging behind him.

"Cut!"

The director's voice crackled in Macklin's ear as Macklin guided the helicopter in a low sweep over the street. The camera crew behind Macklin untensed, exhaling and breaking into easy laughter.

"Fuckin' A! I love workin' on these films," the cameraman said. "Eh, buddy?"

Macklin looked over his shoulder and smiled.

Yeah, great movies.

Down the street, Nick Crecko, *The Bloodmaster*, as played by the notorious homosexual Brock Dale, was heading towards his motor home to take a leak, something he had been dying to do for the last three takes. He was tempted to piss on the car rather than shoot it.

Nick Crecko: The Pissmaster. Somehow, Dale just couldn't see *that* drawing in those luscious box-office dollars.

Macklin swung low over the crew and then brought the chopper down in the middle of the street. Crowds of people pushed against the ropes on either end of the block, watching the chopper, hoping to see Tom Selleck or some other celluloid god step out. No such luck.

Macklin sat in the chopper as the crew unloaded and the engine cooled down. It had been two weeks since his father's death.

Since he had been burned to a crisp…

And still. Shaw had uncovered nothing. Not that Macklin was getting anxious. No, not anxious. *Furious.*

"Do you need me anymore?" Macklin barked into the mike.

"Ah, no, I don't think so, Brett. Thanks." The director was taken aback by Macklin's rough tone and it showed.

Macklin mentally apologized and started the chopper up again. *I'm getting to be a real asshole,* he thought, *a grade A asshole.*

He sailed across the sky, moving towards the setting sun. The freeways were clogged with rush-hour traffic and a thick layer of greenish gunk separated Macklin's chopper from the city below. Sometimes Macklin wished he could stay above it forever and never land. Someday, he just might try it.

Macklin dived low over the Santa Monica coastline, the crashing surf. Sunbathers covered the sand like an army of ants attacking an unattended sandwich. As they took deep drags of the sea air, cars whizzed by thirty yards behind them, belching exhaust on the Pacific Coast Highway.

That's fresh sea air, huh?

The Santa Monica Airport crawled up below him, and he descended, bringing the copter down beside the Batmobile, which was parked close to Macklin's shiny Blue Yonder Airways hangar.

Macklin hopped out of the chopper, stretched, and strode into the hangar. Mort Suderson was crouched under their plane, tinkering with it. *"SAC-RI-FISSSSSSE. That's all God asks us for, a little SAC-RI-FISSSSE. Is that asking too much? Is that going overboard? Is He demanding too much? He isn't asking ENOUGH for the splendor that is His love…"*

A loud roar of applause rose from Mort's transistor radio.

"Simon says PRAISE!"

"PRAISE!" the audience echoed.

"PRAISE!" Simon shrieked.

"PRAISE!" the audience shrieked.

Mort's wrench slipped off the nut and he stumbled, banging his head against the plane. "Fuckin' Christ!"

Macklin laughed, clicking off the radio. "Don't tell me you've found Jesus."

"Huh?" Mort peeked out from inside the plane. "Oh, it's you. He even got *me* to say a couple hallelujahs once."

Macklin grinned.

"You shoulda heard him bitchin' about the Justice Department and the FCC. He says they are Satan's puppets. Christ, that guy has balls, I'll tell ya that. He says God needs more *worthship* if they are going to beat the devil of bureaucracy." Mort tossed his wrench in the toolbox and walked Macklin over to their ancient refrigerator. "Wanna Tab?"

"Sure, why not?"

Mort reached in and pulled two out. "Anything new?"

"Nothing," Macklin said, popping open the soda. "Not one word from Ronny. I don't like it, Mort, my friend, not one damn bit."

"I don't blame you."

"So, how are things going with your lady friend?"

"Depends."

"Depends on what?"

"I met her boyfriend last night. You know, the urologist. Christ, I wanted to take her out and let her play a tune on my meat whistle. Anyway, she opens her door and I say hi and then this big black shadow falls over us I crane my neck up and see this tree with arms and legs towering over us. The guy looks like he picks his teeth with fuckin' two-by-fours. He's wearin' this sweater that must've been knit with crowbars and a pair of faded, tight Levi's that barely restrain this schmeckle the size of my entire body. His hard-on must get mistaken for the Eiffel Tower." Mort gulped down some Tab. 'This is my boyfriend, Smith,' she says. I muster up a smile and introduce myself. 'You can call me Mort,' I say. He grunts, 'I'm just Smith. Call me Smith.' I would've called him Mr. Sinatra if he wanted me to."

Macklin smiled. "I'd get out of this mess now while you still have feeling below your neck."

"Why should I? The Jolly Green Giant lives in Boston. Anyway, he left town today. Strapped to an aircraft carrier, I imagine."

"So? What's the problem?"

"Well, it's his schmeckle. If that's what she's used to, well, look—compared to this guy's fuckin' interplanetary cruise missile, I've got a soiled firecracker."

"I see." Macklin swallowed some Tab. "Well... ah... if you were her, would you want *that* all the time? The thought of something... er... a bit more... ah... manageable might be comforting."

"You might have a point there. Yes, maybe you do. He's drivin' a lumbering old Buick and I've got a sharp little Porsche, small, swift, and deadly. I think you're right."

Macklin clapped his hand on Mort's shoulder. "Listen, I'm going to go give Ronny a call. He must have something by now."

"I hope so, Brett, I really do."

Macklin smiled and stepped into the cluttered office. Papers and maps and old junk mail covered the office like a forest's blanket of leaves. He dropped himself into a creaky wooden desk chair and dialed Ronny's office number.

"Shaw, Homicide."

"Hi, Ron. This is Brett."

"Oh, Mack, I was just going to call you. We're closing in on the boy who killed your father."

"Jesus, I was beginning to think all you guys in Homicide had skipped to Miami Beach or something. Tell me more."

"We've got six guys down for it, though I wouldn't be surprised if more were involved. They're Bounty Hunters, one of a half dozen gangs that are fighting over that neighborhood."

"Do you have them by the balls, Ronny?"

There was a moment of silence. "I wish I could say I did, Mack. We've got a case, but it's not exactly Samsonite, if you know what I mean. One confession and a lot of circumstantial evidence."

"But you've got them."

"We've got them."

"Hey." Macklin's voice was unsteady for a moment. He paused, and then continued. "Thanks. I—"

"Listen, Mack, why don't you come by tonight and have a bite with Sunny and me?"

Dinner with them usually meant sprouts, exotic wine made in somebody's basement or something, avocado things, alfalfa stuff, and protein drinks.

"I think I'll pass this time. The Batmobile needs some attention tonight."

"Okay, another time, then."

"You got it. Gimme a call. I wanna see these guys go down."

"Sure thing, Mack."

Shaw set down the phone gently on the cradle. Sliran came up behind him.

"That patrol car you sent to that kid's house just called in."

Shaw swiveled around in his chair. "Uh-huh?"

"The kid's not there."

"Shit." Shaw glanced at his watch. Where had the two hours gone? He felt a twinge of dread. Did Cruz double-cross him and run? Shaw ran his hands through his hair. "We've got to canvas the neighborhood. Cruz has to be found."

"All right, all right, calm down." Sliran scratched his cheek. "Listen, we've got the other guys, we'll get him. What's the big deal?"

"You're right." Shaw fingered a cassette on his desk. "With this, the case is tied up anyway."

"Tied up all right." Sliran walked away. "Like a noose." He sat down at his desk and looked through the clutter for a moment. Then he reached for the phone. "This is Sliran, Homicide. Have your boys check out the alley on Morrison. That's right. Ah-huh. The alley where Macklin bought it."

CHAPTER FIVE

Saul and Moe stood beside the ambulance, unable to see over the crush of people what all the excitement was in the alley. Moe chewed on some ice, the papercup tilted over his face like a muzzle.

"What's happening to our neighborhood?" Saul said, shoving his hands into his pockets.

"Open your eyes, Saul. Nothing's changed. Nothing at all," Moe said, nearly spitting a mouthful of ice on Saul's shoulder.

"JD's gone."

Their faces were long and tired. Two old basset hounds, sleepy eyed with age. They were falling prey to the sapping forces of the neighborhood.

Saul and Moe were caught suddenly in the glare of headlights as a car skidded to a stop at their feet. Shaw bolted out of the car and broke through the crowd. Sliran emerged casually, pulling out a pack of Marlboros.

"What's going on here, Officer?" Moe asked.

Sliran lit a cigarette and offered the pack to Saul and Moe. They declined. "A kid, one of those ones we think killed Macklin, was roughed up a bit in the alley."

"Is he dead?" Saul asked hopefully.

"No." Sliran slipped through the crowd and walked slowly down the alley towards the huddle of uniforms at the end.

Shaw was kneeling in the grime beside Tomas, the youth's face a smear of blood and dirt. His arms and legs were twisted at obscene angles, his T-shirt in filthy tatters.

"Jesus ...," Shaw muttered. "Tomas, Tomas, can you hear me? Who did this to you?"

Cruz was sobbing. "Get away from me," he sputtered.

"Tomas, I want to help you. Who did this to you?"

"G-get away from me!" he shrieked, suddenly stiffening with pain.

Shaw felt a hand on his shoulder. "Sir, we gotta take this guy away now," the paramedic said. "Save the questions for later."

Shaw sighed. A flash from a camera illuminated the scene, the broken body amidst the trash and dirt.

"Sir, please."

Shaw stepped away as they gently picked up Tomas and put him on a stretcher.

Sliran came up behind Shaw.

"I hope they brought a few baggies," Sliran snickered, idly tossing a bloodied finger in his hand.

⚜ ⚜ ⚜

Dr. Ralph "Cheeks" Beddicker was losing. Baby after baby hit the ground with a splat.

He hunkered down in the plastic chair, his face pressed against his wristwatch. Another baby went splat.

There was a knock on the door. "Come in," Beddicker barked, his cheeks billowing. *Splat.*

Shaw opened the lounge door. His eyes were bloodshot, his tie loose at the collar, and his hair askew. "I need to talk with you a sec."

Splat. "Could you hang on?" He took a deep breath, angered at the break in his concentration. No matter how fast he hit the little button, his fireman never made it to the burning building on time. Another baby kissed the pavement. The game beeped at him. *Splat.*

"This damn watch." Beddicker cursed and finally looked up at Shaw."My son gave it to me for Christmas. It's driving me nuts." He stared silently at Shaw, concentrating on his face like he was going to paint it from memory someday. Finally, he said, "So what can I do for you?"

"How's the boy?"

"Huh? Oh, the mess you guys brought in a few hours ago. Cruz, right?"

"Tomas Cruz. How is he? When can I talk to him?"

"He's alive. He won't run any marathons, though. Both his legs are broken, a couple splintered ribs scratching up his internal organs. He's missing a piece of one finger and he's got a hairline skull fracture.

"Any idea what happened to him?"

Beddicker laughed, his famous cheeks enlarging like blowfish. "He was run over by a freight train." Beddicker shook his head disapprovingly. "Someone slapped the kid around with a block of cement. I dunno. You're the detective. Look around for a blunt object. Like a wall or something."

"When can I talk to him?"

Beddicker stretched. "As far as I'm concerned, anytime you want."

"Thanks, Cheeks." Shaw smiled and dashed out.

Beddicker glanced at his watch. "You're gonna ruin me."

Shaw ran up the stairwell to the fifth floor, bolted out the door, and nearly sprinted to Tomas' room.

"Hold it, Sergeant," a voice yelled.

"Shit," he groaned.

Slimy Sam Dexter, the used-car salesman of attorneys, in his lime green suit and orange tie, swung his empty briefcase cockily as he stepped up to Shaw. "You're not getting near that boy, understand, not until I talk to him." Behind Dexter was Tomas' mother, Hilda, her yellow smile filling her face.

Shaw and Dexter had clashed many times. So far the score was even. Dexter thrived on the low-income, repeat-offender crowd, putting them in debt for life. They preferred Dexter's talons to twenty years of making big rocks into little ones.

"Why don't you rest those gumshoes of yours while I talk to my client?" Dexter swung his briefcase in the direction of the waiting area.

Shaw had no choice. He reluctantly went to the coffee machine and dropped in some change.

"Mrs. Cruz, I'll take care of things now. You go home and I'll swing by later." Dexter patted her on the shoulder.

Dexter walked spritely down the hallway, paused at Tomas' door to see Shaw sitting down with a cup of coffee, smiled, and stepped inside.

The room was dark. Tomas lay in the bed, both legs in traction, his head wrapped tightly in gauze and padding. His eyes were swollen shut and his lips were dark, red scabs barely clinging to his bruised face.

"Hey, Tomas!"

Tomas moaned.

Dexter pulled up a chair beside the bed, "It's me, Tomas, Sam Dexter. Uncle Sam." Dexter laughed. "I'm gonna get you out of this Tomas, just like before."

"It hurts," he whispered.

"I know it does, boy, I know. Now, we've got to talk. The cops are taking numbers outside to see you. We have to get your story straight."

"Uh-huh."

"Now, tell me everything."

It took thirty minutes for Tomas to croak it out, but he did. He told Dexter about calling Shaw, about meeting him in the alley, about taping a confession so his mother and sisters wouldn't fall prey to the Man.

"Who beat you up?" Dexter asked. He was smiling. He could see this case shaping up. Nicely.

"The brothers. I was leaving the alley." Tomas paused, his body shaking with pain. "They were blocking the way, Primo, Baldo, and Jesse. They hit me. They just kept hitting me ..."

Tomas started to cry, which only made it hurt more.

"Tomas, Tomas, listen to me, *listen.*" Dexter leaned closer. "Did Shaw touch you?"

Tomas sobbed.

Dexter nudged him. Tomas cried out.

"Did Shaw touch you? Rough you up a bit?"

"No."

"No?"

"The cop didn't touch me."

Dexter sat silently for a moment while Tomas whimpered.

"Yes, he did."

"What?"

"Shaw came into the alley and beat that confession out of you."

Tomas stopped whimpering. He turned his sightless eyes slowly, painfully towards Dexter's voice. "But my momma and sisters . . ."

"Listen, you just listen to me, boy, and do *exactly* what I tell you. Do as I say and you and your momma and your sisters will be back doin' what you been doin' and Shaw won't bother anyone anymore."

CHAPTER SIX

Brett Macklin sat in the courtroom staring at the gang members with undisguised hatred. The judge could see it. So could the jury. His hatred was so strong you could almost touch it.

Tomas Cruz could feel it but dared not look over his shoulder. He sat still in his wheelchair, his head bandaged and his legs, in casts, sticking out straight in front of him. His facial swelling had gone down just enough so that he could see Dexter beside him, nervously adjusting his paisley tie and brushing imaginary dust off his red jacket.

Primo Manriquez was like a kid at a carnival. To him, this wasn't a murder trial but a *big fuckin' joke.* And the biggest laugh of all was sitting in the first row trying to look *bad.*

"Look at that stupid motherfucker," Primo said, playing with his thin mustache. "Hey, Esteban, look at him."

Enrico Esteban stole a quick glance at Macklin. Suddenly he was glad there were armed officers in the room.

Primo laughed. "Oooooh, he's scaring me. Ooooh."

Teobaldo "Baldo" Villanueva sat stoically. The tall, balding Chicano wasn't worried. Things just happened. If things looked as though they weren't going to work out for Teobaldo Villanueva, well, he'd just have to *make* things work out for Teobaldo Villanueva. That's all.

In Teobaldo Villanueva's world, Brett Macklin didn't exist. For now.

Mario Carrera, snoring loudly, faked sleep.

Jesse Ortega smiled at Primo. To Jesse, Primo was just about the coolest guy around. Next to himself. And Fred Williamson, of course.

Hector Gomez, his arms crossed over his chest, hunched down low in his seat and watched Blake Yates, the prosecuting attorney, as he strolled in front of the jury box carefully reciting his opening statement.

Yates described the gang members as animals with no conscience or remorse, who terrorized a neighborhood and then killed the one man who stood up against them.

Yates paused, his thumb in his vest pocket. "That man was Officer James Douglas Macklin."

Macklin sighed, impatient. *Let's give these punks to the hangman already.* Shaw was restless, unable to get comfortable in his seat beside Macklin.

Yates described the gang members setting Macklin aflame, dwelling on the premeditation necessary to lay such a gruesome trap. Finally, Yates recalled Macklin's final moments, his flaming run across the bus's path and the two deaths it caused.

The Honorable Judge Walter MacFarland watched Yates wide-eyed, seemingly expecting the young assistant district attorney to yank a live chicken from inside his gray, three-piece suit. Six cups of coffee with the morning *Times* and a snort of decongestant, however, always gave MacFarland that look.

"I'd like to call my first witness, Your Honor." MacFarland nodded wearily to Yates. "Sergeant Ronald Shaw."

Shaw groaned. *Ronald Shaw… C'MON DOWN! It's your turn to play Cops 'n' Robbers!* He hated court. He hated testifying. He hated getting up early in the morning. Shaw would have been the happiest man alive if MacFarland banged down his gavel loudly and said, "Never mind, Sergeant Shaw. Go back home to your *Herald Examiner*, the cold toilet seat, and your single daily cigarette."

MacFarland looks like the kind of guy who appreciates the importance of a good shit, Shaw thought as he was sworn in.

Christ, a guy can't function without a morning sit-down and a Camel straight.

"Sergeant Shaw, describe if you will the events leading to your arrest of Tomas Cruz, Enrico Esteban, Hector Gomez, Jesse Ortega, Mario Carrera, Primo Manriquez—"

"Ayyyy, that's me," Primo laughed.

MacFarland banged his gavel down sharply. "Control yourself, Mr. Manriquez, or I'll have the bailiff remove you from the courtroom."

Primo smiled.

Yates sighed. "And Teobaldo Villanueva."

"We began our investigation by questioning people in the area the night of Officer Macklin's murder." *C'mon, Ronny, stay cool.* "From these interviews we learned that Officer Macklin had several run-ins with their gang, the Bounty Hunters, and that they were in the immediate area at the time of his death.

"Go on." Yates leaned against the witness stand, smiling at the jury.

"So I began interviewing some of the gang members about their activities that night. One of them was Tomas Cruz. I gave him my card after I talked with him and I told him to call me if he wanted to talk some more."

"And he did, didn't he?"

"I got a call from him Thursday morning. He asked me to meet him in the alley where Officer Macklin was"—Shaw caught Brett Macklin's eye—"ah … was immolated."

"What happened in that alley, Sergeant?"

"I met him there, like he asked. He said he wanted to confess—"

"Objection." Dexter bolted up from his seat. "Your Honor, may I approach the bench?"

MacFarland motioned for both counsels to step forward. Dexter stepped around his table and grinned.

"Your Honor, I'd like to request that the jury be excused," Dexter whispered, glancing back and forth between Yates and MacFarland. "It has just come to my attention that Shaw's testimony and the evidence he wishes to introduce may be inadmissible."

MacFarland rested his head on his hands.

"Your Honor, Mr. Dexter can't possibly know—," Yates began.

"I've just learned that this so-called confession was not voluntarily and freely given," Dexter interrupted, smiling at Yates. *Gotcha!* "I can prove that Sergeant Shaw beat my client, causing him grievous injury in order to exact this so-called confession from him."

MacFarland frowned and then looked at the jury. "The bailiff will please escort the jury out of the courtroom."

Macklin looked at Shaw. The detective couldn't hide his dread. Shaw didn't like Dexter's tight little smile one bit.

The jury members stood up and filed quietly out of the courtroom. When the door closed behind them, MacFarland sighed. "All right, counselor, call your witnesses."

Dexter bowed slightly with strained grace. "I'd like to call two witnesses, Your Honor. The first is Hilda Cruz." Shaw stepped from the witness stand and passed Cruz as he returned to his seat.

Cruz had traded in her black miniskirt and red spandex top for a flower-print cotton dress, an outfit she probably saved for tricks who wanted a little motherly love.

Macklin whispered into Shaw's ear. "What the hell is going on, Ronny?"

"Dexter says I beat the confession out of Cruz."

Just make them talk.

Tell me, Mack, should I use a rubber hose?

"Did you?"

Shaw turned. "No."

"Where were you early Thursday afternoon, Mrs. Cruz?" Dexter asked politely. It was as if he were questioning the First Lady.

"In the alley with my son."

Shaw drew in a deep breath.

"Why, Mrs. Cruz?"

"Because I don't trust that cop," she yelled, pointing at Shaw. "He has been harassing us, pushing us around as if we were garbage. Every day he's there, threatening us and asking us questions, arresting us for no reason at all except to cause us trouble. I was afraid for my boy."

"Why did your son call Sergeant Shaw?" Dexter asked him.

"To beg him to leave us alone." She turned to MacFarland. "We're law-abiding people, but it don't help no one to be hassled every day by the cops. I'm a single mother and I got to put the bread on the table. I can't have some loony cop bugging us all the time."

"What happened in that alley, Mrs. Cruz?"

"My son asked the cop to lay off us. But *he* wouldn't listen to Tomas. All *he* could talk about was that cop who was killed. The cop kept saying 'You did it and I'm gonna get you for it.' My son said, 'No, no, quit. I didn't do it.' That's when the cop said, 'Don't give me no lip,' and tossed this garbage can at my boy. And then he just started beating him and beating him while my boy begged him to stop. 'Confess, confess' was all that son of a bitch would say."

Tears welled up in her eyes.

"Why didn't you show yourself, Mrs. Cruz, or go for help?"

Hilda Cruz began to weep. "I was scared. I thought he'd kill me." Dexter touched her hand. "Thank you, Mrs. Cruz."

"Any questions, Mr. Yates?" MacFarland asked.

Yates sat silent for a moment. "No questions, Your Honor."

"You can step down, Mrs. Cruz." MacFarland motioned to the bailiff to assist her. The bailiff gently touched her elbow and guided her back to her seat.

Dexter flipped through the papers on his table. "I'd like to call Sergeant Sliran to the stand."

Yates leaned back and whispered to Shaw. "You want to let me in on what's going on, Sergeant?"

"This is bullshit, Yates, absolute nonsense. I never touched the boy."

"Could she have been in the alley?"

Shaw glanced back at Hilda Cruz, dabbing her eyes with a Kleenex. "Yes, maybe, I don't know."

Yates sighed. It fell together with sickening simplicity. "Dexter had this all along."

"What?"

Yates ignored him. "That's why Dexter had a jury impaneled before contesting the confession."

Shaw grabbed Yates. "What are you talking about?"

"It's over," Yates said flatly.

Sliran smirked at Dexter as the attorney approached. "Where were you, Sergeant Sliran, while your partner was in the alley?"

"In the car."

"Could you see Sergeant Shaw talking with Tomas Cruz?"

"Nope."

"Could you hear them talking?"

"Nope."

"Did you hear anything at all from that alley, Sergeant?" Sliran looked at Shaw.

"Sergeant, answer my question. Did you hear anything at all?"

"Some crashes, maybe."

Shaw ran a hand over his face.

"Yes or no, Sergeant, did you hear some crashes?"

"Yes."

"What kind of crashes?"

Sliran turned to Yates for help. Yates sat impassively, his face expressionless. It had ended for him already.

"I dunno, like garbage cans being banged around."

"Did it sound like a fight?"

"Objection." Yates made the obligatory motion, casually, not even looking at the judge. "He's leading the witness on. The witness already described the noises."

"Objection sustained," MacFarland said.

"How long did these noises last?"

"I dunno, a few seconds, maybe a minute."

"And when did your partner come out of the alley?"

"I guess five or ten minutes later."

"Thank you, Sergeant." Dexter smiled at Yates. "Your witness." Yates tapped his fingers on the table. "I have no questions."

The courtroom fell silent. Shaw looked anxiously at Yates, who sat with his head down, doodling on his legal pad. Macklin watched the judge.

MacFarland sighed and cleared his throat.

"The defense has shown that there is considerable doubt as to the validity of the confession. Under the circumstances I rule that the confession is inadmissible as evidence in this proceeding."

Dexter grinned like a monk set loose in a whorehouse.

"Do you have any more witnesses, Mr. Yates?" MacFarland asked.

Yates frowned. The case was lost. Without the confession, there was no way to convict the gang members. "No, Your Honor."

Dexter was jubilant. "Your Honor, the defense respectfully requests that judgment be made in my client's behalf."

"The charges are dismissed."

The youths broke into laughter, clapping each other on the back and shaking Dexter's hand. Macklin stood up slowly, his eyes on the gang members doing their happy dance. Primo flipped him off.

"So that's it, they're free," Macklin said.

Yates was standing, stuffing his papers into his briefcase. "Yep."

"Isn't there anything you can do?"

"No, it's the law, Mr. Macklin."

"The kid confessed."

Yates glanced angrily over his shoulder at Shaw. "*Maybe*, but that doesn't matter anymore."

Macklin grabbed Yates by the arm. "That scum killed my father. You can't let them slither out of here."

"Let go of me, Mr. Macklin," Yates said coolly, carefully. Macklin glared at Yates. Fury raged in the pilot's eyes. Yates, for a moment, feared Macklin would crush his arm like an empty beer can. "Let go."

"Mack . . . ," Shaw said quietly.

Macklin saw his father, screaming in agony, fleeing across the street. He saw the blackened shape, twisted and smoking on the pavement. In that second, part of Brett Macklin died.

Macklin sighed and released Yates. Shaw felt something pass, saw the strange flatness in Macklin's eyes.

The prosecutor rubbed his upper arm. "Believe me, Mr. Macklin, I know how you feel." Yates slipped around Macklin and paused beside Shaw, who was still bewildered by Macklin's unnerving expression.

"You'll be hearing from me, Sergeant," Yates said, leaving.

The gang members began to file out, Primo strutting proudly and grinning as he walked past Macklin. "Hey, Jesse, I feel like some barbecued pork. How 'bout you?"

"Sure," Jesse cackled. "Sure, barbecued pork sounds *good*."

Baldo grunted, strolling casually out of the courtroom with Hector Gomez at his side. Mario, grinning, pretended to sleep-walk out of the courtroom, his arms held out straight in front of him and his eyes barely closed.

Dexter smiled proudly, wheeling Cruz past Macklin and Shaw. "Next time, Sergeant, try to control your aggressive tendencies."

Esteban skirted by quickly, bumping Shaw and Dexter on his way out.

Shaw was left with Macklin. He didn't know what to say. Somehow, sorry just wasn't good enough. Shaw reached out to touch Macklin, hesitated, and walked out slowly, leaving Macklin alone with his thoughts.

Macklin slumped in his chair, the defeat sapping him of the energy to get up and walk out. The unfairness of it all, and his inability to do anything about it, drained him. He felt utterly powerless.

The justice system Macklin had believed in, the system his father had dedicated his life to, had turned around and kicked him in the teeth. Justice wasn't blind. To Macklin, it was comatose. And there was nothing he could do about it. The murderers would go unpunished.

They killed my father. How could the system let them free?

As he asked himself that question again and again, the despair began to fade and he became aware of another voice trying to be heard. He stared at the judge's bench, trying to clear his head so he could hear it.

Macklin enjoyed a moment of mental peace, the judge's bench the only image in his mind. Then he heard the whisper of his anger.

He felt his heartbeat quicken. The whisper was telling him something, he wasn't sure what, but it seemed to lessen the crushing feeling of unfairness. It offered him a way out of his defeat.

The whisper grew into a defiant shout that echoed in his head. The shout, thick with danger and violence, was a stony coldness that drowned memories and feelings and left anger in their place.

The shout became a scream, evoking a fury that burrowed deep inside him and carved a warm niche for itself in his heart. Suddenly Macklin felt energized, alive again, and he understood what the screams were telling him.

Make them pay.

CHAPTER SEVEN

"Lieutenant, this is craziness," Shaw screamed, pacing in front of Lieutenant Bohan Lieu, who was leaning forward in his chair, unbending a paper clip.

"Ronny, I'm sorry. But you know the rules. You're doing desk work until this is cleaned up."

"You don't *believe* that *shit*. I didn't lay a hand on Cruz!"

"It doesn't matter what I believe." Lieu arched his head towards the squad room. Two guys from Internal Affairs were talking with Sliran. "It's what *they* believe."

One of them looked like Liberace, though he dressed better. The other guy, the one who was doing all the talking, was Mr. Regulation. Shiny shoes, short hair, Disneyland employee face. Trouble.

Lieu opened his desk drawer and pulled out a package of Sugar Babies. He popped four into his mouth and offered the open bag to Shaw.

"No, thanks."

Lieu munched on the chewy gob. "I wouldn't get too attached to your victimized attitude, Ronny. You're to blame for most of this mess."

Shaw held out his hand and Lieu poured a few Sugar Babies into his open palm.

"I won't fault you, Ronny, for coming down hard on Tomas. Anyone might have done that." Lieu popped a few more caramel treats into his mouth. "But meeting that kid in an alley and not bringing Sliran in with you was stupid. That was mistake number one. Mistake two was not bringing the kid down here to make his confession. Mistake three was not arresting the kid then and there."

Lieu snapped his fingers. "Three strikes and you're out. A cop with your experience should know better."

Shaw fell into a chair. "You're right," he said glumly. He held out his hand for more Sugar Babies, chewed on them awhile, and watched the Internal Affairs boys grill Sliran. "Well, Lieutenant, what do you see in your crystal ball?"

Lieu pondered a Sugar Baby. "I'd say you're heading into a world of hurt. I'd get yourself a lawyer."

Shaw chuckled miserably. "Anyone got Dexter's number?"

The streets were empty under a full moon that colored the world, through a cloud-streaked sky, with hazy blue shadows. Wind whistled between buildings and the stillness seemed palpable, thick, and uneasy. Shadows became threatening, twitching and darting between crevices and alleys, doorways and other seams in the night.

His shadow fell on the street. His footfalls echoed amidst the gutted, blackened buildings. The lone, unscorched streetlight cast its single unnatural glow on his face as he stood at the alley's mouth.

His eyes were dark, made dull by a fury that had ebbed into a deep, intense anger. He felt almost inanimate, as soulless as the night itself. His shadow lay like a corpse in front of him, stretching into the alley.

He felt utterly alone, unattached to any person, and unable to conjure any joy from the world around him. Unmoving, he stood there struggling to understand and control the changes occurring within him. He feared he might lose any humanity he ever had. It was an agony endured in silence.

He stood. Sunlight slowly burned its way through the night, and the shadows melted away.

He was at the hot-dog stand when Saul arrived at six a.m.

Saul didn't recognize him at first. Looking at the stranger warily as he unlocked the hot-dog stand, he opened the shutters over the counter. The man sat on a stool, his face unshaven, his distant eyes watching the street awaken. Saul tied on his apron and heated up the grill. "You're Brett Macklin, aren't you?"

Macklin turned.

"I didn't recognize you at first." Saul scraped the grill with a spatula. "I've only seen you twice. You didn't look like hell then."

Saul grinned at Macklin. The pilot looked ten years older than when he had seen him at the funeral.

"Listen, Brett, sit right there and I'll fix you up some of my famous eggs." Saul cracked two eggs over the grill, then reached into the refrigerator for a handful of hash browns.

"Your starch special," Macklin said.

Saul saw a hint of brightness in Macklin's eyes. "I see JD told you about my famous breakfast platter."

"And your grease burger."

Saul laughed. "We can still be friends, can't we?"

Macklin grinned. Saul's cheerfulness warmed him, and some of his emotional chill evaporated. "My father walked a beat so he could work off the extra tonnage you put on him."

Saul pointed to the eggs with his spatula. "How you want them?"

"Over easy." Macklin unzipped his jacket and leaned on the counter. "Listen, Saul, I didn't come down here just to eat."

"Big surprise," he said, flipping over the eggs. "Hardly anyone does."

"Dad talked to you—"

"Yes, he did, Brett," Saul interrupted. "And I miss him. Every morning and every evening JD would sit right there, where you are, and just talk. We never saw him as a police officer, you know, walking a beat. He was just another street person, a shopkeeper, a friend."

"Look, Saul, did he ever talk to you about the gangs?"

"A little. Moe and me and your father couldn't believe how violent our neighborhood was getting. We were always hearing stories about kids doing awful things to each other. Why, I can remember when this was a peaceful place to li—"

"What kind of stories?"

Saul handed Macklin his plate of eggs and hash browns. "Horrible things, beatings and shootings and just horrible things, you know. Even your father was shocked. He couldn't figure it out. We'd hear all this talk, but your father just couldn't track down anything. But you know your father—that only made him more determined. He wanted to know where all these stories were coming from and why all this was going on."

Saul buttered two slices of toast and set them in from of Macklin. "The neighborhood's just deteriorating. We noticed it, JD noticed it, everyone noticed it. JD, though, he took it personally. Like it reflected on his ability as a police officer, you know? It seemed like more violence every day. You know things are going bad when vultures like Elias Simon"—Saul pointed his spatula to the Silver Tabernacle looming in the sky behind Macklin—"come down and pick on your bones."

Macklin looked over his shoulder at the towering glass monolith. "Like a vulture?"

"Sure. Comes in here with his fancy duds and con-man smile and his missions and says he's gonna bring Jesus down here." Saul frowned. "Christ'll stay at the Bonaventure. He won't come down here. Simon just came to prey on our fear. People will turn to him cause they're scared and don't know where else to go. *The schmucks.*"

Macklin wiped up the yolk on his plate with a piece of toast and took a bite. "Why do you stay, Saul?"

"Good question."

And apparently not one that would be answered. Macklin pushed his plate away. "What can you tell me about the Bounty Hunters?"

"I wouldn't invite them over for dinner. Why are you asking me all these questions? A walking encyclopedia I'm not." Saul looked at him questioningly and cleared away Macklin's plate. "Good, huh?"

"Delicious. Look, Saul, I'm just trying to understand my father's death. I want to know why he was killed."

"Senseless violence, that's all. Nowadays it happens all the time."

Moe waddled up, the *Los Angeles Times* folded under his arm, and sat on the stool beside Macklin.

"'Morning, Saul. Did ya read the paper?"

Saul had his back to the counter. "Haven't had a chance, Moe. Say hello to JD's son, Brett."

Moe set his paper on the counter and turned, offering his chubby hand to Macklin, who shook it.

"Sorry about your pop. JD and I were close friends. He talked about you, yep. He sure was proud of you."

Macklin tried to smile.

"Couldn't believe they let those punks off. Jesus. What's happening to our legal system?" Moe shook his head. "You know, pretty soon those old farts in the Supreme Court are gonna make it illegal to fight back when some guy jumps you. You'll have to roll over on your back, point to your nuts, and say 'Kick me here and please take my wallet.'"

"What do you know about the Bounty Hunters?"

"Buncha punks, what more do I need to know?"

"Where can I find 'em?"

Moe laughed. "See that street behind you? Just walk out there some night and they'll find you."

CHAPTER EIGHT

The exit signs on the Santa Monica Freeway whizzed past Brett Macklin at seventy miles per hour as he drove the Batmobile towards the patch of glowing, towering names scrawled in the night sky. Crocker Bank. Simon Ministries. Hilton. Transamerica. Jesus Saves. Wells Fargo. They shined blue, green, and bright white against the blackness.

He turned up the stereo, letting Bruce Springsteen run full throttle down "Thunder Road," and veered south away from the downtown skyline towards the softer lights of the neighborhood his father had patrolled.

Earlier that evening Macklin had tried to sleep. But no position in bed was comfortable. His body was damp with sweat and the sheets stuck to his skin. His limbs were tingling so strong, so strangely, that relaxing was a fight. He was tortured by a nameless compulsion that needed no rest. It struggled with him, racing his pulse and making his head throb. He yanked off the sheets, lay for a few minutes, and then bolted from the bed, pacing nervously around the room.

The image of the empty judge's bench and the whisper in his head prodded him again. The next thing he knew he was dressed and slicing through the night, his face reflecting the unearthly green light from the Cadillac's dashboard.

Macklin tried to lose himself in the music. It was no good. The compulsion was louder. No matter how high he cranked up the stereo, no matter how fast he drove, Macklin couldn't force back the compulsion.

The only thing that seemed to ease his tension was the image of himself holding his father's gun, pumping bullets into the gang members that had been set free. That image scared Macklin. It went against everything his father had taught him. Yet it was only when he envisioned himself killing that the painful ache in his stomach ebbed. Only then did he feel any comfort.

The image teased him now. The pain was gone, but the compulsion was as strong as ever.

Macklin followed the curving off-ramp and slid quietly onto the trash-strewn streets of the neighborhood, lowering the volume on his stereo and settling back into his seat. He felt removed from what he saw, as if seeing it on television or from the comfort of a tour bus. This was a foreign land, an alien planet, a world entirely different from the middle-class streets of West Los Angeles.

This was where old General Motors cars go to die, Macklin thought. GM heaven. Monte Carlos, Chevelles, Novas, sharp Buick Rivieras, and pretentious Pontiac Bonnevilles—here they were world-class touring cars. The trappings of ghetto status and loyalty.

Macklin cruised the streets slowly, looking at the faces, learning the terrain. People gathered near an open-all-night liquor store, warming themselves on its neon fire as if it would keep the desperation that stalked this urban wilderness at bay. The people were smileless and had tired, gentle faces.

Teenagers played video games, hung out, strutted, and hit on girls at the Burger Shop. Little placards ran along the flat roofline advertising Chinese food, fried chicken, hickory burgers, and tacos.

The neighborhood people all seemed to be performing to Macklin, acting rough and hard because some script somewhere told them to, because men like Macklin *expected* them to.

Macklin scrutinized the faces.

Maybe he was wrong. They seemed like frightened, angry people. Just like him. Not animals, not creatures he had to punish. Could Shaw have pushed Tomas Cruz too hard? Was the confession what Dexter claimed it was—a lie, the desperate act of a person afraid for his life?

Then Macklin remembered *them*. Primo, Carrera, Teobaldo Villanueva. The violence he saw in their eyes. They didn't bother to hide it. They flaunted it, reveled in it, too.

But did they kill Dad?

Macklin twisted the wheel, the car screeching around the corner in front of Sho-More Adult Films and speeding away from the neon promise of "BIG THRILLS, HARD ACTION, TITILATING FUN."

He passed Saul's hot-dog stand, following the path his father walked before his death. Bars covered all the storefront windows and doors. It was as if the neighborhood were a prison that kept its captives locked on the streets.

Macklin steered clear of the charred section of the block, turned the corner, and headed north towards downtown LA.

There, like a gleaming diamond in a shitheap, was a crisp and clean McDonald's restaurant, resplendent in its bright red brick and golden arches. Unscratched and untarnished, it looked shockingly out of place. The decay that had fed on the neighborhood dared not touch the home of the Egg McMuffin. It was as if the McDonald's were a McHoly shrine on McSacred ground, supernaturally protected from the neighborhood's destructive elements.

It gave Macklin the creeps.

A foot away from the McDonald's parking lot, the supernatural forces ebbed to nothing and entropy began.

The traffic light turned red at the next intersection and Macklin stopped beside a dental clinic that used to be a gas station. The pump islands, minus the pumps, were still there, and the sign that had once read "TEXACO" now lit Dr. Kelly Selvidge's name up in lights.

Dr. Selvidge's neighbor was the green stucco of Christ's Community Church. Huge letters atop the building proclaimed, "GOD BLESS OUR COMMUNITY."

He'd better, sport, Macklin thought, *because nobody else will.*

The light turned green and the Batmobile surged into the intersection. Macklin glanced up at a lighted billboard that announced to the neighborhood that "AMERICA IS GOING TO EUROPE ON PAN AM."

And you're not, the billboard seemed to tease. Your sorry ass is stuck here for good.

Macklin sympathized with the people who had to look at that billboard, that sadistic taunt, every day. The hate Macklin had felt wasn't burning as strongly now. The neighborhood had had a cooling effect on him. The streets didn't radiate violence, as he had expected, as much as despair. He found it hard to resent the place or its people.

But his father had died there in a sick, gruesome way. Somewhere on these hopeless streets walked the bastards that had struck the match.

Macklin cruised down another street, looking for them.

CHAPTER NINE

The moment Teobaldo Villanueva came into the pool hall, people began to worry. Not because he was tall. Not because he was bald. Not because he was rumored to bend crowbars with his teeth. And certainly not because he was Chicano.

Those qualities were nothing to fret about. Everyone in the room *respected* those. The clientele in Crazy Al's pool hall held Baldo in high regard, learning long ago to smile when Baldo was smiling and frown when Baldo was frowning. They knew how to handle it when Baldo was happy or unhappy—it was just a question of how best to avoid him without pissing him off.

But tonight they knew they were in big trouble.

They knew it when there was Hector Gomez buzzing around Baldo like some insane fly drawn to a can of Raid. Hector got that wired only on certain nights.

The second clue was Baldo's eyes, eyes that were nearly pupilless and seemed to recede into his head during those dreaded periods.

The third clue came a few minutes later. It was his conversational technique: a grunt followed by his fist, or foot, smashing violently into something. That something usually resembled a human being at first.

There was no doubt about it. That time of month again. Teobaldo "Baldo" Villanueva was horny. Hector Gomez knew his home might be an oxygen tent if he didn't find Baldo some pussy to chew on soon. Hector wasn't able to find any prospects in the pool hall so he opted for the easy way.

Baldo was sitting still on a bar stool, drinking a beer and growling. Hector put his arm around Baldo. "Hey, man, let's blow this shithouse and get laid."

Baldo nodded and stood up. To him, getting laid was like anything else—eating, drinking, shitting, and puking. You had to do it when you had to do it. Now he had to do it.

"What'll we have tonight, man? A white momma with big tits, huh? Does that sound good?" Hector said excitedly, leading Baldo to the door. "How 'bout some ebony gold, man, some smooth black ass? Maybe a Jap lady, see if it's really sideways, huh?"

Baldo stomped out the door and you could almost hear the people inside the pool hall sagging with relief.

Hector opened the passenger door of the battered '73 Cutlass for Baldo.

"Don't worry, Baldo, my man, tonight we're gonna send some lucky lady to Saturn."

Macklin's black Cadillac pulled around the corner unnoticed as the two youths emerged from the pool hall. At first, in the dim light cast by the pool hall windows, their shapes meant nothing to him. But as he drew closer his mind returned to the courtroom. He eased his pressure on the gas pedal. The car glided slowly on the momentum from the turn.

He had found his prey.

Hector got behind the wheel of his Cutlass and sped into traffic with a lurch and a loud cough from his car's exhaust. Macklin's Batmobile stalked two car lengths behind him.

Macklin followed the Cutlass through the neighborhood, unsure why he was or what he was planning to do. His father's .357 Magnum, an icy voice softly reminded him, rested in the glove compartment.

Hector seemed to be driving aimlessly, suddenly and recklessly making turns at the last possible moment. Macklin was a safe distance behind them but still found himself screeching around corners at fifty miles per hour just to keep up with them.

Lori Ann Bates heard Hector's Cutlass before she saw it fishtail onto the boulevard. She was worrying about tomorrow's anthropology exam and damning the terminally tardy bus line when the sound of tires scraping for a hold on the asphalt interrupted her thoughts.

She watched the car with weary detachment. Just another jerk in a four-wheeled metal-shop project making a fool out of himself, she thought. But her offhand disregard began to ebb as the car's zigzagging motion brought it closer to her. She froze. *This jerk isn't just going to speed by,* she realized. *He's coming for* me*!*

The car suddenly shot forward, as if Hector had heard her thoughts. Lori bolted down the street, looking over her shoulder at the car. To her it was a hungry animal, the headlights savage eyes promising death.

Her conscious mind told her running was useless, but her legs kept straining forward. The car overtook her, skidding to a stop just ahead of her. Before she could stop herself, the passenger door swung open across her path. Jaws opening to greet the prey. A frustrated, defiant scream rose in her throat. Something rough sprung out, grabbed her tightly around the waist, and pulled her inside the car. The door slammed shut and the car roared down the street.

Lori's face was pressed against the vinyl seat and she could smell the sharp odor of male sweat. She felt cold hands crawling up her thigh and quickly rolled over. Lying across Baldo's lap, she looked up into those empty eyes, seemingly devoid of any human feeling, and knew that there would be no mercy for her. She screamed with anger more than fear and reached out to rip them from their sockets.

Baldo pushed her away. She bolted up again. The glare off the rearview mirror stung her eyes. She halted her attack on Baldo, deciding her only hope was to attract the attention of the following car.

Lori tried to fling herself into the backseat. Baldo grabbed her by the hair and wrenched her head back. She held herself in place tightly with one hand and signaled madly with the other at the car behind them.

Baldo reached around, grabbed her face, and pulled hard. Lori reeled back and then pushed forward defiantly, her arm stretching out as if trying to touch the car behind them.

But Baldo was stronger. His suffocating grip hurled her backwards and she felt her head slam against the dashboard. The blow shocked her more than it hurt her, and she thrashed wildly against him. He pulled her forward by the face and then bashed her head against the dashboard again. Her head felt crushed and throbbed with pain. She refused to give in, weakly flailing her arms and struggling for breath. Hector laughed hysterically.

"That ought to calm the bitch down," she heard Hector cackle. "My grandpa used to do that to bass—bash 'em in the head with a big old stick."

Baldo grunted and Lori gritted her teeth to brace herself for the blow. The back of her head crashed against the dash and she stiffened, paralyzed by the dizzying pain. Baldo released her. The pressure on her face disappeared and she could breath.

"Woooowweeeee!" she heard Hector shriek, taking a turn suddenly at high speed. She felt Baldo grab her by the breast to stop her from rolling onto the floor. The car fishtailed and the tires screamed. "Wooooweeee!"

Baldo yanked her up onto his lap, her head lolling against the window. She couldn't see any headlights behind the car anymore. Her only hope was gone. She yelped as Baldo grabbed her right breast and twisted it towards Hector.

"Want some?" Baldo whispered. The burning pain made Lori whimper.

Hector howled. “Later, not while I’m driving.”

Baldo grunted deeply several times in a row, his version of laughter. Lori lashed out for his eyes again and he pulled her to him. She felt his hard lips grind against hers. She dug her nails into his neck, and could feel the spurt of blood as she pierced his skin.

“Bitch!” Baldo grunted, grabbing her by the head and forcing her down to the floor. Her nose pressed into the dirty carpet beside Hector’s leg. Baldo pounded his boot down on the small of her back, pinning her to the floor.

She pushed Hector’s foot against the gas pedal. Hector cried out with surprise, inadvertently twisting the wheel. She could feel the car veering uncontrollably. Lori was no longer thinking of freedom. This was an act of defiance.

The car jumped the curb with a violent bounce. Baldo stomped on her back angrily. The air rushed out of her and pain coursed through her limbs. She held Hector’s foot tightly. Baldo stomped again, the pain overriding her will and releasing her hold on Hector’s foot. Breathless and dazed, she lay limp on the floor.

“Shit, she’s a feisty bitch,” Hector spit, trying to catch his breath. Baldo nodded.

Lori moaned, dizzy and weak, the pain rolling over her in waves. She could feel the car slowing, and then it stopped. She turned on her side.

Lori could make out Hector leaning against the steering wheel above her. “I’m ready for some pussy. How ‘bout you, Baldo?”

Baldo grunted and opened the door. She felt the cool air rush into the car and then suddenly felt herself being dragged by the ankles through the open doorway. She frantically reached for some kind of solid hold. The carpet strands slipped from her fingers and she couldn’t grasp the smooth vinyl seats. Her head banged against the floor as the bulk of her body fell onto the ground.

She was dragged on the loose dirt, her blouse riding up around her shoulders, the sharp gravel scratching her exposed back.

The motion stopped. Through the haze of semiconsciousness, she noticed the fresh, woodsy smell of trees, the absence of street noise, and the lack of light cast by passing cars, streetlamps, and illuminated signs. Then Lori felt Baldo yank down her jeans. The chill raised goose bumps on her skin and she involuntarily contracted her pelvic muscles.

"Give it to her, Baldo, give it to her," Hector, crouched beside them, shrieked excitedly. Lori moaned, shaking her head back and forth, willing this awful nightmare to end.

Her body buckled as Baldo rammed his penis between her legs. It felt like his penis was serrated, his thrusts tearing the flesh from the walls of her vagina. She could feel the warm blood oozing onto her thighs. Baldo grabbed her head tightly, rested his weight on her, and thrust hard.

She cried in pain.

"Tight bitch, huh, Baldo?"

Baldo's weight seemed to crush Lori. The ground was hard and cold against her back and she could feel his hot breath on her face. He began to thrust faster now.

Lori began to feel distant, separate from the abuse being inflicted on her body. She didn't care anymore. Lori looked into his eyes and this time was comforted by the violence she saw there. Death seemed to her like a welcome alternative to this, and she awaited it patiently.

"She loves it, Baldo, they all do," Hector said.

She heard an explosion. Something warm and wet splashed her and she saw Hector lifted off his feet and tossed backwards into a tree. Baldo stiffened above her and she heard the moist squish of his penis pulling out of her. Baldo stood up slowly and looked past her. She turned her head and followed his gaze. Hector lay crumpled against the tree, his chest a splash of red, his dumb, lifeless eyes staring back at her.

Baldo grunted and she saw him turn, expressionless, in the direction of the explosion. A man holding a gun emerged from the darkness.

"You," Baldo hissed, his bloody erection jutting out from between his legs.

"Me," she heard the man say. Lori was jolted by the flash of his gun and another loud crack. She heard the bullet slap into Baldo, who took the impact with the subtle sway of a person slightly nudged by a passerby.

Baldo growled, raised his hands like talons, and rushed the gunman.

The man waited until Baldo was inches away and then fired again, point blank into Baldo's stomach.

But Baldo kept coming, lumbering towards the man like an angered grizzly bear. The man fired again.

Baldo froze, stumbled backwards, and pivoted towards Lori. His penis was gone. The big Chicano fell forward at her feet, raising a cloud of dirt.

Lori closed her eyes, no longer able to disassociate herself from the nausea and pain wracking her body. She didn't hear the man walk over to her, but she felt him reach under her and lift her up.

His arms felt strong and hard. She felt safe. In his arms, bobbing with each of his long strides, she felt herself unhinge. Closing her eyes tightly, her body convulsed with deep agonizing sobs. The tears burned her skin and rolled down her face onto his arms.

She sensed herself being lowered to the ground. His arms slipped out from under her. Panic began to creep into her sobs.

"Don't leave me now!"

"Shh-h-h-h," he said, gently touching her cheek. "S-h-h-h."

Then she heard the ring of a dime dropping into a pay phone, the clicking of the dial rolling, and the murmur of his voice, a few words.

"Ambulance ... rape ... police ... hurry.

She strained to open her eyes. Tears and pain blurred her vision. As he walked away, she could barely see the man's dark shape blending into the night.

"Who are you?" she called out shakily, unsure if the receding shape was a person or just a trick of the light.

It could have been the wind, a whisper, or herself replying. But she could have sworn the shape said:

"The jury."

The story broke the next afternoon.

"Mr. JURY KILLS RAPISTS, SAVES WOMAN," the *Herald Examiner* touted in their evening edition, while the more sedate *Los Angeles Times* read, "TWO RAPISTS KILLED, MYSTERY GUNMAN SOUGHT."

Shaw watched it on the evening news, his arm around Sunshine, Guess lying at his feet.

"This is the park where a twenty-two-year-old UCLA student thought she would die at the hands of two vicious rapists who abducted her at a nearby bus stop late last night." The square-jawed reporter looked over the shoulder of his tailored suit into the clearing. "Then, out of those trees there, a man stepped out and gunned down her captors, who police have identified as twenty-four-year-old Hector Gomez and twenty-six-year-old Teobaldo Villanueva."

The screen showed the bus stop where the girl was abducted. "Police say the victim had just visited her grandparents and was waiting here for her westbound bus when Gomez and Villanueva drove up and grabbed her, taking her to a secluded park a few miles away." The reporter's face now filled the screen. "There, police say, she was in the midst of being raped when this mystery man saved her, carried her to a phone booth, and placed an anonymous call to authorities. Who is this mystery man? He identified himself only as 'the jury' and disappeared."

Shaw changed the channel.

"... while Police Chief Jed Stocker urged the Good Samaritan to assist police in their investigation by making himself known."

Frustrated, Shaw hit the remote control again.

"The question remains: Who is Mr. Jury and will he strike again?"

Shaw turned off the set. "Wonderful. That's all we need, some lunatic vigilante shooting up the streets. The news media has taken this thing and blown it all out of proportion."

Sunshine stroked Shaw's thigh absently. "Lighten up, Ronny. So what's the big deal if people indulge their Superman fantasies a bit?"

"Because it's liable to spur this guy on. Sunny, this Mr. Jury is nothing more than a killer."

"A killer who saved that girl's life."

"This time. Next time he decides to kill a couple of guys it may not be so clear-cut."

They were silent for a moment. "Hey, Ronny, weren't those two of the guys who—"

"Yep. I won't be sending a wreath to their funeral."

As Brett Macklin watched the news in the garage, sitting on the hood of his Cadillac, he kept reliving the previous night. He couldn't dredge up any guilty feeling. They were animals, and if he hadn't stopped them, they would have ravaged the girl, possibly killing her. After what they had done to his father ...

Macklin leaned forward and changed the channel.

An old man, with skin like a peanut shell, bent towards the newsman's microphone. "I think they should give this Mr. Jury guy a medal."

Next up was a woman trying to balance her teething child in one hand and pull up her slipping bra strap with the other. "I'd sleep better at night knowing Mr. Jury was in my neighborhood. There just ain't enough cops out there."

A man with "accountant" written all over his face was stopped on a busy street. "Mr. Jury? Just another maniac with a gun. He probably shot those guys because they didn't give him his turn with the girl."

A crisp-looking businesswoman was quizzed in front of an impressive building. "I think it's great. We *need* a guy like him." She smiled into the camera. "I just hope Kryptonite doesn't bother him."

Macklin snapped off the set and went to bed. He slept like a baby.

CHAPTER TEN

"A Job Well Done Means More Jobs to Come."

Melody stared at the maxim, which she had needlepointed in a sampler and hung on the wall, and smiled to herself, patting the naked man atop her on the back.

"Oh God, *please* don't stop!" she shrieked, faking an orgiastic squeal.

The mattress creaked underneath her as the man quickened his pace. *Business ain't bad today,* she thought to herself, hoping she would handle three more guys before quitting time. Her body rocked under him. If she was real lucky, she could make it home in time to catch the nightly *Hawaii Five-O* reruns on Channel 13.

She glanced up at the water stains on the ceiling. They were like clouds to her. Each day they looked like something different. Today they were a giant clam with arms and legs like a man. His thrusts were beginning to hurt her.

"Oh God, I can't take it!" she screamed joyfully, her way of saying 'Hurry up, already, I ain't got all day, buddy!' to her customers. It usually worked, and this man was no exception. The man tensed up, groaned deeply, and fell on her, sweating. Melody glanced over his heaving shoulders at her wristwatch. Ten minutes had passed. Great.

After a few moments, he recovered and propped himself up on his elbows, grinning the way one would expect a person to grin after enduring an orgasm that could change a person's eye color.

"Shit, Melody, you're gonna kill me. I don't know if I can handle you twice a week," the beefy taxi driver said between sharp intakes of breath.

Melody grinned and gave his penis a playful squeeze.

"You've been saying that for six months, sport." She slid out from under him and reached for her clothes. Artie was one of her "old dependables." He paid in advance and always came back for more, despite the guilt he said he felt about sneaking away from his three-hundred-pound wife and four delinquent kids.

Melody slipped on her panties and tight, black leather pants, straightened up, pressed his face between her breasts. To him, she knew, she was nothing more than two breasts with legs. "See you next week, sweetie." She gave him a pat on the head, stepped back, pulled a low-cut top over her head, and walked out of the room.

Melody, her brown eyes glowing, dashed down the stairs and into the lobby. She winked at Alfred, the skinny, elderly hotel desk clerk, and sauntered outside into the bright afternoon sunlight.

Just then an old, black Cadillac with huge, sloping fins slid to a stop at the curb in front of her. *Nifty car,* Melody thought as she bent down and peered inside at the driver. There was something familiar about the driver's narrow, blue eyes, the hard, uncompromising set of his jaw, the sharp cheekbones and dark skin.

The man smiled a warm, sad smile that both attracted her and made her wary. Cop or fun-loving fuck? She couldn't quite read this tall, muscular man in the leather flight jacket.

"Hello, Melody, how are you?" he asked, opening his door and rising from the car.

"Depends," she said, meeting his even gaze as he walked around the car towards her. She tried to figure out which smile to flash. The boy-can-I make-you-feel-good smile or the I'm-so-innocent-I-could-be-Florence-Henderson smile. She ended up sporting an awkward, nervous grin of uncertainly. At least it fit.

"I'm Brett Macklin." He took her hand and led her to the car. "My father talked about you quite a bit."

She broke into a big, happy smile. "Brett Macklin, I'll be damned. How did you know who I was?" She opened the passenger door and got into the car. She just gave herself the rest of the day off.

"Saul told me where to find you." Macklin closed her door, walked around to the driver's side, and got in. "And once I saw you, well, I knew I had found the Melody my father spoke of."

He guessed she was in her mid – to late thirties. She was clearly a hooker, but there was, in an odd sort of way, a certain innocence about her. That was probably half of her charm and what had amused his father. JD often jokingly referred to Melody as his girlfriend. Brett was never sure whether or not his father ever was sexually involved with her. It didn't really matter. She was one of the few signs of hope JD found on his desperate beat.

She blushed. She always thought she was beyond blushing. "You know, Brett—I guess I can call you Brett—you look a lot like your father."

Macklin smiled, easing the Batmobile into traffic. "Thanks. Where can we go to talk?"

"How about my place? I can make some tea." She pointed down the street. "Take a left, go two blocks, and then make a right. It's the apartment building on the left. They call it 'gracious living' on the sign out front. What a line, huh? I'll make some tea just like your father liked it."

"Sounds good to me." Macklin felt slightly uncomfortable. His father had talked about Melody in glowing terms, always avoiding how she made her living. He never told Brett outright that she was a hooker. Brett didn't quite know how to behave.

Macklin was pleasantly surprised by how nice and conventional her apartment turned out to be. She could see what he was thinking and teased him. "What were you expecting? Something seedy, a bed in the middle of the room with sticky sheets? Maybe some mirrors on the ceiling and centerfolds from old *Hustler* magazines on the wall?"

"Something like that."

The place looked like an ad for Levitz furniture snipped out of the newspaper. Crisp and clean, with a sofa and love seat and dinette set seemingly plucked from a "Suburban Newlyweds' First Home" display, comfortable and inexpensive.

In every corner of the room was a hanging plant, and the walls were covered with grass cloth. "I put the grass cloth up myself," she said, switching on the room lights. "I did it a piece at a time, a week at a time. That crap is expensive, you know."

Macklin nodded, noticing the little antiques, the spoon collection, and the nondescript sort of paintings found in Holiday Inns across the nation.

"This is where most of my money goes, Brett. I don't buy fancy jewelry or relatively new used cars," she said. "I mean, this is where I live. This is me. I want to make it my castle."

Macklin sat on the couch.

"And I never bring my clients here," she added quickly, "This is *my* place, you know?"

Macklin nodded. "You brought Dad here, didn't you?"

"Oh, yeah, all the time. He was a teddy bear. A lovable teddy bear. He always made sure I was happy and not getting hassled too much. Occasionally he'd have to lock me up, you know. That was his job. I had no quarrel with that."

"Did he ever talk to you about what he was working on?"

Her smile waned. "You mean about the people who killed him?"

"Yes, I do." He looked at her sternly.

She sat down on the love seat across from him. "You know, he and I would sit here and talk, for hours sometimes, after he got off duty. That's all we did, talk. No screwing. Not that I didn't try." She shrugged her shoulders. "It meant a lot to me, his friendship, you know?"

"It meant a lot to him, too, Melody."

She sighed and nodded. "So what do you want to know?"

"Anything. Everything. What did he tell you about the gangs?"

"The gangs." She drew her legs together into the yoga position. "Well, Christ, I don't know. The gangs. They bugged him. He had a hard time dealing with all the sadistic stuff happening on the streets. He'd ask me about things he'd hear on the streets and ask me what I was hearing. I was hearing the same shit. This gang was out to slit that gang's throat, you know. Last week, a Laser went over into Street Sharks territory and boned one of the Street Sharks' girls. So, the Street Sharks went over to this burger joint, the Laser hangout, and blew 'em all to hell."

She paused for a moment. "Thing that bugged your father was that no one ever knew which Street Shark's girl it was that was screwed or which Laser did it. Seems the Street Sharks got all pissed off about something they only heard about, you know? Thing was, your father said a lot of people were hearing a lot of things but weren't seeing a lot of things. Gangs are decimating each other over stuff that they hear happened but maybe didn't happen. See? JD couldn't figure out where all these rumors and stuff that was pissing off the gangs was coming from."

"What did he do about it?" Macklin asked.

"What could he do? It scared the shit out of him. He saw the violence escalating, the neighborhood going to hell, and he couldn't nail down the cause. He saw people getting all pissed off and freaked-out about stuff that never happened. I wish I could have helped him, but what could I do? I listened to him yell and scream and be frustrated. I made tea. And then he was killed, boom, just like that, out of my life."

She stopped talking. Macklin saw her sparkling eyes well up with tears.

Melody looked up at the ceiling as her tears spilled out and rolled down her cheeks. "I probably loved your father." She looked across at Macklin and sniffled, trying to smile. "I probably did."

Macklin stepped over to her and kissed her on the cheek. "He probably loved you, too." He touched her shoulder. "Thanks."

"Hey, anytime, Brett." She wiped the tears away from her eyes with the palms of her hands. "Really, come by anytime." Her face said please.

Macklin smiled. "I will. Good-bye, Melody."

Grace Dettmer tightened her grip on the steering wheel and gritted her dentures as her husband Harold slipped his hand between her legs.

Ever since he had read *that* article, the one that said "spontaneity, unpredictability, and unusual locales" will revive comatose libidos, life had been unbearable for Grace.

This evening would offer no respite. She tried to ignore his ardent fumbling and concentrate on driving home. There had been no time, no place, that was free from his irritating passes. One night she had opened the refrigerator and he leaped out, covered in chocolate body spray. Another time, she went to get a pillowcase out of the closet and he pushed her in, held the door shut, and talked dirty to her for thirty-five minutes. Last week Harold followed her into the dressing room at May Co. and suggested that she "try him on."

And now he was fondling her as she drove their white, 1965 Mustang southbound on the Harbor Freeway. They had bought the car new, right off the showroom floor, back when it looked like Harold's corner newsstand could grow one day into something that would make B. Dalton and Mr. Walden cower in fear.

That day never came and Grace still picked him up every night at 10 p.m. when she finished her shift at Denny's. It was now 10:22 p.m.

One lane over and two car lengths behind Grace and Harold was a cameo beige Toyota Tercel driven by Lester Grevich, and insurance salesman from Redondo Beach on his way back from a boring party at his sister's house in Studio City. His wife would have come, but she hated his sister and was constipated to boot.

Lester's car was a mobile Neil Diamond concert. Everyone he knew hated Neil Diamond. His wife absolutely forbade him to play Diamond's music in their apartment. So, whenever he got in the car, he grabbed at the chance to crank up the Sanyo and groove to "Sweet Caroline."

It was 10:23 p.m.

Suzanne McNaughton, a struggling actress in a town filled with struggling actresses, was right behind Lester in a 1972 blue Impala. And she had to go wee-wee real bad but didn't want to stop at a gas station. She just wanted to get home.

Grace was, to her great surprise, actually beginning to tingle *down there* as the Mustang sped towards the Third Street overpass. Neil and Lester were rockin' their way through "Done Too Soon," and Suzanne was breathing deeply, muttering to herself. "Hold on, babe, c'mon, hold on."

That's when Grace saw the woman fall from the overpass. The body slammed into the Mustang's hood and bounced into the windshield, shattering it and showering Grace and Harold in bloody glass. Grace jerked the wheel sharply, sending the car spinning out of control. The woman's body slid off the hood and dropped into the path of Lester's Tercel.

Lester saw the Mustang spin into the center divider, slapping the cement and crumpling up into an unrecognizable mass of metal. He had just a split second to ponder why the Mustang had lost control. Then the Tercel bounced hard. Lester's head slammed against the roof and he felt something crush under his wheels. He looked into his rearview mirror to see what he had hit and didn't notice the eighteen-wheeler in front of him. The impact tore the car's roof, and Lester's head, right off.

Suzanne saw the Tercel flatten the twisted body and screamed, the floodgates of her bladder bursting open as she pounded her foot against the brake pedal. The car skidded over the body. Suzanne, warm urine soaking her legs, could feel the locked tires catching the body and grinding it into the asphalt as the car slid under the overpass and plowed into Lester's Tercel.

From a dark office in a high-rise building east of the freeway, the slender man watched the accident through powerful binoculars. He was pleased.

Police cars and rescue vehicles surged around the snarled traffic, tearing up the freeway shoulder towards the wrecked cars. He watched the firemen extract Grace and Harold, their features obscured by blood, from the mesh of gnarled steel. Two officers guided a shaky, crying woman from a smashed blue sedan. A short, stocky truck driver paced beside his rig, casting nervous glances up at the police and television news helicopters that circled over the scene, bathing it in light. A black body bag lay next to the tiny Japanese car crumpled under the back of his truck.

The slender man adjusted the binoculars and pressed a tiny red button. The lens zoomed in on a huddle of firemen working around the blue sedan. The man could just make out the pale white skin of the crushed woman's leg jutting out from under the car's rear wheel. He smiled.

The man lowered his binoculars and admired the night vista.

"That takes care of little Melody," he whispered coolly to himself. The city lights burned brightly, casting an eerie glow on his narrow face. The light accentuated his sharp cheekbones and shadowed his deep-set blue eyes, making them seem even more intense.

He turned and sat down at his desk, picked up the phone receiver, and dialed. It rang twice before he reached the second party. "You did well. I congratulate you."

"We've still got a problem," the other man said, not bothering to mask his irritation.

"Really?" the caller replied whimsically. "What is it, pray tell?"

"Brett Macklin," he snapped.

"Brett Macklin," he repeated softly, letting the name hang in the air. "What do we know about him?"

"What do you mean? He was that cop's son."

"No, no backstory. What's this man's history?"

The caller sighed. "Went to UCLA, graduated with a degree in aeronautical engineering, and grabbed an entry-level job at Hughes helping to design helicopters. He got bored, locked horns with some of his bosses, and needed to get physically involved in his work."

"So he learned how to fly."

"Yeah. He got to like flying a hell of a lot more than talking about it in the office, you know? So, when his flight instructor put his cheap-shit airline up for sale, his star student borrowed and hocked and scraped up enough cash to make him an offer. The guy sold it to him and Macklin's been running the show ever since."

"I see. Macklin seems like an ordinary man. He'll pose no threat to us."

"Look, he's asking a lot of questions."

"Good," the slender man interrupted, admiring the skyline again. "I think we can expect Mr. Macklin to tie up some of our loose ends."

"Until he becomes a loose end," the other man said.

"Exactly. Now, you be a good boy, watch him closely, and keep cleaning up after him."

"Okay," he replied reluctantly, "if that's the way you want to play it."

"It is." The caller paused. "Don't worry. The moment Mr. Macklin becomes trouble is the moment Mr. Macklin dies."

CHAPTER ELEVEN

They were still washing Melody off the freeway an hour later when Brett Macklin got out from under his latest acquisition, a rusty gray 1959 Cadillac four-door, and turned on his workbench radio.

"... and Merlin the Talking Dog's trainer, Al Metzger, says that at least one network has approached him with the idea of featuring his canine chatterbox in a situation comedy..."

Macklin walked around the car, inspecting the dents and scratches for the umpteenth time since he found the car. It had been rotting on blocks in a forgotten corner of a used-car lot, an irresistible target for rocks, dirt clods, and pellet guns. He got the battered relic for $300.

"Things moved slowly on the gubernatorial campaign trail today with opponents Lieutenant Governor Elliot Wells and our own Mayor Lucas Breen the guests of honor at two separate dinners held to raise money for their campaigns.

"Neither Breen nor Wells, who is still slightly ahead of Breen by five percentage points in the polls, used their podium time to criticize one another. A change of pace or the lull before the storm?" The newsman chuckled. Macklin groaned at the forced humor.

"Traffic is still tied up on the southbound Harbor Freeway tonight as CHP officers clean up the scene of a grisly four-car pileup that has left two people dead and two others seriously injured. Police say the accident occurred when Melody Caine, a thirty-four-year-old prostitute, fell to her death from the Third Street overpass in front of oncoming traffic. Witnesses said that

two unidentified men threw Caine off the overpass into oncoming traffic and then fled."

Macklin froze.

"Caine was initially struck by a car driven by an unidentified Culver City woman who lost control of her vehicle and slammed into a center divider. The woman and her husband, both suffering serious injuries, were rushed to County USC medical center. One man was killed when—"

Macklin, trancelike, reached over slowly and turned off the radio. He rose, switched off the garage light, and walked out to the Batmobile, closing the garage door behind him.

Macklin opened the car door and sat down behind the wheel. He could see his father, aflame, screaming across the path of a bus. Macklin turned the ignition key and pumped the gas. The Batmobile roared, and he saw Melody, her energetic smile replaced by a grimace of sheer terror, being hefted over the side of the overpass into traffic.

"No more," he muttered, opening the glove compartment and pulling out his father's .357 Magnum. "No more."

Macklin stalked the neighborhood again. He parked his car in a dark alley and took to the streets on foot. He had no doubts this time about his intentions. Anger coursed through him like an electric charge, propelling him down the street with long, determined strides.

First his father. Now Melody. The bastards had gone too far. Macklin wouldn't abide any more of their killing. It was time to fight back. When he found the Bounty Hunters he was going to make them pay. In blood. It was the only kind of payment they seemed to understand.

People on the streets moved aside for him, sensing the violence in his walk. Macklin didn't even see them. The only faces he would register belonged to the Bounty Hunters.

Macklin rounded a corner and saw three figures under a streetlight. A hawk-nosed man, a cigarette dangling from his lips, sat on the hood of a red '68 Trans Am. The man, clad in a white undershirt, black baggie pants with exaggerated pleats, and shiny black shoes, gestured broadly with his hands as he spoke to two guys standing on the sidewalk.

One of the duo was Macklin's height, six feet tall, and thin, with a jet-black Mohawk that ran from the top of his forehead to the nape of his neck. He looked like a scrawny Chicano imitation of Mr. T. Tight Sassoon jeans hugged his lanky legs right down to high Converse high-top tennis shoes. Shirtless under a denim vest, his hairless chest was adorned with a dozen brassy-looking dime-store necklaces.

The other was a sparsely bearded youth in a red fleece sweatshirt, the hooded jacket unzipped to his sternum. A scar cut a jagged line across the bridge of his nose and down under his right eye.

They noticed Macklin before their friend did.

Macklin ignored them. It was the hawk-nosed man he wanted.

Jesse Ortega muttered. Cigarette smoke seeped out of his pointed nose and curled upwards. "It's *him*."

"Who?" the scarred man asked.

"The asshole from the courthouse, Julio, that's who." Ortega tossed away his cigarette and stood up.

"Shit," Mr. T. laughed.

Ortega, flanked by Julio and Mr. T., blocked Macklin's path. Macklin stopped just in front of them, perspiration beading between his shoulder blades forming an itchy wet spot.

"Hey, look, Faustino, it's Charles fuckin' Bronson." Ortega grinned at the man with the Mohawk. Julio circled Macklin, appraising him. Macklin eyed him warily.

The sound of something slicing the air drew Macklin's attention away from Julio. Faustino smiled menacingly at Macklin and twirled a crudely made nunchucks in his hand.

Macklin was familiar with the Okinawa weapon, made with two heavy sticks connected by a small chain. His father had brought home a few he took from kids on the street. It was a popular weapon among the gangs because it was easily made, concealed, and brandished.

Macklin took a deep breath. Sweat rolled down his back. He could sense the urgent tension in the air, the imminent violence, explosive needing only the igniting spark.

He heard the slap of flesh and glanced back at Julio, who stood tapping the palm of his hand with a small Dodgers' souvenir bat. Macklin arched an eyebrow in surprise. Where had *that* come from?

Smiling, Macklin faced Ortega and Faustino. "Aren't you boys out past your bedtime?" he asked casually.

"Maybe you wanna take a swan dive off an overpass, motherfucker," Ortega hissed with a tight grin.

Macklin sighed. "If you're looking for trouble, little man, you just bumped into the West Coast distributor." He shot a grin over his shoulder at Julio. "Why don't you all crawl back under your rock before you get hurt?" That was the spark.

Faustino moved first, swinging the nunchucks at Macklin's head. He ducked and hammered his fist into Faustino's stomach. Faustino buckled, the air escaping from his lungs with an audible, gagging cough. Macklin jabbed his elbow into Faustino's head, knocking him aside.

Macklin turned swiftly and saw the bat crashing down towards his head. He sidestepped Julio's blow, grabbing him by the shoulders, and rammed his knee into the man's groin, feeling the testicles flatten against the rigid pubic bone.

Julio screamed in agony and folded over against Macklin's chest.

Then Faustino threw the nunchucks around Macklin's neck and yanked back fiercely. Macklin choked for air and grabbed at the cold links, desperately trying to free himself before Faustino could snap his neck open like a walnut between the sticks.

Faustino grunted, wrenching Macklin around by the neck to face Ortega. Macklin's head pulsed from lack of air and felt as though it might burst.

Ortega's eyes were alight with fury. "You made a big mistake coming down here like you fucking own the place, Mr. Big Man."

Faustino tightened his grip. Macklin winced, pulling at the chain.

His chest ached under the vice-like pressure of his lungs straining for oxygen.

"I'm gonna slit you open, motherfucker." A switchblade flashed in Ortega's hand. Smiling, Ortega stepped towards him, knife held out.

Macklin reacted without thinking. He reached back and grabbed Faustino's neck, lifting himself up and lashing out at Ortega with both legs. Macklin's feet slammed into Ortega's chest and sent him reeling. Faustino fell backwards, bringing Macklin with him.

Their impact against the cement jarred Faustino's hold on the nunchucks, and Macklin rolled free, pulling the Magnum out from his belt in the same motion and firing at Julio and Faustino.

The powerful report of the .357 echoed twice from the graffiti-smeared walls around them. Gray, smeary blobs of brain tissue blended with a spray-can-painted message.

Crouched, he aimed the gun at Ortega and breathed in the air hungrily. To Macklin's surprise, he felt good. Light-headed, exhilarated.

Macklin stood slowly, the throbbing in his head waning, and stepped past the two bodies toward Ortega.

"If I were you, little man, I would run."

Ortega back-trotted nervously, uncertain if Macklin would shoot him in the back if he turned.

"I said run, boy."

Ortega turned and burst into a full, weaving run. Macklin shoved the gun back under his belt and watched Ortega flee. It was another concession to his anger. He wanted to play with Ortega a bit. Macklin wanted Ortega to taste the terror his father must have felt.

Ortega, just rounding the corner, looked over his shoulder and saw Macklin bolt towards him like a low-flying missile.

"Shit," Ortega hissed, spittle dampening the edges of his mouth. He ran, sucking in air in rhythmic huffs, hard and deep, like a locomotive, spewing spit and snot. Nearly tripping over himself, Ortega careened to his right into an alley and into the shadows. He could hear the steady, even clop of Macklin's feet in his wake.

The alley fed into a parking lot. The expanse was bathed in a yellowish light from bulbs dangling overhead from a crisscross of wires that stretched between two tired buildings. Ortega ran across the open lot, under the network of lights, weaving between parked cars to the next alley.

Ortega, his body quaking with his labored breaths, looked madly over his shoulder for Macklin, hoping he couldn't keep up.

Macklin sprinted smoothly into the parking lot, grinning, the gun held casually in his right hand.

Ortega turned, fear tightening his face, and stretched his legs forward into the alley. Each breath was a hot dagger thrust down his throat. His feet slapped a puddle and he stumbled forward, his arms flailing.

He recovered clumsily, looking back again as he fell into a run. The darkness ahead was split by a shaft of moonlight that shone on a cyclone fence cutting across the alley. Ortega leaped towards it. His hands twisted like claws. The fence rocked against his weight as he slammed high into it, grabbed hold, and crawled up. He straddled the fence between his legs and glanced back.

A man's shadow stretched on the alley floor towards the fence. Footfalls echoed in the darkness.

"Damn the motherfucker." Ortega jumped from the fence, turned, and saw Macklin break out of the shadows.

"You're mine," Macklin yelled as he scaled the fence.

"Fuck you!" Ortega flipped Macklin off and bolted out of the alley into the street, right in front of a taxi.

The car skidded and hit Ortega a glancing blow. The youth sprawled across the pavement.

"Hey!" The baseball-capped driver shoved his head out the window. "Watch it, dumb fuck!"

Macklin dropped off the fence and saw Ortega pick himself up and limp across the street to a decaying, boarded-up tenement. Ortega jumped up and pulled down the fire-escape ladder, climbing it furiously until he reached the third-floor landing.

Macklin waited until the taxi drove away before emerging from the dark cover of the alley. He saw Ortega force open the double-sashed window and dive inside the building. No thoughts burdened Macklin as he slowly crossed the street to the age-beaten, colorless structure, long ago abandoned and left for dead.

Macklin scaled the ladder carefully, paused on the landing, and cocked his head towards the dark hallway beyond the window. All he could hear was the creaking of the door swaying in the night breeze. He stepped to the right edge of the window, pressed his back to the wall, and peered with a sideways glance down the length of the hallway. Moonlight spilled through a cracked window at the far end. The rest was blackness.

Macklin crossed quickly to the opposite side of the window, holding the gun up beside his head, and looked inside again. All he saw was more darkness. He sighed and looked down through the iron grating at the alleyway below. It was now or never.

He turned. A face stared back at him through the window. It was his reflection in the glass. The face didn't seem like his own: humorless, rigid, a disquieting smile playing on the lips.

Macklin closed his eyes, took a deep breath, and tightened his grip on the gun. A second later he swung his leg over the sill, paused, and pulled himself through, ready to shoot anything that upset the darkness. Nothing did.

He moved slowly towards the cracked window at the end of the hallway, both hands around the gun, muzzle tip up and held out confidently in front of him. His eyes darted from side to side, his ears straining to hear the slightest sound.

Ortega lashed out of the darkness, slashing Macklin's gun hand with a switchblade. Macklin's hand tightened reflexively, the loud crack of gunfire splitting the night as the blade sliced open his hand.

Macklin stumbled backwards, startled, the Magnum slipping out of his injured hand and clattering to the floor. Suddenly Ortega was an inch away from his face, ready to plunge the knife into his neck. Macklin sidestepped and felt the blade sliding smoothly into the flesh of his upper right shoulder.

They tumbled backwards towards the cracked window. Ortega drove his knee into Macklin's chest, knocked him straight up, and then hit him across the face with a hard right punch.

Macklin slammed back against the wall. The impact jarred the air out of his lungs. He fell forward and took a feeble right swing at Ortega's head.

Ortega, grinning, dodged the blow and drove his fist into Macklin's stomach.

Macklin doubled over, gagging for air. Ortega whipped his knee into Macklin's chin. A blinding white pain erupted in Macklin's head. He no longer sensed his body. He was just a weightless pain sailing through the air.

A second later he could feel his limbs again and knew he was lying on the floor. He could hear Ortega panting for breath. Macklin's vision was a blur.

Ortega's shape leaned over him in slow motion, though Macklin knew it was all passing in an instant. Macklin was aware of the searing pain in his shoulder.

He could vaguely sense Ortega crouching over him, raising the knife, savoring the brief moment before plunging it again and again into Macklin's chest.

He's going to kill me.

The realization slapped him. For a split second, his head cleared. Macklin twisted to the left and dodged Ortega's savage knife thrust.

Macklin kicked Ortega's knees and heard a crack. Ortega cried out, reeling backwards and dropping the knife.

Macklin stood up quickly. He was overwhelmed by a wave of nausea and dizziness and nearly fell again. Swaying, Macklin saw Ortega crawling for the switchblade. Rage took Macklin over, consuming his pain and momentarily revitalizing him.

He kicked Ortega in the side with a loud grunt. Ortega rolled into the wall and scrambled to his feet. Macklin faced Ortega and smiled.

"C'mon, little man," Macklin hissed.

Ortega swung wildly with his right hand. Macklin ducked and grabbed Ortega's arm, pinned it behind Ortega's back, and pushed Ortega headfirst through one of the few window panes to escape vandals' rocks.

Ortega's scream mingled with the sound of shattering glass. Macklin pulled him out quickly. Jagged glass stuck up from the sill like teeth.

Macklin twisted Ortega's arm with one hand, gripped the man's head with the other, and thrust him slowly through the window again. He stopped when Ortega's neck nearly rested on the pointed glass shard sticking up from the sill. Blood streamed down Ortega's cheeks and dripped onto the glass bits.

"Who killed the cop?" Macklin stared into the back of Ortega's head and forced the words out through deep, raspy breaths. "Who? Who killed him?"

"Go fuck yourself, asshole," Ortega groaned.

Macklin twisted Ortega's arm up and forced his neck down against the shard. Ortega's body thrashed under him as the glass touched his skin, drawing blood.

"Are you getting the point? Huh? I want answers. Who killed the cop?"

Ortega stiffened, afraid the slightest movement would drive the sharp glass deeper into his neck.

"Talk to me," Macklin said, "or the next time you make a sound it will be out of both sides of your throat."

"I-it was Primo. P-Primo torched the pig."

"Where can I find him?"

Ortega hesitated. Macklin pushed Ortega's head down against the shard.

Ortega whimpered. "Okay, okay," he whined, "the scrap yard two blocks o-over, h-his old man owns it. Y-you can find Primo there."

"How about the others, where can I find them?"

"Shit, I-I can't tell you that..."

"Talk or I'll impale you right now."

Ortega spilled out the information in one long, agonized breath.

Macklin lifted Ortega off the shard and tossed him against the wall.

Ortega grunted painfully and slid to the floor. Macklin walked down the hallway, picking up his gun and the crimson switchblade. His bloody shirt clung to his chest and his shoulder pulsed with pain.

"You're crazy, man, a goddamned crazy motherfuckin' lunatic," Ortega yelled. Macklin kept walking, his back to Ortega.

Macklin turned slowly.

His voice was soft, almost a whisper. "You're a tombstone, buddy."

He raised the Magnum slowly, saw Ortega's eyes widen in fear, and then pulled the trigger.

Ortega's head exploded, splashing blood and brain against the wall.

Macklin stood locked in place. The gunshot echoed off the walls. His stomach contorted, and bile bubbled inside him, struggling to get out. He had just killed a man, not in self-defense, but in cold blood.

Macklin winced, fighting back the urge to vomit.

When he opened his eyes again he could only stare at what was left of Ortega—the splintered head and the greenish goo dripping off the wall onto the bloodstained torso.

The shakes started in Macklin's knees and spread up his body. He shivered like a naked man in a snow flurry.

What have I done? he asked himself meekly.

Only gave the scum what he deserved. The reply was strong; self-assured, as if coming from a different man hiding behind his conscious mind.

The shakes disappeared and Macklin was in control again. His body was bathed in sweat and the pain was coming back. Soon it would be too strong ... Macklin turned away and walked weakly down the hallway into the night.

CHAPTER TWELVE

His body spiraled through a tunnel of thick fog. Wisps of mist whirled in front of his eyes. The fog suddenly split and a black wall closed in on him. The impact, rather than smashing him, left him floating motionless in darkness. Light began to seep into his dark world and he became aware of the coldness underneath him.

He began to sense the contours of his body. A flame burned deep inside his left shoulder. His head pounded in time with his heart. The light cut the darkness into indistinct gray shapes.

"Brett? Can you hear me?"

The gray melted and gave way to dimension and color. Macklin stretched his hands and felt wood underneath him. A table.

Macklin blinked hard, concentrating on tuning in his vision as if it were a television picture.

When he opened his eyes he saw Mort Suderson leaning over him.

"Good morning." Mort smiled grimly.

"Hi." The reply scratched Macklin's dry throat.

"You look like hell." Mort's breath looked like smoke in the cold air.

"I always do in the morning." Macklin leaned upwards, and Mort, seeing Macklin wanted to sit up, wrapped his arm around Macklin's shoulders and guided him.

Macklin closed his eyes, feeling nauseous. The nausea subsided and he opened his eyes again. He sat on the edge of the table, facing Mort. Behind Mort he saw his Cessna and realized he was in his hangar at the Santa Monica Airport. The hangar was always freezing in the morning.

Macklin fingered his shirt. It wasn't damp with blood. He wore fresh clothes.

"How did you get here? Where did these clothes come from?"

Mort dragged over a stool and sat down in front of Macklin. "You don't remember?"

"Remember what?" Macklin mumbled, running his tongue over a loose tooth on the upper right side of his mouth.

Mort frowned. "I found you about an hour ago, just after six a.m., lying against your car. You were bloody and beat to hell. You were mumbling all sorts of unintelligible shit. When I mentioned taking you to a hospital you started screaming 'no' and passed out."

Macklin lightly poked his cheeks. They were sore to the touch and were slightly swollen.

"So I carried you in here, cleaned you up as best I could, and put you in some clothes I found in your office." Mort sniffled. "You've got to see a doctor. Those knife wounds are nasty and my spit 'n' glue patchwork isn't going to be enough."

"No doctors, not yet."

"Sure, sure." Mort waved Macklin away and started pacing in front of him. "Guess you had a rough night."

"Uh-huh," Macklin groaned.

"Uh-huh," Mort mimicked. "That's it? Just uh-huh? Listen, pal, I think you owe me more of an explanation than that. What the fuck is going on?"

Macklin looked into his friend's eyes. "Mort, let's forget it. I—"

"No," Mort interrupted, staring into Macklin's eyes. Macklin had never seen such angry determination in his friend before. "Tell me now or I'll walk to that phone and call you an ambulance."

"Have you heard about Mr. Jury?" Macklin asked wearily.

"Yeah, so?"

"You're looking at him."

Mort pursed his lips and exhaled his breath in a dull whistle.

A loud screech outside caused them both to turn their heads towards the hangar door. Macklin heard a car door slam shut and the clap of feet on the pavement. He glanced at Mort just as Sergeant Sliran, a cigarette dangling from his lips, yanked open the hangar door.

"Good morning, Sergeant," Macklin chirped, pushing himself off the table. The nausea rose in him again. "What are you doing here?"

Sliran tossed his cigarette away and stormed up to within inches of Macklin's face. "Make it easy on me, Macklin. Gimme the gun and assume the position against your plane."

"Watch out, it's supercop." Mort grinned.

Sliran glared at Mort. "Don't push it, Suderson. I'll serve you your teeth for breakfast."

"C'mon, Sliran, we get the point. You're a real tough asshole. We're petrified. Get to the point or get the hell out."

"Last night you went downtown and blew Jesse Ortega's brains out."

"Really?" Macklin stared into Sliran's eyes. "Gee, and I thought I was here last night with Mort, working on the plane." Macklin maintained eye contact with Sliran, overcoming the urge to glance at Mort. His heartbeat quickened.

How far would his friend go to cover for him? One contradictory word or expression from Mort, and Macklin was ruined.

"Jesse Ortega was acquitted, you know, for torching your daddy," Sliran said.

"I know," Macklin said evenly.

"That's motive."

"Sure is. Only problem is I didn't do it."

"Coincidence, huh?" Sliran sneered.

"Sounds like it to me. I know it's hard to accept, Ortega being such a saint and all. Who would want to hurt him?"

"Mr. Jury. The bullet that blasted open Ortega's head came from the same gun used on Hector Gomez and Teobaldo Villanueva. Funny, so far Mr. Jury has only killed people on your shitlist. Quite a coincidence."

"So call *That's Incredible!* Arrest me or get the hell out of my hangar."

Sliran scratched his neck. "Look over your shoulder, Macklin. You so much as spit and I'll haul your ass behind bars."

"Out." Macklin smiled. "Now."

Sliran stomped out, slamming the door behind him. Macklin turned slowly towards Mort and then fell back against the table.

Mort licked his lips. "Did you kill Ortega?"

"Yes." Macklin sighed. He didn't know what more to say. Right now, all he wanted to do was sleep. Macklin moved away from the table and stumbled toward his office.

"I'm gonna sleep for a few hours in my office, okay?"

"Sure," Mort mumbled.

Macklin shuffled into the office and sat down carefully on the torn reclining chair behind his desk. His whole body sagged, aching everywhere all at once.

He leaned forward, pulled open his desk drawer, and rummaged around the pencils and paper clips and folders until he found a small plastic bottle of Tylenol. He emptied the pills out in the drawer. Three open Tab cans lay amidst the clutter on his desk. He reached for one, shook it, and heard some liquid swirl inside. Macklin placed two pills in his mouth and swallowed them with a mouthful of flat, sweet soda.

Macklin sat back in the seat, rested his feet on the desk, and closed his eyes. Sleep caught up with him quickly.

His dream took him back to the tenement. To Ortega. Again there was the fight, the shattered glass, the blood. Again the .357 Magnum spit fire. But this time it was Macklin's head that burst, a stream of blood shooting out of his neck like a geyser. The blood became a shape. The shape became a name. The man was Brett Macklin's twin.

The scum got what he deserved.

The scum . . . the scum . . . the scum . . . deserved . . . deserved.

"Wake up, Mack."

He was being shaken. Pain pushed the sleep away and he opened his eyes. Shaw stood above him, unsmiling.

Oh shit, not again.

"What time is it, Ron?"

"Noon."

Macklin had slept for about four hours. He felt like he needed a couple more days.

"Oh shit. I was working late last night and, well, I guess my body sort of closed up shop." Macklin tried to sit up smoothly, quickly, to hide his pain. He hid it from Shaw. The charade didn't work as well on himself. It was all he could do not to wince.

"Someone showed up downtown last night, raised hell, and killed Jesse Ortega."

"So Sliran told me."

"Yeah, Sliran woke me up this morning with the news."

"Are you a suspect, too?"

"Oh, I guess so." Shaw pulled up a chair. "Internal Affairs has decided to go all the way with the beating thing. I've got a long haul."

"I'm sorry."

"Don't be," Shaw snapped. "Listen, Brett, we don't need some Lone Ranger coming down and turning the streets into a war zone. People can get hurt."

"Why are you telling me this, Ron?"

He ignored Macklin. "People like your father."

Macklin's face reddened. "People like my father are and have been getting hurt. Every single day. At least this Mr. Jury is doing something about it. At least someone is fighting back. What the hell are you doing about it?"

"Oh, c'mon, Mack. Don't give me that old police-can't-do-the-job bullshit. You're smarter than that," he said.

"Listen, Ron, save your speech for someone else. I'm not your Mr. Jury."

Shaw stood up and headed towards the office door. "You aren't some superhero, Mack. You'll bleed just like the rest of us."

He turned and walked out.

Macklin sighed and stood up. He saw Mort leaning against the doorway. "He has a point, Brett."

"Mort, my friend, put yourself in my shoes. What would you do?" Macklin asked.

"Blow the fuckers away."

CHAPTER THIRTEEN

Two large breasts pressed into Brett Macklin's face. He could see her nipples, hardened by the coolness of the hangar, poking against the fabric of her white uniform. He felt her fingers gently brush his chest. His eyes were drawn to her deep cleavage, tantalizingly exposed by a zipper open to her sternum.

"Ouch!" Macklin yelled, a sharp pain in his shoulder shattering his calm. "That hurt worse than the damn knife did in the first place."

"You'll thank me later," Cheshire Davis said as she removed the syringe from Macklin's shoulder and stepped back.

Macklin, sitting shirtless on the edge of the hangar table, heard Mort approaching from the office behind him. "Hey, Cheshire, he should be thanking you *now.* We owe you one."

Mort held out a Tab to Cheshire and shot Macklin a scolding look. Macklin tried to shrug; the pain made him wince.

"Forget it, Mort. Without your sister I don't know whether I would be a nurse today. I practically rode through school on her shoulders." Cheshire chuckled, shifting her gaze to Macklin. "Actually, Brett, you're being very good. We'll give the anesthetic a chance to sink in, and then we'll start sewing you up."

"Terrific," Macklin deadpanned, already feeling his shoulder tingling. Mort laughed.

"Well, wish I could stay and see the action, but I have a lunch date." Mort smiled at Cheshire. "Thanks again, Cheshire."

"Like I said, no problem." She set down the can of Tab beside Macklin and reached into her handbag, pulling out the curved needle and brown catgut thread.

"Mack, I'll leave you to settle the bill." Mort waved and walked out the door.

Macklin sighed. The awkwardness of the situation made him feel uneasy. He was left at the mercy of a complete, albeit attractive, stranger. His uneasiness made the silence in Mort's wake tangible, and the hangar became cavernous.

She moved close to him again, her breasts filling his view. It only made him more uncomfortable. He glanced up into her friendly brown eyes. "I'm sorry if I seem rude. I really do appreciate you coming down here so quick."

He was vaguely aware of the needle piercing the skin around his wound.

"I had nothing to do for lunch, anyway." She smiled. "Mort said you couldn't see a doctor. Something about protecting a friend."

"Yeah, a buddy of mine got bad drunk, you know, started waving a knife around. I tried to take it away from him and he accidentally stabbed me." Macklin, afraid she'd see the lie in his eyes, gazed at her bosom. "If I went to the emergency room, there would be questions, maybe the police. I really don't want to get the guy in trouble. It was heavy troubles that got him that drunk in the first place."

"Yeah, I see your point. You're being very good about it."

Macklin didn't say anything and spent the next minute or two shifting his eyes between her face and her breasts.

"You keep yourself rather fit, Brett."

"Thanks."

"How do you do it?"

"Jesus," Macklin said evenly.

"Huh?" She stopped sewing for a moment, looking at him oddly.

"I put all my faith in Jesus. Through him, both my body and soul are revitalized."

"Jesus," she muttered narrowing her eyes.

"Our savior," Macklin added.

"Ah-huh." She pulled a stitch harder than she had to. "You know something, Brett?"

"What?"

"You're full of shit." A big smile lit up her face and they both started laughing.

She finished treating Macklin's wounds fifteen minutes later. As she hurriedly gathered her things, glancing at her watch, Macklin slipped on his shirt and stood up.

"What do I owe you?" Macklin asked.

"Owe me?" She arched an eyebrow quizzically and rubbed her chin. "Dinner."

"Dinner?" Macklin smiled.

"Yeah, dinner." She nodded, pleased with herself. "How about tonight?"

Macklin chuckled. "All right, tonight it is. Where would you like to go?"

"My apartment. I'm the best cook I know."

They reached the door. Macklin opened it for her.

She told him her address. "It's right on the beach. You can't miss it. Come by at seven."

"I wouldn't miss it."

She grinned and Macklin understood how she'd gotten her name.

Cheshire purred.

"Oh, you *are* beautiful, Brett Macklin," she whispered, her eyes closed, her body rocking in the waves of pleasure radiating from between her legs. He thrust gently, keenly aware of her body undulating as her enjoyment grew.

She didn't sense his emotional distance, only his glistening skin and his sexual artfulness, the mounting pleasure that brought a flush to her body and swelled her breasts.

Macklin could feel her orgasm coming, the pleasure intensifying and the tension growing more difficult for her to bear. She arched her back, pushing her hips against him. Her hands tightly grasping the rungs of the brass headboard behind her.

She began to thrash as the pleasure blossomed, flaring out and touching her everywhere. Cheshire stiffened suddenly, exhaling slowly, her lips stretched into a surprised, satisfied grin.

And then she fell back, the grin becoming a laugh. She wrapped her arms around Macklin and pulled him down to her.

"You little shit, you," she said, biting his lip. "Trying to kill me, are you?"

Macklin kissed her lips, her cheeks, her neck.

"Your game hens and wild rice were an aphrodisiac," he said. "And I think you put something in the wine."

Cheshire stiffened again and held her breath as Macklin slid one strong hand between her legs and explored the wetness there, moving from one silky fold to the next.

"Oh Jesus," she moaned. "You're still hard."

"Uh-huh." He smiled, stroking her.

Cheshire shook her head. "Brett, you've got to be kidding. You don't think… my body can't take it!" She laughed.

"Again," he purred, licking her nipples and thrusting slowly.

It was one a.m. when Cheshire fell asleep, exhausted. That was what Macklin wanted. He was wide awake, sticky with sweat, listening to the waves breaking against the shore. When he was sure she was solidly asleep, he slipped silently out from under her heavy brown comforter, dressed quickly, and left the apartment. He took the stairwell to the street, careful to avoid being seen.

The Batmobile was parked across the street against the backdrop of the crashing surf. The grill glistened like moist teeth in the moonlight. Macklin ran to the car, started it up, and drove away, reaching out with his right hand to open the glove compartment.

CHAPTER FOURTEEN

Time had not been kind to the Grand View theater. Its tiny ticket booth was barely standing, serving as a trash can for passersby and a urinal for every street urchin wanting to take a piss.

Bits of glass from the shattered marquee crunched under Macklin's feet as he walked carefully on the cracked tile of the theater's entranceway. He looked at the soiled plywood sheets nailed haphazardly over the lobby doors. Taking a deep breath, he felt the coolness of the gun against his stomach. Macklin would rather have been lying snug under Cheshire's heavy comforter, her body curled against his, than standing outside the crumbling theater. But his compulsion nagged at him. His need for revenge overwhelmed his need for peace. The abandoned Grand View was now Mario Carrera's home. Ortega had told him that before swallowing a bullet.

Macklin slipped around the right edge of the windowless building to the back exit, stepping into the darkened recess to test the doorknob. It was unlocked.

Macklin frowned and looked at the door, hoping God would suddenly bless him with X-ray vision. He hated not knowing what was beyond the door.

Suspense only twisted his stomach and made him want to shit. He pressed his shoulder against the cold steel, unzipped his leather flight jacket, and drew his gun from under his belt.

The door creaked as he cautiously eased it open an inch. He stopped abruptly and listened. Sweat tickled his face.

He heard nothing. *Oh sure, nothing.* Macklin scolded himself. The last time he thought there was nothing, he was nearly stabbed to death.

He struggled and leaned against the door. The rusty hinges of the metal door complained loudly in the darkness. Suddenly Macklin heard a roar from behind the door, and an instant later a maelstrom hailed against the door and slammed it shut. Macklin stood for a moment, his heart beating in his throat, and then ran hand over the tiny bulges in the steel.

The son of a bitch has a shotgun.

Macklin stepped four paces back and, using his good shoulder, hurled himself against the door. Diving into the theater, he rolled into a row of seats as the shotgun exploded from above, the pellets rebounding off the wall behind him.

Macklin, curled against the seats, panted for breath. The theater smelled of age, musty and damp. He gave his eyes a second or two to adjust to the dark. Judging from the wide dispersal of pellets embedded in the door, Macklin thought Carrera couldn't have been too close, perhaps near the lobby. *But where is he* now?

There was only one way to find out. Macklin bolted up and fired into the darkness. The theater quaked and he saw a flash to his left, about ten feet up, in the center of the theater. He ducked as the blast tore off a chunk of the seat beside him. Macklin took a deep breath and pumped three bullets to the right of where he had seen the muzzle flash. An agonized scream mingled with the sound of his gunshots.

Macklin dropped back behind the seats, listening. Was Carrera dead, injured, or lurking somewhere nearby? His stomach ached. Macklin licked his lips and sprang into the aisle, gun forward, ready to fire. Darkness and silence greeted him. Crouched, Macklin moved slowly up the aisle. He expected Carrera to leap out in front of him, the shotgun spitting death.

His stitches itched, blood seeping out between the strands. A painful reminder of his last foray into the shadows. Fear pressed in on him, building walls and making the large theater feel claustrophobic. Macklin stopped as the incline peaked. His heart pounded as he touched the lobby door with the tip of his gun.

Macklin imagined Carrera behind it, a sadistic smile on his face, the shotgun lovingly cradled in his arms and pointed at the double doors. He closed his eyes, swallowed, and crouched like a linebacker squaring off against a defensive end.

Macklin burst through the doors, knees bent, his arms forming a triangle with the gun at its point.

He spun, trying to catch the slightest movement in the shadows. Macklin untensed, grateful Carrera wasn't there. To his left, the ruins of the refreshment stand crouched in the corner, a twisted relic of tortured metal and broken glass. The light from a streetlamp outside filtered though a crack in the plywood-covered entranceway and cast an eerie glow over the thick layer of dust on the floor, illuminating a smear of footprints leading to a staircase on the right.

Macklin warily eyed the staircase, shrouded in the shadows. His entrance into the lobby had been loud. He feared Carrera must know exactly where he was now. As he moved towards the stairs, he saw that the first flight led to a landing. The second flight, hidden from his view, he assumed stretched up and back towards the lobby.

Macklin thought out the risks. If he went up the first flight, he could curl around the landing and walk right into a shotgun blast. He strained to see more, knowing it was impossible. Hugging the right-hand side of the stairs, Macklin moved carefully up, step by step, his back pressed against the wall. If Carrera was around the corner, Macklin was a dead man. *I'll take the asshole with me.*

Macklin sprang onto the landing and slammed against the wall with a loud thud. An empty staircase reached up to the second floor. A weak light moving back and forth escaped under the projection room door. Macklin stared at the door as he moved up the flight of stairs.

The guesswork was over. *Carrera is in the projection room,* Macklin thought, *and he knows I'm coming through the door.*

Macklin glided across the floor and stopped beside the door, his ear pressed to the wall. He heard Carrera's raspy breaths. Macklin's shirt clung damply to his chest and back.

He stepped back from the wall and positioned himself in front of the door.

One.

Two.

... three!

Macklin kicked open the door and burst into the room, crouched low in a deadly firing stance. He froze. Mario Carrera was crumpled under the projection window in a pool of blood, holding a flashlight over his chest and staring with morbid fascination at the blood frothing up from his gurgling chest wound.

Carrera's right hand lay loosely on his blood-specked shotgun, which was propped on his thigh and pointed at the doorway where Macklin stood. He glanced at Macklin, an obscene smile on his face. "Come to finish me off, huh?" he wheezed.

Macklin saw Carrera's hand twitching on the shotgun.

"I know you." Carrera started nodding, breaking into a laugh that shook his body and spilled more blood onto the floor. "Yeah, yeah, I know you."

A finger slipped around the shotgun trigger.

"You're that cop's kid." Carrera dropped the flashlight. It rolled through the blood and stopped at Macklin's feet. Their eyes met.

"You shouldn't have killed him," Macklin whispered.

Carrera smiled again. Instinct tossed Macklin sideways into a stack of empty film reels as Carrera raised the shotgun and fired. The blast masked the explosion from Macklin's gun. Macklin saw the bullet tear through Carrera's skull and split it apart. The halves of Carrera's head splattered onto the floor.

Macklin rose to his feet slowly. He put the gun under his belt, zipped up his jacket, and walked out of the room.

Macklin crept back into Cheshire's apartment just as the digital clock ticked to 4:32 a.m. He tiptoed to her bed and shed his clothes, slipping into the sheets beside her.

She rolled over instinctively, her arm falling across his chest, and buried her face against his neck.

He closed his eyes. In ten minutes, he was where dreams and heroes dwell.

CHAPTER FIFTEEN

He woke three hours later near orgasm, Cheshire's head between his legs. She looked up, brushing her hair out of her eyes and smiling at him. "Rise and shine, Brett."

"It looks like I already have," he said, sitting up and kissing her. His hands cupped her breasts, brushing her nipples erect with his thumbs.

"Mmmm," she moaned.

Their lovemaking carried into the shower, where they lathered up and climaxed under jets of hot water. They dried each other off and dressed quickly, stumbling into the kitchen just after nine a.m.

"Oh shit." Cheshire glanced at the clock over the kitchen sink. "I'm late. I'm gonna get killed."

"Breakfast is out, then?" Macklin frowned. "And I was going to take you to eat on Rodeo Drive," he added teasingly.

She raised her hand as if to hit him. "Smart-ass."

There was a loud, insistent rapping at the door.

"Shit, who could that be?" Cheshire droned, dashing to the door and yanking it open.

Sliran stood in the hallway.

"Shit." Macklin, seeing Sliran over Cheshire's shoulder, sat down wearily on the arm of Cheshire's couch.

Sliran wordlessly shoved Cheshire aside, waving his LAPD identification in her face.

"You're pressing your luck, stud," Sliran sneered, approaching Macklin. "You should have waited until Jesse Ortega was cold before you went out killing again. What a fuckin' idiotic thing to do. Now you can't dance around the room singing coincidence."

"Sliran, what are you babbling about?"

"C'mon, Macky boy, save the innocent routine for the gay boys at Soledad. Last night you used Mario Carrera for target practice."

"I was here last night. You figured that out after talking to Mort or you wouldn't be here now."

Sliran glanced at Cheshire. She stood beside the open door, her arms crossed angrily over her chest. "Yeah, I can see you've got a tight little alibi. It doesn't wash, Macklin, not with me."

"What is this guy talking about?" Cheshire shrieked.

Macklin, ignoring Cheshire, stood up and faced Sliran. "You don't have a warrant and I don't recall Cheshire inviting you in. So either cuff me or get out."

"No cuffs, at least not today. I came here to give you a little news." Sliran adjusted his shades. "While you were pumping bullets into Mario Carrera, a couple of your daddy's friends bought it. That little Jew, what's his name?"

"Saul, Saul Rosencranz," Macklin replied tonelessly.

"Yeah, he and a guy named Moe Biddle got their heads bashed in and dunked in the French fryer. Sizzled the skin right off. They looked like a coupla pieces of fried pigskin. Couple of blue suits found 'em and are still puking."

Cheshire grabbed Sliran by the shoulder and spun him around. "Get out of my apartment. Now, or I'll call my lawyer."

Sliran straightened out his jacket. "Sure, sure, I'll go. See you soon, Macky boy." He winked at Cheshire and strolled casually out the door.

She slammed the door shut behind him and turned to Macklin, who sat back down on the couch arm, his hands on his knees. "Brett, are you okay?"

Macklin nodded. "I'm fine, I'm fine. Just leave me alone for a second." A heavy guilt weighed down his shoulders. The past few days were a blur of bloodshed.

"Mort told me about your father. Does all this have something to do with that?"

Macklin didn't hear her. His thoughts were on Melody, Saul, and Moe. The three people he had sought out for help uncovering the reasons behind his father's murder were now dead. Macklin didn't believe in coincidences any more than Sliran did. Someone, he realized, was following his tracks. Anyone he had talked to might be next.

Cheshire stood awkwardly by the door. She wasn't going to get any explanations from Macklin. Not now anyway. "Are you sure you're okay?"

"Yes," he snapped. "Now, go. I'll lock up for you."

She considered the situation for a moment, started to say something, and then opened the door. "You'll give me a call tonight?"

"Yes, I will." He smiled apologetically. "I'm sorry I yelled at you. It's just... there's a lot coming down on me right now. One of the guys who killed my father was gunned down last night. Sliran thinks I did it."

"Anything I can do to help?"

"Nope, I just need a few minutes to get my thoughts together."

"Okay." She lingered a second or two and then walked out.

Sizzled the skin right off...

Macklin closed his eyes tightly and covered his face with his hands.

He saw Brooke and Cory, their heads being forced into the boiling oil, their bodies convulsing spasmodically. Macklin's head jerked up.

Macklin dashed to Cheshire's phone and dialed Brooke's number at the Westwood Art Gallery, where she worked.

"Hello, Gallery West," Brooke answered gaily.

"Hi, Brooke, this is Brett."

"Brett, it's good to hear from you," she said brightly, and then, more somberly, she added, "How are you feeling?"

"Fine. Listen, how would you like to take a little vacation?"

She laughed. "I'd love to. Paris sounds nice."

"No, I'm serious. You and Cory, on me. You could go visit your father in Boston."

"C'mon, Mack, that's very grand of you, but there's just no way. Cory has summer school and I'm just swamped here. Besides, wouldn't it be better if you waited a few weeks and snuck away for a few days, just you and Cory? I think she'd like that."

"Brooke, listen to me," Macklin said, trying to keep the fearful edge out of his voice. "You've got to trust me. It's not safe for you two to stay in the city."

"Not safe? What do you mean?" she snapped. "Mack, why don't we discuss this later—"

"No," he interrupted, tightening his grip on the receiver. "You're in danger of being hurt by the same people who killed my father. " He told her about Melody, Saul, and Moe. "Please, go away for two weeks."

"Mack," she said cautiously, as if trying to diffuse a bomb with her words, "you're talking nonsense. Listen to yourself. I know your father's death hurt you very much, but—"

"Brooke, damn it, do this one thing for me. Take my Visa card and go away. *Please.*"

Brooke didn't reply. Macklin listened to her breathing.

"Mack, how do you know we're in danger? Aren't you being a little paranoid?"

"Please, Brooke. Don't ask me questions. Just trust me. Please. Go away, anywhere you want. Do it for me."

Brooke sighed.

"Brooke, all I'm asking is that you take a vacation. A week or two. Is that so bad? You'll enjoy it."

"Okay, I'll go. But not because I need the vacation or believe your paranoid fantasies. I'm doing this for you and Cory. I'm afraid if I don't do it you'll nag me for days and probably scare the hell out of Cory in the process."

"Thanks," Macklin said with relief.

"Save it. When I get back, you had better explain yourself. Don't ever think you can get away with a stunt like this again."

"Okay. I'll get you on the first plane out tonight."

"What? Mack—"

"Call your father. I'll swing by tonight and take you to the airport."

"Shit. All right, Mack. While we're gone, I hope you get your head straight." She hung up.

Macklin set down the receiver, picked it up again, and started to dial the number at the hangar to warn Mort about the possible danger he was in. Then he realized Mort was in the copter, flying for *The Bloodmaster* crew.

He left Cheshire's apartment and drove straight to the hangar, where he spent the day catching up on paperwork and canceling some of his charters. He managed to get Brooke and Cory on a seven o'clock flight out of LAX and picked them up and took them to the airport. They ate some of the rancid, pasty glop the airport coffee shop called food. Just because they had a captive clientele next to the departure gates was all the reason the food operators needed to overcharge people for food that, Macklin thought, probably violated the Geneva Conventions, or at least the constitutional strictures against cruel and inhuman punishment. Brooke sat silently, poking at a gray mass the restaurant billed as chopped steak. Cory tried to entertain Macklin with stories about her friends.

At the gate, Macklin kissed Cory and then hugged Brooke.

"Mack," she whispered angrily, "you're crazy."

Macklin pressed his lips against her ear. "I don't want you getting killed."

The television screen captured the images of a score of uncomfortable people, some dressed in suits and squinting into bright television lights and flashbulbs, others pointing to the cameras and lights. The cramped press room at Parker Center seemed even more claustrophobic than usual. Faces flickered across the screen. Police Chief Jed Stocker, separated from the throng by an unbalanced podium, sweated under the blinding lights and tried to read casually from his prepared statement. It was hard to tell if the greenish cast to his complexion was caused by the television, or if it was something he ate.

"... I assure you we are vigorously pursuing a number of leads we are certain will expose the identity of this savage vigilante."

"Chief, you're calling him a savage vigilante," Al Zimmer, of the *Herald Examiner*, yelled through a mouthful of Wrigley's gum. "There are some people who think he's a hero."

"Thanks to you the press, Mr. Zimmer. He's committing murder, and that's against the law."

"Hasn't the number of gang-related crimes decreased dramatically since Mr. Jury started his crusade?" asked a UPI reporter. Stocker, and even some of the reporters, found it hard to tell whether the reporter was a man or a woman. The reporter always wore a plaid shirt and jeans.

"True," Stocker replied, looking for breasts on the UPI reporter. "But that hardly justifies—"

"A *Herald Examiner* poll shows most of the people in this town would like to pin a medal on the guy," Zimmer interrupted. "You arrest Mr. Jury and you're liable to be lynched."

"The law is the law. Mr. Jury is breaking it."

"Can you be more specific about your investigation? Do you suspect a renegade cop? Perhaps more than one vigilante is at work," said Jessica Mordente, the slim, dark-eyed reporter from the *Times*.

"We are exploring all avenues of inquiry, Ms. Mordente." Stocker rocked against the podium. "To say more would compromise the investigation."

"Do you have any witnesses besides the rape victim?" Mordente continued.

"As I said, I can't say much more at this point."

"It sounds to me like you don't have anything, Chief," Mordente snapped. "Just how eager are you to apprehend Mr. Jury?"

"We are doing our best. Believe me, ladies and gentlemen, we want Mr. Jury behind bars."

Mayor Lucas Breen, sitting in his dark office in city hall, kicked off the television set with his bare foot and looked across his cluttered desk to Stocker.

The chief sat stoically in his chair in front of Breen's desk, his eyes on the now blank TV set.

"Good job, Jed," Breen sneered, leaning back in his high-backed leather chair. "You should know spewing bullshit like that to the press is like squirting blood into a shark's face."

"Give me a break, Lucas, what was I supposed to tell them?" Stocker sighed and closed his eyes. "'Ladies and gentlemen of the press, Mr. Jury is a political problem and we need more time to figure out the best way to handle it so our careers won't be ruined. He makes the LAPD look foolish, but the city seems to love him. So for now, we're making him an honorary police officer and issuing him a license to kill.'"

Stocker stood up and paced back and forth in front of Breen's desk. "Under the circumstances, *sir*, I think I did pretty damn good."

"Really? You think you have them fooled?" Breen stroked the thick hair on his chin. "You're no further along in the investigation than you were a week ago."

Breen sniffed, leaning forward and searching his desk for a container of nasal spray. "Damn allergy drives me fucking nuts." He found the container and squirted twice in each nostril, inhaling hard. "Jed, I want to be governor of this state. I'm moving up in the polls and giving Elliot Wells a real battle."

The mayor pulled imaginary lint off the American flag beside him. "I think I can win. Mr. Jury, whoever the hell he is, isn't helping me."

He glanced at Stocker. "Or you."

Stocker stopped pacing and turned to face Breen.

"Don't look so surprised, Jed. It's no secret you want this office when I go. If you don't catch Mr. Jury soon, we're both going to be serving fries at McDonald's."

"We're doing our best," Stocker said quietly. "We have a lead, a small one. Remember that cop that got torched?"

"Mackinaw or something, right?"

"Macklin, James Douglas Macklin. Some of Mr. Jury's victims were arrested for Macklin's murder and released on a technicality. The detective I've got heading the investigation, Neal Sliran, thinks Macklin's son, Brett, might be our man."

"So bring the son of a bitch in."

"We can't. We have nothing on him. In fact, we have nothing, period. No description to go on, no physical evidence except for the bullets we dug out of the victims. We're looking for a ghost."

Breen smiled. "He'll make a mistake and he'll fall." He looked at Stocker. "Just make sure you have someone there to catch him. Then bring this caped crusader to me."

CHAPTER SIXTEEN

The lights of Los Angeles gleamed and flickered below him. The night vistas always held an element of unreality, with their satisfying and startling visions. Some nights the lights were an endless field of precious jewels, glimmering and glistening, his for the taking. Other times the lights were torch-carrying enemies approaching ominously and whispering his name.

The lights were different tonight, slowly banding together into a new vision. He watched them carefully while absently tracing the gold-embossed book on his desk with his finger.

His polished white marble desk, eight feet long and four feet wide, dominated the room. The hand-rubbed teak paneling would have given the expansive office a hushed warmth if it were not in constant conflict with the unsettling sight of his desk. Adding to the contrast was a portrait of himself, behind his ornate leather desk chair, and flanked on either side by picture windows that afforded him a breathtaking view of the city. His blue eyes in the portrait blazed with power and confidence.

His eyes narrowed now as he stared at the city below him, watching the lights coalesce into a vision that was just beginning to become clear.

The phone rang.

The mood was broken and the lights became just lights.

He reached back and grabbed the receiver angrily. "Yes?"

"It's me." The voice was rough and resonant. Unmistakable. "We've got that shit on the run now. He's called in reinforcements."

"Big guns?" he asked wearily, turning and leaning on the desk with his elbows.

"Just one. A guy named Kirk Jeffries from New York. He's a wizard with statistics and can isolate a candidate's weak points with astonishing accuracy.

"He's one of those young computer geniuses and looks like one, too. A real sorry-looking asshole. But he's probably the nation's third or fourth best pollster.

"No one understands the guy's methods, but everyone knows they work. On your side he's an invaluable weapon."

"I take it he's with the enemy."

"Yeah, and it's a damn shame, too. He worked with me on my first campaign and made sure I said just the right crap to sway the iffy numbers my way. I'd love to have him on my side. But the guy is a loud-mouthed prick. Isn't a team player. He didn't know his place. I gave him the boot when it was clear I had the campaign won and I didn't need to put up with his shit."

"What sort of threat does he pose?"

"A big one. He knows a lot about me. Too much. We have to take him out of the picture. He arrives here in two days."

"Simple enough. We'll have him killed in the usual fashion."

"I don't think that's a good idea. Not with this Mr. Jury crap. Let's kill him simply." There was a pleading tone to his voice that, coming from him, was shockingly out of character.

"Macklin is harmless." He took a deep breath, forcing back his rage. He became enraged at the slightest hint of cowardice or lack of confidence. "We control him."

"This could explode in our face, you know, and ruin everything."

"Stop whining," he snapped, startling himself and the caller. He struggled to control his temper. With measured restraint, he spoke slowly and methodically, "You sound like a child. I'll handle this. I know what I'm doing." He sat up in his chair. "We're going to succeed. Have faith. After tonight's show, you'll have God on your side. I'm going to endorse you."

"Terrific," he snorted. "It will come in handy when they crucify me. I don't suppose you have a crown of thorns I could borrow?"

The caller hung up. The other man sat for a moment in silence, tapping his fingers on the leather-bound book. Someday he might have to kill that man. The caller was already showing signs of weakness that couldn't be tolerated.

He reached for the phone and dialed.

"Yeah?"

"I have another elimination for you to arrange," he said smoothly. "Same price, same procedure. As usual, make sure he looks like another innocent victim caught up in gang warfare. Be absolutely certain."

"Okay, okay. What is the guy's name?"

"Kirk Jeffries. He's coming into town in two days. I trust you can get the details on your own?"

"Yeah, I got sources. What about Macklin?"

"I told you, let him have his fun, and then you can have yours. Just do as I tell you."

"Macklin should die now."

His anger flared. "Do as I say! That's what I pay you for."

He slammed down the phone. Someone knocked timidly at his door. "Enter," he yelled.

The huge oak door swung open and a woman wearing only a white bathrobe stepped meekly into the room, closing the door behind her. She was slender and tanned, her breasts full, her legs long and smooth. She had a euphoric, punch-drunk look that labeled her as one of his many, nameless, utterly devoted minions.

She approached him slowly, stopping just in front of his massive desk. He walked around the desk, came up behind her, and turned her by the shoulders to face him.

He looked at her with father-like warmth. But inside the frustrations were boiling, had brought him to a breaking point. He recognized the symptoms well and struggled to reveal none of them to the girl. Touching her hand tenderly, he led her to the center of the room.

He motioned with his head to her bathrobe. "Take it off," he commanded.

The robe slipped off her soft, brown skin and fell to a clump at her feet. Her empty, trusting gaze met his as she obediently dropped to her knees. "I love you, my savior."

Her placid acceptance of his whim made him nauseous. She was empty and useless, utterly devoid of redeeming value. Yet he had made her that way. A part of him wanted her like that. *Needed* her like that.

Elias Simon smiled. "I love you, too, my child."

He turned as if to walk away and then spun, giving her a sharp kick in the jaw that snapped her neck with a crack. The blow catapulted her young, budding body across the room and sent her stunned soul seeking explanations in the next world.

He felt much better.

CHAPTER SEVENTEEN

Brett Macklin lay naked in bed, his sheets a wrinkled heap at his feet, staring across the room at a killer.

He stared into his own bloodshot, dull eyes reflecting back at him in the mirror above his bureau. The eyes didn't have any of the humor he had always seen in them before. They were a soldier's eyes, eyes that had in the last week dispassionately witnessed slaughter, torture, and depravity. All of it in live-action, full-color, six-track Dolby stereo.

What have I become?

It was a question he couldn't answer. Not yet. Not until the killing had ended and he could go hide somewhere and rebuild himself. Reconstruct his world again. His father, a constant authority figure in his life, a symbol of unshakeable stability, was gone. The justice system that had been his father's religion, a system that had earned his unquestioning devotion, a system he had taught his son to respect and obey, had betrayed them both. And the man Brett Macklin thought he knew best, himself, was now a stranger to him.

He sat up, resting his back against the headboard.

Macklin was startled by his new single-mindedness of purpose, this violent determination to eradicate the slime that had taken his father, then Melody, and then Saul and Moe. A single-mindedness of purpose he easily gave in to even though it defied all his morals, his entire sense of right and wrong. How long had he really been living with this stranger? How had it manifested itself in the past? How would it shape his future? The reflection cast its unwavering gaze upon him and he knew tonight he would kill again.

⚜ ⚜ ⚜

The room sizzled. The cool night breeze and the whirring fan didn't change a thing. They just couldn't compete with Busty Keaton. This woman could melt the polar ice cap.

But tonight she was farther south, trapped forever on scratched celluloid, dancing on Primo's wall. She writhed and contorted in front of him, her fingers between her legs, her head tossing madly from side to side.

"Yeahhhhhh." Primo grinned, taking a deep drag on the best weed he'd ever had. Beside him, on the metal desk, the old projector could barely keep the images up, rattling and whining as it sucked in the film and spilled it out around Primo's feet.

She fell to her knees, bent backwards, and opened herself up to him. "Hey, momma, c'mere and sit on my lucky bar stool," he cackled, pulling on his crotch.

The small, wooden box of a building seemed to close in around him. Sweat glistened on his forehead and chest, dampening his open shirt. It was just him, the heat, and Busty in the scrap-yard office, having a party.

His gritty body odor and the pot smoke mingled with the smell of years of cigarettes and cigars, cheeseburgers and belches, rusting scrap metal and dusty windowsills. The infrequent visitors to the scrap-yard office did their business in a hurry, talking fast and making sure they didn't bump into whatever must have shit and then died there.

Stacks of yellowed invoices and forms lined the walls that surrounded the two desks in the center of the room. In one corner, a soiled army cot rested in the shadows beside an old Frigidaire. For Primo, this was home sweet home.

Primo found the shack comforting. Especially at night. Here he always felt relaxed, safe. Nobody, not even that spineless bastard blowing away his friends, would dare bother him here. A Saturday night special lay beside the projector and a switchblade was in his back pocket, pressing against his buttocks.

Primo's eyes widened as Busty bent forward and pressed her face between her legs.

"Holy shit," he muttered. It was the most fantastic feat he had ever seen. For the first time in his life, he felt something akin to respect. Primo involuntarily shivered. It wasn't a reaction to Busty's amazing contortions. It was something else, a tickle between his shoulder blades. He tried to shrug it off. But the irritation continued, making it impossible for him to enjoy Busty's orgiastic writhing.

He looked over his shoulder at the window behind him. Brett Macklin stood outside, expressionless, his breath fogging the glass.

Primo grabbed his gun off the desk and swiveled, pumping three bullets in rapid succession into the window. The glass shattered and a cool breeze swept into the room. "Ha-ha! Blew the fuck out of you, asshole!"

Primo, his gun smoking, stalked up to the window and peered over the sill. There was no body.

"You're dead, fuckwad," Primo yelled at the stacks of metal sheets, twisted car bodies, and rusted piping. "I'm gonna cut off your balls and make you eat 'em!"

Primo climbed out the window and crouched on the cold dirt, the gun held out in front of him. As he walked into the shadows cast by the scrap piles, he could hear Busty Keaton squealing wildly in the office.

The crazy motherfucker Mr. Jury picked a fight with the wrong guy. "I'm gonna shish-kebab your fuckin' head, motherfucker. No one fucks with Primo." He walked in smooth strides around a heap of urinals, sinks, and busted refrigerators. Goose bumps rose on his damp skin, chilled by the cool air blowing through the scrap yard.

He heard a whistle behind him. "Hey, shorty, lookin' for me?"

Primo whirled around. Something icy splashed on his face, stinging his eyes and soaking his upper body.

Coughing, Primo stumbled backward, his vision blurred. A strong odor filled his nostrils and burned the tender membranes.

"What the fuck," Primo spit, stumbling back against the refrigerator. The smell of the substance was overpowering. His heartbeat built quickly into a frenzied pounding. "Gasoline," he hissed fearfully.

Primo, still unable to see clearly, broke into a run. He stumbled over a pipe, sliding face first into the dirt.

He frantically scrambled to his feet and saw two figures standing five yards away, both Brett Macklin. Blinking hard, tears streaming down his face, Primo raised his gun and pointed at the double vision of Brett Macklin.

"You're dead, asshole." Primo fired. Macklin threw himself sideways to the ground and felt the bullet whiz past his ear. The spark from the gun barrel ignited Primo's arm. Macklin saw the split second of surprise and terror in Primo's eyes before the fire consumed Primo's face. A high, wild scream escaped from Primo as the fire engulfed his body and drew it into a tiny, twisted curl of bubbling flesh.

Macklin stood up slowly, the smell of burned meat heavy in the air. He felt nothing. Not even hate.

CHAPTER EIGHTEEN

The sirens comforted Esteban as he strolled down the street. The sound was a natural part of the night, the babbling brook and the wind whistling through the trees of his urban wilderness. Mother Nature here was a robot made of asphalt and steel, grease and tar, with eyes of dirty glass and lungs of soot.

Grit and gravel and shards of glass crunched under his feet.

He embraced the warm smell of exhaust in the air and the sound of screaming sirens. It gave him a fleeting sense of security as he made his journey to Primo's place. There, he would be safe.

Mr. Jury was after them, and Primo could protect him. Alone, Esteban felt utterly defenseless and vulnerable. Primo made him feel strong. Primo made him feel a lot of things. Primo got him women, which he knew he could never get himself, drugs, booze, and money. Primo was father, friend, and foe.

Esteban knew his value to the gang was not as a violent commando. He was an errand boy and a punching bag. It was a perilous existence, but he liked to see people scared. He enjoyed it when they set that cop on fire. It made him feel strong. Made him feel like he had balls like Primo and Baldo. Sometimes it even made him come.

His allegiance was to anyone who could protect him and keep him entertained in this fashion. Primo and the gang did both exceedingly well. But there was another who did it better, who offered him more and gave him some sense of power. Someone who, until Mr. Jury came along, scared him more than Primo.

He saw the flames when he turned the corner. A crowd of people lined the fence of the scrap yard, and police cars were parked everywhere. Panic stormed through his guts. *Not Primo!* he thought to himself. Primo was too macho, too tough. Without thinking, Esteban stepped off the curb and walked across the street.

He heard the loud wail of a horn. Turning his head, he saw a pair of headlights closing on him. The coroner's wagon screeched to a halt inches from him.

"Watch out, boy, you're going to get hurt," a white-clad driver yelled. Esteban fled without looking back. He fled until his chest was tight with pain and his legs felt like lead.

Lost, scared, and out of breath, Esteban felt his bladder opening and then the warm wetness trickling down the side of his leg.

"Oh God," Esteban whined. "I'm next."

After what seemed like hours, his breathing slowly returned to normal. The shaking became chilly, infrequent quivers, and the pain ebbed in his chest. Esteban realized he had to think his way out of this. He wasn't like the others Mr. Jury killed. Esteban had an ally. A powerful ally. He would go to him for help.

Yes, he would help me, Esteban thought, straightening up. *I won't die.*

Esteban, comforted now, opened his eyes and turned away from the wall. And stared straight into a gun barrel. Esteban shrieked, throwing his hands up in front of his face.

Brett Macklin cocked the gun.

"Wait! Wait!" Esteban pleaded, his voice cracking. "Look, I'm not the one you want, man. Look, I'm small-time, okay?"

"Convince me," Macklin said softly.

"It's bigger man, really, it's bigger. I'll help you. Look, the cop wasn't burned 'cause of us. See, the mayor wanted him killed. The mayor told us to kill the cop."

Macklin touched the gun to Esteban's forehead. "You'll have to do better than that."

Esteban moved backward, his shoulder scraping the wall. "You're making a big mistake if you waste me. Look, I can help you. Get me safe and I'll talk."

Macklin kept silent.

"Huh? Okay?! I'll talk, just get me safe."

Macklin stared into Esteban's eyes. "You want me to swallow this bullshit about Lucas Breen? Breen didn't stroll down here and ask you to kill my father."

"No!" Esteban squealed, nodding his head up and down, eager to please Macklin. "But someone did for him, really, I know, so for Christ's sake keep me alive to prove it. I'm better for you alive. Christ, you can always kill me later, right?"

Macklin lowered his gun and grabbed Esteban by the collar. "All right, punk, this story had better be good. Your life depends on it."

"Yeah, yeah, it'll be good." He looked fearfully into Macklin's eyes.

He released Esteban and started walking down the street. Pushing Esteban in front of him.

"Why was my father killed?" Macklin asked.

Esteban swallowed. "Look, alls I know is that he was asking too many questions. He wanted to know everything about what every gang was doing. You know? Everything he heard on the street he wanted double-checked."

"Like what?"

"I dunno. Like if he heard the Black Belts messed up with the Cougars, he wanted me to find him someone who saw it happen. Someone who could prove to him that it was true."

"Why?" Macklin roared, grabbing Esteban by the arm and dragging him closer.

"I don't know!" Esteban yelled frantically. "I just did what he asked, you know?"

"What does this have to do with Lucas Breen?"

Before Esteban could answer, a gunshot rang out from across the street. Macklin dove behind a parked car, dragging Esteban down with him.

Macklin hadn't been quick enough. The right side of Esteban's head was gaping open, blood gurgling through a splintered mess of hair and bone. Esteban's body rattled, splashing blood on the car.

Macklin raised his gun and peeked around the front of the car. He could barely see the gunman standing in the shadows beside the building directly across the street. Macklin bolted up, firing the Magnum twice in the same motion.

The bullets glanced off the brick beside the gunman, who ducked and returned Macklin's fire.

Macklin pulled back as one bullet ricocheted off the car's front grill and another shattered the windshield.

Macklin heard the footfalls as the gun man abandoned his cover and ran down the alley. Macklin rose and sprinted across the street, hugging the walls of the building for cover as he dashed down the alley after the assailant.

He saw the gunman dart out of the alley and take cover behind a car. Macklin hurled himself against the wall as the gunman fired and felt the hot bite of the bullet slashing his forehead.

Macklin fell forward on his knees, blinded by the pain, blood streaming down his face. He blinked open his eyes and, reaching back to the wall to steady himself, stood up.

Wiping the blood out of his eyes with the back of his hand, he slid along the wall to the street. Remaining in the shadows, he scanned the street. Parked cars lined both sides. No one was in sight.

Cautiously, he emerged from the alley and stepped dizzily into the street, the gun held shakily in his hand. The street was quiet. Macklin lowered his gun and sighed. Whoever it was had escaped.

Then Macklin heard a roar down the street to his left. He spun and saw a sedan racing towards him. He spread out his legs to brace himself and aimed the gun carefully in front of him, firing twice into the windshield of the oncoming sedan before leaping out of its path onto the hood of a parked car.

As the sedan thundered past, Macklin caught a quick glimpse of the driver before he tumbled off the hood and onto the sidewalk.

Macklin stood up slowly, swayed unsteadily, and watched the car screech around the corner and disappear. Blackness closed in on him and he fell against the parked car, sliding to the sidewalk.

Groaning, Macklin willed himself to stand. He grabbed the car door and pulled himself up, his eyes closed, a fleeting image of the gunman flashing in his head. Macklin couldn't hold the image long enough to identify the man, but he knew one thing. The gunman was no stranger.

Macklin heard the echo of footsteps from the alley. The police must have been drawn to the gunfire. Macklin trudged down the street in the same direction the speeding sedan had gone.

He turned the corner and quickened his pace, his strides smoothing as the pain in his head waned and his sense of balance returned. Gradually, his walk became a sprint, his battered body protesting with innumerable aches as he forced it to move quickly through the night.

When he was certain no one was following him, he jogged along the twisting, circuitous route to his car, which he had parked a mile away from Primo's scrap yard. His face was twisted in anger. He had expected to be free of this whole nightmare by this evening, his father's death avenged, his life assuming some semblance of normalcy.

The gunman changed all that.

Macklin drove himself faster, straining his legs, trying to run the deep disappointment, the physical pain, and the burning rage out of him. Running for Macklin was like flying, a sort of freedom, a perch above it all from which to reflect. It gave him the distance to observe things more clearly.

But nothing was clear anymore.

The facts just didn't make any sense to him.

He had thought his father had been just another victim of a sadistic gang folly. Now it appeared to be more than that. Melody and Saul had told him his father had been puzzled by gang violence in the neighborhood.

What was it Melody had said? Macklin asked himself. Something about rumors, lies, that were sparking gang violence. Yes, that was it. People were acting on rumors about events that never occurred. Gangs were exacting deadly retribution from rival gangs over affronts and attacks that never happened.

JD was investigating those rumors, where they were coming from and why, when he was killed.

Macklin was falling into his rhythm now, his feet padding gently and softly on the pavement, his body shifting into that exertion-fed physical and emotional high.

Now Melody and Saul were both dead. Macklin had no doubt it was because they had talked to him. Why were they killed? What danger did they pose, and to whom?

Again the gunman's fleeting image toyed with Macklin. *I've been a fool,* he thought. Someone is following me, picking off anyone that can get me closer to the truth about my father. How long has the killer been on my tail? Why and for whom?

Why am I still alive? Surely, he's had dozens of opportunities to kill me. That question, for the moment, seemed the most puzzling. Why hadn't the gunman killed him along with Melody, Saul, and Moe? Was the bullet that killed Esteban meant for him?

Macklin slowed a few yards short of the Batmobile, parked beside the gray rubble of a demolished building.

The killing wasn't over—that was clear to him. Macklin tried again to hold the gunman's image long enough to recognize it. Find the gunman, Macklin knew, and he'd find his answers. And his freedom.

Then again, it occurred to him, he might not have to find the gunman. The gunman might find him.

CHAPTER NINETEEN

Brett Macklin lived in the sort of single-story house a child might draw—symmetrical, a front door flanked by two windows and topped with a pointed roof.

The sea breeze that cooled Macklin now as he rose from the Batmobile had done its subtle damage to his home, gradually stripping off the white paint in tiny flakes and exposing the turquoise underneath.

Three old Cadillacs rested on his unkempt front lawn like tired, grazing cattle. The neighbors were constantly complaining about it, threatening to legally force him to get rid of the "ugly relics," but so far they were all bark and no bite.

One of the cars was a mere skeleton, a rusted four-door body on blocks that Macklin had hoped to transform into a blazing red classic. He stood beside it and tried to rekindle his enthusiasm, remembering how excited Shaw had been when Macklin gave him the blue Cadillac convertible. It was pointless. The Brett Macklin who had been childishly eager about the project was gone. Those sorts of visions seemed beyond his reach now.

He took the Magnum out and tossed it inside the gutted hulk and then trudged up the front steps, inserted the key in the deadbolt, and turned the knob. Wearily, he pushed open the door and stepped over a pile of mail, closed the door, and switched on the light.

Macklin went into the closet-size hall bathroom under the stairs and looked at his face in the mirror. His hair was stuck to the caked blood on his forehead.

"Shit, do you look like hell," he told his reflection. He twisted on the faucet and splashed his face with cold water.

The water refreshed him and washed away the blood. When Macklin looked into the mirror again, he was surprised to see that the bullet had barely nicked his forehead.

"It's always the little ones that bleed the most," he said to himself. After drying his face off with a towel, he clicked off the light and went into the kitchen.

A week's worth of dishes sat soaking in the sink, nearly submerged in brownish water, soggy bran flakes, and bits of fat. It gave the compact kitchen a sour smell.

The cupboards looked bleached, badly in need of restaining, and the countertops, yellowed with age, wouldn't shine if soaked for a month in Formula 409. The floor, however, was brand-new, designed to look like a cobblestone path. Because Macklin rarely swept the floor, it was easy to mistake it for one.

Cleanliness was of little concern to Macklin. There were only two rooms in the house Macklin cared about anyway—the bedroom and the garage. The rest of the house was just space to throw his stuff.

Macklin sauntered over to the refrigerator, opened it, and searched for the makings of a quick meal. He discovered some leftover pepperoni pizza wrapped in foil. He pulled out the pizza and a Schlitz, and closed the refrigerator door with his rear end. As he carried the food to the table, he noticed the light blinking on his telephone answering machine on the counter. So he hit the "play" button with his elbow as he passed the machine.

He dragged a wooden chair out from under the small butcher block with his foot and sat down.

Beep. "Hi, Brett, this is Cheshire. I haven't heard from you. Let's get together, okay? Gimme a call at home or at the hospital. Bye!"

Beep. "Fred Jenkins here. You have just won $1,000 worth of savings for just $39.95. That's right Mr.... ah... Mr. Brett Macklin. Our coupon book, being held in your name for a limited time, will entitle you to a treasure trove of values, $1,000 worth, for just a piddling $39.95. Call me, Fred Jenkins, at 555-7497 to claim your $1,000 in spending power!"

Beep. "I think the warp drive is busted on my Caddy. Scotty, can you give it a look-see? " It was Macklin's former brother-in-law, the proud owner of one of Macklin's rebuilt '59 Cadillacs. He smiled as he chewed a mouthful of pizza. "The thing shakes 'n' groans and the rockets in the back just aren't spitting out the flaming thrust I'm used to. See ya. Bye."

Beep. Static. *Click.*

A hanger-upper. *Asshole.* Macklin swallowed some beer and took another big bite out of the pizza slice.

Beep. "Hey, old buddy, it's me, a haunting voice from your past, eh?" Kirk Jeffries still sounded as though someone had just poured a can of Drano down his throat. Macklin remembered the last time he saw Jeffries, two years ago, soaking in the rain waiting to see a *Dirty Harry* movie. "I'll be making my triumphant return to the sunny southland tomorrow. I've been having wet dreams about the Chicken Shack, so what do you say we meet there tomorrow night at seven thirty? Grab Ron and we can relive our college days. If you can't make it, gimme a call at the Beverly Wilshire."

The blank remainder of the tape hissed. Macklin enjoyed the silence and then heard footsteps outside. He looked at the backyard door.

The door slammed open and two figures sprang into the kitchen, holding guns.

"Freeze, Macklin," Sliran barked, poised in front of Macklin and aiming his gun at his head.

Macklin, holding a slice of pizza in front of his mouth, looked over his shoulder. Two uniformed cops stood in the hallway, their guns trained on him. Macklin turned back to Sliran and shrugged, dropping the pizza on the table and raising his hands. "C'mon in, guys, make yourselves at home."

Sliran motioned to the officers. They hooked their hands under Macklin's shoulders, pulled him out of the chair, and pushed him against the wall.

Macklin smiled at Sliran as an officer frisked him. "You better have a warrant."

Sliran dropped a folded paper on the table beside the beer. "You're under arrest, Macky boy."

"The charge?" Macklin asked, turning from the wall.

"Jaywalking. Fuck, what do you think it is?" Macklin's arms were twisted behind his back. The handcuffs snapped closed. "It's murder, Macky boy. It isn't legal in this state to kill people. You're going down, just like I promised."

Sliran met Macklin's tired gaze. "Get him out of my sight and read him his rights."

The officers led Macklin out.

Sliran picked up the can of beer, took a few gulps, and noticed the sound of static from the answering machine for the first time. He went over to the machine and hit the "rewind" button, sipping the beer as the tape whirred.

"It's not a clean bill of health, Ronny, but at least you have your job back," Lieutenant Bohan Lieu said from inside the restroom stall.

Shaw, standing at the urinal relieving himself, frowned. "What exactly are you telling me, Lieutenant?"

"I'm giving you your gun and badge back—that's what I'm telling you. The board can't prove you actually beat Tomas Cruz—"

"I *didn't* beat Tomas Cruz," Shaw interrupted. He zipped up his fly and flushed the urinal.

"Okay, sorry," Lieu yelled over the sound of the water cleaning the urinal, "but there was enough to prove you leaned too hard on the kid."

The soap dispenser squirted a green glob into Shaw's hands. "Why doesn't soap look clean anymore?" he muttered to himself. He turned on the faucet and rubbed his hands together under the hot water.

"What does that mean, Lieutenant?" Shaw asked.

Shaw heard the toilet flush and the sound of Lieu fumbling with his belt. "It means I'm going to have to slap you on the wrists for unprofessional methods unbecoming of a police officer."

The stall door swung open and the portly Asian lieutenant stepped to the sink beside Shaw. "A formal reprimand is going into your file, Ronny."

Shaw shrugged, pulling a paper towel out of the dispenser. "I can accept that. I've got a question, though."

"Shoot," Lieu said, reaching past Shaw for a paper towel.

"Yates was after my ass. It looked like I was gonna drown in shit creek and no one was going to throw me a life preserver. What happened?"

Lieu smiled and walked towards the door. "It's the Mr. Jury case, Ronny. We need your help."

"What? What do you need me for?"

Lieu and Shaw stepped out of the men's room and into the brightly lit hallway crowded with police officers scurrying to and fro. "Sliran is questioning a suspect right now. I want you to take a look."

Lieu pushed open the door to the room adjoining the interrogation room, flicking on a light as he walked in.

Shaw strode up to the two-way mirror, which allowed observers to look in on interrogations unseen. Lieu sat down in a chair behind him.

Shaw caught his breath and felt a hot flush warm his face.

Brett Macklin, looking haggard and pale, seemed to be staring right at him. Shaw stepped back even though he knew all Macklin saw was his own reflection. Macklin sat at a long table in a straight-back, uncomfortable chair occupied only an hour before by a transvestite drug dealer trying to plea-bargain his way out of an armed robbery charge.

Sliran, his tie loosened below an open collar, sat on the table's edge beside Macklin, smoking a cigarette and deliberately exhaling the smoke into Macklin's face. Another detective, a sunken-cheeked, fifteen-year veteran of the force referred to by his peers as "skull face," stood wearily against the door.

His hand shaking, Shaw reached out and turned on the speaker.

"C'mon, Macky boy, it's late." Sliran's voice sounded tinny over the loudspeaker in the observation room. "I want to go home and poke my girlfriend, you know?"

Sliran took a long drag on the cigarette, blowing out the smoke slowly and deliberately into Macklin's face. "You don't even need to talk much. Just say two words: 'I confess.' Can you do that? Read my lips. 'I confess.'"

Sliran tapped the reel-to-reel tape recorder in front of Macklin. "Say it into the tape recorder. Better yet, say, 'Yes, I blew Teobaldo Villanueva's nuts off.' Say, 'Yes, I shot Jesse Ortega's head clean off and then did the same to Mario Carrera.' Say, 'Yes, I torched Primo Manriquez 'cause he burned Daddy to a crisp."

Shaw winced at Sliran's insensitivity.

"Say, 'Then I put a few holes in Enrico Esteban.' See how easy that is?" Sliran smiled. "There, now you try it."

Macklin sighed and stood up. "Bye."

Sliran pushed him back down in his seat.

"You're not going anywhere, Macky boy."

Shaw clicked off the speaker and turned his back to the window. "Okay, I saw the show. Now what?" He said hoarsely.

"What do you think, Ron, about Macklin?" Lieu tilted the chair back against the wall.

Shaw folded his arms over his chest. "Don't play games with me, Lieutenant."

Lieu smiled. "Please, Ron, don't get hostile. I know Macklin is your friend. That's why I need your help. You know him better than anyone. Do you think he's Mr. Jury?"

"Brett Macklin is like my brother," Shaw said softly.

Lieu shrugged. "That's not what I'm asking."

Shaw turned around and looked at Macklin again, sitting stoically in his chair and facing the mirror. As long as Shaw could remember, he and Macklin had been the closest of friends. Nothing had ever changed that. Not until now.

Shaw couldn't deny there had been a change in Macklin. He had seen it happen in the courtroom. Macklin was impossible to reach. He had grown into himself. Shaw was hurt and concerned that Macklin didn't come to him to work out his grief over his father's murder. The Brett Macklin Shaw knew would have.

Shaw remembered when Macklin's marriage dissolved, the long hours he spent talking with his distraught and bitter friend. They had healed that wound together. His father's death had to be devastating, the release of the accused killers even more painful. Had these two forces, Shaw asked himself, combined to change Brett Macklin? *To change him into a killer?*

It was a thought Shaw tried to ignore. One by one he had watched the Bounty Hunters turn up dead. Each time he had tried to kid himself into believing Brett Macklin couldn't possibly be pulling the trigger. *Yet*... The detective in Shaw told him Macklin was the obvious, most likely killer.

Emotionally, it was impossible for Shaw to accept.

Shaw had lied to himself during those long sleepless nights since the trial. He'd told himself some warped, justice-seeking citizen had chosen the Macklin case as his first vigilante cause. He'd told himself it could be a rival gang destroying their enemy. After a while it seemed that any possibility, even aliens from outer space using the gang for target practice, seemed more reasonable than Brett Macklin being the killer.

Both Shaw and Brett had been raised under JD Macklin's watchful eye. He had instilled them both with a deep respect for the law. Yes, he taught them, the law is sometimes blind. Sometimes the innocent are punished and the guilty set free. Those inequitabilities are a rarity. By and large, the law afforded justice and peace.

It was JD Macklin's example, his total devotion to the cliché of law and order and justice for all, that led Shaw to police work.

Macklin's love for his father, Shaw believed, would stop him from playing judge, jury, and executioner.

But in that courtroom, Shaw had seen something roll over and die inside Brett Macklin. In the passing of a second, the closeness he felt towards his friend had disappeared.

Shaw hesitated, staring at Macklin through the glass. The man Sliran was questioning didn't look like the man Shaw had grown up with. The face was changed. Harder, angular, lined, the eyes reflecting a joyless rigidity.

The face of a killer?

"Yes," Shaw whispered, turning to face Lieu again. "Yes, I think he could be."

"So do I. That's why I want you to help Sliran on this."

"That's ridiculous," Shaw snapped. "First of all, you already have him—you don't need me. Secondly, I can't put my friend away. I just can't do it."

Lieu stood up and squeezed Shaw's shoulder. "Ronny, we're friends. If you don't clear this thing up for yourself, it will eat away at you for the rest of your career. The self-doubt, the fear that you let Macklin get away with it, will devastate you. And we really don't have Macklin. He'll be out of here in the morning."

Lieu walked towards the door. "He may be innocent. We have nothing on him, nothing that will hold up in court, anyway. Gut feelings aren't enough to convict a man, I'm afraid." He smiled. "The case file is under the chair. Take a look at it."

Lieu left the room. Shaw stared at the door for a few moments, glanced at Macklin in the interrogation room, and then reached under Lieu's chair, pulled out the file, and sat down to read it.

Fifteen minutes later Shaw had read through the file. He waited until Sliran had finished his questioning and had "skull face" lead Macklin to his cell before he emerged from the observation room.

Shaw found Sliran standing in the hallway, cursing at the coffee machine.

"Eh, Shaw, how's it going?" Sliran kicked the machine, his back to Shaw.

"Life could be better. I'm back on active status," Shaw replied, approaching Sliran.

Sliran pressed the "coffee" button again. "Great." He gave the machine another kick.

"And I'm working on the Mr. Jury case." Shaw punched the side of the machine and then nudged the front with his shoulder. A cup fell into the slot and coffee poured into it. "Cream?"

"Sure," snapped Sliran.

Shaw punched the machine just below the selection buttons. Cream dribbled into the paper cup.

Sliran reached for the coffee. "Well, there isn't anything to work on. You buddy has got a lifetime lease on a federal apartment." Sliran started down the hall.

Shaw smiled grimly, falling into step beside him.

"Don't kid yourself, Neal, Mack will be out of here"—Shaw glanced quickly at his watch—"if he can get hold of a lawyer, oh, by about three o'clock tomorrow afternoon."

"Maybe."

"No maybe about it, Sliran. You don't have a damn thing on him."

Sliran stopped. "Why the hell are you on this case? This guy is your little buddy. You'd love to let him skip out the door and blow away a few more punks, huh?"

"Give me a break," Shaw groaned. "You know as well as I do you have nothing. Not a shred of solid evidence. Why didn't you have him tailed after the first killing? Why didn't you warn the gang members or at least have them watched? For Christ's sake, Sliran, that's the most obvious thing to do. Everything we've got now is circumstantial. There's nothing to build a case around.

"We're going to have a hard time proving Brett Macklin is Mr. Jury, and all thanks to your stupidity." *And what about me? Am I murderer for not stopping Mack?*

"I'll prove it," Sliran said. "With or without you, Shaw. Preferably without." He pushed Shaw aside and stomped down the hallway.

The cell door closed behind Brett Macklin. He stood still for a moment, his back to the door, the sound of the lock clicking into place still echoing in his head.

The charge is murder, Macky boy.

Macklin knew his lawyer would arrange his release by tomorrow evening. He knew Sliran had nothing to hold him on. He knew he would never have to pay for his crimes.

Pay? Hell, you're paying now.

Macklin fell onto the hard bed, a padded shelf jutting from the wall a foot above the floor. His body ached. He couldn't tell whether it was from weariness or frustration.

Macklin had lied, bled, cried, and killed to balance the scales. It wasn't enough. Vengeance and the truth still eluded him.

How much longer do I have to wait? How much more do I have to give?

Macklin rolled over and faced the wall. He didn't know where to begin looking for the answers. He did know his biggest obstacle.

Now there was Mr. Jury to reckon with.

Sliran would assume it was over, that Macklin had had his revenge. *Maybe,* Macklin thought, *some of the heat will be off now.* Sliran would still poke around but would be an endurable nuisance. The only real threat is...

Macklin rolled onto his stomach and buried his face in the crook of his arm.

C'mon, Mack, say it.

Shaw.

Macklin closed his eyes.

Shaw. He could stop me.

Stop you? Stop you from what?

Killing again. Getting even.

Nothing is going to stop you, Mack. Nothing.

For the hundredth time Macklin tried to fit the pieces of the puzzle together into one coherent picture. The rape. The Mr. Jury headlines. . The trial. Melody's smile. Lucas Breen. The sedan with the shattered windshield screeching around the corner. The images were a blinding collage that wore Macklin down into an uneasy slumber.

His dreams showed him a summer night that was quiet and warm. JD Macklin walked casually down the street, his uniform neatly pressed and his badge shining. Shopkeepers, drawing iron gates closed over their doors and windows, acknowledged Macklin with a friendly smile or a quick, reflexive glance.

JD turned a corner and the night seemed to darken. This street was completely empty, the air still, the buildings somehow older and taller and uglier than the ones he had just passed. His stride was easy and comfortable, his footsteps echoing as he crossed in front of the alley.

A whistle called to him.

JD Macklin, smiling, turned and saw Brett standing behind him, wearing black, holding the Magnum at his side.

Brett Macklin raised his arm slowly and aimed the gun at his father's head. And then blew the bewildered look right off his face.

CHAPTER TWENTY

Rush hour the next day began about three p.m. The cars heading east on the Santa Monica Freeway slowed to a crawl at the Robertson turnoff. Mort Suderson knew a car didn't move faster than twenty miles per hour at this point unless it had machine-gun turrets mounted on the hood and a stunt driver behind the wheel.

Mort was blessed with neither. So it took him nearly an hour to get downtown in his lime green '78 Chevette, a car he referred to as his "pussyfart little shitmobile." The car doubled as his filing cabinet, crinkled Tab can depository, picnic table, and home entertainment center. Mort had installed the stereo system himself, cutting a huge hole in the dashboard and stuffing everything but a turntable in the space. Twice the stereo had been stolen and twice the thieves had cut around it, leaving an even bigger hole.

His latest stereo was held in place with two rolls' worth of electrical tape and periodic applications of Scotch tape, Elmer's glue, and rubber cement. Mort thought it gave the car character.

Genesis' "Just a Job to Do" was shaking the Chevette as it sputtered to the curb in front of the police station. A weary Brett Macklin, his clothes wrinkled and hair askew, stood on the sidewalk.

Mort reached across and unlocked the passenger door. It creaked loudly as Macklin pulled it open and fell into the torn bucket seat.

"Thanks for coming down, Mort." Macklin cleared a space for his feet among the Big Mac containers, the Tab cans, and old newspapers.

"No problem." Mort pulled into traffic and slammed on the brakes. Macklin threw out his arms, bracing himself against the dashboard. The motor home Mort nearly sideswiped honked as it passed. Macklin leaned back and sighed.

Mort smiled apologetically and moved away from the curb, weaving through traffic to the freeway.

They had traveled for a few minutes in silence when Mort cleared his throat and spoke hesitantly. "Well, it's over now."

"No, it isn't," Macklin whispered. "It may just be the beginning."

Mort reached under his seat, looking for something amidst the clutter. "I guess you'll be needing this, then." He pulled out the .357 Magnum and offered it to Macklin.

Macklin looked at the weapon and then glanced at Mort. He took the gun in one quick motion and set it on the floor by his feet.

"I came by the house just as the cops took you away. I did a little search of my own," Mort explained, turned down the radio. "I figured if I could find the gun, so could Ron. I figured it would be better if I was the one who found it.

Shaw.

Surely Shaw knew about his arrest. Macklin nervously wondered what Shaw's reaction would be. Would Shaw become an enemy or an ally? It was a question Macklin presumed he would have to face sooner than he liked.

Macklin looked at Mort and smiled. "You don't have to do this, Mort. If I fall, I don't want to drag you down with me."

"Look, I know what I'm doing. You helped me when no one else would."

"You don't owe me anything, Mort. If you did, you've paid me back double already."

"Brett, if you need help ... ah ... finishing things, I'm here."

Macklin put his hand on Mort's shoulder. "Thanks, Mort, I appreciate it.

"But I really don't want to get you any more involved than you already are at this point. It's better for the both of us. I really don't know what I'm going to do. There are so many unanswered questions."

Mort nodded and turned up the radio. They drove the rest of the way without talking, absorbed in their own thoughts. Macklin wasn't really thinking—his mind had slipped into neutral and he was absently watching the cars as they passed.

Mort pulled up in front of Macklin's house. "If you need to reach me, Brett, I'll be flying the chopper tonight for *The Bloodmaster* crew."

"All right." Macklin opened the door and got out. "Thanks again, Mort."

He closed the door.

"See ya, Brett." Mort waved and drove away.

Macklin yawned, unlocked the door, and was halfway to the bedroom when he remembered that Kirk Jeffries was in town. As drained as Macklin was, he thought some time with his old friend might be therapeutic. Perhaps it would bring a little of the old Brett Macklin to the surface again. It also meant seeing Shaw.

He went into the kitchen to call and invite Shaw. Sunshine answered the phone. The usually talkative Sunshine was abrupt, treating Macklin like an obnoxious salesman she couldn't wait to get rid of.

Shaw wasn't in, but he would be back soon. Macklin asked her to have him come by his house at seven o'clock if he was interested in joining Macklin to see Jeffries.

The conversation left Macklin feeling ill at ease. Sunshine's behavior was a sign of what he could expect from Shaw.

Macklin sighed and then walked to the bedroom, where he quickly stripped and showered, first with hot water to soothe his aches and pains and then with cold to revive and invigorate. He dried himself and slipped into a worn-out pair of Levi's 501s, his favorite basic blue rugby shirt, and his dirtied Adidas.

Feeling warm and relaxed now, Macklin went to the entry hall and gathered up the scattered mail, carrying it with him to the kitchen table, where he began sorting through it.

For the next half hour he comfortably lounged there in the familiar clothes and familiar habits and familiar smells of his old, single life. The mail was something refreshingly routine, and it was nice. For those few minutes before Shaw drove up in hiss blue, 1959 Cadillac convertible and started honking, Brett Macklin felt almost normal again.

Macklin opened the front door and groaned inwardly. Shaw had that solemn look on his face that meant a "big talk" was coming. He wanted to yell "see you some other time, Ronny," go in the house, and lock the door. Instead, he closed the door and sprinted to the car.

"It's looking good, Ronny." He stroked a fin as he walked around the back of the car and got in the passenger side.

Shaw pulled away from the curb, made a U-turn, and headed north.

Macklin glanced at Shaw, who drove as if he was wearing an iron neck brace.

"Okay, talk to me. Don't sit there like a mortician."

"I don't know, Mack. It seems to me you'd be rather comfortable with a mortician. You've boosted their business to a new high this month."

"You think I'm Mr. Jury."

Shaw turned and met Macklin's gaze. "I *know* you're Mr. Jury. Everybody does. Don't kid yourself. You may as well make a uniform and write it in gold on your chest." Shaw scratched his neck.

"Relax, Mack, it's just you and me in the car. No hidden recorders, no camera. Nothing a murderer like yourself should be concerned about."

"I'm not a murderer," he replied.

"You're a killer, simple as that. The only difference between you and the guys who killed your father is that you're alive and free." Shaw studied Macklin's face. "For now."

"If you're so sure I'm your man, why don't you stop me? Why are you with me now?" Macklin asked. Shaw turned away. "I'll tell you why. You know, whether it's me or somebody else, you'd like to shake Mr. Jury's hand and say, 'job well done.'"

"Mack, your way is wrong."

"Do you have any doubt they killed my father?"

"No," Shaw said, barely audible.

"How many other people have they beaten, raped, harassed, or killed?"

"I don't know."

"*You don't know.* Well, I know something. I know that no one is going to miss those vicious animals. I know that a lot of people are breathing easier at night now that they are gone. That's not to say I'm your man. But somebody has to do it. We can't let a bunch of punks hold an entire city hostage."

"That's not the point. You thought you had reason to kill—"

"Come on, Ronny," Macklin interrupted."I told you I wasn't Mr. Jury."

Shaw looked at him skeptically and continued, "... and so did they. Reason doesn't mean a damn thing. It's still murder. You can lie to me, but you can't lie to yourself."

"I'm not living a lie. You are. The cops won't ever win. You know that. It just keeps getting worse. The law protects the criminal and punishes the victim."

Macklin lowered his voice and settled back into his seat. "The time has come for someone to draw the line, for someone to tell these punks they can't prey on people anymore."

Macklin looked away from Shaw to the passing skyline, "It's time for us to take our city back."

As Shaw banked around the La Brea turnoff and surged north towards Hollywood Boulevard, he thought about what

Macklin had said. Shaw knew that in many ways Macklin was right. He knew the frustration of watching the law let the guilty free. He could see crime growing in the face of constant cutbacks in police budgets and manpower. He felt the helplessness as people saw their neighborhoods fall under the control of warring gangs. He realized all the LAPD could do was police the results of the violence and not the violence itself.

And he had let Macklin kill.

La Brea met Hollywood Boulevard and Shaw steered the car to the right. Hollywood Boulevard, a tired whore trying to turn one last trick, a street that wasn't made to grow old, stretched out in front of them.

Macklin watched the tourists swarm around the footprints as they waited for the Hollywood Tour bus. To him, the street was dying. Tourists would look in vain for the mythical glitter and find just another neon street full of empty dreams, broken promises, and the make-believe hope that thrives wherever reality doesn't live up to fantasy.

Trendiness had packed up and moved west to Beverly Hills and Westwood, which, unlike Hollywood, were kept as antiseptic and clean as the dreams they were selling. Not that the dreams were any more real—they just looked and felt better. Desperation, which Macklin saw flaunting itself in Hollywood, hid in the shadows of Rodeo Drive and Westwood Boulevard, barely noticeable amidst the sea of BMWs.

The Chicken Shack was an island in a parking lot looming up on Macklin's left. It looked like a street party. Motorcycles crowded the parking lot. Male hookers plied their trade from metal picnic tables facing the boulevard.

A crush of garishly dressed punk rockers, with Mohawk haircuts and blaring stereos, milled around the yellow hut in large clusters.

Standing amidst it all, as if illuminated by a spotlight, stood Kirk Jeffries. He leaned against the counter that wrapped around the hut, munching hungrily on a massive chicken leg, the flat end of his bulbous note spotted with chicken grease.

Shaw squeezed his Cadillac convertible between one of the rows of motorcycles and a Plymouth Duster that looked as though it had been parked under the space shuttle launching pad.

Their discussion still weighed heavily on both of them. Grimly, Shaw and Macklin avoided each other by looking at Jeffries for a moment.

Macklin was pleased that Jeffries hadn't changed in the two years since he had last saw him. Jeffries' breast pocket was still bulging with a half dozen long cigars. Jeffries liked to shove the cigars deep into his mouth, gnawing on them until they were ragged and black. The habit had yellowed his teeth and given him smokestack breath.

A huge belt buckle that spelled KIRK held up his Sassoon jeans under his bulging belly, which was hidden by a blue checked shirt open wide at the collar to expose his hairy pigeon chest. His only concession to fashion, Macklin noticed, was a new pair of Sperry Top-Siders.

Shaw nudged Macklin without looking at him. "Look, he's still got that damn watch."

Wrapped around Jeffries' wrist was a gold watch that seemed to be about two inches thick, a timepiece that could probably deflect cannonballs and low-flying nuclear warheads with ease.

Jeffries, reaching for another piece of chicken, noticed Macklin and Shaw staring at him.

"You guys gonna sit in that meat wagon like a coupla pimps or join me?" Jeffries barked, his lips stretched into a side smile that afforded the punker near him a good look down his sooty throat.

Macklin and Shaw looked guiltily at each other, grinned, and got out of the car.

"Wait," Jeffries yelled, holding up a chicken breast. "Don't exert yourselves on my account." He wrapped his left arm around the bucket of chicken and moved to a bench beside Shaw's car.

Jeffries set down the bucket and grabbed Macklin in a bear hug, still holding the chicken breast. "It's good to see you again, Brett."

Before Macklin could reply, Jeffries released him and hugged Shaw. "Christ, Ronny, is that a gun or are you just glad to see me?"

Jeffries burst into his choke-wheeze of a laugh, which he silenced with a big bite of chicken.

"Sit down and grab some chicken before I eat it all," he said while chewing.

Macklin reached for a leg, thick with the Chicken Shack's famous batter. "Still as quiet and reserved as ever, aren't you, Kirk?"

"Don't believe in holding back, Brett, you know that."

Shaw expected Jeffries to stop taking bites out of the breast and just swallow it whole.

"Here you are making money left and right and you still don't know how to eat like a human being," Shaw said, only half joking. He took a wing from the bucket and pulled it apart.

"Fuck you, Ronny," Jeffries deadpanned. Macklin roared with laughter, nearly gagging on his mouthful of chicken.

Jeffries, preferring not to notice Macklin's laughter, glanced at the crowd around the yellow hut. "Queers have taken the place over, but the chicken is still the best. Shit, you two look good."

"Thanks," Macklin said.

"How do you guys do it?" Jeffries asked.

"We don't eat here anymore," Shaw replied.

Jeffries roared and noticed the grim expressions on his friends' faces. "What's the matter with you two? You're like a coupla rocks."

Macklin smiled. "We've had a long day. So, how long are you staying in town this time?"

"I'm here for a few months, at least until the gubernatorial race is over. I'm gonna help Elliot Wells clobber that son of a bitch Lucas Breen."

"Vengeance is sweet," Shaw said, looking Macklin in the eye.

"Damn right it is," Jeffries said. "I've been waiting for a shot at old Prickface for a long time."

"What exactly happened between you two?" Macklin asked. "You never did spell it out for me."

Jeffries held up his hand, signaling a pause while he swallowed a mouthful of chicken. "Breen hired two guys to do a number on Francis Reed, that councilman that ran against Breen in the mayor's race. These guys followed Reed around night and day and got some pictures of him screwing his secretary. Reed was married at the time, had two kids at UCLA. Breen came into my office one day, ranting about how he had Reed beat. He tossed the photos to Reed and told him to pull out or else he'd give the photos to the press. When Breen left the office I burned the fucking photos."

"Shit," Macklin muttered.

"Not shit, a shitstorm. Reed yelled my head off, fired my ass, and told me I had just kissed my career good-bye."

Shaw shook his head in disbelief. "Why didn't you go to the press, tell them what you knew?"

"C'mon, Ronny, it would have blown up in my face. It would have brought Breen down, you're right about that, but it would have tainted us all. Besides, I haven't always been a saint myself. I just never stooped *that* low."

"Old Prickface," Jeffries continued, "is going to lose, boys. So, if I were you, I'd get some money down in this campaign."

"Speaking of money"—Shaw pulled apart a wing—"you must be bathing in it."

"Hell, yes, don't know what to do with it all. Frankly, I'd do this work for free." Jeffries started chomping on the chicken bone. "It's a game to me, making the statistics into gemstones for me and turds for the other guys."

The bone swallowed, Jeffries leaned forward and contemplated the bucket. "What can I do with money? I could buy bigger cigars, I guess, get new hubcaps for my Jag every month, piss it away on overpriced food and overrated women.

"Hey, I'm a simple guy, you know?" He threw his hands up and raised his eyebrows as if to say "See, look at me from head to toe, I really am simple."

Jeffries took a leg from the bucket and nearly swallowed the whole thing, bone and all, in one eager bite. "As long as I can keep the old brain stoked, I'm happy."

"You don't care what the candidate stands for?" Shaw asked.

"So the candidate's a Democrat. Republican? A homosexual cat-hating, schmuck-baiting, leisure-suit-wearing Martian? It means nothing to me. Work with any of them if it's a challenge. Unless it's a small-time asshole like Lucas Breen."

"You sound happy," Macklin said.

"I am." Jeffries wiped his face with a yellow Chicken Shack napkin.

"Remember when we all worked on that cheerleader's campaign for student body president?" Shaw asked.

"We were all trying to sleep with her," Macklin added.

"I *did*," Jeffries said proudly, poking himself in the chest with his thumb.

"Bullshit." Macklin grinned at Shaw. Shaw looked away. Macklin self-consciously sustained the smile.

"Sure did," Jeffries said. "I was so happy about it I got drunk afterwards and tried to piss off the ninth-floor dormitory ledge."

"It's a good thing you were wearing that hooded sweatshirt," Macklin said.

"Yep, otherwise you would have grabbed a handful of air and I'd be part of the dormitory landscaping." Jeffries laughed. "Boy, I wish I was twenty again."

Macklin was distracted by the sound of tires skidding on the street. He saw a brown pickup truck, with three scruffy guys in the bed, make a screeching U-turn in front of the Chicken Shack and then bounce into the parking lot to Macklin's right at high speed.

"What the hell?" Shaw muttered, dropping his chicken and looking over his shoulder.

Macklin watched the truck smash through the row of motorcycles beside them and skid behind the Chicken Shack. The three passengers in the truck squealed with delight.

Macklin stood up just as the truck reappeared around the opposite end of the shack and saw one of the youths toss a flaming bottle towards them.

"Duck!" Macklin yelled, throwing himself down against the picnic table. He sensed the Molotov cocktail streak over his head and heard it shatter inside Shaw's car behind him.

Macklin turned and saw the flames licking the upholstery he had worked so carefully to restore. Jeffries bolted up from under the table and scrambled towards the Chicken Shack, running low past the wrecked motorcycles.

Macklin saw the truck whip around, screeching on a parallel path beside Jeffries. A youth raised another firebomb in his hand.

"Stop, Kirk!" Macklin yelled.

The firebomb landed among the motorcycles and exploded. He saw his friend hurled through the Chicken Shack window by the force of the blast.

Shaw, crouched beside the picnic table, sprang up, gun in hand, and fired at the truck, which skidded behind the building again.

Enough is fucking enough. Macklin's anger took control of him. Enraged, he pushed through the frenzied crowd and ran towards the other side of the Chicken Shack. The truck fishtailed around the edge of the building. Macklin took a running leap onto the hood of a parked car and then flung himself into the speeding truck. He slammed into a man poised to throw another lighted Molotov cocktail and knocked him over the side of the truck.

Macklin, lying stunned on his side, saw the burning man roll screaming in the truck's wake. One of the two remaining men jumped on Macklin, pinching Macklin's head between his hands. He slammed the back of Macklin's head against the floor of the truck, which sped into the street across the path of opposing traffic.

Macklin reached out for his assailant's neck, digging his thumbs into the soft flesh. The man's eyes bulged. He let go of Macklin's head and grabbed at Macklin's wrists, gurgling as he tried to loosen the choking grip.

Macklin felt himself thrown from side to side as the truck swerved sharply, weaving in and out of westbound traffic on Hollywood Boulevard.

Out of the corner of his eye, Macklin saw the other man swinging a bottle down towards his face and reacted instantly. Macklin jerked his choking assailant down on top of him. The bottle shattered against the assailant's head.

Macklin rolled out from under the unconscious man and fell against the tailgate, his back jammed into the right corner.

The remaining man, on his knees, looked from his bloodied friend to Macklin.

"You son of a bitch," the man shrieked, lunging at him.

Macklin yanked the tailgate handle with his left hand. The tailgate opened and Macklin fell back, desperately grabbing hold of the truck with his right hand. The man slid past Macklin and out of the truck headfirst, splattering like an insect against a motor home's shiny grillwork.

Macklin's body dangled over the passing road, his feet skipping on the asphalt. The racing truck snaked wildly around cars, whipping Macklin back and forth as he struggled to pull himself back in.

The car careened to the right and Macklin's body swung to the left, allowing him to lift his leg onto the tailgate and pull himself aboard.

Macklin, gasping for breath, crawled up the bed to the cab, braced himself against the side of the truck, and shoved his foot through the window behind the driver's head.

The driver yelped, twisting the wheel. The truck rammed against the side of a Hollywood Tour bus, jarring Macklin and flinging him to the opposite side of the bed.

"Look, it's the Fall Guy," a pregnant bus passenger from Wenatchee, Washington, squealed, excitedly snapping pictures of Macklin as he reached inside the cab and tried to take the wheel of the speeding truck.

The truck slammed against the bus again. The passenger rocked, watching Macklin push the driver's head away with one hand and grab the steering wheel with the other.

The bus driver braked and the truck careened sideways across the bus's path into oncoming traffic. A Datsun glanced off the passenger side of the truck and sent it spinning out of control through the front window of Frederick's of Hollywood in a storm of glass, plaster, and lingerie.

CHAPTER TWENTY-ONE

Time stopped on Hollywood Boulevard like a movie freeze-frame.

Then, out of the settling dirt and debris of Frederick's gaudy purple building, a figure emerged, staggered, and collapsed on the Walk of Fame.

Two police cars, sirens blaring, screeched to the curb. The car doors flew open and the officers burst out, guns drawn. Three ran into the crumbling storefront while the other went to Macklin, who lay twisted on Jack Palance's star, moving slightly and groaning as if shaking off the last remnants of a Sunday morning sleep-in. Macklin opened his eyes and saw a policeman leaning over him.

"Jesus," the officer said, holstering his gun. "Take it easy, an ambulance is on the way."

The officer scurried back to the squad car to call for backup and rescue units.

"Fuck the ambulance," Macklin mumbled, his face smeared with blood, plaster, and flecks of glass. He propped himself up on an elbow, fought back the dizziness, and then stood up shakily.

A large crowd had formed around the store and Macklin stumbled into it, the people moving out of his way as if he had a deadly infection.

"Hey, you, wait!" he heard the officer yell through the gathering crowd behind him.

Macklin turned to a taxi parked at the curb, glanced at the surprised, obese driver, yanked open the door, and dived in the backseat.

"Take me down to the Chicken Shack," Macklin coughed, lying down on the seat. The police officer, who had lost sight of Macklin in the crowd, ran past the taxi.

The driver glanced at Macklin in the rearview mirror, "After *that*, you wanna eat?"

"Are you gonna drive or do I walk?"

The driver stared at Macklin a moment longer, looked at the confusion of the street, and then sighed, turning the ignition and pumping the gas. "A fare's a fare," he mumbled.

Macklin closed his eyes as the car pulled away from the curb and pressed his face against the seat, hoping the worn cushion would deaden the throbbing pain in his head.

The accident had happened so fast. The truck had burst through the glass like a rocket, slamming into a gold-painted pillar and folding into it like an accordion, crushing the driver. Macklin remembered sailing through the windshield on impact, landing in a cluster of nightgown-clad mannequins.

"Hey, guy, you ain't puking on my seats, are you?" the driver barked.

"Please drive, okay?" Macklin sat up and looked out the rear window. The pandemonium on the street was now several blocks behind them.

"You look like hell, mister."

"It's okay," Macklin groaned. "I got another hour or so before my act at Chippendales."

"If it's like your last act, I hope the audience is armed," the driver said.

Macklin closed his eyes and leaned his head against the window. It felt like someone was pounding a stake through the middle of his head.

He thought about the days since his father's funeral. Tranquility given way to an endless succession of bloodshed. In his old world, his old life, people didn't throw Molotov cocktails at him while he ate dinner.

It didn't make sense.

Opening his eyes, he saw a long line of cars stopped in front of the taxi. Billows of smoke colored the sky brown about two blocks away.

The driver threw up his hands. "This is as far as you go. I can't get any closer."

"Okay." Macklin said, pushing open the door and stepping out onto the street. "What do I owe you?"

"Nothing. Just stop bleeding in my cab."

"Thanks." Macklin closed the door and walked down the street towards the smoke. Each step brought stabs of pain in his left side, his right knee, and his head.

As he neared the Chicken Shack he could see the parking lot was thick with smoke from the exploding motorcycles and the flames feeding off Shaw's Cadillac.

Two motorcycle cops growled into the parking lot, followed by a fire truck. Macklin, pushing through the crowd of onlookers, saw Shaw run from inside the Chicken Shack to meet the policemen. Raising his arm over his face to shield himself from the heat and smoke, Macklin dashed across the parking lot behind Shaw's back.

Squinting, Macklin made his way to the Chicken Shack hut. He stumbled through the doorway and saw Jeffries lying on a bed of shattered glass and fried chicken.

He leaned over his friend, scanning the rotund body for injuries. A mean gash cut across the right side of Jeffries face, from his forehead down to his chin. A jagged piece of bone, starkly white and speckled with blood, tore through the skin of his twisted right arm.

"I'm still alive, if that's what you're wondering," Jeffries whispered, his voice tinged with fear.

"Welcome to LA." Macklin picked shards of glass off Jeffries' face. "How do you feel?"

"Horrible. It hurts like hell. You wouldn't have some aspirin on you, would ya?"

"Nope."

"Ah, fuck it. I'll just suffer. I'll be a martyr, a war hero."

Macklin grinned with relief. Now he knew Jeffries was okay. "Don't you think you're going overboard? A war hero?"

"Hell no. Los Angeles is under siege. You can't eat in this town without risking your life. The last guy Wells brought in was gunned down at a Chinese restaurant, for Christ's sake."

Jeffries suddenly drew in his breath sharply, his eyes closed tightly. Macklin put his hand on Jeffries' shoulder as his friend untensed.

"Take it easy, Kirk. It's just pain."

Jeffries chuckled, the wave of pain appearing to ebb. "It's only pain. You're such an asshole, Brett."

"Kirk, did you tell anyone you were going to be here?" Macklin asked, not sure why.

"Nope. Just you."

Macklin felt an off, light-headed feeling, completely different from the dizziness he'd felt before. It dulled his pain and sent adrenaline surging through his veins. His heartbeat quickened.

"Are you sure?"

"Ya, I'm sure."

Macklin stood up slowly. The answers that had eluded him he sensed were within his reach now, swirling around his psyche, ready to come together into one truth.

He walked out the door into the smoke, feeling apart from the activity around him. Firefighters dragged hoses to the flames. A paramedic ambulance skidded to a stop at the curb.

Bits of dialogue crackled in his head.

... We'd hear all this talk but your father just couldn't track down anything...

Gangs are decimating each other over stuff that they hear happened but maybe didn't happen... Maybe you wanna take a swan dive off an overpass, motherfucker...

... The mayor told us to kill the cop...

Look, alls I know is that he was asking too many questions…

…Freeze, Macklin.

The gunman's face, the face behind the cracked windshield of the speeding sedan. It was coming into focus.

Freeze, Macklin.

Sliran. The gunman was *Sliran*!

Why would Sliran want Esteban or Macklin dead? How did Sliran fit into his father's murder? Or this attack?

Macklin looked back at the Chicken Shack, remembering Jeffries' words. *I'm gonna help Elliot Wells clobber that son of a bitch Lucas Breen…* What had happened to the last guy Elliot Wells had brought in to help him?

He was killed.

In a gang massacre.

The mayor told us to kill the cop…

Shaw was leading a team of paramedics to the Chicken Shack when he saw Macklin, trancelike, emerging from the smoke.

"Mack!" Shaw yelled, angry and surprised.

Macklin, apparently in a daze, ignored him and walked to a police motorcycle. Shaw broke away from the paramedics and ran toward Macklin, who straddled the cycle and kick-started it.

"Stop, Mack," Shaw yelled. "Stop!"

The cycle shot forward and Macklin roared past Shaw, veering away from the traffic-clogged street onto the sidewalk.

Shaw, flushed with anger, watched people leap out of Macklin's path as he raced down the sidewalk.

"That guy just took my cycle!" a voice screamed.

Shaw turned and saw an officer approaching behind him. "Put out an APB on Brett Macklin…"

The motorcycle purred to a stop on a side street across from the rear of the police station. Macklin, hidden in the shadows beside a brick building, looked at the police station as if it were Neal Sliran himself. He could feel the hate growing inside him and tightening his chest.

Macklin picked up the microphone.

"Dispatch, this is"—he made up a number—"Unit 232. Patch me in to Sergeant Sliran."

"Roger, 232, stand by," the woman's voice crackled over the speaker.

"Unit 232," a man's voice came over the speaker. "This is Sliran, go ahead."

Macklin brought the mike close to his mouth, a grim smile on his lips. "I'm still alive, Sliran, and I'm coming after you!"

"Who is this?" Sliran barked.

Macklin let him listen to static for a moment. Then he spoke slowly and carefully. "The Jury."

Macklin clicked off the radio and waited. Two minutes later he saw the back door of the station fly open and Sliran rush out, get into a Ford Galaxie, and screech out of the parking lot.

Macklin smiled, gliding smoothly into traffic a few cars behind Sliran.

CHAPTER TWENTY-TWO

The Elias Simon inner-city mission glowed in the dark. The building looked to Macklin as though it had been carved out of a block of marble, a one-story square monument to the power of religious television.

Macklin crouched behind the juniper bushes that lined the parking lot adjacent to the mission. He had been there for the last twenty minutes, watching Sliran smoking a cigarette in his car, parked directly across the street from the mission. Sliran tapped the dashboard nervously, casting glances over his shoulder every few seconds.

Macklin was impatient, too. His foot was falling asleep and his head still ached from the crash. And he wanted to go over and break the bastard's neck right now.

He was seriously considering just that when he saw Sliran look over his shoulder again and not turn back.

Peering over the top of the juniper hedge, Macklin saw the beam from a pair of headlights slice the darkness. A black Cadillac limo snaked around the corner towards the mission. Macklin ducked as the lights raked the top of the hedge and the car turned into the parking lot. Sliran, as if on cue, got out of his car, snubbed out his cigarette, and sprinted across the street.

Macklin raised his head again and saw the uniformed black chauffeur emerge. The chauffeur bent down to open the passenger door. Macklin saw the flash of blond hair, the blue suit, the slim, dancer's body. Sliran walked up and spoke to the man in animated gestures. The man turned to speak and Macklin saw his face. Elias Simon.

Macklin raised an eyebrow. *So Simon is pulling the strings. How does he fit in?*

The evangelist put his arm around Sliran's shoulder and led him into the mission. The chauffeur sat back down in the front seat of the limo.

The interior light was on. He could see the back of the chauffeur's head. The chauffer was reading a newspaper, spreading it out against the steering wheel. Bent low, Macklin dashed as lightly on his feet as he could to the limo.

He pressed himself close to the back right tire. Reaching into his pants pocket, Macklin pulled out his keys, careful not to jingle them. He picked out a long key and pressed the tip of it into the tire's pump nozzle, letting the air hiss out. Satisfied that the limo wouldn't leave for a while, Macklin dashed stealthily to the gleaming office building of Simon's mission.

Macklin found himself in one end of a portrait-lined hallway leading to a circular central reception area. The hallway smelled of freshly laid shag carpet. Macklin hugged the walls, passing portraits of Jesus Christ, Ronald Reagan, Oral Roberts, and Elias Simon as he quickly moved down the hallway. All the men were seen from the waist up against the same radiant sun. The oval-shaped reception area was lit by the bright moon shining through a rooftop skylight. There was a round desk in the center of the room near a wall-size portrait of Simon holding a Bible against his chest with both hands.

Two hallways branched off from the reception area. One was directly across from Macklin and led to a pair of arched, oak chapel doors with stained glass in the middle. One of the doors was ajar and Macklin could hear the muffled sound of voices from inside.

Macklin bounded in three steps to the chapel doors. He pressed his back to the wall and peered through the crack between the doors. He could see the first three rows of wooden pews. At the front of the room Simon, his arms folded against his chest, was leaning against a podium. Jesus Christ hung from the cross behind Simon and, head lolling on one shoulder, stared down at the evangelist.

Sliran paced angrily in front of Simon.

"Don't bitch at me, Simon. I wasn't the one who let Macklin run all over the goddamn city."

"How did he find out about you?" he asked softly.

"Shit, I don't know. Does it matter? If you had let me kill him the moment he started asking questions..."

"Building a case against Macklin would have been a case against us as well. Others could have been led to us. Had you killed Macklin, his black friend would have started to ask questions." Macklin saw Simon's face harden. Simon seemed to be fighting back his anger. "My plan was virtually foolproof, economical and efficient. Macklin would have eliminated any trail we had left. But you have ruined it all with your insipid handling of the Jeffries matter."

Macklin exhaled slowly, a sickening feeling swelling in his chest. *They used me. Everything I've done has served them. All the killing. All the pain.*

"Ah, fuck you, Simon."

Simon lashed out, grabbing Sliran by the neck with both hands. Macklin flinched, as startled as Sliran by the sudden strike. "You spineless lump of useless flesh! You have jeopardized everything!"

"It was *perfect*!" Sliran screamed, his hand pulling at Simon's wrists. "It was perfect to get rid of them all in one fell swoop. How was I to know Macklin would escape?"

Simon tossed Sliran back into the pew. "You should have consulted me. Had I known Jeffries and Macklin were connected I would have handled the matter in a more direct fashion." The evangelist, his back to both Sliran and Macklin, ran his hands through his hair and took a deep breath. "You made a stupid, stupid decision. And now you have compounded that stupidity."

Sliran, his face red and panting for breath, straightened up into a sitting position. "Simon, look—"

"*Think!*" Simon whirled to face Sliran. "Think for one *fucking* moment. For once in your life summon some intellect. Why do you think Macklin threatened you?"

"To put a scare in me," Sliran said quickly, "show what a big man he is."

Simon smiled thinly. "Exactly. Now, why would he want to do that?" His voice was acidic and patronizing. "I'll tell you why. He wanted you to panic. He wanted you to run. He wanted you to lead him to *me*."

Macklin spun and saw the chauffeur standing behind him, grinning, a gun equipped with a silencer in his right hand.

"Isn't that right, Mr. Macklin?" he heard Simon yell from the chapel. A chill rolled down Macklin's back. The chauffeur motioned with his gun towards the chapel doors. Reluctantly, Macklin turned and pushed open the doors, stepping into the chapel.

Simon, flashing his famous TV smile, stepped down the aisle towards Macklin. Sliran, surprised, stood up.

"So, you are the troublesome Brett Macklin." Simon looked back contemptuously at Sliran, who was visibly shaken by Macklin's arrival.

"I thought you'd look less like a circus clown in the flesh, Simon," Macklin said.

Simon chuckled. "That's good. You're living up to the brash image I had of you. Don't look so hurt, Mr. Macklin. This meeting was inevitable. You are predictable to a fault. You are here, just as I knew you would be."

Macklin felt broken inside. Simon was right. He had been manipulated from the start.

Simon looked over his shoulder at Sliran. "Luck seems to be on your side tonight, Sliran." Simon met Macklin's gaze. "Your luck, I'm afraid, has just run out."

Macklin sensed the quick motion behind him. The back of his skull exploded with pain and the floor rushed up to meet his face.

Pain. As the blackness faded, that was the first, overwhelming thing he became aware of. It was comforting. It meant the chauffeur hadn't blown his head off. It meant he was still alive. He concentrated on the pain, using it to visualize his predicament.

A cold, stinging pain radiated from his wrists and coursed down taut, aching arms that seemed stretched to their limit. He shook his feet and felt empty space beneath him. *Shit,* he thought, *I'm strung up.*

Macklin sniffed. His nostrils filled with the room's dank, musty odor.

The air was still. A warehouse? *No,* he thought, *the air is too heavy and oppressive.* Something smaller, more enclosed. A garage, a basement perhaps.

He listened for a sound of others in the room. Breathing or motion. He sensed neither. Slowly, he opened his eyes. It took a second for his eyes to focus. A single lightbulb dangled from the ceiling a few yards away. He saw the circuit breakers mounted on the wall, the dust and cobwebs, the boxes and discarded office furniture, the four steps leading up to the door on the far side of the windowless room. A basement.

Macklin looked up and saw that his hands were bound by a pair of handcuffs that, under the weight of his body, had sliced into his flesh. The handcuffs were draped over a pipe that was about the width of a broomstick and stretched the length of the room, a valve interrupting the span about halfway across. He wrapped his fingers around the chain and pulled. The steel bit into his wrist, making him wince with pain. He let go. Blood streamed down his arms and dripped onto the floor.

The pipe, and the cuffs, were secure, as he knew they would be. He was securely, and undoubtedly, Simon's prisoner.

There was a loud clank behind Macklin and the sound of an engine grinding to life. Pulleys squealed as cables went into motion. Macklin twisted and saw the bottom of an elevator shaft behind him, the rising counterweight telling him that a car was on its way down. The elevator car stopped at the lobby level and Macklin heard footsteps approaching the basement door. He closed his eyes as Sliran, Simon, and two of his men came in.

"Bring him around," Simon told Sliran, "and then find out what he knows."

"Gladly." Sliran advanced on Macklin, studied him for a moment, and then put everything he had behind a hard blow to the stomach.

The air rushed out of Macklin and he buckled. Before he could recover, Sliran swatted him across the face repeatedly, snapping his head sharply from side to side.

"Enough." Simon leaned against a stack of cartons. Sliran reluctantly stopped, stepping back from Macklin. He swung back and forth, moaning.

"C'mon, Macky boy. Tell us what you know," Sliran said, grinning.

Macklin's eyes fluttered open. His cheeks stung and his ears were ringing. Tears rolled out of his red eyes as he gasped for breath. "Know about what?"

Sliran raised his hand to strike Macklin but was halted by a strict glance from Simon. Sliran let his hand drop to his side and regarded Macklin with undisguised fury.

"Mr. Macklin, I'm a reasonable man. A pious man. I hate to see a fellow human being suffer. There's no reason for you to suffer." Simon stepped up to Macklin and lifted Macklin's face up by the chin. "I'm going to kill you. Okay? We won't kid each other. You can die easily, swiftly, one bullet though the head. Or, you can die slowly in agony. I can let Sliran here do what he pleases. Put an open flame under your testicles. Snip off your cock with shears and make you eat it." Simon spoke with the casual air of a person discussing the weather. "Perhaps he'll be more civil and just twist off your nose with a set of pliers, or remove your teeth, one by one. Either way, we'll get what we want."

Simon released Macklin's head, letting it drop against his chest. "The choice is yours, Brett. May I call you Brett?"

The last thing Macklin wanted to do was help the asshole. But talking would keep him alive for a few more minutes. The longer he stayed alive, the better his chances for somehow surviving. Besides, if he was going to die, he wanted to die knowing the truth.

"Gimme a sec," Macklin gasped.

"Surely." Simon smiled. Sliran looked disappointed.

Macklin wasn't sure what he knew. His father had been looking into seemingly baseless rumors of gang violence, which were, in turn, spurring more gang violence. Then his father was murdered by a gang. Why had they killed him? Esteban said the mayor ordered it through someone else. That someone was Sliran, who blew Esteban's head off. How did it all fit together? Political enemies of Lucas Breen being killed in the midst of gang warfare. Why?

"The floor is yours, Brett," Simon said, his voice laced with impatience.

"Okay," Macklin swallowed. "You're using gangs to kill anyone who stands in your way or endangers Lucas Breen's shot at Sacramento."

"Good guess," Sliran sneered, lighting a cigarette. "Can I kill him now?"

Simon grinned. "Relax, Sliran, let the man finish. Go on, tell me more."

"My guess is that Sliran here, through gang members like Esteban, purposely stokes gang tensions by concocting events that never occurred. I assume it's to pit the gangs against each other in such a way that your enemies get killed in the midst of it all."

Simon clapped. "Bravo."

"Why? Why not just kill them?"

"Don't be an idiot, Brett. If someone is assassinated, people investigate. If the gangs kill them for us, the victims become just another statistic. No one sees a larger picture."

"I see," Macklin whispered. It was diabolically logical. "So I get it now. Sliran would feed his Estebans on the various gang stories they would go around and feed to their fellow gang members. These Estebans would say a rival gang had committed a serious affront that demanded immediate, violent retribution. Perhaps sometimes the Estebans wouldn't have to lie. Maybe Sliran would get his rocks off kicking in a few heads and make it look like a rival gang did it. My father asked too many questions. He had to be killed.

"Sliran saw Shaw meet with Tomas Cruz and arranged for the kid to have the shit kicked out of him. Invalidate the confession so the gang members didn't end up in jail and accidentally spill something about your operation."

Macklin swallowed, shifting his gaze between Simon and Sliran. As soon as he ran out of things to say, Simon would let Sliran indulge his sadism.

Macklin didn't kid himself. There would be no swift end. Sliran would make him suffer.

"And you, Brett, performed wonderfully as my garbage man. You cleaned up any trail we might have accidentally left," Simon said, impressed with himself.

"With the exception of this mishap, things went smoothly."

"I can't figure out, though, how you got these few gang members, these contacts, to help you." Macklin needed time.

"It was easy." Simon walked up to Macklin. He stood so close Macklin could smell the wintergreen mouthwash on his breath. "They were sent to our missions by probation officers who wanted to take part in a community service. I don't think we disappointed the probation officers."

Macklin took a deep breath. Anything he said now was absolute guesswork.

"You bought the gang members off, appealing to their greed with money, drugs, maybe even guns. I don't suppose many of them lived long enough to enjoy their rewards. After all, the more you used them the more they knew, and replacements were always easy to find."

"You're very good at this. If I had known that before, I wouldn't have let you live so long."

"I don't know, Simon. If I were in your shoes, I probably would have done the same thing. Let the son of a bitch tie up any loose ends that could lead to us and then get rid of him."

"You sound very smug and self-assured for someone in your position, Mr. Macklin."

Macklin glanced up at his cuffed wrists and frowned. "You can't win them all."

"This has been fun, Mr. Macklin."

"There is just one thing I can't figure out," Macklin offered tentatively.

"Imagine that," Sliran growled, "just one thing."

"You and Breen," Macklin said. "A symbiotic relationship. I suppose you have the power, through your ministries, to influence voters and pump money into his campaign. Breen has the power to keep the law from rummaging through your dirty laundry, and his support adds a legitimacy and prestige to your ministry. Together, using God and government, you two can control a lot of people and do a lot of damage. No doubt, you both dream about the presidency. Quite a relationship."

Macklin smiled. "I wonder who owns who."

Simon stiffened. "Well, it seems you've uncovered quite a bit. You get an A-plus for ingenuity. Now we can end this uncomfortable business with a simple question. Who have you shared your knowledge with?"

Macklin's heart started to pound. He was at a dead end. Silence would stall death. And lead to torture. To say he had told no one would lead to a similar end. Anyone he named, just to buy time, would be killed. Silence, now, seemed to be the only avenue.

"That sure put a muzzle on him," Sliran said. "He finally shut the fuck up."

"Loosen his tongue," Simon whispered, meeting Macklin's defiant gaze.

Sliran gave his fury free rein. He beat Macklin like a punching bag, unrelenting in his feverish assault until Macklin slipped into merciful unconsciousness.

"Stop," Simon hissed, angry at himself for letting Sliran lose control—he wanted answers, not a corpse.

Macklin's chin rested against his chest, his breathing erratic and body slack, swaying gently from the force of Sliran's blows.

Simon lifted Macklin's head by the hair and examined his eyes with his free hand. "Sliran, you miserable fuckup. Look what you've done. He's no good to us now."

Sighing, Simon released Macklin and walked slowly over to Sliran, whose face was damp with sweat from the exertion of the beating. Without warning, Simon slapped Sliran across the face and sent the cop reeling into the cartons. Sliran was about to spring on Simon but saw the two lieutenants tensing. Besides, Sliran wasn't sure he could take Simon.

"We'll deal with Macklin later." Simon looked down at Sliran as if he had just caught him jerking off in church. "In the meantime, get rid of Shaw."

Sliran struggled to his feet, uncomfortably aware of Simon's hard gaze. "With pleasure."

The cop took one last look at Macklin and then walked out, followed by Simon and his men. The door closed.

A moment later the pulleys whined and the elevator climbed up the guide rails of the shaft at five hundred feet a minute.

CHAPTER TWENTY-THREE

Shaw's eyes burned. They were dirty and sleepy and he had rubbed them too much. He expected his eyeballs to shrivel up and just drop out of his sockets onto the stacks of files.

Soon it would be morning and sunlight would assault his tired eyes. Loud noise would grate on his ears, cutting through the Tylenol wall around his headache and setting it bursting free.

"Shit," he muttered, letting his head drop onto the desk. It had been a hard few hours. He had ridden with Jeffries to the hospital and asked him about his conversation with Macklin.

Something Jeffries told Shaw had bugged him as he drove home from the hospital, poking and prodding him until he made a U-turn and headed back downtown to the station.

Now, just a few hours shy of dawn, Shaw was left with his notes. And his discovery.

Over the last two years a dozen people related somehow to the Elliot Wells campaign had been killed in the midst of gang skirmishes. It was far too big a number to be a coincidence. But it was far too big a mystery for an exhausted, sleepy cop to take on at three a.m.

And he wasn't so sure he wanted to take it on when he was fully awake, either.

"Shit," he said again, picking up the legal pad and scanning the list once more.

It was no wonder the connections had not been made before. An old woman who had contributed money to Wells' campaign was gunned down in Beverly Hills in what seemed like just another case of gang joyriding. An influential lawyer, popular with California politicians and a noted Wells supporter, was killed during a gang fight in a downtown parking lot. A well-known media consultant, brought in by Wells to design a new media campaign, was butchered in a gang massacre at a Chinese restaurant. Alone, the murders had none of the earmarking of a premeditated assassination. Together, they made a sickening tapestry of conspiracy and death.

Someone was manipulating the gangs. But how and why?

The man with the motive was obviously Lucas Breen. Yet, it could be anyone with a grudge against Elliot Wells.

Whatever it *could* be, Shaw knew he could prove nothing. At least not yet.

"Putting in overtime, Shaw?"

Shaw dropped the notepad and looked up. Sliran leaned against the open doorway to the empty squad room.

"What are you doing here, Sliran?"

"I'm covering for Locklear this morning. What's all that shit on your desk?"

Shaw sighed. "Background. I'm just checking up on some hunches of mine."

"Really," sneered Sliran. "I got some hunches, too. I bet you help Macky boy load his gun every night, huh? Maybe he comes home after he blows a few guys away and tells you all the grisly details so you two can jerk off together."

Shaw stood up and stretched. "Jesus, Sliran, aren't you a little old to be playing school-yard bully? I'm not going to take a swing at you, so save it. I'm too tired to give a damn what crazy crap is thriving in that narrow mind of yours." He set his legal pad on top of the stack, picked it up, and headed towards the door.

Sliran didn't move.

"C'mon, Sliran, you gonna block my way all night, trip me, or what? I want to go home and go to bed, okay? You can get me at recess tomorrow."

Sliran stepped aside. “Fuck off, Shaw. You and Macklin are on borrowed time.”

Shaw walked past him into the hallway. “Scary line, Sliran. On that note, I bid you good night.”

Sliran watched Shaw disappear down the hall, lit a cigarette, and then went over to Shaw’s desk and began looking through the drawers. He’d catch up with Shaw later, and then kill him.

Brett Macklin hung from the pipe, his consciousness whirling in a dizzying netherworld of nausea and gnawing pain.

Get rid… with pleasure.

Shaw.

The words sailed in and out of the confusion and ache, slowing his journey through it and bringing his thoughts with each repetition.

Get rid of Shaw.

With pleasure.

Things were slowing, the words becoming clearer, the pain becoming more acute. His stomach suddenly heaved, vomit spilling out of his mouth and nose in deep wrenching gags and splattering on the basement floor.

His stomach empty, his body sagged and he felt chilled, shivering, his sides aching from bearing his weight and the stress of his violent regurgitations. Nostrils swelled with vomit.

What a great day this *has been,* Macklin thought, breaking into painful laughter, vomit dripping out of his nose.

The laughter was just what he needed to force back the helplessness and summon whatever energy and resolve he had left.

The laughter ebbing, he regarded the handcuffs and pipe anew, scrutinizing them for any exploitable weakness. His eyes narrowed on the valve several feet down the length of the pipe. The valve. He felt a surge of hope. The valve meant he was not bound to one continuous length of pipe but to two smaller pipes connected by the valve. If he could free the section of pipe he was attached to from the valve, he could escape.

Gritting his teeth against the pain, Macklin began to swing his body, the arcs becoming larger and less agonizing with each pass. When the momentum was at its peak, Macklin strained the muscles of his lower back and brought his legs up and wrapped them around the pipe. He stayed like that for a moment, eyes closed, catching his breath and fighting back the waves of pain that swept his body.

Relax, it's just pain.

Opening his eyes, he saw the pipe directly over his face. With a deep breath, he slid along the pipe, drawing his body along with his legs. The valve grew closer. A clock ticked loudly in his head. Each second brought Shaw closer to death—if he wasn't dead already. Or Sliran could return and exact his excruciating brand of revenge.

Macklin stopped as his feet slid against the valve. Gripping the pipe tightly with his hands, he dropped one leg and stretched it under the valve to the other side of the pipe. He repeated the move with the other leg. He pulled himself along the pipe again until the valve was just over his midsection.

Okay, Mack, now the fun starts. He reached up for the valve with his cheek pressed against the pipe, and grabbed hold of it. Straining against the valve wheel, he tried to twist the entire valve structure down towards him.

It didn't move.

Shit!

Macklin summoned his strength again, pulling down the valve wheel. There was a creak and the subtlest of movements. A flake of rust fell into Macklin's right eye, stinging it.

Blinking, he pulled again. Another creak. A tear rolled out of Macklin's eye, taking the rust with it. *Maybe,* he thought, *things aren't as bleak as they seem.*

Pulling again, he turned the valve a bit more. That's when things started looking bleak to Macklin again. First he heard the hiss, and then he smelled it.

Gas.

He was handcuffed to a gas line. Macklin felt sweat break out between his shoulder blades. The more he loosened the pipe from the valve, the more gas would escape. Macklin quickened his efforts, damning fate, holding his breath to avoid taking in the noxious fumes. The valve structure turned slowly, the valve wheel pulled down now nearly over his midsection.

Turning his head away from the pipe, Macklin took another breath. Macklin could already feel the sour-tasting gas working against him, the queasiness riding over him. He reached over the pipe, grasped the valve wheel, and tried to finish his first counterclockwise turn of the valve structure.

The gas whistled softly in his ear.

Macklin didn't know how much longer he could fight the effects of the pungent gas, his vision already blurring and his head pounding, and still summon the strength to finish turning the valve structure and free the pipe.

Moving as if in slow motion, the gas hissing in his face, Macklin twisted the valve structure around the pipe two more times, willing himself to stay conscious. He felt the blackness threatening to overtake him.

There was a scrape, and the pipe slipped free from the valve, the gas whistling though the narrow gap between the two. Semiconscious, Macklin dropped his legs from the pipe and slid forward, the handcuffs slipping through the gap. He hit the floor on his knees, sending shockwaves of pain through his body.

Macklin wanted to curl up and let the blackness win, but something deep inside urged him to *move*!

Grimacing against the pain, dizzy from the gas, Macklin stood and hobbled across the room, falling against the boxes and knocking one of them over. Hundreds of small white candles spilled out and rolled across the floor.

Macklin saw Sliran's matchbook on the floor amongst the candles and picked it up, opening the flap. There were plenty of matches. He glanced at the candles, the pipe, and then the candles again.

I'll blow that son of a bitch Simon right into the heavens, Macklin thought. *I'll sip a beer and watch the fireworks from my front porch.*

Managing a battered smile with his cracked and bloodied lips, Macklin grabbed a handful of the candles and carried them up the steps with him. Up here, the air was clear of gas. He lit first one candle and then another, placing them behind pipes, beside wiring, until he'd set half a dozen of them. He didn't know how long it would be before the gas got up here in the right concentration to explode. He just hoped it would be long enough to get him out. He had read too many newspaper stories about gas explosions turning office buildings into so much dust.

He took one last look at his handiwork and then eased open the door and slipped quietly into the brightly lit, glass-enclosed lobby. Peering cautiously around the edge of the wood-paneled wall, he could see that he was at the far end of the lobby, a long stretch of marble floor separating him from the bank of elevators against the wall on his left and the glass doors on his right. Between the elevators and the door was an empty guard's desk.

From Macklin's angle, it was impossible to see if the guard stood on the other side of the elevator bank, just behind the desk, or whether the lobby was clear.

It didn't matter. Macklin had no choice. Within minutes the gas could reach one of the candles and cause a catastrophic explosion.

Macklin wanted to be long gone when *that* happened.

As Macklin emerged from behind the wall and started sprinting towards the glass entranceway, he heard a chime and saw a flash in the corner of his eyes. He stopped and turned back just as the elevator doors parted, revealing Simon and three of his men.

"Get him!" Simon yelled, hitting the twenty-second-floor button.

Macklin scrambled back to the basement, throwing his body against the door and leaping into the room.

The dozens of candles flickered at him around the room. He was cornered.

The grind of the elevator machinery caught his attention. There was no other way. He dashed madly across the room to the elevator shaft, jumped, and grabbed a beam on the undercarriage of the ascending car. Macklin was whisked up into the shaft just as the guards spilled into the basement.

The elevator raced up the shaft like a rocket. His injured arms, again tortured by his weight, seemed ready to snap apart. He willed himself to hold on. The cracks of light seeping through the doorways of passing floors gave him a dizzying sense of motion. His legs dangled in the darkness.

The car came to a shuddering halt, nearly knocking Macklin from his perilous hold. Macklin swallowed. *What the hell do I do now?*

Macklin wrapped his legs around the guiderail on his left. He looked down. A speck of light below was all he could see of the basement. At any instant the gas could reach one of the candles. The explosion would send a fireball up the shaft that would fry Macklin alive. In that case, he had only moments, or one wrong move, and he could fall twenty-two floors. They'd have to wipe him off the floor with a sponge.

He grabbed for the slippery guiderail with both hands. For an instant, he had no handhold, tottering dangerously over the open shaft, held from death only by his legs. His handcuffed hands grasped the rail. Breathing deeply, he quickly shimmied down the rail the fourteen feet to the next crossbeam, which looked no wider than four inches to Macklin. His foot hit the beam. Still holding on to the guiderail, he glanced up at the elevator. If it descended, it would snap off his head and slap his headless torso right off the beam.

Lowering himself so that his legs straddled the crossbeam, Macklin began to pull himself along it to the center ledge in front of the twenty-first-floor doorway. Macklin was relieved to see that the outcropping was twice the size of the crossbeam he now straddled. Grabbing a guiderail for support, he pulled himself up to a standing position on the cement ledge. Macklin pushed apart the twenty-first-floor doors and stumbled into the hallway. The bright fluorescent lights burned his eyes. Across the hall was a door marked "STAIRWELL." He ran to it, flung open the door, and vaulted up the steps two at a time until he reached the twenty-second floor.

Opening the door slowly, Macklin saw the elevator door across from him and a wall on his right. To his left was a glass doorway and a secretary's desk. On the paneled wall behind the desk the words "SIMON MINISTRIES" were written in marble letters. Macklin eased the door shut behind him and locked it by turning a bolt above the knob. Stepping to the elevator, he pressed the "down" button. The doors slid open. Macklin reached inside to the control panel and flicked the tiny switch from "run" to "stop."

Now, Macklin thought, *it's just the two of us. I may die trying, but I'm taking you with me.*

He opened the door to Simon's office foyer. Two hallways branched off from the foyer. He took the one on his right. Macklin followed it slowly, hugging the walls, passing offices along the way. The hallway curved to the left and Macklin saw the oak doors of Simon's office. As Macklin edged closer, more of the office became clear. He could see the huge marble desk. Beside it, Simon stood, his back to Macklin, staring out the window at the city below.

Macklin, his heart pinging furiously, stepped through the doorway into Simon's office. Simon turned. Macklin froze. Simon smiled, seemingly undaunted by Macklin's appearance in his office.

"You are a tenacious man, Brett." Simon rubbed his cheek and walked toward Macklin. "I respect you. It's important you understand that before I kill you."

Macklin bent low, his hands out in front of him. The compulsion, the killing instinct, commanded him now, overriding his fears. Although he knew he could hardly defend himself handcuffed, he was swept up in the tide of absolute hatred.

Simon yelled and leaped into the air, his right leg lashing out towards Macklin's head. Macklin sidestepped, raising his arms to protect himself. He felt a sharp pain as Simon's boot glanced off his right forearm. The blow knocked Macklin sideways.

Macklin stumbled, quickly retaining his balance. Simon whirled around on the ball of his left foot and faced Macklin.

They circled each other. Simon smiled. "Killing is a release, a sport. I think you would have grown to enjoy it as much as I do."

Simon's right leg snapped up. Macklin jumped back, grabbing Simon's ankle, and lifted. Simon, unbalanced, tumbled backwards into the marble desk with a loud grunt. Macklin took advantage of the opening. He swatted Simon across the face with his fists and followed through by ramming his right elbow into Simon's belly. Macklin felt the air rush out of Simon's mouth.

Macklin had left his right side exposed. Simon jabbed Macklin sharply in the kidney and pushed him away. Macklin, lurching to the side, momentarily paralyzed by the blow, pivoted to face Simon. As Macklin turned, Simon brought his knee up and slammed it into Macklin's jaw. Macklin's head exploded with pain and he fell backward, his body hitting the floor.

On impact, Macklin rolled on his side, instinctively trying to get distance. Simon's foot crashed down beside him. Macklin, on his back, lashed his legs out at Simon, smashing his heels into Simon's groin. Simon cried out, doubled over, and stumbled back.

Macklin bolted up and aimed a wild punch at Simon's chin. The blow spun Simon around. Macklin yelled, spread his wrists apart, and flung his hands over Simon's head. Macklin jerked, the handcuffs digging into the flesh where his hand met his wrist as the chain tightened around Simon's neck. Simon clawed at Macklin's bloody wrists.

Macklin was oblivious to the pain. Even if the cuffs dug so deep they scraped bone, he wouldn't release his choking hold on Simon.

Simon, twisting and turning, pushed Macklin backwards. Macklin lost his balance and they plunged to the floor. The impact jarred Macklin's hold for a second and Simon tried to squirm under Macklin's arms. Macklin rolled over on top of Simon, sat up straight, and with a guttural cry, leaned back and gave the chain one final, merciless yank.

Simon's body convulsed. Macklin, gritting his teeth and wincing, refused to lessen the force he exerted against the chain. He felt something snap inside Simon's neck. Simon gurgled and then stiffened, dead weight against Macklin's chain.

Macklin held tight for a moment longer, the cuffs slicing deep into Macklin's flesh, and then released Simon. As Simon's swollen face struck the floor, the building was rocked by a tremendous explosion. Macklin fell forward onto Simon's back. Water burst out of the sprinklers on the ceiling, creating a virtual rainstorm. Another explosion, like a thunder clap, shook the building.

Macklin struggled to his feet, reaching out to the marble table for support. The building shook under him. He heard something growl beneath the floor. Macklin walked around the desk to the window, pressing his face against the wet glass. An explosion in the middle of the building spit glass and flame out into the air. Smoke encircled the lower floors, obscuring his view. But he could see tentacles of flame lash out to other buildings, setting them ablaze.

There was no escape. The rumble of explosions was growing more forceful. Fire was eating its way upwards through the floors below his feet. Water soaked him. He would have to wait here and hope he could keep the flames at bay. It was a foolish hope, he knew, but the only hope he had. And what would happen to him if he was found there, standing beside Simon's corpse?

A light from outside blinded him. Shielding his eyes, he heard the beating mechanical rhythm of a helicopter drawing near. Macklin ran out of Simon's office, through the shower in the hallway, to the foyer. The elevators had blown open. Flames licked out between the twisted metal, scorching the ceiling and setting the wall aflame. The sprinklers spat in the face of the firestorm. Macklin had to get to the stairwell.

Raising his arms across his face, Macklin pushed open the glass doors and ran though the hallway, under the canopy of flame, to the stairwell door. The heat around him was excruciating. He felt at any instant he would just erupt in fire. He reached out for the bolt, recoiling. The knob was red hot. The flames roared around him. Macklin twisted the bolt, searing his fingers, and dropped his burned hand to the doorknob, turning the red-hot metal and throwing his weight against the door. It flew open. He tumbled into the smoky stairwell, gasping for air. Barely able to see through, he bounded up the two flights of stairs to the roof.

He opened the door. The cool wind slapped him in the face. Through his teary eyes he could see that the helipad in front of him was ringed with flame. A gaping hole at the far end of the roof spewed fire and hot metal into the sky like a volcano. That must have been where the fireball, streaking up the elevator shaft, had burst through the roof. The helicopter wouldn't be able to land. Macklin ran, diving through the flames onto the helipad. He hit the ground rolling, his right pant leg aflame. Desperately he rolled over the leg, drowning the flames. The helicopter neared the building, whipping the flames with its rotors. Macklin, his pants smoldering, stood up and waved his arms madly in an effort to attract the pilot's attention. The helicopter searchlight pinpointed Macklin amidst the flames and bathed him in white light. An explosion ripped though the center of the building, knocking him over and rocking the structure as if it were jetsam in a stormy sea. A wisp of flame shot out of the rooftop hole at the helicopter. The pilot pulled the copter up as if riding a wave, then dropped it back down again over Macklin.

Macklin stood unsteadily, the building swaying under him. The helicopter hovered low over Macklin. He was able to read the familiar call letters.

It was *his* helicopter.

A rope ladder tumbled out of the helicopter and landed in front of him. He stared at it, wondering how the hell to climb up the thing with his hands handcuffed. He grabbed the side of the ladder, pulling himself up and letting the rope fall between his legs. Macklin then rested his heel on the nearest rung and brought his other heel up onto the next, higher rung.

The helicopter veered away from the building, swinging Macklin over the flames and off the roof over the city. Macklin grasped the rope tightly, his arms pulsing with pain. He began to inch his way up the rope ladder, using his legs to grasp the rungs and his hands for support. The rope swayed over the city.

Macklin pulled himself into the chopper, glancing over his shoulder at the blazing building. He saw the flames wrapping around the silver Tabernacle like vines.

"Are you okay?" Mort yelled over the loud whine of the whirring blades. Turning away from the blaze, Macklin moved to the seat beside Mort and closed his eyes. Much of the pain that had been dulled by the anger and fear was returning now. "I've had better days," Macklin murmured. "I'm just glad you showed up when you did."

"So am I." Mort looked at Macklin with obvious concern. "I just wrapped up shooting downtown with the *Bloodmaster* crew when I saw the Silver Tabernacle blow." His questions spilled out in a rush. "What the hell were you doing there? Why are you handcuffed? What the fuck is going on?"

"Mort, I can't explain it all now. We have to get to Ronny. He's in danger."

Mort sighed. "Then your job isn't finished yet."

"Not yet."

Mort motioned to the back of the copter. "You'll find your gun in the utility box. You left it in my car. I brought it up here with me so I could keep my eye on it."

Macklin leaned back in his chair. He hoped he wasn't too late to save Shaw. Losing his closest friend to a bullet would be too much. Simon and Breen had already taken too much from him.

The Silver Tabernacle, receding as the copter streaked westward, stood against the night like a giant torch, glowing orange and yellow. Suddenly its base was rocked by a massive explosion. The silver obelisk, its shattered windows staring at the night through flaming eyes, rocked unsteadily like a drunk full of too much muscatel, and then toppled toward the earth.

CHAPTER TWENTY-FOUR

Everything was pissing Shaw off as he drove home. The lunatic drivers on the street, the feel of his smoke-stained clothes against his sticky skin, the noise masquerading as music on his radio, and most of all, the gutless, rubber-band-powered engine of the Ford Fairmont he had just rented from Hertz.

Why in hell don't they put engines in cars anymore? Shaw wondered.

He was afraid he might have to get out and push the car home. All he wanted to do was put the day behind him, crawl into bed, and slip into one of those deep, dreamless sleeps that leave you looking like hell when you wake up but feeling great.

If Guess was locked outside, and if he disconnected the phone, and if he put a muzzle on Sunshine, he figured he could sleep until late that afternoon, take a good shit and sneak a Camel, make himself a thick corned-beef sandwich, and *then* worry about getting a new car, untangling the Elliot Wells murders, and finding Brett Macklin.

Shaw steered his car onto the driveway behind Sunshine's Bug and felt his body sag with relief. A warm bed was just beyond the busted porch light.

With a tired grunt, he got out of the car and started towards the house. Sliran stepped out of the shadows beside the garage, blocking Shaw's way.

"Sliran, what the hell?" Shaw groaned.

"Just cool it, *boy*."

"*Boy?*" Shaw took a step towards Sliran, who drew his gun with a smile.

"Yeah, you heard me. It's time to pay the piper."

"Sliran, you're certifiable," Shaw whispered, looking at the gun with disbelief.

Sliran advanced slowly, towards Shaw, who stepped backwards towards the street. "I'm going to enjoy killing you, Shaw. I never liked the idea of niggers on the force to begin with."

Sliran raised his gun level with Shaw's chest. "Say good-bye, nigger."

Shaw winced as a thunderous burst shattered the night. Shaw, realizing he wasn't hit, the gunshot still ringing in his ears, looked at Sliran.

Sliran's wide eyes regarded Shaw questioningly. With stunned horror, Sliran lowered his head and saw the blood spilling out of his chest. Sliran raised his head, his lower lip twitching, his gun shaking in his hand. Someone whistled from the darkness behind Sliran.

Sliran whirled around, holding his gun arm out.

"MAAAACCCCKKKKLLLLIIIINNNN!"

The angry cry had barely left Sliran's mouth when the bullet smashed into his head, splattering Shaw with bits of hair and brain. Sliran's body hit the ground as the last syllable of Macklin's name passed his lips.

Shaw wiped his face, smearing the blood and brain matter. He looked up from Sliran's twitching body and saw Macklin emerge from the shadows, the Magnum held loosely in his handcuffed hands. Macklin's face was hard and guiltless. Their eyes met, Macklin's unflinching gaze showing Shaw a violent resolve and not a shred of remorse. Shaw didn't expect any.

"Are you okay, Ron?" Macklin whispered.

"Yeah." Shaw could barely get the sound out of his throat. Sliran's blood ran down his cheeks. Shaw could feel his own expression on his face. A mask of sad acceptance, of reluctant and painful surrender. Brett Macklin was Mr. Jury. A murderer. A killer who had just saved his life.

Shaw broke his gaze at the sound of blades slicing the air. The helicopter suddenly descended from the sky behind Macklin, coming in over their heads and kicking up a whirlwind of leaves and dirt as it landed behind Shaw in the street.

With one final, quick glance at Shaw, Macklin dashed to the chopper and climbed in. The helicopter rose and veered away, disappearing into the night sky as suddenly as it had appeared.

Shaw sat down on the curb and watched lights flick on behind drawn curtains, listened to dogs barking excitedly and sirens drawing near. It seemed to him that tomorrow would never come.

Just after dawn. It was Lucas Breen's favorite time of day. The air was still. The sky was deep blue, undershadowed with warm pinks and bright yellows. The city sleeps quietly. He usually had the park's tree-lined paths to himself and could jog in peace.

Then there were mornings like this. The smog layer was a thick green blanket over the city. Smelly, ratty-looking bums seemed to be everywhere, crossing his path and asking for change.

The quiet was broken by the city workers cutting foliage under the pedestrian bridge, feeding branches into a loud, incessantly whirring shredder.

Breen carried a Walkman loaded with a classical music cassette for just such an occasion. He slipped the earphones on his head and kept the bums at bay with an angry growl and a glare that promised mutilation.

He jogged casually across the bridge, barely hearing the shredder over the pleasant sounds of the Beaux Arts Trio. Another scruffy transient emerged from the shrubbery ahead of him and stood in his path.

Breen narrowed his eyes and put on a little extra juice. He wanted the bum to know he'd tackle him if he didn't slither right back into his bush.

But the ragged-looking man didn't cower or scamper away like the rest. As Breen neared him, he noticed the blood caked on the man's arms, the malice in his blue eyes.

Breen slowed, studying the man's face.

"Oh my God," Breen whispered, abruptly turning and running back the way he had come.

Brett Macklin.

Breen scrambled to the pedestrian bridge. Macklin, no longer bound by handcuffs, ran close behind.

His breath coming in ragged gasps, Breen heard Macklin's steps grow louder, closer. Then he felt steely arms around his legs and he went down hard. Breen rose quickly, shrugging Macklin off him like an old jacket.

He whirled around and slammed his fist across Macklin's chin. Macklin flew back against the bridge railing. Before Macklin could recover, Breen drove his fist into Macklin's stomach. Macklin felt a burst of pain and doubled over, pushing himself forward and ramming his head hard into Breen's midsection.

Breen backed into the opposite rail. Macklin straightened up, gathering breath into his lungs, and heard the crash of shattering glass. Breen held a broken beer bottle in his hand. Macklin leaped back as Breen swung the jagged bottle towards his face. Breen stepped forward and swung again. Macklin grabbed Breen's wrist, stopping the swing, and they tumbled backwards.

Macklin felt his back slam into the railing again. He bashed Breen's wrist into the railing, trying to force the mayor to release his hold on the bottle.

Breen's knee shot up into Macklin's balls. Macklin doubled over against the excruciating pain and drove his knee into Breen's groin. Breen lurched forward, his head hitting the rail. The bottle dropped out of Breen's hand and into the shredder.

Macklin heard a crunch and then tinkling as the bits of glass were spit out into the bed of a truck.

Macklin ducked out from under Breen, moved behind him, and wrapped his arms around Breen's hips. With Breen's crotch over his neck, Macklin lifted Breen up over the rail. Breen grabbed the rail in a desperate attempt to stop the fall. Macklin grunted, pushing as hard as he could. Breen flipped over backwards, losing his grip. Screaming, Breen fell onto the foliage shredder. It sucked him in by the legs and spit him out the chute as a fine red mist.

The city workers, busy chopping branches from a nearby tree, didn't even notice.

Macklin turned away and picked up Breen's fallen Walkman as the music hit its final crescendo.

EPILOGUE

Los Angeles mayor Jed Stocker sat behind his desk and let the two men in his office digest what he had just said.

He thought he had put it rather succinctly.

It had been a turbulent few months for the city since Breen's disappearance. The unsolved murder of Elias Simon. Jed Stocker's landslide victory against city councilman Derby Locke in the mayoral campaign. Crime had risen dramatically. Worst of all in Chinatown, where rival gangs battled for territorial rights. Each day the newspapers reported a new massacre or rape or bombing or random killing and the inability of the police to do anything about it. Few gang members were arrested. Those who were didn't stay behind bars long. Witnesses were killed or intimidated into changing their stories, and the new mayor, Jed Stocker, needed a solution.

"So you've got problems in Chinatown," Brett Macklin said wearily, standing in front of Stocker's desk, his hands in his pockets. "Big fucking deal. I still don't understand why you had Ron drag me down here."

Shaw, who sat on the couch against the wall to Stocker's right, wondered the same thing. He didn't like the idea of hauling Macklin downtown. It hurt. An upholder of the law, Shaw had docilely watched while Stocker covered up the Sliran killing and let Macklin go free. The only way Shaw could live with himself was to consider Macklin dead. Yet Stocker wouldn't let him do that. Stocker wanted Macklin watched and put Shaw in charge of the surveillance. Shaw hadn't personally seen Macklin since Sliran's death, but he had read the reports.

Macklin had become a virtual recluse, seeing his ex-wife and daughter only once, Cheshire three or four times, and spending most of his time flying, often sleeping at the hangar.

Then came Stocker's call early this morning. He wanted Macklin in his office at nine a.m. sharp. Whether Macklin wanted to come or not. Shaw faced the assignment with dread. Seeing Macklin would stir Shaw's inner turmoil once again, and Stocker's unexplained desire to see Macklin worried him.

Shaw knocked on Macklin's door and saw a friendliness in Macklin's eyes when his door opened. Shaw expected Macklin to bluntly refuse to come along.

Macklin didn't. It was almost as if Macklin knew he had no choice. Or had been expecting it.

They rode downtown in claustrophobic silence, not even looking at each other.

Stocker smiled at Macklin. "I told you about the problem in Chinatown because I want Mr. Jury to take care of it."

Shaw stiffened. *No! This can't be happening.*

Macklin chuckled and turned towards the door.

"I can nail you right now for a dozen murders," Stocker snapped, staring at Macklin's back. "With ease. Sergeant Shaw, tell Mr. Macklin how easy it would be to put him behind bars." Stocker picked up a thick manila file. "It's all in here. We've got enough evidence here to convict you half a dozen times. Airtight."

Macklin turned slowly, glancing at Shaw. The detective couldn't bring himself to speak. He couldn't believe what he was hearing.

The mayor wanted Macklin to kill for him. And he wanted Shaw to help.

"Fuck off, Stocker," Macklin said ruefully. "I'm not doing anything for you."

"Wrong," Stocker said flatly. "The scum on the street are scared shitless of you, and we're gonna use that fear."

Macklin met Stocker's gaze. "One man can't stop them."

Shaw's mouth was dry. The mayor and Macklin were talking about murder.

"C'mon, Macklin. These guys are no different than the men who killed your father. Go after them the same way. I'll make sure you get no heat from the police." Stocker glared at Shaw as if the glare would suffice as an order. Shaw felt sick.

"No," Macklin said. "I'm through. I'm not killing anymore."

"You will." Stocker stood up and came around the desk to face him. "You're mine, Macklin. For better or worse, I own you. Besides, I think you're still angry. You want to keep fighting."

"I'll think about it," Macklin said evenly. "But when I'm done, I want that file."

"No deals," Stocker said quickly.

"We'll see about that," Macklin said as he turned towards the door. "We'll just see about that."

(UPI) LOS ANGELES—Police believe the mysterious vigilante "Mr. Jury" came to the rescue of a Chinatown pharmacist Wednesday night, killing three gang members who allegedly forced their way into his drugstore and began assaulting him when he refused to pay them protection money.

Lee Kwon, fifty-one, said he was closing the doors at about nine p.m. when the three men pushed their way in past him and started to break merchandise.

When Kwon tried to stop them, the men allegedly pinned him against the wall and began punching him, demanding "protection money" as they threw their blows.

"Then this man walked in the store," Kwon said, "came up behind them and whistled. I had already turned the lights out, so I couldn't see his face." The men released Kwon and sprung on the stranger, "who pulled out this big gun and just shot 'em down, bam, bam, bam, just like that. Then he picked up a Snickers bar, handed me thirty-five cents, and just strolled out..."

THE END
Brett Macklin will return in
ADJOURNED

ADJOURNED

BY LEE GOLDBERG

Originally published in paperback as *.357 Vigilante #2: Make Them Pay* under the pen name "Ian Ludlow" by Pinnacle Books, June 1985

Special thanks to Jerone Ten Berge for the cover art and Eileen Chetti for the proofreading.

PROLOGUE

The little girl with pigtails scrambled onto Santa Claus' lap. Old St. Nicholas, stark naked, wrapped his arms around her and, with a hearty "ho ho ho," asked her what he could give her for Christmas.

Santa gaped joyfully at the girl sitting stiff backed on his fleshy legs. His heavy hairless chest lolled on the swell of his stomach, his pale skin flushed baby's-bottom pink. The girl stared blankly at the brightly wrapped empty gift boxes that cluttered the floor around them. Behind Santa and the girl, a Christmas tree strewn with blinking lights glowed against a wood facade paneled with red Masonite strips designed to look like brick.

"Don't leer so much, Santa," Wesley Saputo groaned, combing his hand through his brown hair and sharing an irritated smirk with Lyle Franken, the chunky cameraman. "We're looking for fatherly warmth here."

Santa squinted against the bright lights, trying to see Saputo in the darkness behind them. A bead of sweat rolled down Santa's cherubic face.

"Sure, I can do that," Santa sputtered, shifting uncomfortably in his seat, a splinter of wood from the hastily built throne pricking his butt.

The girl reflexively clutched at a roll of flesh on his stomach to steady herself.

"Good, good. That's why I pay you," Saputo said wearily. Then, more softly, he asked, "Okay, Cassie, how are you doing?"

The ten-year-old girl squirmed at the mention of her name. Her usual exuberance had been sanded down to shyness by her nakedness, the strange way the man in the Santa Claus beard and cap looked at her, and the heat and glare of the bright movie lights.

"Fine," she mumbled, toying with one of the red bows in her cherry red hair. "When do we get ice cream and go to Disneyland?"

"Not long, Cassie. Don't you want to be a star?" said the voice behind the lights.

"Uh-huh."

"Okay," Saputo crooned. "Then let's do like I told you. Be nice to Santa the way I said."

Saputo heard footsteps approaching slowly behind him in the darkness of the warehouse. Glancing over his shoulder, he saw a tall figure wearing a long, dark blue U.S. Navy pea coat with the collar turned up against his neck. Saputo felt a tremor in his chest. Tice.

Saputo swatted Franken's side. Franken, who also doubled as production designer and throne builder, turned from the viewfinder and followed Saputo's gaze.

"Good afternoon, gentlemen," said the man, wiry and thin, as he emerged from the shadows and glided toward Saputo and Franken like the surf crawling up the sand.

"Shit," Franken groaned, turning back to the camera.

"Keep shooting," Saputo quietly told Franken and, with anxiety fluttering in his chest, approached Tice.

Tice always made Saputo nervous. It was Tice's face that did it. His features seemed to Saputo like sharp cuts of flesh carved by the quick, slashing strokes of a razor. Tice had narrow slits for eyes, a jagged scar for a smile, a needlelike nose, and strands of stubby black hair that coated the top of his skull like a thin layer of paint.

And it was the way Tice spoke. No matter how loud or hushed his voice, Tice's words always sounded to Saputo like a whisper. Yet it was always audible, never muted, stealthily enveloping any conversation. A vocal oil slick.

"Mr. Orlock is looking forward to more of your work," Tice said, looking past Saputo to the Christmas set. Saputo glanced back and saw Santa caressing Cassie's thigh.

"So am I." Saputo nodded.

"He wants you to know it's nice to have you back," Tice said emotionlessly. He apparently didn't share Orlock's enthusiasm.

"It's nice to be back," Saputo agreed. *It's nice not having my dong tied to some fucking penile plethysmograph, he thought. It's nice not getting electrocuted every time I see a sweet, hairless cunt and the machine tells some jerk-off shrink I've got a hard-on. It's nice being free.*

Without Mr. Orlock's help, Saputo knew, he might still be in that gray nuthouse, where everything smelled like rubbing alcohol.

"He is expecting a lot of product in a very short time. You can come through, can't you, Wesley?"

"Sure, no problem. Just keep the money coming."

"But there is a problem, Wesley," Tice replied melodically. "You haven't been keeping up your side of the bargain."

Saputo's heart skipped a beat. "What do you mean? This picture will be done soon. It's on budget. What's the problem?"

"Where did you get the girl, Wesley?" Tice inquired softly.

Saputo saw Santa spread Cassie's legs apart. "A runaway. I... ah... found her cowering under the Santa Monica Pier," Saputo said in a matter-of-fact tone, watching the scene unfold in front of the cameras. He had taken her here for the night, and then, this morning, Saputo tied Cassie's hair into pigtails and took her to the International House of Pancakes.

While she ate her breakfast, a pancake happy face with a pineapple smile and whipped-cream hair, Saputo told her how he wanted to take her to the biggest, bestest ice cream parlor on earth. Then to Disneyland, where they would stay for days. All she had to do was be in a movie about Christmas.

You love Christmas, don't you? he had asked her. *Santa Claus will be in it. He'll have lots of presents. All you have to do is have a good time and tickle Santa. Then you can have all the ice cream you want and then we'll play together for as long as you like.*

She said it sounded fun and asked for a glass of chocolate milk.

"That wasn't wise, Wesley," Tice said, breaking into Saputo's thoughts. "You're not being very smart."

Saputo shrugged, shifting his attention back to Tice. "Got a better idea?"

Tice's gaze stabbed into him. "I'll get you the children, you make the movies. That's the bargain. It wouldn't be healthy for you to get caught again."

"Yeah, sure." Saputo held up his hand, pushing at the air between them, anxiety dancing in his chest again. "Take it easy, no problem. I don't want to go back to prison or the hospital again."

"That isn't where you'd be going, Wesley." Tice grinned and walked back into the shadows.

Asshole. Saputo trudged back to the set.

The camera was still whirring, Lyle Franken's eye glued to the viewfinder. Franken's gaze narrowed on Cassie's pigtails ... soft, tuggable pigtails that bounced with every movement of her head. Franken liked girls best when they wore their hair that way. And the girls sometimes liked him. They liked Franken because his short stature and his rolls of fat gave him the accordion shape of a cartoon character crushed by a huge boulder.

Franken saw Santa's eyes bulge with pleasure and wished he could be in that makeshift throne with Cassie buried between his legs. *Santa's Little Helper,* Franken was certain, was going to be a classic film.

Saputo stepped behind Franken and off to one side, sharing similar thoughts. But, unlike Franken, Saputo *would* get his turn. Oh yes, he certainly would.

"Great, Cassie, just great." Saputo grinned, his tobacco-stained teeth sticky with saliva. There were no fucking machines to zap his hard-ons away now.

"Cut," Saputo said heavily. Santa Claus held Cassie against his heaving chest. Her eyes were vacant, her face sickly pale.

Franken stepped back from the camera and patted Saputo on the back. "The lab boys should be able to get this off in three days. This is going to be a big one, Wesley. I can feel it in my—"

"I know where you can feel it," Saputo interrupted, staring at Cassie, a grin spreading on his face. Franken's chirpy coughs of laughter spilled out in a rush as Saputo went to Cassie and picked her up off of Santa's lap.

She was dead weight in his arms. Pliant.

Saputo swallowed dryly. "Okay, boys, it's a wrap. You guys can clean up here."

Franken jealously watched Saputo head towards the warehouse door with Cassie. "Be gentle, Wesley."

"I always am." The door closed behind him.

Sergeant Ronald Shaw had seen a lot of dead bodies. Not many made him cry. He struggled to keep his tears away from the half dozen other officers huddled in the pounding rain as they stood staring at the bloated corpse of a ten-year-old girl.

Even in death, lying in the mud beside the raging waters surging down the drainage canal, Shaw could see her beauty. Shaw looked at her vibrant red hair, caked with dirt, and saw her face, now a lifeless pearl white, and imagined the way she must have glowed when she smiled. Shaw couldn't stop staring. The water that had washed her up from God knows where lapped gently against her, tossing her tiny pigtails.

"Sergeant Shaw?" a voice from behind him ventured carefully. The black homicide detective, stirred from his thoughts, looked back, wiping his eyes with the back of his hand.

A snout-nosed man hiding under the biggest brown umbrella he had ever seen approached him. Shaw, no longer lost in the emotion of the moment, felt the stinging wetness of his rain-soaked clothes against his skin. In Shaw's rush to get here from the office he had left his umbrella drip-drying in the garbage can beside his desk.

The man offered his black-gloved hand to Shaw and held his umbrella over them both. "Sergeant Clive Barer, Sexually Exploited Child Unit, Juvenile Division. We've met once before."

Shaw reached out and shook Barer's hand, the leather glove slick in Shaw's wet grasp. "It's been a long time, Clive. Five years."

Barer shrugged. "I wish we weren't meeting again this way." He took a step toward the overpass that stretched across the canal a few yards away and offered shelter from the downpour.

Shaw followed, glancing back at the girl, her neck bruised a teal blue where crushing hands had choked the air out of her. The rushing water beside her charged along the cement canal south into the distant, stark industrial wastelands of Commerce and Southgate.

"Who found her?" Shaw asked, looking forward and trudging alongside Barer through the mud.

"A guy on the freeway lost a suitcase off the top of his car. It landed down here. You know, one of those Samsonite things," Barer said, lowering his umbrella as they walked under the overpass. "Anyway, he came down to get it and found her."

The roar of the rain drowned out the sound of the cars. Shaw could feel rumbling on the San Bernardino Freeway overhead. He shivered and wondered when he would see Noah's Ark sail down the canal.

"Do you know who she is?" Shaw asked.

"Yeah. Cassie Reed, ten years old, lived with her divorced mother in West LA. A week ago Cassie's mother gave the kid a spanking for not doing her chores and sent her to her room," he replied. "She never saw the kid again."

Barer cleared his throat. "Did you see the kid's neck?"

Shaw nodded.

"Familiar, isn't it?" Barer sighed.

"Yeah," Shaw said. "But I put Saputo behind bars. There's no way he could have done this."

Barer shook his head wearily. "He was released on parole two months ago."

CHAPTER ONE

Listening to the Bowel Movement made Los Angeles mayor Jed Stocker grimace. The tinny electronic sound and screeching lyrics blaring over the stereo speakers across the room made Stocker feel like he wasn't in his office but strapped into a dentist's chair having his teeth drilled.

Without Novocain.

An insistent pounding at the door, which at first Stocker thought was part of the song, gave him the excuse he needed to leave his desk and twist the stereo's volume down low.

"Come in," Stocker yelled gratefully, the last note of the song ringing in his ears.

Sergeant Ronald Shaw stepped in, closing the door behind him. "I got here as quickly as I could." He noticed the album cover for the Bowel Movement beside the stereo. It depicted a toilet, the open seat cover fanged like the mouth of a hungry shark, chasing a Ronald Reagan look-alike out of the bathroom. "I didn't know you liked that kind of music, sir."

Stocker removed the record from the turntable. "I don't. My son, Jed Jr., known as Faced to his fans, just became the lead singer of this new-wave group. This is their latest album. I decided to give it a chance. He told me the only way to enjoy it is loud."

The mayor flung the record like a Frisbee into the garbage can beside his desk and clapped his hands together. "I think I've just discovered the only way to enjoy that record."

Shaw chuckled. "Why does he call himself Faced?"

"It's shorthand for shit-faced." Stocker walked back to his desk and settled into his high-backed leather chair, the city's seal on the wall behind him. "And on that point, I'd have to agree with him. The kid has so much crap in his veins he never knows night from day." He nodded in Shaw's direction. "Sit down, Sergeant."

Shaw took a seat facing Stocker, who was flanked on one side by the state flag and on the other by the national flag. "What can I do for you, sir? Your message was rather vague."

Stocker scooted his chair forward and opened a file that was on the desk. "It's about your investigation into the murders of those young girls." He shuffled through the papers for a moment before finding the one he wanted. "Oh yes, here it is."

Leaning back in his chair, propping the file open in his lap, Stocker shot a scornful glance at Shaw. "Well, Sergeant, thanks to you, the city is being sued for three million dollars."

"Look, Mayor—," Shaw began.

Stocker continued, raising his voice over Shaw's. "A trio of sharp Century City lawyers representing Wesley Saputo is charging you with harassment. They say he hasn't been able to move an inch without bumping into a badge."

"C'mon, sir, I'm only doing my job," Shaw insisted. "In the two weeks since we found Cassie Reed beside the canal, two more girls have been kidnapped, raped, and strangled. The murders fit Saputo's MO. I've only been doing what any conscientious cop would do. I've brought him in for questioning, obtained a search warrant and gone through his house, and maintained constant surveillance."

Stocker shook his head. "I appreciate enthusiasm. As former police chief, and now as mayor, I expect my officers to take the extra step. But, Sergeant, you've gone too far."

Shaw felt his face flushing with anger. "What do you want me to do, let him go on raping and killing young girls?"

Shaw had seen it happen before. Men like Saputo are labeled mentally disordered sex offenders, sent to a cushy state hospital for a few years, and then put back on the street. Shaw didn't know who was sicker, Saputo or the shrinks who set him free.

"Don't smart-mouth me, Shaw," Stocker thundered. "You have to face reality. His lawyers say you don't have any evidence against him, not a single fingerprint and no semen matchup."

"I know it's Saputo," Shaw shot back. "True, we have no prints. But all of Saputo's victims were girls between the ages of ten and twelve. Same thing now. All of Saputo's victims were raped, sodomized, and strangled. Again, so are the new victims. We couldn't get a blood type off of Saputo's semen five years ago because he is a nonsecretor. The person who raped these girls is also a nonsecretor."

"So, to summarize, you don't have shit," Stocker stated, tossing the file onto his desk.

Shaw tapped the arm of his chair with his fingers, trying to keep cool. "I'll get the evidence, you can count on that. I'll make sure they put him behind bars forever."

"How are you going to do that?" Stocker asked. "Saputo's lawyers are going to seek a restraining order from Superior Court Judge Lewis Nile this afternoon, and I think they'll get it. Any further attempts to bring Saputo in for questioning and the lawyers will haul us to court."

Stocker scowled. "Face it, you botched this one, Shaw. You came on too strong and now we can't get near him."

Shaw glared at Stocker. "Are you telling me to let this guy go?"

"No, I'm telling you to call Brett Macklin."

The words, like a sharp punch to the solar plexus, stole Shaw's breath. He stared at the mayor for a moment in disbelieving silence.

"I want these murders to stop, but I don't want Saputo and his lawyers getting a chance to give the press a show," Stocker explained. "I don't want Saputo turned into some kind of fucking martyr. The city doesn't need a slew of negative headlines screaming about police harassment."

"The city doesn't need a vigilante, either. Fighting crime with crime isn't the answer," Shaw cautioned. "Let's not make the situation any worse."

"How could it get any worse, Sergeant? You just got done telling me that Saputo is killing children. I'm telling you the LAPD can't get near him." Stocker held up his hands despairingly. "Do you have a better idea?"

"There has to be another way, a legal way," Shaw insisted.

"There is no other way," Stocker shouted. "I want Macklin on this. *Now.*"

⚜ ⚜ ⚜

He ran madly down the street, the World War I fighter plane riddling the asphalt on either side of him with bullets. The plane streaked across the cloudless sky above the office buildings, banked, and barreled down on him again, the gun turrets spitting slugs.

He dived onto a parked car, rolled across the hood, and fell onto the sidewalk behind it. Bullets chewed up the street toward the car. He flung himself forward as the bullets raked the car and punctured the gas tank.

The car exploded, ripping the air and hurling a pulsating ball of flame into the sky. The plane roared away, preparing to bank again.

He stood up, flames licking out for him, and pulled the Magnum out of his waistband.

"Fuck this," he mumbled, strolling into the street, shrouded by a veil of smoke. He stopped in the center of the street and straddled the broken white dividing line, daring the plane. "Come and get it."

The plane dropped down low and came for him.

The flames from the car sounded like a windstorm, the staccato beat of the bullets chipping away at the street a savage hail.

He raised his gun. The plane filled his vision. The engine's roar filled his ears. The bullets clamored for him.

He fired twice.

The plane vomited deep black smoke and curled sharply in a skyward arc, sputtered, and dived. Rocking uncontrollably, the plane glided unevenly toward the entrance of a parking structure behind him, as if it suddenly thought it was just a fancy Ford station wagon.

The plane's wings were ripped away as it skidded through the entranceway into the darkness on a carpet of sparks and smoke. A split second later, an explosion tore through the structure, the building splitting open like a popcorn kernel.

He lowered his gun and, as people started to peek out of the doorways and windows they had been hiding behind, walked leisurely down the street.

"That was fantastic!" Mort Suderson yelled, slapping the floor in front of the television. The film's end credits rolled across the screen as Nick Crecko, the Bloodmaster, disappeared into the sunset against the Los Angeles skyline. "Wasn't it great, Brett?"

"C'mon, Mort, it was crap," Macklin groaned, reaching toward the VCR atop the TV set.

"Wait! Don't turn it off yet. Don't you want to see our credit?" Mort looked at Macklin as if he were crazy. Macklin, raising his hands in a show of acquiescence, stepped back and watched the screen.

Aerial transportation provided by: Blue Yonder Airways

"That's us!" Mort pointed at the set, wagging his finger excitedly. "That's us, boss! We're stars!"

Macklin clicked off the VCR and hit the "eject" button, tossing the videotape onto Mort's lap. "All we did was fly the film crew around. No one is going to nominate us for an Oscar."

Mort reached up, braced himself on a couch cushion, rose to his feet and stretched. "Christ, Brett, I love hard-core police drama."

Macklin went into his kitchen, which adjoined the living room. "That was shit, Mort. C'mon, a fighter plane chasing a guy through downtown Los Angeles? Who are they kidding?"

Mort, glancing back to make sure he wasn't being watched, brushed potato chip crumbs off his faded blue jeans onto the shag carpet and then followed Macklin into the kitchen. "It's exciting. It isn't supposed to be Shakespeare."

Macklin opened the refrigerator. "What would you like, Mort?"

Mort eyed the six-pack of Schlitz longingly but knew better. Booze had already fucked up his life enough. "Gimme one of those Diet Cokes."

Macklin grabbed a beer for himself and handed Mort the diet drink. "I have a hard time separating what I know about the filmmakers from the film itself. Brock Dale, the guy who played macho Nick Crecko, is a whimpering homosexual, an egotistical little hemorrhoid in the ass of humanity."

"You've got to forget that." Mort snapped open the Diet Coke and took a big gulp. "On screen, he's the invincible Bloodmaster. Has been for years." Mort ambled into the living room and dropped himself onto Macklin's couch.

"Has-been is right." Macklin, sipping his beer, leaned against the kitchen doorway. He could hear raindrops tapping the roof. "But I have to admit, it was a nice way to kill a lazy, rainy afternoon."

"Yeah, I tell you, I'm going to fucking sue the Beach Boys," Mort said, pausing to swallow a mouthful of Diet Coke. "Did they ever mention weeklong rainstorms in their songs, huh? No. The sun was always shining and everybody was getting laid. Do you see the sunshine? Do you see me getting laid?"

Mort shifted his gaze to the Duraflame log burning in the fireplace beside the TV. "But that's going to change."

"The weather or your sex life?" Macklin quipped.

"Who gives a shit about the weather? I can't do anything about that. I can fix my sex life. I'm going to make a few changes."

"Like what?"

"I'm thinking of changing my name," Mort offered cautiously. "I've thought it out and I think I'd make a good Mortimer *Neville.* It's sexy, it's now, and it's a happening name. It's me."

Macklin stared silently at Mort.

"It's a great name, huh?" Mort continued, nervously filling the silence. "A real *fuckable* name. A guy with a name like that could get so much action he'd have to get his schlong insured against injury."

Mort stood up and started pacing in front of the fire. "Of course if I'm going to be that active with the ladies, I'm going to need an operation."

"Operation?" Macklin asked uneasily.

Mort stuck his tongue out, shoved his index finger under it, and approached Macklin. "I'm gonna have this little connection here snipped off," he slobbered. "It'll make my tongue longer. I think it's too short and I'm not adequately satisfying women with it, you know? I also plan to drop a few hundred bucks into some new clothes."

The sound of the front door slamming shut drew their attention to the entry hall. The two men turned and saw a frowning Cheshire Davis, still in her white nurse's uniform, carrying two bags of groceries into the house. "That's disgusting, Mort, nauseating."

"How long have you been standing there?" Mort said, his face reddening.

She walked past Mort into the kitchen, her eyes scolding him. "Long enough, Mort."

Macklin started to laugh.

"Ah, fuck you, Brett," Mort shot back, reaching for his pseudo-sheepskin-lined Levi's jacket lying in a heap on the floor. "It isn't funny. I was born handicapped, with a deformed tongue."

Macklin, rocking with laughter, spilled his beer on the floor. Cheshire, unpacking the groceries, began to laugh as well.

"It isn't funny!" Mort shouted. "I'm correcting a birth defect."

Realizing that he was making no headway with either of them, Mort gave up, stomping to the front door in a huff and yanking it open.

Macklin's laughter stopped abruptly. He saw Shaw standing in the doorway, his gray trench coat soaked with rain.

Mort looked over his shoulder at Brett for some kind of cue.

"See you later, Mort." Macklin caught his breath, his smile ebbing. Mort hesitated for a moment, uncertain whether to leave or not, then brushed past Shaw into the rain.

"Can I come in?" Shaw asked sheepishly.

Macklin looked over his shoulder at Cheshire, who was busy stuffing food into the refrigerator and apparently hadn't heard Shaw's voice. Macklin sighed, approaching Shaw quietly. He made no motion to invite him in.

"What is it?" Macklin demanded, careful to keep his voice low. He knew what Shaw wanted. Every morning Macklin awoke and wondered, is this the day they come for me again? The fear that his wondering might actually be longing kept him up nights.

"Mayor Stocker wants to see you," Shaw said.

Stocker wants you to pick up your gun again, a voice teased Macklin. *He wants you to dig it out from under the floorboards, slip the six bullets into the chamber, and squeeze the trigger. You'd like that, wouldn't you, Macky boy? You'd like that a lot.*

"No," Macklin said.

Shaw swallowed. "Look, Mack, you don't have any choice."

Macklin looked over his shoulder toward the kitchen. Cheshire was out of sight, probably putting food into the refrigerator. He faced Shaw again. "My life is becoming whole again. Do you want to shatter that?" He was asking the voice inside him. Not Shaw.

"No, I don't," Shaw replied, anger seeping defensively into his voice. "You know how I feel about it. But it's not in my hands."

Shaw immediately regretted the tone of his voice. None of the sympathy he actually felt came across.

To Shaw, Macklin's ocean blue eyes suddenly dimmed, his face tightening into the savage look of determination that made Shaw doubt this was the same Brett Macklin he had grown up with. The look that symbolized the man Macklin had become since his father, a beat cop, was set aflame by a street gang. The look of a killer who made sure each of those gang members ended up in a burial plot.

It was that look, and the lawlessness it represented to Shaw, that made it impossible for Shaw to ever enjoy the deep friendship they'd once had.

"When does he want to see me?" Macklin's words seemed to have a serrated edge.

"Tomorrow morning. Nine o'clock."

"All right, I'll be there." Their eyes met for a second that felt like days to Shaw. He thought he saw a spark of vulnerability in Macklin's eyes and was about to say something, to reflexively grasp for their old closeness, when Macklin slowly closed the door in his face.

CHAPTER TWO

The punker with the tangerine orange Mohawk held a sawed-off shotgun, Macklin was sure of that. Macklin had seen him out of the corner of his eye as he drove past the Quick Stop market on his way to Stocker's office.

Macklin pressed the gas pedal to the floor. The black Cadillac shot forward. At the next intersection, Macklin twisted the wheel, whipping the car into a screeching U-turn and gliding it to a stop at the street corner a quarter block up from the market. He wasn't even thinking now. His anger was doing the thinking for him.

He didn't have his gun, but he wasn't going to let that stop him. The wooden skeleton of a building under construction adjoined the garage-size Quick Stop market. Macklin assumed he could find a weapon at the construction site.

Macklin bolted out of the car and splashed through puddles on the sidewalk into the roofless structure beside the market. Crouching, Macklin searched the muddy concrete floor for a suitable weapon. He was about to settle for a damp two-by-four when he spotted a steel level lying amidst wood shavings and scattered nails. Picking it up, he swung it. The level was heavy in his hand. *Yes.* He smiled. *This will do.*

He slipped out the back of the structure into an alley and approached the market's back door. Cautiously, Macklin turned the doorknob with his left hand and slowly pushed the door open with his shoulder.

The door opened into a closet-size storeroom lined with cardboard boxes. Macklin closed the door carefully behind him and could hear voices from just outside the door across from him.

"L-look, I-I don't have the combination to the safe, r-really," Macklin heard a young man plead in a voice made shrill with fear.

"Bullshit!" the punker rasped. "Open the fucking safe, or I'll blow your head off!" The punker sounded angry and impatient. Macklin thought it was only a matter of seconds before the punker lost his cool and the cashier would be splattered all over the room.

"Open it!" the punker shouted.

Macklin eased open the storeroom door and entered the market unseen. The market was bathed in fluorescent white, three aisles running across the floor to the cashier, who was boxed in by counters cluttered with magazine displays and jars of candy. The punker, wearing snakeskin pants and a vest made of chains, shifted his weight in front of the counter, holding the shotgun six inches from the pimple-faced cashier's neck.

The cashier dumped a handful of change and curled bills onto the countertop in front of the punker.

"Here, that's all we have in the register," the boy stammered. "I don't know the combination to the safe, you have to believe me."

"You got two seconds to learn it, maggot," the punker barked.

Macklin stepped into the aisle behind the punker and crept forward, raising the level over his head. The cashier caught the movement behind the punker and, for an instant, stared right at Macklin.

Macklin frantically waved his hand, motioning the cashier to look away.

"Time's up, asshole, open it!" The punker jabbed the shotgun into the cashier's stomach. Macklin was two feet away.

"You're unbalanced, buddy," Macklin hissed.

The punker whirled around. Macklin swung the level at the punker's head like a baseball bat and felt the dull smack of steel against flesh. The punker fell, reflexively squeezing the trigger. The shotgun jerked, spitting fire. Macklin threw himself sideways into the candy rack, and the cashier screamed, leaping back against the Slurpee machine.

Macklin felt the shotgun pellets scorch past his right ear and heard them chew into the ceiling. Bits of plaster rained down like snowflakes.

Bracing himself against a shelf of Baby Ruth bars, Macklin rose carefully, deafened by the ringing echoes of the shotgun blast. Brushing plaster off his shoulders, he looked down at the twitching punker. Blood seeped out in frothy rivers from the left side of the punker's head, which now had the unnatural curve of a peanut shell.

Macklin shifted his gaze from the punker to the cashier, who cowered in shocked silence against the Slurpee machine. Cherry-colored ice fell out of the machine in huge globs.

"Are you okay?" Macklin asked, stepping up to the counter.

The boy nodded as if in a trance.

Macklin rested the level against his right shoulder and smiled reassuringly at the boy. "Why don't you stop leaning on the machine and come here for a second?"

The boy stared quizzically at Macklin for a moment and then suddenly realized his back was against the Slurpee lever. The boy jumped forward as if electrocuted, his back coated with red ice. A smile that shifted rapidly between embarrassment and relief filled his pimple-scarred face.

"Thanks. You ... ah ... saved my life."

"No problem," Macklin said. "Would you do me a favor?"

"Of course!" the cashier eagerly responded.

"When the police ask you what I look like, tell 'em I'm about five foot four, three hundred fifty pounds, and Asian. Get my drift?"

The cashier looked confused. "S-sure. Anything." Macklin smiled. "Thanks." He stepped toward the door and then stopped, returning to the counter.

"Listen, could I have a large coffee?"

"Yeah, sure, a large coffee." The cashier spun around, grabbed for the coffeepot, and poured Macklin a cup. The coffee spilled out in a rush and flowed over the rim of the disposable cup. The cashier didn't notice. He set the pot down and, forcing a broad smile, shakily handed Macklin the cup of coffee.

Macklin, the level in one hand and the coffee in the other, turned his back on the cashier, stepped over the punker, and strode to the door. "See you later. Thanks for the coffee."

"W-wait," the boy yelled as Macklin pushed open the front door with his shoulder. "Who are you?"

Macklin, his back to the cashier, smiled to himself. "The jury."

It was 9:45 when Macklin flung open Mayor Stocker's office door and sauntered in.

"I said nine o'clock, Macklin," Stocker barked, rising from behind his desk. Shaw, sitting on the vinyl couch against the wall to Stocker's right, groaned inside. The meeting was getting off to a great start.

Macklin shrugged. "I got held up."

"Well, I don't give a shit." Stocker jerked a finger toward the two chairs fronting his desk. "Sit down, Macklin."

Macklin stayed where he was, in the center of the room, and shoved his hands deep into the pockets of his Levi's 501s.

"Make it quick, Mayor." Macklin's words came out with measured evenness. It gave Shaw an unsettling chill.

Shaw glanced at Stocker, expecting an angry retort at Macklin's impudence, but none came. Stocker slid past the state flag and sat on the edge of his desk.

"Sergeant, tell Macklin our problem."

Macklin glanced at Shaw.

No, it's your problem, Stocker, Shaw thought. *I can take care of this within the law. I don't want Macklin involved.*

"Three little girls have been raped and strangled in the last month." Shaw looked at Stocker as he spoke, avoiding Macklin. Shaw felt if he directed his words to Macklin, he was somehow condoning the actions Macklin was going to be asked to take.

"Go on, Sergeant," Stocker prodded impatiently.

Shaw sighed, straightening up. "We know who's doing it," he continued reluctantly. "A psychopathic pedophile named Wesley Saputo. Five years ago, Saputo was in the kiddie-porn film business. Backed by Crocker Orlock, a wealthy magazine distributor, Saputo made hundreds of low-low-budget films and then released them worldwide through a complex underground pedophile network."

Shaw paused, glancing at Macklin to gauge his reaction. There was no change in the pilot's hard expression. "We were able to arrest Saputo and a couple of his cronies when his cameraman, a greasy character named Lyle Franken, was caught in an LAPD sting operation trying to sell kid-porn photos. One of the photos was a blowup from a Saputo film. It was a picture of a twelve-year-old girl who had recently been found raped and strangled."

Macklin turned to his left, his back to Shaw and Stocker, and stared out the window at the city's skyline. The buildings poked out through a thin layer of smog. Sunlight fought in vain to break through the noxious haze.

"Franken became a nonstop talker under pressure and we were able to send Saputo away on kiddie-porn charges. We couldn't pin a thing on Orlock," Shaw said. "He managed to keep himself at arm's length from the operation. But he was behind it, no doubt about that."

Shaw paused, his feelings of frustration regarding the Saputo case stoked again by the retelling. He found himself getting caught up in the sort of anger that drove Macklin. The tension wrapped itself, boa-like, around his neck, and squeezed. He fought against it, striving for cool detachment.

Shaw didn't want to feel like a part of what was going to take place in this office. "Saputo was labeled by the state shrinks as a mentally disordered sex offender, spent some time at Patton State Hospital, and then at Soledad. He was released on parole in September. The murders began in November."

"That's a fascinating story, gentlemen," Macklin said, his eyes scanning the city's steel peaks and asphalt valleys. "What does it have to do with me?"

"Kid porn has been nearly dead in this city for five years," Stocker replied. "Orlock had the money, but his talent was behind bars. Saputo is out now, and Orlock isn't about to let his star filmmaker get caught again. Orlock's cadre of high-powered Century City attorneys jumped on us and wrangled a court order that forbids us from harassing Saputo. We get within ten miles of him, and his lawyers drag us into court.

"Saputo has to be stopped before he kills again, Macklin," Stocker said evenly.

Macklin turned slowly to face Stocker. An amused smile played on Macklin's lips. "What you want me to do is kill him."

Shaw felt his stomach muscles tense up. He wanted to get up and walk out now, before he got in any deeper, but his body wouldn't move.

"No, we want you to stop him." Stocker's words came out as crisp and smooth as the stride of a man carrying a live bomb.

You mean kill, Shaw thought, *you rotten son of a bitch. And Mack will.*

"I won't be your executioner, Stocker. Then I'm as bad as the people you want me to"—Macklin paused, a grin growing on his face—"the people you want me to stop."

Macklin paced in front of Stocker. "I think we need some due process here."

"What?" Stocker's eyebrows arched in angry disbelief.

"Saputo *could* be innocent." Macklin glanced at Shaw and was pleased to see the beginning of a smile.

Some of the iciness Shaw felt toward Macklin was melting. *Maybe this madness could end,* Shaw thought. *Maybe Mack is seeing that his way is wrong. Maybe…*

"Funny," Stocker said, walking toward Macklin, "you weren't exactly Mr. Due Process when you were avenging your father, were you? Saputo *is* guilty. We both know that. What's your problem? What more evidence do you need?"

"I'll gather the evidence I need while you and Shaw find someone, a judge or something, who can be our judicial review," Macklin said. "This third party can pass sentence. I want the judgment on whether to stop someone to come from him after a careful review of the evidence I gather. I want the decision called by someone besides you or me. I don't trust either one of us, Stocker."

Stocker laughed uproariously. "Macklin, you are out of your fucking mind. The answer is no. Period. You do as you're told."

Macklin smiled. "You don't give me orders. Suggestions, perhaps, but not orders."

Stocker stepped within a foot of Macklin. "Are you forgetting I can have you arrested for multiple murders right this fucking second? You are in no position to tell me a damn thing!"

Macklin could smell the spearmint mouthwash on Stocker's breath. "You may be able to put me behind bars, but I can destroy you, the LAPD, and the whole city government," Macklin replied softly, undaunted by Stocker's rage.

"You're dreaming, Macklin."

Macklin pulled a cassette tape out of his pocket and tossed it to Shaw. "Play it," he demanded sharply, staring Stocker in the eye.

Okay, let's see what your game is, Mack, Shaw thought, sauntering casually across the room to Stocker's stereo system, popping in the cassette, and hitting the "play" button.

Static hummed over the speakers. Shaw heard a faint voice and turned the volume up.

"*... so you've got problems in Chinatown.*" Macklin's voice was clearly recognizable over the speakers. *"Big fucking deal. I still don't understand why you had Ron drag me down here."*

"I told you about the problem in Chinatown because I want Mr. Jury to take care of it..."

Stocker paled at the sound of his voice on the tape. Macklin's gaze remained fixed on Stocker's scowl-drawn face.

"Every conversation we had about the gang warfare I ended in Chinatown is on tape." Macklin said, obviously pleased with himself. "I walked in here wired."

"*... these guys are no different than the men who killed your father. Go after them the same way. I'll make sure you get no heat from the police...*"

"Turn it off, Shaw," Stocker yelled.

Shaw didn't move. He wanted to see Stocker roast for a minute. Maybe if Stocker heard himself he'd see the lunacy. Maybe he'd understand. Maybe this crazy vigilante bullshit would end.

"*... You're mine, Macklin. For better or worse, I own you.*"

"You never did, Stocker. And you never will." Macklin calmly walked over to the stereo and ejected the tape. "This is my version of mutual assured deterrence. You screw me and I'll screw you."

Macklin handed the tape to Stocker. "Keep this one as a souvenir."

The mayor grabbed the cassette and yanked out the tape, tearing it. He tossed the ruined cassette into the garbage can.

"Okay, you've both played your trump cards, now what?" Shaw spoke up, drawing their attention. *It's time,* Shaw thought, *to inject some reality into this.* "How do we find someone who can play God, decide who lives or dies? What you're talking about is still murder."

Shaw let out a sigh of futility. "But you two have forgotten that, haven't you? All right, let's deal with this on a less philosophical plane. How do we find someone you and the mayor can both live with?"

Shaw walked in a broad circle around Stocker and Macklin. "What do we do, gentlemen? Approach someone and just say, 'Hello, we've got an assassin working for us. Would you mind playing referee?' Suppose we approach the wrong man and he goes to the *Los Angeles Times*?"

"You'll just have to find the right man, Ronny," Macklin said.

"I will?" Shaw half smiled. "Guess again."

Shaw was the one person under Stocker's influence whom Macklin could trust, the only person Macklin knew would look out for his interests as well as the LAPD's. "Ronny, revenge won't work as justification anymore."

"It never did, Mack." Shaw shook his head. "You're kidding yourself if you think anything will justify it now."

"Injustice, Ronny, that's our justification," Macklin replied. "The law isn't working. Too many criminals are going free and too many innocent people are getting hurt."

"Oh, spare me the ethical bullshit and let's get to the point, okay?" Stocker shuffled to his desk and fell into his seat. "We're talking about a fourth man. Someone else who knows, Macklin, that you're Mr. Jury."

"And knows you're encouraging me."

"What kind of man are we talking about?" Stocker ran his hands through his hair. Macklin had him by the balls. He had to show Macklin just how crazy the idea was. "A neoconservative ex-judge like Sinclair Thompson, a lunatic liberal lawyer like Frank Swift, or a mercurial Harlan Fitz clone? Face it, Macklin, the three of us are in it alone. We are inextricably bound to each other."

"Harlan Fitz . . . ," Macklin mused.

"A big-mouthed, headline-mongering ex-judge turned talk-show personality who has his head securely up his ass," Stocker snapped. *Jesus, why can't Macklin understand?* "The guy can't figure whether he's on our side or the ACLU's. He's a jackass. We both hate him. Case closed. We're back to square one."

"I've never heard of Harlan Fitz," Macklin mused, "but he sounds like our man. If both sides can't stand him, he must be doing something right."

Macklin walked toward the door. "Ronny, you approach him while I scope out Mr. Saputo."

Before either Stocker or Shaw could object, Macklin was gone.

CHAPTER THREE

There's no business like show business, it's like no business I know…

The needle was stuck on Brett Macklin's mental turntable. Ethel Merman belted out that lyric again and again in Macklin's head as he glided toward the red light at Overland and Culver Boulevard. He could understand why the song droned on. It was the toll charge the neighborhood exacted for driving through.

The MGM Studios water tower, with the logo of the company's latest film emblazoned on it, loomed a few blocks up under a blanket of bruised clouds. To his right he saw the Veterans Memorial Building fountain, frothy water gurgling through the sprockets of three intertwined steel strips fashioned like movie film.

This is movieland, he heard the neighborhood try to convince him, *and there is glitter here. You may not see it, but it's here.*

The neighborhood merchants apparently saw it, somewhere behind the age-beaten Premiere Motel or beside Celebrity Hair Styling or around the corner from Al's Star Burgers.

Macklin didn't see any. Maybe Wesley Saputo, riding in a tan four-door Seville two cars in front of him, did. The light switched to green and the traffic crawled eastward on the rain-slicked street toward downtown Culver City.

Macklin studied the buildings as he passed them. They looked like the facades pretending to be buildings on a Hollywood backlot. Cement and gray, art deco, fantasyland, urbanity. If one could buy a business district at Ralph's, Macklin thought, this would be in the plain-wrap section.

He sighed. He'd driven past here a thousand times and never cared about appearances before. Now he cared. *Shit,* he thought, *am I bored.* To drown out Ethel, he clicked on KROQ-FM and turned up the volume. A rebel yell from Billy Idol shook the car. Ethel sang on, undaunted.

Macklin had been following Saputo around for two days and had canceled several charter flights to find the time. He was beginning to get mad about all the money he had pissed away to play cops and robbers. Time Macklin could have spent in the air, flying charters and thereby paying the bills that cluttered his office, was killed in his car outside Saputo's apartment building listening to Dire Straits and Bruce Springsteen tapes.

At least Mort is flying, Macklin thought. *It's a good thing, too, or I wouldn't have the money to pay him.*

Macklin wouldn't have been upset if Saputo had at least done something incriminating. But Saputo rarely left his weed-landscaped mustard yellow Mar Vista apartment building except to run down to Safeway for groceries. Macklin was beginning to wonder if Stocker and Shaw knew what they were talking about.

Saputo turned right where Culver met Venice Boulevard and then veered left onto Robertson. Macklin followed, yawning, noticing with irritation that the afternoon was giving way to evening. The city was now enjoying the chilly afterglow of a day of cold, hazy blue sunshine.

The Seville wound through a mazelike path of side streets lined with bland, boxy, one – and two-story industrial buildings before pulling over beside a windowless warehouse. Macklin drove past the warehouse, made a U-turn two blocks away, and came back. He stopped behind a cement mixing truck parked kitty-corner from the warehouse and turned off his ignition.

He watched Saputo rise from the passenger side of the Seville. Three hairless grizzly bears stuffed into camel-colored slacks and Sanka brown corduroy jackets emerged from the car after him.

Macklin had no doubt the three apes packed some heavy artillery under those carved-granite shoulders.

Macklin studied Saputo, who strutted toward the warehouse door in his Jordache jeans, tan polyester jacket, and red silky dress shirt unbuttoned down to the bulge of his stomach. A gold chain tapped against his bony chest with each footfall.

It was Macklin's first opportunity to look at the man. In the next brief second or two, Macklin knew Stocker and Shaw were right. He saw it in Saputo's self-impressed gait, in the narrow I'm-fucking-your-wife-and-your-daughter-too grin, in the eyes that conveyed a school-yard bully's childish defiance and disrespect.

Macklin saw Saputo slip a key into the steel door, which was the bottom right corner of a much larger door that could slide up to let in trucks. Saputo stepped inside, two guards galloping after him like pet dogs. The third man stayed outside grimacing, apparently unhappy at having to perform sentry duty.

Macklin settled back in his seat, pushed a Doors tape in the Sanyo, and prepared for a long wait. The guard lit a cigarette, reached down with one hand to adjust his balls, and began to pace in front of the warehouse, blowing smoke out of his mouth in tiny circles.

A van wound around the corner in front of Macklin, the headlight beams cutting a swath in the darkness toward his head. Macklin ducked as the light passed through the car and glanced at his watch. It was 8:04 p.m. Roughly three hours had passed since he had parked outside the warehouse.

Macklin sat up and saw the van pull up to the warehouse door. The driver honked twice. The sentry, facing Macklin's direction as he appeared around the edge of the warehouse, tossed away a glowing cigarette butt and walked around the back of the van to the driver's side.

The driver and the sentry knew each other, Macklin assumed, because the sentry stayed there chatting as the steel warehouse door rose noisily. Bright light spilled from inside the warehouse and bathed the van in whiteness. The van surged forward, and Macklin could see the end of a laugh on the sentry's face. The warehouse door dropped quickly, swallowing the van and the light. But not before Macklin caught a glimpse of the van's license plate.

Macklin scribbled the plate number down on a notepad beside him, adding to the list of plate numbers he had copied from cars parked around the warehouse.

The sentry walked toward Macklin without noticing him and then turned around the edge of the warehouse, disappearing from Macklin's view.

Macklin scratched his cheek. Hmmm.

His buttocks ached, and he was sick of listening to his tapes. And nothing was happening outside the warehouse. All the action was inside. Macklin figured those were good reasons to get up, stretch, and give the warehouse a careful look-over.

He opened the door, stepped outside, and bent over, touching his toes. His back cracked audibly. Macklin frowned. *I'm turning into a fat old man.* Lately, Macklin had come to accept that he wasn't the muscular youth who had dashed through UCLA on a track scholarship anymore.

Macklin closed the door, careful to muffle the sound, and sprinted stealthily across the street to the shadows of the office building beside the warehouse. *By now the sentry is directly behind Saputo's warehouse,* Macklin thought. *If I'm alert, I can circle the building undetected, staying behind the sentry.*

Abandoning his cover in the shadows against the building, he dashed lightly on the balls of his feet across the alley to the side of Saputo's warehouse. As he moved along the wall, he noticed the cement expanse had no doors or windows.

Macklin slid his body around the back of the warehouse and saw the back of the sentry disappearing around the opposite side.

This wall, too, had no openings. He sprinted across the length of the warehouse and paused before rounding the next corner. Peering around the wall's edge, he saw the sentry standing next to a garbage bin. The sentry struck a match on the edge of the bin, his fleshy face momentarily illuminated as he lit the cigarette that dangled between his puffy lips.

The sentry flicked his smoking match away and shuffled along the asphalt to the front of the warehouse. As soon as the sentry rounded the corner, Macklin crept quietly over to the trash bin. He noticed that a rust-coated padlock clamped the bin closed.

What kind of trash is so important that you lock it up? Macklin wondered, tugging on the padlock. He stared at the bin, letting his imagination assume the worst. In his mind, he could see his nine-year-old daughter, Corinne, amidst the trash, neck sliced open, maggots squirming over her bloated, decaying face.

He shivered, his stomach churning.

You've got a sick mind, Mack, a real sick mind.

Macklin dashed back, the way he had come, to the rear of the warehouse and crossed the alley to the rear of the adjacent office building. He went around the side of the building and paused, glancing to his left to see where the sentry was. The sentry was out of sight, probably beginning his circle around the warehouse again. Macklin trotted to his car and got inside.

He took a deep breath and studied the warehouse. *What are you doing in there, Wesley?* Macklin reached out to the glove box with his right hand. Sitting beside the .357 Magnum was a baggie full of cut carrots. He pulled out the bag, closed the glove box, and clicked on the stereo. Munching on his carrots, he scrunched down in his seat and waited, letting his mind wander to thoughts of Cheshire.

He was glad Cheshire had the night shift this week and wouldn't be stumbling into the house until after midnight. She'd be less aware of his absence and would be less likely to question his excuses.

Cheshire was spending four to five nights a week at Macklin's Venice home. Macklin remembered how uncomfortable it had felt at first, how scared and pressured her presence had made him feel. But those uncomfortable feelings had ebbed with surprising speed and were replaced by an urgency, a need to spend time with her.

Macklin found it all so ironic. Becoming involved with her had never been part of his plans. They had met nearly a year ago, during the horrible weeks after his father's murder.

She had gone to nursing school with Mort's sister and had patched up the stab wound Macklin received in a deadly struggle with one of the gang members who had killed his father.

He used her then, making love to her and spending the night with her as an alibi. While she slept, Macklin snuck away to kill one of the murderers.

But after his father had been avenged, Macklin continued to see her. In fact, she was the only person he saw. He couldn't bring himself to see his daughter, Cory, or Brooke, his ex-wife. Not after what he had done. Not after what he had become.

Cheshire was part of his new life. Cory and Brooke were part of his old life, a life sacrificed to the driving compulsion inside him that the public called Mr. Jury. For now, despite his love for Cory, Cheshire was all he had.

He felt that being with Cheshire was rebuilding him. He was beginning to feel that he might be able to recapture some of what he had lost.

The small warehouse door opened, interrupting Macklin's introspection. Wesley Saputo, accompanied by his two guards, emerged from inside and sauntered to the Seville. Saputo was hyped up, talking excitedly, his hands moving quickly to illustrate some point. They waited for the sentry to join them, and then the four men got into the Seville. The headlights flashed on and the engine roared to life.

Macklin ducked down as the Seville sped past him. When the car had turned the corner, Macklin started up his car and drove to the edge of the warehouse, stopping next to the trash bin. Leaving the engine running, he got out and opened the trunk.

He pulled out a pair of bolt cutters and a Glad trash bag and closed the trunk. His face etched with determination, Macklin pinched the padlock between the cutting blades and snapped the clasp. Dropping the bolt cutters, he lifted open the trash bin.

The sour stench of decay smacked him, curling his face into a wince. *God, what a smell.* Breathing through his mouth to avoid the smell, Macklin leaned into the bin, searching through the rotten food, empty bottles, and cans. He grabbed handfuls of damp, slippery paper and three typewriter ribbon cartridges and shoved them into the bag.

Closing the bin, he picked up the bag and his bolt cutters and returned to the car. Macklin turned on his interior light and examined the contents of the bag.

A wave of nausea rocked Macklin as he gazed at three soiled, torn, and yellowed photos of naked girls, no older than ten or eleven, being fondled by men with hungry grins.

The bastards…

He shoved the photos back into the bag. *I'm going to stop this shit,* Macklin thought. *What Saputo is doing is inhuman.* Macklin flipped off the interior light, started the engine, and drove away.

Had Macklin looked in his rearview mirror, he would have seen the dark form standing at the edge of the warehouse behind him, watching.

The thin man turned and walked casually to a coal black BMW, parked in the shadows across from the warehouse. In what seemed like one fluid, choreographed motion, he opened the door, sat down, and reached for the telephone between the seats.

"Mr. Orlock?" The man's words slithered out snakelike—soft and smooth. "This is Tice."

"Good evening, Tice," Orlock replied lightly.

"The stranger followed Wesley to the warehouse and just broke into our trash."

"Really?" Orlock laughed. "Our trash, huh? We can't have that, Tice, now, can we?"

"No, sir," Tice whispered.

"A man's trash is sacred."

"Yes, sir." Tice smiled thinly.

"You'd better kill the fiend."

"As you wish." Tice clicked off the phone.

CHAPTER FOUR

Cheshire was curled up in the corner of the couch in her yellow terry-cloth bathrobe watching *Late Night with David Letterman* when Macklin came in the front door carrying a small grocery bag.

"Mack, I thought you'd never get back," Cheshire said as he rushed past her into the kitchen.

"I'm sorry, there was more office work at the hangar than I thought." Macklin set the bag down on the kitchen table. "But I got you a little surprise to make up for it."

Cheshire rose from the couch, turned off the television, and trudged barefoot into the kitchen. "What?"

Macklin melodramatically yanked a quart of chocolate ice cream from the grocery bag. "Ta-da!"

Cheshire laughed. "I appreciate it, honey, but it's too fattening."

Macklin frowned. "Fattening? Cheshire, are you going to deny yourself one of life's greatest pleasures?"

"Yep."

"Okay." Macklin shrugged, turning his back to Cheshire and reaching toward the kitchen cabinets above the sink for a bowl.

"Forget the bowls, Brett," Cheshire said. He turned around and saw her holding two spoons in one hand and yanking open the quart with the other. "Half the fun is just digging in. It doesn't give you time to think about the calories."

He grinned, shaking his head disbelievingly, and took a spoon from her, plunged it into the ice cream, dug out a huge portion, and eagerly stuffed it into his mouth.

"Good?" she asked with an expectant smile.

"*Great.*" He pointed to the ice cream with his spoon as if she needed urging on.

"I'm going to savor this," she said, wagging her spoon at him.

"Okay already, so eat."

Cheshire stabbed the ice cream with her spoon, carved out a thick wedge, and sucked the end of it into her mouth. She closed her eyes and rolled the ice cream between her cheeks. "Mmmmmmmm," she purred.

"Good?" Macklin asked.

She opened her eyes and nodded, the motion tipping her spoon. The remaining ice cream in her spoon spilled off inside her bathrobe.

Cheshire shrieked, dropping the spoon on the table.

"Shit!" she snapped, quickly untying her bathrobe.

Macklin saw the ice cream roll between her breasts, the chill raising goose bumps on her tan flesh and drawing her nipples into sharp points. He took her hand as she reached back for a towel.

He looked into her hazel eyes, stuck his free hand into the ice cream container, and clawed out a handful of chocolate. She tilted her head to one side and regarded him quizzically. Smiling, he smeared it deliberately over her left breast. She tossed her head back and gritted her teeth, drawing in a fast, deep breath.

Macklin's heart raced as he massaged a handful of ice cream over her other breast. Rivers of chocolate ran down her stomach and onto her panties. Leaning over, Macklin began to lick the ice cream off her breasts while one chocolate-covered hand massaged the warmth between her legs.

Cheshire moaned deeply, her nipples hard, pulsating points of chilly pleasure. Her icy ecstasy was invigorating, overpowering. She tore open his shirt, reached behind him, and plunged her hands into the carton, grabbing two handfuls of ice cream and rubbing it onto his back.

Macklin arched his back in reaction to the cold, pressing his wet, sticky lips into her neck and his hips against hers. She took his face into her hands and kissed him, her fingers entwined in his hair. Macklin eased down her panties, filled his hands with ice cream, and pressed the chocolate between her legs. She gasped in shock and pleasure, her mouth open in a wide smile.

"Goddamn, Brett Macklin!" she cried, her breaths coming hard and fast. She growled playfully, unbuckled his belt, and yanked down his pants. His erection strained against his bikini briefs. She took a handful of ice cream with one hand and pulled down the briefs with the other.

Macklin laughed. "Cheshire…"

"Yes?" She giggled mischievously and then wrapped her ice cream–filled hand around his stiff penis. Macklin choked back a scream. Cheshire laughed, dropped to her knees, and ran her tongue slowly up the shaft of his penis.

Macklin moaned and finger-painted her back with chocolate fingers. He'd never felt so hard.

She reached for more ice cream, knocking over the empty container. Macklin clasped Cheshire by the shoulders, pulled her up, and kissed her, wrapping his arms around her and drawing her tight against him. Pushing her back against the kitchen counter, he entered her. She wrapped her legs around his waist, her hands grabbing his ass.

They moved against each other slowly at first, but their eagerness took over and soon they were undulating quickly, sharply, streams of melting chocolate ice cream streaming down their heaving bodies.

They let out surprised, muffled shrieks as they came, shivering with chills of cold and pleasure.

Macklin tried to catch his breath, his cheek against Cheshire's breast. He could feel her heart pulsing. "Now, that's what I call a chocolate sundae." He grinned.

Cheshire threw back her head in a wild, satisfied laugh. "I love you, Brett, you sneaky little shit, I really do."

Macklin closed his eyes and felt something stiffen defensively inside him. He had the momentary impulse to walk away from her. Defying the urge, he suddenly lifted her up into his arms. She shrieked playfully. Laughing with more gaiety than he felt, he carried her upstairs to his bedroom, where they showered, dried each other off, and made love again under the heavy comforter. They drifted off to sleep, snug in the warmth afforded by each other's arms.

Cheshire woke up at 6 a.m., ravenously hungry, yearning for a big country breakfast. She slipped out of bed carefully, trying not to wake up Brett, and crept naked down the stairs into the kitchen.

She paused in the doorway to the kitchen and surveyed the mess, hugging herself and feeling goose bumps on her shoulders. The empty ice cream container lay on its side on the kitchen table. Dried rivers of melted ice cream ran down the wood cabinets and settled on the floor in brownish puddles. It looked like the aftermath of a precocious child's fun or a wild raccoon's scavenging.

She frowned, knowing Brett would find a way around helping to clean up the mess, and stepped toward the refrigerator. The cold floor shattered whatever remnants of sleep remained. She tiptoed hurriedly across the floor as if she were walking barefoot on an ice rink.

Shivering, she hunched in front of the refrigerator and pulled it open. A wave of cold air splashed against her and the bright light from inside stung her eyes.

Oh, so cold!

Being cold didn't feel so bad last night, did it?

Cheshire grinned nastily. *No, it didn't.* She peered into the refrigerator. She frowned again. The refrigerator looked like some kind of icy mausoleum. There were dozens of tiny aluminum – and plastic-wrapped bundles of indiscernible food lining the shelves like so many corpses. No eggs. No milk. No margarine.

If she wanted a country breakfast, she realized, it would have to be frozen pizza, leftover chicken, Schlitz beer, and some stale Grape-Nuts cereal. Damn! She wanted to surprise Brett with a big, rousing breakfast.

No, be honest. You just want to be a pig!

She closed the refrigerator and bounced on her feet, trying to stay warm while she considered her options. Cheshire wasn't about to let the sorry selection in the refrigerator ruin her plans.

Nope, she was going to have her country breakfast. At home. In bed. *Maybe,* she thought, *we can even play around a bit before I have to get my butt in gear and head to the hospital.*

Safeway is just three blocks away, she reminded herself. *Throw something on. Brett's sleeping like a baby. It will take a few sticks of dynamite to wake Brett up. Hurry. You can still have your country breakfast.*

Cheshire dashed up the stairs, slipped into a pair of faded jeans and a loose-fitting white sweatshirt, tucked her feet into a pair of sandals, and stole Brett's car keys and a few bucks off the dresser. She was down the stairs and out the door in twenty seconds.

The crisp, cold air slapped her as she dashed across the porch and through the front lawn, soaking her feet on the wet grass as she ran to the driveway between the rusted, decrepit Cadillacs that languished in the yard until Brett found the spare time to restore them.

Half-frozen beads of dew gave the black Cadillac in the driveway the icy look of an Eskimo Pie. Cheshire, anxious to get warm, quickly unlocked the door and got in. She slid the heater control to high. Cheshire wanted a warm blast as soon as possible.

She pumped the gas pedal, slipped the key into the ignition, and turned it.

The fiery explosion sent a hot wind crashing through Brett Macklin's bedroom window. Instinct tossed Macklin off the bed in the turbulent split second when the hellish roar rocked the house and blew a windstorm of glass shards sweeping through the room. Macklin, confused and twisted amidst the sheets on the floor, thought it was an earthquake.

He blinked open his eyes and sat up, still groggy from sleep and dazed by the sudden shudder that had tossed him out of bed. His thoughts, like the bedroom, were in utter disarray. Macklin propped himself up on the bed and, facing the window, saw the heavy brown smoke spiraling upwards outside and smelled something burning.

What the fuck happened?

Macklin ran to the window, oblivious to the broken glass slicing his feet, and looked down.

He saw a car door, charred and smoldering on the steaming lawn.

Cheshire…

Macklin whipped his head around. Cheshire wasn't in the room. Naked, he frantically bolted out of the room and raced down the stairs, flinging open the front door and jumping off the porch onto the grass. Rounding the corner of the house, he felt the burning heat of the blaze before he saw the bright yellow flames eating out the inside of the Batmobile.

Macklin ran toward the car but was pushed back by the searing heat. He could see the ravenous flames chewing into the vague, smoky outline of a person in the front seat.

He tried to scream her name, but his overwhelming feeling of hopeless frustration stole his breath. His lungs were being strangled by something strong and cold, something he had felt before only months ago.

Macklin closed his eyes and fell to his knees.

Forgive me, Cheshire, forgive me…

CHAPTER FIVE

Shaw had a sickly feeling of déjà vu as he stood watching the firefighters douse the smoking, gnarled remains of the Cadillac.

He relived a warm, still night in a poverty-stricken South Central Los Angeles neighborhood. The black detective remembered the gutted, smoldering remains of the RTD bus, the body bags in the street, the unrecognizable charred lump of sizzling flesh that had once been LAPD Officer JD Macklin.

The RTD bus had wound around the corner when Brett's father ran, aflame, across its path. The bus driver swerved to miss him. The bus roared into oncoming traffic, smashing into cars and bursting into flames that nearly reduced an entire city block to smoldering ash.

Brett Macklin had seen those flames, too. And from them, Mr. Jury was born.

Shaw, grimacing, turned away from the firefighters and approached Macklin, who sat on the porch steps in his maroon cotton bathrobe. Macklin stared coldly with glazed eyes at the wall of pajama-clad neighbors gawking at him on the sidewalk and listened to the steady streams of soot-blackened water rushing down the driveway and splashing into the gutter.

"Mack?" Shaw ventured softly. Macklin showed no sign of having heard him.

"Mack?" He repeated, shaking Macklin's shoulder. "Are you okay?"

Macklin's head shot up. "Am I okay? What kind of goddamn question is that?" His anger flared, lighting his eyes with rage and shattering his shocked lethargy. "Sure, Ronny, I'm just great. My lover was blown to bits in my driveway this morning. Am I okay? Sure, I've never felt better."

Macklin stood up, pushed Shaw roughly aside, and stormed toward the front door of the house.

Shaw made a move to follow him and Macklin whirled around, lashing out and striking Shaw in the chest with the palm of his hand.

"A year ago my life was ripped apart by a bunch of savages," Macklin yelled. "They set my father on fire, they poured gasoline on him and watched him burn. When they tossed that match on my father, they also set fire to my life." Macklin nodded toward the driveway. "I was beginning to think maybe, just maybe, I could become a normal human being again. Fuck, those savages won't let me."

Macklin, his face flushed with anger, poked Shaw hard in the chest with an accusing finger. "You won't let me."

Macklin yanked open the front door and slammed it shut behind him. Shaw sighed and stared at the closed door, torn between leaving and going inside. An old feeling, one of friendship and need, drew him toward the door, while a strong, new feeling of distance and repulsion pulled him away.

"Shit," Shaw muttered to himself. "I hate this job."

Shaw cautiously eased open the door and peered into the house. Macklin, pacing back and forth in the living room, froze for an instant when he saw Shaw and leveled a gaze ripe with violence at the black detective.

Shaw entered the house anyway, eyeing Macklin with the wary attention of a man who accidentally crosses a lion's path in the jungle. Shaw closed the door softly behind him and took a tentative step into the entry hall.

Macklin turned away and continued pacing, ignoring him. Shaw slipped his hands into his pants pockets and remained standing in place, feeling awkward and claustrophobic.

"I can't face my daughter anymore, not after what I've done." Macklin kept pacing, his gaze cast to the floor. Shaw could barely hear him. "I'm afraid the blood on my hands will smear her, that the horror will take her like it's taken everyone I've touched since Dad was killed. I love her more than anything in this world, and I can't hold her.

"It's a disease, a fucking disease!" Macklin yelled suddenly, startling Shaw. Macklin ripped a framed print from the wall over the mantelpiece and swung it like a bat against the opposite wall again and again, until he had shattered it to bits.

"Don't you see? The same disease that took my father is infecting me." Macklin advanced angrily on Shaw and grabbed him by the neck with both hands. Shaw fought to stay calm. "It eats away at me late at night. It pokes and prods me until I break out in a cold sweat and grit my teeth to hold back the screams."

Macklin shook him. "*I want to kill!* I want to cut these savages away like a tumor. Do you understand? There's a side of me that wants pure carnage, and goddamn it, you're feeding that. You and Stocker and the slime on the streets—you're pushing me into it, begging me to do it. I can't help myself. I want to even the scales, make it right again. I need to make it right again."

Macklin stared into Shaw's eyes and saw himself. Macklin saw his wild eyes, his sweat-dampened face, his cheeks red with fury, his jaw tight with rage.

Make them pay.

For the first time, Macklin saw the face behind the voice that had driven him to kill. The voice that was urging him to kill again.

Make them pay.

Macklin gently released Shaw and saw the reddish impressions his fingers left on Shaw's throat. Macklin took two steps back and held up his hands in a show of surrender.

Shaw hoarsely cleared his throat and took a deep breath, his hands still in his pockets.

"Last night she said she loved me," Macklin whispered. "For a minute I thought I could have it all again. Happiness. Peace. Someone to love. And in a split second it's gone. Up in flames. I can almost hear someone laughing at me."

Macklin stepped up to Shaw again and gently rested his hands on Shaw's shoulders. "I'm sorry, Ronny. It's just that... I don't want to lose anyone else. I know you can't accept who and what I am now. But try. This time you came to me—this time you asked me to do it. You're part of what I've become."

He drew Shaw close into a tight embrace. Shaw felt stiff, uninvolved, as if he were watching it all on television, but he wrapped his arms around Macklin anyway.

"I'll try to be a friend to you," Shaw whispered raspily. "But what you're doing is wrong. It's against everything I believe, everything your father believed. I can't turn my back to that."

Macklin leaned away from Shaw. "Ronny, you and I grew up together. We are brothers."

"That's what makes it so hard." Shaw shrugged off Macklin's arms and turned toward the door. "Remember what you said to Mayor Stocker about law and order, judicial review. Don't betray yourself by picking up a gun and playing vigilante again."

Shaw opened the door, stepped outside, and paused for a moment, his back to Macklin. Sunlight bathed Shaw and cast his shadow on Macklin.

"I'm sorry about Cheshire," Shaw said. "I want the people who did this as badly as you do." He pulled the door closed, shutting out the sunlight and leaving Macklin alone in the dim, smoky living room.

"No," Macklin said to the closed door. "No, you don't."

⚜ ⚜ ⚜

"*Judge for Yourself!*" the toothsome host yelled, a huge grin stretched across his face. "The show that puts you behind the bench and sentences you to prizes like ... *a brand-new car*!"

The studio shuddered with shrieks of glee and hundreds of clapping hands. The clatter sounded to Shaw, standing behind the window of the control booth to the rear of the audience, like a flock of deranged birds.

The stage curtain behind the host opened. Lights flashed. Buzzers rang. A buxom brunette drove a glossy silver Oldsmobile Cutlass across the stage, parking it in front of the massive judge's bench that dominated the set.

The cameras panned over the audience, zooming in on the clapping, cheering, screaming, hysterically happy women bobbing in their seats. The show's synthesizer-borne theme song blared over the speakers beside the flashing "APPLAUSE" signs above the stage.

The host swept his hand over the set behind him. "Now, meet our two contestants!" Two smaller judges' benches, one occupied by a woman with an overbite and the other by a black marine, appeared on either side of the set as if under the host's magical control.

Shaw shifted his weight uncomfortably. He didn't like being here. The emotional echo of his heated encounter with Macklin this morning was strong. Now here he was watching this. The contrast made him slightly dizzy. Or perhaps it was just the claustrophobic control room, the heavy cloud of cigarette smoke, the dreamlike glitz and blitz of the game show.

Or Shaw's fear. Coming here could be, he realized, the biggest mistake of his life.

"Okay, two, zoom in on Dirk," the director said into mouthpiece of his headset in a voice that sounded like it escaped from a throat filled with splintered wood. The camera-two TV monitor filled with the host's face.

"... just predict the judge's verdict on these real, small-claims cases and you win!" The perpetually grinning host sauntered behind his podium on the far side of the set. "And now, here's our judge, the Honorable Harlan Fitz!"

"Camera three, close on Fitz, cue the commercial," the director mumbled perfunctorily. These same shots, Shaw assumed, were called day in and day out.

Harlan Fitz appeared at the bench, in his traditional judge's attire, with what Shaw thought to be a tired grimace on his face. Fitz was a broad-shouldered, strong fifty-five-year-old man, and his face had aged well. Shaw noticed it hadn't fattened or sagged with time. A gray-brown mustache and beard gave him a scholarly look. Age showed itself only in the few lines across his brow, the puffy bags emerging under his eyes, and the slight recession of his hairline.

The *Judge for Yourself* theme music swelled as Fitz took his seat, and the audience clapped like performing seals ready to do tricks.

The host pointed at the camera. "Stay right there—the excitement begins right after this!"

"Okay, bring up the music. Camera one, pull back wide." The director raised his hand, his index finger extended. "Aaaaaand"—he whipped his arm down and jabbed the woman beside him—"roll commercial."

The commercial filled the screen. A good-looking woman, apparently a lawyer, ran through the courtroom, breezed through an executive board meeting, and whisked past the maître d' of a fine restaurant to a table.

"Gee, Mary, how do you stay so active?" her plain-looking harried female lunch companion asked, her voice dripping with absolute awe.

Mary reached into her purse. "New You–brand tampons!"

Shaw sighed, switching his attention from the monitor to the stage. Technicians scurried on the set like ants. Fitz sat stoically at his bench, staring blankly into the audience. Shaw felt a little sad. This wasn't the Harlan Fitz who had once been a feared judge and outspoken critic of the inadequacies of the law.

Shaw thought back to the Public Disorder Intelligence Division file on Fitz he had read after the meeting with Macklin in Stocker's office several days ago. The report attributed Fitz's retirement to political and personal pressures. It concluded that Fitz was overwhelmed by the futility of battling what he saw as the inadequacy of the law and became disheartened by the lack of cooperation from fellow judges. Exasperated and exhausted, he retired.

Fitz became a nomadic media personality, a frequent guest on radio and TV programs. According to the numerous newspaper clippings of interviews done with Fitz that Shaw read in the PDID file, Fitz thought he could educate the public, initiate change. The media exploited Fitz's outrage, Shaw believed, ignoring the man's insights and turning his vehement attacks on the legal system into entertainment.

Shaw studied Fitz now as the director signaled the cameramen that the commercial break was nearly over. Shaw thought Fitz looked lost. He prayed to God that he was reading Fitz right. That assumption was his long shot. Macklin—the city, for that matter—depended on that.

Yet once the commercial was over, Shaw watched Fitz come alive, whittling away what little confidence Shaw had in his all-important assumption.

Fitz played the game with wit and vigor, appearing both knowledgeable and authoritative. Even interested. That was no small feat. The contestants were argumentative morons with no concept of the law or, it seemed to Shaw, simple logic.

Once the next commercial break came, Shaw noticed the judge sag, the glow disappearing from his face. Unlike the toothy host, when the cameras went off, so did Fitz.

Maybe, Shaw thought, *just maybe there is some hope.*

After a few more cases were heard, Ms. Overbite broke the 0-to-0 deadlock with the black marine and won the game. Then came the "judge-off" for the car. She had to match Fitz's decision on a particular case. Shaw didn't hear the host read the question, but it had something to with premature ejaculation, mud wrestling, break dancing, and a set of broken skis.

Ms. Overbite closed her eyes and clutched the host. Her lip quivering, she announced her decision. She looked hopefully at Fitz. A prerecorded drum rolled. A hush fell on the audience. Fitz held up a gavel-shaped placard with his answer scrawled across in felt-tipped marker. Their decisions matched.

The woman screamed joyfully, jumping around the host like a hysterical kangaroo. As the audience went wild with applause, Shaw slipped out of the control room and into a narrow slate gray corridor. He shuffled toward a door a dozen footsteps away. Harlan Fitz's name, hastily handwritten in capital letters on a sheet of typing paper, was affixed to the door with yellow masking tape. As Shaw neared Fitz's door, his fear grew. He knew that Fitz had frequently—and publicly—chastised the ill-prepared prosecutors, careless cops, and sleazy lawyers who let criminals slip through the justice system unscathed. That's what had gotten the PDID interested in him. But Shaw also knew his proposal could just piss off Fitz even more. The judge could go to the press.

And then comes the end of the world.

Shaw turned the doorknob and stepped inside. He immediately felt cramped for breathing space. The windowless room seemed to him to be barely larger than his car. The lack of circulation gave the room the hot, oppressive quality of an oven recently used to cook a batch of Arrid Extra Dry. A white wood table and lightbulb-lined mirror claimed half the room, and two folding chairs were propped against the opposite wall.

He opened a chair and sat down, crossed his legs, and waited.

It will work out, Ronny.

Shaw laughed to himself. *Yeah, sure.*

He heard footsteps outside, and before he could brace himself, Fitz pushed open the door.

"I see you found my dressing room, Sergeant." Fitz grinned, dropping heavily into the folding chair opposite Shaw. Gone were the judge's robes. Fitz was in the sweat-dampened shirt and jeans he had worn under his robes, which he had rolled up into a ball and placed on his dressing table.

"What did you think of the show?" Fitz asked, slapping Shaw's knee.

"It was very entertaining," Shaw replied.

Fitz laughed. "Bullshit."

Shaw smiled awkwardly, not knowing whether to join in Fitz's laughter.

"You probably hated it more than I did," Fitz said. "Look, a guy has to make money. Maybe I'm educating someone out there, who knows?"

"Well, it educated me, if that means anything," Shaw replied. "It's the first time I've even been behind the scenes, so to speak, of a TV show. I'm impressed."

"Thank you. You're very kind, Sergeant." Fitz's smile waned. "So why exactly do you want to talk with me?"

Shaw shifted uneasily in his seat. "Well, that isn't easy." He dropped his gaze and pondered his feet. Unable to think of an easy way to approach it, Shaw opted for the bottom line. "What do you know about Mr. Jury?"

"I know he's a vigilante who has killed half a dozen people."

"That's all?" Shaw asked, chancing to look at Fitz. The judge frowned.

"What more do you want, Sergeant? The guy is running around doing what most of us would like to do."

"Would you call it a sort of justifiable homicide?" The remark didn't come from Shaw but from the script Shaw chose to perform. It was as if he was part of an undercover operation, playing a role. Nothing, to him, could ever be said to justify Macklin's actions.

"Just what are you getting at, Sergeant? I just got done playing the only game I want to for today." Fitz folded his arms across his chest and pinned Shaw under a stern gaze.

"What if I were to tell you Mr. Jury is interested in introducing some due process into his vigilante justice?"

"I'd say it's still vigilante justice," Fitz replied. He stared into Shaw's eyes, trying to see something there. Shaw wanted to get up and run.

"And I'd say it seems Mr. Jury is a better man than I thought," Fitz said slowly. His eyes narrowed. "Am I talking to Mr. Jury?"

"No," Shaw responded quickly. Too quickly, he thought.

"All right, Sergeant," Harlan Fitz groaned testily. "Let's quit the sparring. Make your point."

"What would you say if Mr. Jury wanted you to be that due process, to evaluate evidence and determine who, within the scope of the law, is guilty and innocent?" Shaw's throat felt raw, stone dry.

Fitz's stare didn't waver. The silence in the room was a crushing weight on Shaw's shoulders that grew heavier with each hourlong moment.

"I'd say my phone number is in the book."

CHAPTER SIX

That next afternoon Mother Nature got angry. She blew the rain clouds away with fierce, gale-force winds that blasted through the city, ripping trees out of the ground, tearing off roofs, severing power lines, and smashing in plate-glass windows.

People on the street, who were still recovering from five days of pounding rain, were caught by surprise and were tossed around like leaves by their wind-opened umbrellas. Tourists must have thought they were watching a sadistic *Mary Poppins* sequel in the making.

The merciless weather, along with a merciless editor, kept Jessica Mordente away from her desk at the *Los Angeles Times* and out on the street for most of the day. Her Thomas Brothers street map was her bible as she raced around the city interviewing the victims of Mother Nature's wrath.

She talked to an irate starlet in Beverly Hills whose pink Rolls-Royce was crushed by a tree. Then Mordente sped west to the Santa Monica Pier, where the wind had kicked one of the city's notorious vagrants into the sea. After two more hours of on-the-spot reporting, Mordente shoved her three full reporter's notebooks into her purse and headed downtown for the Times building.

Mordente remained in front of her computer terminal for the rest of the afternoon, piecing together a story from her notes and frequent telephone interviews. It was nearly 7 p.m. before she was able to switch off her screen, relax, and grab a bite to eat. She left the newsroom and wearily trudged down the hallway to the elevator, taking the jolting ride to the cafeteria.

Her stomach growled, Get me food!, all the way up to the tenth floor. She strode into the cafeteria, bypassed the salad bar, and zeroed in on the grill. The gangly Mexican cook, dwarfed by a white hat resembling a mushroom cloud, greeted her with a cheerful grin.

Mordente placed her order hurriedly in Spanish, asking him for two grilled turkey and cheese sandwiches. While he prepared her sandwiches, she whirled around the circular buffet, snatching a handful of chocolate chip cookies, a bag of Doritos, and a tall paper cup full of black coffee.

She took her sandwiches with a thankful smile, rushed through the cashier's line, and settled down to eat at a table by a window. The moment her rear end touched the seat and her nose took in the aroma of the hot food, she could feel herself beginning to unwind. Outside, she could see the red numbers on the Times building clock glowing against the dark backdrop of the Civic Center buildings. Today, she realized, had felt like a week.

Her stomach took control of her body now, ordering her to grab a sandwich and wolf it down in six hungry bites. She did. Mordente had learned long ago how to handle her body. She knew she could occasionally put her stomach on hold for an entire day, but when the food was on the table, she had to let her stomach call the shots. That was the deal she had struck with her stomach. She understood her body and had worked out agreements with her bowels, hair, bladder, teeth, uterus, and, most important, her lower back.

The quick consumption of sandwich number one had taken the edge off her hunger, and her stomach allowed her to approach the rest of the meal in a more relaxed manner. Sipping her coffee, which was so hot it nearly scalded her tongue, she folded open the paper to the Metro section.

She scanned the narrow story running down the first column about the robbery of another bank by a gang who hid their faces with rubber Halloween masks. This bank was robbed, it seemed, by Yoda, Jimmy Carter, and a werewolf. She glanced at a feature photo of an elderly woman in a wheelchair rolling down the street, a duck on a leash following along.

Midpage, just under the fold, she found her lengthy roundup of southland wind damage. She read it with a sense of mild achievement and a renewed feeling of fatigue.

She was about ready to follow the story to the jump when she saw the tiny boxed article below hers. It was just a glorified filler, so unimportant that no by-line was attributed to it, but she looked at it anyway. Sometimes these short stories were interesting.

> VENICE—A Hollywood nurse was killed Wednesday morning by an exploding bomb rigged to the ignition system of her boyfriend's car.
>
> Cheshire Davis, 32, was leaving the home of 35-year-old Brett Macklin at about 6 a.m. when the blast occurred. Police say she triggered the bomb when she tried to start his car, a vintage 1959 Cadillac.
>
> The blaze resulting from the explosion was quickly contained by firefighters before it could do more than superficial damage to Macklin's home.
>
> A police spokesman said there is no apparent motive for the bombing and, refusing to venture an explanation of any kind, noted an investigation is under way. Macklin is owner and operator of Blue Yonder Airways in Santa Monica and has no history, according to police sources, of any "criminal associations."
>
> The early morning blast jolted residents living as far as two miles away from Macklin's home, police say.

Mordente felt that annoying tingle between her shoulder blades that told her there was something more to the story than she caught at first glance.

She read the story again. *So maybe one of 'em had a jilted lover that tried to get even.* The tingle didn't fade. Mordente gave the story a third goingover, wondering what it was about the article that nagged at her.

Then it hit her. That name... Macklin... she had heard it somewhere before. She got up, her hunger forgotten, and dashed down the stairwell to the Times morgue.

The smoke from the fire was trapped in Brett Macklin's house. It clung to the walls, his body, the furniture. Everything he ate or drank in the house tasted charred.

He spent the morning moving aimlessly through the house, trying to hide from it. But the smell was everywhere. And so was Cheshire. Everywhere he turned he was confronted by her presence—the houseplants Cheshire had brought over and nurtured; the dish towels she had made while they watched old movies on TV together; her makeup scattered on the bathroom countertop; her comforter, covered with broken glass, in a heap on the bed.

Macklin felt smothered, on the verge of screaming. Death was everywhere, closing in on him. Yet he couldn't leave the house. Something kept him there. He picked up the glass, shard by shard, from the bedroom and made the bed. He got down on his hands and knees and scrubbed the chocolate ice cream off the kitchen floor. He cleaned the house like a robot, unthinking, performing the tasks as if controlled by some irreversible computer program.

By late afternoon, there was nothing else to clean, nowhere to hide. He was forced to feel. He felt the coldness gradually sweep over him, numbing the dull ache of sadness as it had months before.

He paced in the living room. The coldness inside him was melting under the searing heat of a new emotion. It scorched through him, fed by his sadness. It flushed his skin, tightened his face muscles, and quickened his heartbeat.

His depression was gone, beaten. A familiar voice spoke to him again.

Make them pay.

Macklin rebounded, snapping out of his depressed lethargy. He called up a local rent-a-car place and had them deliver a full-size Chevrolet Impala. He took the Glad bag filled with Saputo's trash, put it in the trunk, and drove to Kmart, where he bought a pair of plastic gloves to examine the typewriter ribbons.

While Mother Nature drop-kicked transients into the Pacific Ocean, crushed European luxury cars, and swatted homes off the Hollywood hills, Macklin was sitting alone in the cavernous Blue Yonder hangar at the Santa Monica Airport, wading through Saputo's trash.

First, he studied everything that had been typed on the ribbons by reading them backward, following the three lines of letters in a W-shaped trail and jotting them down on a legal pad.

The ribbon contained memos to kiddie-porn distributors that promised new films within several weeks and a regular production schedule. Also, Macklin read through sales copy for the kiddie-porn films and products:

"... *Kiddie Call Girls*, *Moppet Cock Suckers*, and *Cuddly Clit* offer the demanding man hot child sexuality at its erotic best..."

"... lifelike Latex blow-up dolls with warm vaginas and budding tits that make them the best lay imaginable ... whenever you want it!"

"... they're young, they're wet, they're 200 glossy black-and-white pictures of the horniest sweet candy *ever*..."

Macklin stared down at the legal pad, then glanced at the remaining stacks of papers, photos, and film. Bile, hot and acidic, bubbled up in his throat. He dashed to the bathroom, leaned over the toilet, and vomited in deep, aching heaves that left him light-headed and shaky kneed.

Bracing himself against the sink, he straightened up and flushed the toilet. He felt as if he had puked up everything except his heart and lungs. He turned on the faucet, cupped his hands under the cool water, and splashed his face a few times. Then, his face damp, he meekly ventured a look at himself in the mirror.

His skin was chalk white. The only tinge of color came from the dark circles that underscored his eyes and gave them a sunken, empty look. Macklin splashed his face again, as if he could wash the face he saw in the mirror off his own.

Dabbing his face dry with a rough paper towel, Macklin shuffled back into the hangar and decided to forget the piles of paper for a while and see what the film strips had to offer. *Best to do it on an empty stomach,* he thought. *All I can do is gag.*

He sat down on a stool and fed the torn strips of celluloid, which he presumed were outtakes, rejects, and damaged film, through his tiny Super 8 viewer. The same viewer he had used to edit home movies he shot of Cory. Brooke nursing Cory at the hospital. Cory walking for the first time. His father playing with Cory. Cory nearly hidden under JD Macklin's LAPD hat. Cory's seventh birthday party at Disneyland.

He spent the next two hours in front of the viewer. Most of the film was outtake footage for a good reason. The endless yards of blurry, indiscernible shots and scratched film had made Macklin's eyes stinging red. Macklin yawned, tired of the vague shapes, overexposed film, and lingering shots of genitalia.

Macklin wearily fed another three-foot-long strip of film quickly through the editor. Something bright flashed for a split second on the tiny screen, catching his attention. He pulled the strip backward, careful not to rip the sprockets on the feed. Another bright flash amidst the blur of frames. Macklin brought the film through again slowly and stopped at the bright frame.

The shot was hazy, but in comparison to the rest of the film, it was Oscar-winning cinematography. A young girl, perhaps ten years old, sat on a stool, her legs crossed, at the edge of a movie set. It must be a wild shot, Macklin thought, taken accidently and not part of their movie. Lights and rafters, as well as several people, could be made out in the background.

She looked serene, calm.

Not like she would be, Macklin thought. Not swollen and green, naked and covered in mud. Not rotting beside a rain-swelled canal.

Macklin clicked off the viewer. *Not dead.*

A loud rapping at the hangar door startled him. Macklin, tearing the frame from the strip and putting it in his shirt pocket, quickly swept everything on the table into the Glad bag.

The knocking became irritated and persistent.

"Hang on!" Macklin yelled as he dragged the bag along the floor into his darkened office. He closed the office door and sprinted across the hangar. Macklin took a deep breath and opened the door.

A gust of cold wind blew into the hangar. Standing against the night, under a narrow cone of light cast by a dirty bulb above the door, was a dark-skinned woman in khaki pants, a white woven silk blazer, and a brown blouse.

She looked at him with curious green eyes that sparkled like olivine stones. "Brett Macklin?"

"Yes?"

"My name is Jessica Mordente," she said politely. "I'm with the *Los Angeles Times*."

A fucking reporter, Macklin thought, *a vulture.*

"I've got a subscription," Macklin said curtly, closing the door. She jammed her foot in the way, forcing the door open a crack.

"Good. Then you'll see the story that exposes Mr. Jury."

Macklin's stomach muscles tightened defensively as if he were preparing to ward off a blow. "Move your foot, lady, or you're going to lose it." Macklin stared into her eyes and felt a tremor of nervousness at the determination he saw there. A sense of apprehension squeezed him, viselike. He'd be damned, though, if he'd give up any ground. "I'm in no mood for journalistic bullshit."

"Come now, Mr. Macklin, couldn't we talk for just a moment?" she said with exaggerated care, as if talking to a temperamental child. It made Macklin want to throttle her. "Aren't you even a little interested in Mr. Jury?"

"Not the slightest."

Mordente shook her head and spoke evenly. "I think you are, Mr. Macklin. Very much." She met his scornful gaze. "Mr. Jury's first victims were the men suspected of killing your father. Interesting, huh?"

"He made a good choice."

"Now someone has planted a bomb in your car and killed your girlfriend." She saw Macklin's face harden. "I think Mr. Jury is going to strike again, real soon."

"And I think you're about to acquire a permanent limp."

Mordente laughed coyly. "Well, Mr. Macklin, a polite good night to you, too." She turned her back to him and walked away, waving her hand at him. "See you around."

Macklin slammed the door shut and fell back against it. His heart raced. The world was closing in on him again. Harder this time. Macklin took several deep breaths, exhaling them slowly, trying to calm himself. *I don't care if they find out who I am, what I am.*

Then why are you so rattled, Macky boy? Macklin pulled the piece of film out of his pocket and studied it.

Because I don't want anyone to stop me until I've evened the score.

CHAPTER SEVEN

Erica Tandy stretched her legs out as far as they could go and tried to touch the darkish cloud with her toes. She almost made it, but the swing resisted at the height of its climb. The swing fell back and she tucked her legs, trying to grab the air and pin it between her calves and the underside of her thighs.

It was Friday, the second clear day after so many rainy days when she couldn't come out and play. She had the whole muddy park to herself. It was chilly, but the crisp wind cooled the perspiration, prompted by her energetic swinging, that she could feel on her back.

As she swung backward over the ground, she looked down at the big hole in the dirt, carved out by the dozens of kids who dragged their feet as they rode the swing. It was brimming over with dirty water, so she bent her legs closer to her to prevent her toes from skimming the puddle.

The swing carried Erica back, high up into the air again. The swing froze for a split second and then fell forward. She extended her legs, tightened her grip on the chain and felt the swing race downward and begin its climb toward the sky.

It stopped with jolt that flung her face forward toward the dirt. She grasped the chains tightly, holding herself in the swing. Angrily, she whipped her head around to see what had so suddenly halted her skyward arc.

Erica saw a man standing behind her, holding the chain above her hands. At first she was scared because he looked like that awful man called Mr. Dark she had seen in that spooky movie on HBO. She remembered Mr. Dark had these pictures of kids on his palms and would squeeze his hands real hard until blood dripped out of his fists. "Hi there," the man said, smiling warmly. He brought the swing down to him slowly. She kept her eyes on his. She didn't like his thin eyes at all. They were too far into his head, as if they were trying to hide from her or something. "Your mom told me I'd find you here."

"Why?" she asked, stepping shakily off the swing. The man glided around in front of her. She became powerfully aware of the enormity of the park and the absence of any other children. It made her chilly, even though the red sweater Nana had made her for Christmas should have kept her warm.

"Because she has a special lunch planned." He put his hand on her shoulder. His black gloved hand felt heavy, like a iron clasp. "A party."

"A party?" she asked shyly. She felt him guide her away from the swing set toward the street.

"With cookies and cake." He walked up beside her, his hand firmly grasping her shoulder. "A surprise party for ..." He let his voice trail off.

"For Daddy?" She eagerly filled the conversational lapse.

"Yes," he agreed in a praising tone. "For your father."

The fear, like a cloud that had obscured the sun, floated away and she felt warm again. Surprising Dad would be fun! The stranger's eyes didn't look so bad now. Instead of Mr. Dark, he was beginning to look like Rick Springfield, though she had never seen Rick dressed like this, with a big scarf and overcoat.

"You have a van just like my uncle's," she said. He reached past her and opened the van's passenger door.

"He helped me pick it out." Tice smiled. She climbed in, and he closed the door behind her.

⚜ ⚜ ⚜

Shaw stood very still in the center of Macklin's living room, holding a magnifying glass over his eye with one hand and a strip of movie film up to the light with the other.

"It's Orlock," Shaw whispered.

Macklin barely heard him. "What did you say?"

"In the background, behind the girl." Shaw lowered his arms and faced Macklin. "Crocker Orlock is standing there."

"Great." Macklin clapped Shaw on the back. "Nail the son of a bitch, then give me a few seconds alone with him and I'll find out who killed Cheshire."

"Hold on, Mack." Shaw held the film out to Macklin. "We can't get him yet."

"Why the hell not?" Macklin shouted into Shaw's face. "What more do you need? It's all there on the film. For God's sake, Ronny, you've got Orlock with a kidnapped girl who turned up dead."

Shaw tossed the magnifying glass on the couch and ran his hand through his hair. "Mack, this film is virtually useless. It doesn't prove a thing."

"Ronny, are you out of your mind? What's the matter with you?" Macklin yanked the film from Shaw's hand and waved it in front of the detective's face. "Look at this closely. It links Orlock with everything. Murder. Kiddie porn. Do I have to gift wrap him and drop him off at police headquarters for you?"

Shaw jabbed the film with his index finger. "You're gonna have to do better than that. It won't stand up in court. For starters, it's illegally obtained evidence—"

"So say it was given to you by an anonymous Good Samaritan," Macklin interrupted impatiently, a scowl of frustration on his face.

"Number two," Shaw continued, ignoring Macklin's remark, "we can't positively identify Orlock. The more we blow it up, the blurrier it will get. His attorney can talk a jury out of this with ease."

"You know it's Orlock! You recognized him!" Macklin yelled.

"Yeah, so what! Grow up, Mack. Truth can be disproved by a good lawyer living off a fat retainer." Shaw sighed. "Thirdly, even if we can convince the jury it's Orlock, we can't prove he kidnapped her. Look, what the film does prove is that Crocker is dirty."

"You knew that already, Ronny."

"But now I *know* that."

Macklin fell back wearily against the wall and slid down into a sitting position on the floor facing Shaw, who stood in front of the fireplace. "Okay, did you get anything from the list of plates I gave you?"

"Yeah, that paid off. The warehouse is owned by Orlock through a maze of dummy companies and leased to Saputo by an independent, legitimate rental agency. The van also belongs to Orlock, as does the Seville you saw Saputo driving."

Macklin looked up at Shaw and spoke very carefully. "I think it's time Mr. Jury takes care of it."

"Really?" Shaw smirked. "Remember your grandiose speech about due process?"

Macklin nodded.

"Does it still hold, or do you run out of here now, guns blazing?"

Macklin stared silently at Shaw for a full minute. "It still holds."

"Good." Shaw pulled a slip of paper out of his pocket and tossed it into Macklin's lap. "He's expecting you."

Shaw went to the front door and walked out.

Macklin glanced at the crumpled paper in his lap and picked it up. He unfolded it slowly and read it twice.

Harlan Fitz. 555-9182.

⚜ ⚜ ⚜

Whenever life got complicated, Harlan Fitz sought refuge in the Greasy Spoon, where club sandwiches start at $6.50 and chocolate ice cream is white.

The bookcase-lined walls made him feel like he was back in his judge's chambers, and the aroma of cooking food gave the popular Century City restaurant a warm, homey quality that he found relaxing.

The Greasy Spoon was nestled between what Fitz would have called two twenty-story stereo speakers; the dressed-for-success executives knew them as the Twin Towers, two silver monoliths rising above the exclusive cluster of office buildings just outside Beverly Hills.

Fitz sat at his favorite table, tucked into a shadowy corner in the back, and nursed a Bloody Mary while watching the ebb and flow of the Friday noontime crowd. He could hear the rumble of the Santa Anas sweeping through the city, which had been lulled into complacency by a deceptively calm morning.

The usually trim, slim, and prim Century City executives emerged at noon like preprogrammed robots from their high-rent, high-rise offices and marched into the Greasy Spoon looking mop topped and harried. Fitz noticed that even actor Peter Graves, huddled amongst the crowd awaiting tables, appeared disheveled. Having seen *Mission Impossible*, Fitz knew how rare that was.

Fitz ordered a second drink and glanced nervously at his watch. He was watching for the mysterious vigilante to show up and half hoping the man wouldn't. He didn't kid himself. Just agreeing to meet with Mr. Jury and not going to the police made him an accomplice. Then again, if Shaw was any indication, the LAPD wouldn't give a damn anyway.

He buttered a pencil-thin breadstick and noticed, uneasily, that his hand was shaking just a bit. Fitz couldn't decide whether what he felt was fear or excitement.

Macklin sat at the bar, as he had for the last two hours, watching Fitz across the room and glancing at faces, hunting for anyone who might be a cop or reporter waiting to snare Mr. Jury in a nice trap.

When Macklin spotted Peter Graves, he almost bolted out of the restaurant. For a split second fiction became reality for him and he thought the Mission Impossible team had come to get him.

Shit, Macky boy, take it easy. Macklin swallowed the remainder of his beer, slid off his bar stool, and headed toward Fitz's table, a manila envelope under his arm.

Macklin neared the round table. "Excuse me, are you Judge Fitz?"

Fitz's head shot up quickly, the voice startling him. He studied the approaching man and found himself squinting back at the blue eyes that were unabashedly sizing him up.

"Yes," Fitz replied, recovering his composure, and motioned to the seat in front of him, "You must be"—Fitz cut himself off and shrugged—"the mystery man."

Macklin's stony expression was broken by an ironic grin. He folded his six-foot frame into the padded wicker chair and offered Fitz his hand as he sat down. "My name's Brett Macklin."

Fitz straightened up in his seat and shook Macklin's hand. Macklin's grip was strong and firm, giving Fitz the impression that Macklin was a man who was self-assured and aggressive, a fighter. Or, Fitz wondered, am I just reaffirming my preconceived notions?

"You must be as nervous as I am, Mr. Macklin."

Macklin nodded, setting the envelope in his lap. "More."

"Have any trouble finding me?"

"Not at all. You said look for the darkest corner of the restaurant and you'd be in it." Macklin shrugged. "You were right. Besides, I caught a few minutes of your show on TV before I came."

A freckled, pale-skinned waitress, her ample girth bound by a nannyish black apron, came to the table.

"I see your friend has arrived, Judge. Are you ready to order?"

"I'll have another Bloody Mary, thanks," Fitz replied.

"Scotch on the rocks," Macklin said. The waitress nodded at them both and bustled toward the bar.

Fitz leaned back in his seat, watching the waitress go, and chuckled. "Why did I expect you to ask for the drink in a dirty glass?"

Macklin shifted uneasily in his seat. "I didn't come here to trade one-liners with you. This isn't easy for me."

Fitz was about to speak when the waitress appeared again, giving them their drinks. The judge took a sip of his drink and then stirred it with his swizzle stick.

"Mr. Macklin, are you at all familiar with California history?"

"Slightly," Macklin said wearily, lifting his glass to his lips.

"In the mid-eighteen hundreds, San Francisco was being eaten alive by crime. The police, the courts, the city government, they were all thoroughly infected by corruption and did nothing. The citizenry took to the streets themselves, hunting down criminals, conducting trials, and then strictly punishing the offenders." Fitz took another sip of his drink and regarded Macklin solemnly. "Popular opinion then, and now, is quite supportive of those vigilantes. An opinion leader of the era, a seaman-turned-lawyer named Richard Henry Dana, said the vigilantes rescued the city, restoring morality and good government."

Fitz smiled, meeting Macklin's gaze. "He said the vigilantes were"—his voice took on a high, melodramatic tone as he quoted from memory—"'the last resort of the thinking and the good, taken to only when vice, fraud and ruffianism have entrenched themselves behind the forms of law, suffrage and ballot, and there is no hope but in organized force whose action must be instant and thorough.'"

Macklin saw the judge's hand tighten into a fist on the table. "Mr. Macklin, I believe that same environment, that same laxity of the law, exists today. It sickens me. And until now I've felt helpless to stop it. Your desire for due process proves what I suspected before, that you aren't a murderer, but a man of principle trying to restore order."

Macklin looked around the room, afraid someone might have overheard. None of the patrons seemed to be paying any attention to them. "Can we take a walk? I really don't feel comfortable talking here."

Fitz laughed self-consciously. "Of course. Forgive me. I wanted to at least meet here, on familiar ground, where I could feel comfortable. This was the only place I could think of besides home, and that's always out. I never bring work home. That is my sanctuary. I will not let it be touched by matters like this."

Macklin nodded somberly. His home could never be a sanctuary, not now. Every facet of his life had been irrevocably touched by the disease that took his father first, then Cheshire. Slowly but surely, he knew, it was infecting him as well.

They left the restaurant and were struck by a strong gust of wind that whipped up their hair as they made their way to the escalator. They didn't talk as they rode it down to the second floor of the parking garage.

Macklin breathed through his mouth. The garage was thick with car exhaust fumes trapped inside the structure by the raging winds. Their footsteps echoed through the dark garage as they walked silently between aisles of parked cars to Fitz's metallic blue two-door '79 Buick Regal. Fitz unlocked the passenger door, motioned Macklin inside, and then walked around and got in as well.

"There, now we have some privacy." Fitz put his key in the ignition, twisted it to the alternator setting, and then turned on the stereo. Classical music played softly over the speakers. "First, I need to know a little more about you. How did you become a vigilante?"

Macklin told his story, beginning with his father's death and ending with his surveillance of Wesley Saputo, glossing over Cheshire's murder without knowing why. He kept the encounter with Mordente to himself, as he had with Shaw. He thought it was pointless to scare either of them.

"I see," Fitz said quietly. "What kind of material evidence have you collected?"

Macklin handed Fitz the envelope. "These memos and a strip of film that shows Orlock with a child the police later found raped and strangled."

Fitz lifted the flap and thumbed through the items in the envelope, his face hardening.

When the judge got to the film strip and held it up to the interior light, Macklin spoke up. "Shaw tells me he can make out Crocker Orlock in the background. He says that isn't enough to prove Orlock's complicity."

Fitz grunted. "He's right, I'm afraid. I need more evidence that ties Orlock directly to the films and thereby the murders." He returned the envelope to Macklin. "The problem is all the evidence against Orlock will be circumstantial. To make up for that, I need a preponderance of evidence to feel comfortable finding guilt."

"You want more evidence." Macklin opened the car door. "I'll get it. What about Saputo?"

"He should never have been released from jail," Fitz responded, staring out the windshield at the rows of parked cars. "Your evidence, coupled with what Sergeant Shaw told me, leaves no doubt in my mind that Saputo is back in business. In time, it might be possible to gather evidence that can be used in a courtroom, but even then I don't know if a conviction could be secured or if he'd even remain behind bars."

Fitz started the engine and then glanced at Macklin. "So shut the bastard down."

CHAPTER EIGHT

Richard Nixon and Darth Vader held Uzis and stood in the bed of the pickup truck E.T. had just driven through the bank's plate-glass window.

"Everyone facedown on the floor," Nixon yelled over the shrill alarm. "If I see anyone's face, I'll blow it off."

The nine lunch-hour customers and the dozen bank employees didn't argue with the three men in the rubber masks. Everyone in the convex, window-walled bank lobby dropped to their knees and flattened themselves on the glass-strewn floor.

E.T. left the truck's engine running and bolted from the cab. He vaulted over the bank counter and moved quickly to each teller's window, stuffing handfuls of money into a large gunnysack.

Darth Vader, standing in the truck's bed with Nixon, caught a movement on the floor. An old lady was raising her head. "Get down!" he barked.

"I can't," she whined, looking up. "There's a sharp piece of glass tha—"

Vader squeezed the trigger of his Uzi. Her body stuttered back along the floor as bullets bit into her head and spit out blood. Fearful screams from the panicked employees and customers joined the frenzied wail of the alarm.

"Goddamn it, why did you do that?" Nixon shouted. "C'mon, we've got enough cash, let's get out of here!"

"I don't believe I saw you boys sign a withdrawal slip." A voice behind the three robbers stopped them cold. They turned and saw Brett Macklin standing in the doorway, the .357 Magnum at his side.

Macklin caught a jerk in E.T.'s gun arm, crouched, and spun on his heels, firing twice. The slugs punched into E.T.'s stomach, lifting him up and tossing him back into a row of desks.

Macklin then threw himself sideways as Nixon raked the doorway with retaliatory gunfire. The bullets chased Macklin, shattering the glass above his head as he scrambled behind the bank counter. The customers quivered on the floor, the staccato beat of gunfire echoing in their ears.

Vader climbed into the driver's seat of the truck, shifted it into drive, and pressed the accelerator to the floor. The truck shot forward, knocking Nixon off balance. Macklin popped up behind the counter and fired.

The bullets slapped Nixon off the moving truck and sent him toppling backward into a potted palm. Macklin strode from behind the counter just as the truck smashed through the plate-glass window on the opposite end of the bank. Raising his gun arm, Macklin looked down the length of his barrel at the truck screeching madly south on Century Park East. And then he squeezed the trigger.

The truck burst apart in a red-orange thunderclap of flame, gnarled metal and glass shards streaking through the air. Macklin shoved the gun under his waistband, pulled his leather jacket over it, and rushed out of the bank just as it erupted into chaos, the frightened people on the floor clambering to their feet.

He dashed onto the sidewalk and trotted up the street against the current of Century City businessmen charging to the bank. His heart was racing and his body was drenched in sweat.

It had all happened so fast. He was driving out of the parking garage across the street when he spotted the robbery taking place. He screeched to a stop a few yards from the bank, grabbed his Magnum, and ran inside.

His only regret now was that he had arrived too late to save the elderly woman. Macklin got into his car, which he had left double-parked and still running, and sped away from the bank, glancing in his rearview mirror at the blazing truck and the growing crowd of people in his wake.

Macklin steered the Impala into the left-turn lane onto the westbound stretch of Santa Monica Boulevard. At the same moment three police cars, sirens blaring, skidded behind him onto Century Park East and raced to the bank. Breathing deeply with relief, Macklin pulled the gun out of his waistband, tossed it into the glove box, and slammed it shut.

Jessica Mordente swung her legs over the yellow tape marked "DO NOT ENTER" that surrounded the bank and stepped carefully through the shattered window.

Broken glass crunched under her heels as she strolled across the lobby, listening to the rumble of voices that filled the bank. Flashbulbs on LAPD cameras spit light into various corners of the glass-walled lobby. Uniformed officers and detectives were scattered about in huddles, interviewing the bank employees and customers. To Mordente's left, beyond the teller's counter, she saw men in white lift a black body bag onto a stretcher.

She carefully stepped around the blood-specked chalk outline of a body drawn on the floor and headed toward a familiar face. FBI Special Agent Chet Navarro stood at the other end of the room, half-turned toward the street, where firefighters hosed down the steaming, blackened remains of the pickup truck.

Mordente admired Navarro's lean physique, well displayed in a tailored gray suit. Her eyes lingered on his firm, strong legs and followed them up to his tight, round buttocks, nicely hugged by pleated slacks. She remembered how soft that fine ass felt squeezed in her hands.

She pressed her hand against the small of his back. "How's my favorite Fed?"

Navarro turned, surprised. "Jessie, how did you get in here?"

She smiled. "Does it matter?" Glancing past him, she could see the bank camera mounted high on a pillar.

"No," he said, slipping his arm around her shoulder and steering her outside. "I haven't seen you for quite a while."

"Can you believe this place?" she asked. They walked through the broken window onto the sidewalk. "It looks like a small war took place here."

"A small war *did*," Navarro replied, unbuttoning his collar and loosening his tie with his free hand. They followed the black skid marks left by the truck to the street. "Some Good Samaritan blew the fuck out of the rubber-mask gang. So now you can take your life savings out of your mattress and put it in the bank again."

"Anyone see this Good Samaritan?" she asked.

"No, everyone was lying facedown on the floor."

She stopped and stared into his amber eyes. "What about the bank camera?"

"What about it? You know, I've missed you, Jessie." He put his hands in his pockets and looked around self-consciously. "You're impossible to reach."

She stepped closer so that he could feel her breath on him. "I've missed you too, Chet. Maybe we could get together. Tell me, do you think you got a picture of the mystery man?"

"I don't know."

"I'd like to see it," she said softly.

"Jessie." He started walking toward the street again, stopping at the barrier of yellow tape. "You know I can't let you print the photo unless the Bureau clears it first."

She caught up with him. "Who said anything about printing it? I just want to see it."

Navarro frowned, swung his legs over the yellow tape, and held out his hand to help Mordente over. "I don't think so. I could get in a lot of trouble, Jessie."

She took his hand and climbed over the tape. "I don't want you to get in any trouble," she said, squeezing his hand reassuringly. "But I would like to see the photo. And I'd like to see you, too. It's been a long time, hasn't it, Chet?"

"How about dinner?" he asked tentatively.

"Sure, we can have dinner at my place." She patted him gently on the side and walked away. "I'll give you a call to see how your investigation is going."

As she walked to her Mazda RX-7, she felt Navarro's eyes on her. It made her feel attractive. And powerful. She knew she'd get that photo somehow, and she had a strong hunch about the face she'd see staring back at her from it.

"Orlock residence, who's calling please?" The voice sounded to Brett Macklin like an eerie cross between Jack Palance and Charles Bronson.

"John Smith," Macklin replied sarcastically. "Give me Orlock."

"I'm sorry, he's busy right now," the man said politely, then, more sternly, "I'll take a message."

It was a command, not a considerate offer.

"Take this down, buddy. Tell Orlock to get on the phone or his kid-porn operation will be on the front page of tomorrow's *Times.*"

"It's all right, Tice," another voice intruded on the line. "I'll deal with the gentleman." Macklin heard a click as Tice hung up his extension. "All right, Mr.... ah... Smith, what can I do for you?"

"Listen, that's what. You and I are about to become partners in the candy business."

"I'm not in the candy business, Mr. Smith."

"Don't screw around with me, Orlock. I'd just as soon step on you as deal with you, but the eastern interests I represent don't share my opinion of you."

Orlock laughed. "C'mon, Mr. Smith, this is ridiculous. I'm a very busy man, with no time for poor James Cagney impersonations. Just who are you and what are you talking about?"

"Let's meet and discuss that."

Orlock sighed. "Good-bye, Mr. Smi—"

"I'm looking at this photograph of you," Macklin interrupted. "It's quite amusing. Maybe you know the one. You're standing behind a little girl."

Macklin paused to let his words sink in. "A little girl who a short time later was found facedown in a canal, bloated, her neck broken. I'm sure the district attorney and the *Times* would love copies of the picture. What do you think, Orlock?"

"Perhaps I can juggle a few appointments and chat with you," Orlock said. "Where and when would you like to get together?"

"Your warehouse in Culver City. I want to see your operation."

"I have no operation, as you call it, Mr. Smith. I rent the warehouse to various—"

"Seven o'clock tonight." Macklin slammed the phone down. The clap echoed through the empty hangar. He plucked the black suction mike, purchased for just a buck or two at Radio Shack, from the telephone receiver and clicked off the cassette recorder it was attached to. There was nothing incriminating on the tape, but it was nice to have.

Macklin leaned back in his torn vinyl office chair, rested his feet on his paper-cluttered desk, and gazed through the doorway at his JetRanger helicopter and his Cessna in the hangar. *I'm a pilot, not a cop,* he told himself. *What the hell am I doing?*

But he knew that as exciting and beautiful and relaxing as flying was for him, there was something essential missing that prevented him from feeling content with his life, something he once had when he was on the UCLA track team. It was a sense of utterly consuming physical challenge, of pushing his limitations to the point of agony. The pain always ebbed, though, and left an afterglow of exhilaration that charged him until the next challenge, when he would give just a little bit more.

In the Quick Stop market. In the bank today. He had felt that charge, that sweet addictive charge, again. *Admit it, Macky boy. It's never felt better …*

Macklin swung his feet off the table, knocking stacks of paper to the floor.

"Shit." He bent over and spent a moment attempting to assemble the papers before giving up and kicking them. Paper scattered around the room, settling on the floor and chairs and boxes and cabinets like giant, mutated snowflakes.

He punched the door and walked into the hangar.

It's no life, no matter how good it might feel, Macklin lectured to himself. *A man can't live that way.*

We'll see …, a voice inside chided him.

"Hey, Brett, what the hell happened to your house?"

Macklin turned and at first glance didn't recognize the man coming in the hangar wearing reflecting sunglasses, a pink satin scalloped shirt, and designer jeans.

"Mort?" Macklin asked incredulously.

"Of course it's me." As Mort came closer, Macklin noticed his friend's uncharacteristically dark tan and the cloud of Pierre Cardin aftershave that surrounded him. "But not for long. I'm nearly Mortimer Neville."

"You're nearly out of you mind. What is all this shit?"

Mort patted himself on the rear. "One pair of Sassoon jeans." He tapped the rim of his glasses. "Porsche shades." He ran his hand down the scallop cut of his shirt. "One genuine Morey

Geyer scalloped shirt from Palm Springs, and, to top it all off"—Mort unbuttoned his collar to expose his hairless chest—"a summer tan from Al Bonzer's Sunset Strip tanning boutique."

Macklin groaned. "Jesus, Mort, you look ridiculous."

"Listen, Brett, your opinion doesn't count. You have no taste." Mort took off his sunglasses, folded them, and slipped them into his breast pocket. "Cheshire does. I went by the place to model my threads for her first and get a real opinion, but I couldn't find her. What happened to the place anyway? It's scorched."

Macklin suddenly realized Mort didn't know, that his friend had been back in Los Angeles for only a few hours.

"Hey, Brett, what's wrong?" Mort said, the glow disappearing from his face. "You look like you're about to puke."

Macklin didn't know how to begin. There was no right way. "Mort, she's dead."

"Huh?"

"Cheshire, she's been murdered." Macklin grasped Mort's shoulder. "Someone put a bomb in my car and she was blown up."

Mort squinted his eyes quizzically and tilted his head toward Macklin. "What?"

"Cheshire is dead," Macklin said carefully.

Mort swatted Macklin's arm away. "It's you, isn't it?"

"What?" Macklin snapped.

"Mr. Jury. The killing. It isn't over, is it?" Mort glared at Macklin. "*Is it!?*" he yelled.

Macklin frowned and exhaled slowly. "No, it isn't, Mort. I'm not sure it ever will be."

Without warning, Mort smashed his fist into Macklin's stomach and, before Macklin could recover, followed through with an uppercut that sent Macklin sprawling onto the floor.

"Fuck you, Brett, just fuck you."

Turning his back to Macklin, Mort walked toward the hangar door.

"Mort," Macklin rasped, propping himself up on his elbows. "Wait, I need your help!"

Mort kept walking.

"Damn it, Mort, I loved her, too!"

Mort stopped, his shoulders sagging.

Macklin stood up shakily. "We can make them pay, Mort. Together."

Mort looked over his shoulder. "Who are they?"

"A bunch of psychos who kidnap kids, force them to have sex in porno movies, and then kill them." Macklin held out his hand to him. "Will you help me?"

Mort turned around slowly and sighed. Macklin waited, his hand out.

"Please?" Macklin prodded.

Mort nodded, reached out, and shook Macklin's hand. "I'm sorry I hit you. I was pissed. I know it isn't your fault."

"It's all right, I don't blame you. I thought it was over, too."

Macklin told Mort about his meeting with Stocker and Shaw, the surveillance of Saputo, his meeting earlier that day with Harlan Fitz, and the phone call he had just made to Orlock.

"What do you want me to do?" Mort asked.

"I want you on the roof of the building across from the warehouse, taking pictures and covering me," Macklin said. "If I get into trouble, call Shaw."

"All right."

"You have a gun, don't you?"

Mort hedged with silence. He hadn't used a gun since his alcoholic days on the LAPD chopper patrol.

"Yes or no, Mort? Do you have a gun?" Macklin knew Mort had been a crack shot once and thought he probably wasn't too bad now.

"Yes," Mort said. "But, Mack, I haven't fired a gun since—"

"No arguments," Macklin interrupted. "It will protect both of us."

Macklin yanked a pen out of his breast pocket. "Gimme a piece of paper, Mort."

Mort pulled a wrinkled Blue Yonder Airways business card out of his back pocket and handed it to him. Macklin glanced at the card, gave Mort a disapproving look, and turned it over.

"Here's where I'm meeting Orlock." He scribbled down directions and gave the card back to Mort.

"It's a date," Mort said, studying the card.

"Good, then I'll see you tonight." Macklin headed toward the door.

"Wait a minute, Brett."

Macklin turned around.

"If they put a bomb in your car, they must know who you are," Mort said. "They must know you're not a representative of some eastern syndicate."

"I don't think they ever saw my face," Macklin replied. "My hunch is they saw me tailing Saputo, got my license number, and didn't bother to do any other checking before they decided to play it safe and kill me."

"And what if you're wrong?" Mort argued. "What if they know you're just a cocky pilot?"

"I'll have to stay alive long enough for you to rescue me."

CHAPTER NINE

Shaw sat on the edge of his couch and leaned close to the portable black-and-white TV, which was sitting on a blue plastic milk crate in the center of the living room.

Tuxedo-clad superspy Pete Cypher stood in the underground garage of his apartment building watching three sword-swinging ninja warriors kick his blazing red Corvette convertible into a pile of fiberglass dust.

"As you can see, Mr. Cypher, we mean business." The portly Frenchman in the wheelchair grinned, stroking the chameleon in his lap. *"Where is the electrofremeon nodule?"*

Cypher arched his eyebrows in mock surprise. *"I thought you knew."* He shot a glance at the rubble that had once been his car. *"It was in the glove compartment."*

"Oh, Pete Cypher is smooth," Shaw whispered, glancing over his shoulder at his white girlfriend. "C'mon, Sunshine, you gotta see this. Cypher is gonna flatten these guys any second now with his laser ring or his flame-throwing shoe."

"Uh-huh," she mumbled without looking up from her paperback copy of *Loose Change*. Curled up in a red vinyl bean bag, Sunshine was braless in her gauze blouse, her long brown hair falling across her chest and clear down to her Indian wraparound skirt.

Shaw shrugged, decided it was her loss, and stared intently at the screen again.

"Very amusing, Mr. Cypher," the Frenchman quipped, *"but that isn't reason enough to keep you alive. I want it now."*

Cypher grinned. *"Then I'll just have to give it to you."*

Shaw laughed. "Here it comes, Sunny. Cypher is gonna do his thing."

"Uh-huh," Sunshine replied.

Someone knocked at Shaw's door.

"Shit. Sunshine, could you get that?" Shaw didn't shift his attention from Pete Cypher.

Sunshine peered at him over the top of her book. "You've got two legs and two hands."

"I can't," Shaw whined. "I've invested forty-five minutes in this. You've read that book three times. Okay? Please?"

Sunshine sighed, pulled herself up, and trudged to the door.

"Hello, my name is Jessica Mordente. I'm a reporter with the *Los Angeles Times*," Shaw heard a woman say. "Is Sergeant Shaw in?"

Shaw groaned. Cypher squinted at the three ninjas and pointed his digital wristwatch at them.

"Come in, Ms. Mordente," Sunshine said.

"Thank you," Mordente replied.

Shaw reluctantly rose from the couch, his eyes on the set, and back-stepped toward the door. *What has Cypher got in his watch?*

"Ronny!" Sunshine shouted.

Shaw whirled around, startled, and flashed an apologetic smile at Sunshine and Mordente.

"Sergeant Shaw?" Mordente ventured, offering her hand to him.

"Yes," Shaw replied, a questioning look on his face, and shook Mordente's hand. "What can I do for you, Ms. Mordente?"

"Please, call me Jessie. Everyone does."

"Right," Shaw said, leading Mordente to the couch. He stopped to watch a pin-size missile blast out of Cypher's watch and zoom toward the terrified ninjas.

"Ronny, why don't you turn off the TV so we can talk?" Sunshine urged. Shaw reluctantly switched off the set and sat on the arm of the couch beside Mordente.

"So, what's your story?" Shaw asked glumly.

"Mr. Jury." Mordente replied.

Shaw felt the anxiety flare in his chest and shrugged, as if her remark meant nothing to him. "Well, I could have saved you a trip," he casually remarked. "It's an ongoing investigation, and I can't release any information."

Sunshine shot a curious look at Shaw as she picked a discarded pair of her wooden platform shoes off the living room floor.

"I think Mr. Jury is the man who foiled that bank robbery this afternoon," Mordente said.

So do I, Shaw thought. "You may be right. Then again, you may not. It's speculation at this point, and I'm in no position right now to discuss the case." Shaw narrowed his eyes and wondered what she was after. "Really, why don't you contact our press relations office in the morning? It's been a long day and—"

"Do you have any evidence in the Mr. Jury case?" she interrupted. "Any fingerprints, witnesses, suspects?"

"Look, I already told you. I can't discuss the case." A stroke of anger colored his voice. "We have leads we are actively pursuing."

"That's the same speech Stocker used to give me back when he was chief of police," she commented dryly. "C'mon, Sergeant, hasn't anything changed since then?"

Shaw didn't like the way this conversation was going. He felt as though his words were footsteps in a mine field. "That's all I can tell you. I don't want to risk jeopardizing the investigation. You already know what I'm authorized to tell you. The only description we have is from a cashier in a Quick Stop market. He says Mr. Jury is a short Asian with a weight problem."

"Sergeant, you once arrested Brett Macklin because you thought he was Mr. Jury," she said evenly. "Isn't that true?"

Sunshine came beside Shaw and wrapped her arm around his waist.

"Not exactly," Shaw said, wishing he had Cypher's watch right now. "But we did bring him in for questioning." Shaw's heart pounded. She couldn't know the truth, could she? "Just what are you getti—"

"Why did you arrest him?" she interjected pointedly, her words coming in a rush. "What evidence did you have linking him to the murders? Was it simply his revenge motive or something more that led you to arrest him? Is he still a suspect?"

Shaw stood up, strode silently to the front door, and held it open. "Ms. Mordente, that's enough for tonight. You want to interview me, you call the press information office in the morning and we'll go from there."

Mordente scratched her cheek and smiled. "What are you afraid of, Sergeant?"

"I'm afraid you're not going to leave and the whole evening will be shot to hell."

She stood up and shifted her gaze between Sunshine and Shaw. "You have been friends with Brett Macklin for a long time. I think if he was Mr. Jury, you might be tempted to cover up for him."

"Stop playing games with us," Sunshine shot back. "You're saying Mack is Mr. Jury and you're accusing Ronny of covering for him."

"Mack and I are close friends, Ms. Mordente," Shaw said. "I'd be lying if I said it wasn't painful having to question him about the Mr. Jury killings. But you're right. He had motive." Shaw leaned against the wall. "The fact is, Brett Macklin is a man who has had to endure a lot of personal tragedy lately. Someone out there got mad about that and decided to do something about it."

"How do you know that someone isn't your friend? It's the logical assumption, Sergeant."

"Ms. Mordente, I'd like to watch a little TV, make some popcorn, spend a quiet evening at home, okay?" Shaw tilted his head toward the door. "Let's call it a night."

Mordente acquiesced. "All right." She pulled a card out of her skirt pocket and gave it to Shaw. "Here's my card if you want to reach me." Mordente glanced at Sunshine. "Thank you both for your time."

Shaw closed the door behind Mordente and tore up the card into scraps. *It's finally happening,* he thought, *what I knew would happen all along.* He felt a chill ride over him, raising goose bumps on his flesh and making him shiver.

He walked into the living room and stood beside the fire, the heat warming his back. The heat against his back only made the iciness over the rest of his body more acute. *Someone is picking apart our flimsy cover-up,* he warned himself. *It's only a matter of time now before the whole thing comes crumbling down and crushes us all.* He recognized his chills for what they were—the same chills he felt as a child whenever the doctor wanted to give him a blood test or throat culture. The chills of unadulterated fear.

Sunshine crossed her legs and sat down in front of him. "I hate to admit it, Ronny, but she has a point."

Shaw tossed the bits of paper into the fire and sat down on the couch behind her. He willed the fear out of his voice. "Sure she does. That doesn't make it the truth."

"But it is the truth, isn't it?" she asked softly, staring into the fire.

"No," he told her quietly, one last lie in the whole string of lies that he felt, with aching certainty, would soon become his noose.

Luck didn't seem to be on Mort Suderson's side Friday night. His windbreaker wouldn't zip up, and there was no dry place to squat on the roof of the building across from Orlock's warehouse.

Sitting on the roof was like wading in a stagnant pond. A vast puddle of rainwater stretched across the roof, reaching into all the corners that afforded the best view of the street below.

There was no way around it. Mort had to get wet. His socks were soaked sponges inside his wet tennis shoes and made his feet feel like solid blocks of ice.

Mort sniffled and wiped his nose with the back of his hand. He cursed himself for not bringing his heavy Levi's jacket. He squatted in the far left-hand corner of the warehouse roofline, two stories above the street, Orlock's warehouse in front of him, an alley to his left. The last, dimming rays of the sun gave the greenish haze above the city a sickly glow. It reminded Mort that the poison air didn't disappear at night—it simply hid in the darkness.

He glanced at his watch. It was 6:30 p.m. Perfect, he thought. He wanted to settle in early.

The gun felt snug against him in his LAPD-issue shoulder holster, and the Canon AE-1 hung around his neck. With nothing else to do, he decided to play with the camera. He sighted Orlock's warehouse through the viewfinder, adjusting the zoom lens. If he wanted to, he knew he could snap clear pictures of the bolts on the steel warehouse door.

This is going to be easy, Mort thought.

He aimed the camera at the moon, playfully thinking he'd take a few pictures of craters.

Mort heard something splash in the water behind him. He lowered the camera and jerked his head around. His eyes caught the flash of steel an instant too late. The wrench slammed into the side of his head, and a blinding burst of intense pain consumed him. In the fraction of a second before darkness swallowed his thoughts, Mort realized he should have guessed there would be others who wanted to settle in early.

Tice wiped the blood off the wrench with a white handkerchief and slipped them both into the pocket of his overcoat. He examined his black-gloved hands to see if any blood had splattered them. They were clean. His thin lips stretched into a self-satisfied grin as he casually glanced down at Mort, who lay at his feet wide-eyed but unseeing, tiny rivulets of blood crawling down his cheek.

Tice lifted Mort by the armpits and dragged him through the water to the building's edge. Then, with the heel of his black shoe, he pushed Mort over the edge with a sharp kick.

Mort's body fell silently, landing in the trash bin in the alley below with a dull thud.

Brett Macklin parked the Impala across from Orlock's warehouse thirty minutes later and immediately noticed the thin, long-legged man in the black overcoat standing out front.

Macklin switched off the ignition and stared at the man. The guy gave Macklin a bad feeling in his gut. Macklin thought the man could make a good living playing Gestapo agents in low-budget World War II movies. That thought didn't do much to quell Macklin's uneasiness.

Thank God there's someone with a gun watching out for me, Macklin thought. He opened the car door and walked casually toward Orlock's warehouse. As Macklin neared, he could see a tight grin on the man's face.

"Mr. Smith?" the man hissed, approaching Macklin.

Macklin recognized the voice. It was Tice, the man who had answered Orlock's phone.

"Yeah," Macklin said.

Tice suddenly drove his fist hard into Macklin's stomach, catching Macklin completely by surprise. Macklin choked forward, gagging, the air forced out of his lungs. Tice stepped close to Macklin, who was hunched over and gasping for air, and grabbed a handful of Macklin's hair. Steadying Macklin's head, Tice rammed his knee into Macklin's neck and released him.

Macklin tumbled backward and lay inert on the pavement, wheezing and skirting the boundaries of consciousness. He was completely paralyzed with pain, sapped of the air necessary to move. Yet he was aware of Tice bending over, opening his flight jacket, and removing his .357 Magnum.

A long white Lincoln limousine snaked around the warehouse and slid to a stop in front of them. Tice grabbed Macklin by the collar and lifted him up, slamming him back against the warehouse wall. Macklin blinked open his eyes and saw the tinted rear window of the limousine slide down.

A man with heavy purple lips sneered at him from inside the car. The skin on the man's face was pale, stretched tight over his skull and hugging the sunken contours of his cheeks and the broad ridge of his brow.

"No one treats me like a common thug, Mr. Smith," Orlock said. "You're a stupid man. A dead man."

C'mon, Mort, Macklin thought, *come save me from this.* "Aren't you forgetting something?" Macklin coughed out between labored breaths. He was a rag doll in Tice's hands. "Kill me, and your picture goes to the DA and the press."

Orlock shrugged carelessly. "I'll take that chance." Macklin hadn't counted on that at all.

"Good night." Orlock waved at him and then leaned back in his seat, disappearing from view. The window hummed closed and the limousine moved away slowly. The warehouse door opened. Tice yanked Macklin forward, twisted his right arm painfully behind his back, and led him toward the doorway.

Macklin glanced at the warehouse across the street. *Mort, where the fuck are you?*

"Your friend has taken the night off." Tice grinned as if he had read Macklin's thoughts. Tice's words struck Macklin like a blow.

Ahead, Macklin saw Wesley Saputo standing in the doorway. Macklin could see Orlock's van parked beside Saputo and the plywood, plank-supported back sides of movie sets in the center of the warehouse.

"Mr. Smith," Saputo said, "you are going to be a movie star."

"I am?" Macklin sputtered. "A romance? A light comedy, perhaps?"

Saputo stepped back and let Tice and Macklin edge past him. "No," Saputo laughed. "A snuff film."

CHAPTER TEN

Macklin stumbled over a confusing latticework of electrical cables that crisscrossed the expanse of the huge warehouse as Tice urged him forward toward the sets. Large, standing movie lights bathed the center of the warehouse hot white.

His eyes followed the cables from the lights to a battered junction box, held together with electrical tape, on the floor to his left. Beyond it, in the far corner of the warehouse, Macklin could see stacks of film canisters, bottles of thinner, and gallons of paint.

"Move, Mr. Smith," Tice growled, and wrenched up Macklin's arm. Macklin winced at the sharp pain, his tendons threatening to snap like taut rubber bands.

Macklin stumbled clumsily alongside Tice. Saputo and two of the gorillas Macklin had seen when he had staked out the warehouse fell into step beside them.

They weaved through several standing movie sets—a kitchen, a doctor's office, and a classroom—to a dining room. A birthday cake sat on the table amidst party favors and balloons. Two of Saputo's crewmen stood on ladders adjusting lights while Lyle Franken put a canister of film into the movie camera.

Macklin saw a little girl wearing a pink-and-white-checked gingham dress sitting at the end of the table, her tear-streaked face drooping with sadness, a red-striped cone-shaped party hat askew on her head. A cardboard cake covered with unlit candles sat in the middle of the table, surrounded by gifts and party favors. A blond-haired boy, who Macklin guessed was perhaps ten years old, was wearing black bikini briefs and playing with a half dozen Hot Wheels toy cars in one corner of the set.

"Hey, who is this? What's going on?" whined a heavyset man with a thick mustache. Standing beside him was a gangly woman in gray leather pants and a pink Camp Beverly Hills sweatshirt, a cigarette stub dangling out from under her upper lip.

Saputo smiled. "Mr. Smith here is the star of our next picture."

"Can you fit our son Jimmy into it?" the woman asked, her cigarette bobbing. Macklin saw the boy raise his head at the mention of his name.

"I don't think so." Saputo grinned at Macklin, as if the two were sharing in a friendly, secret joke.

"We could use the extra money," the father said. "The kid has been a pain in the ass for ten years."

"Ten years and nine months," the mother added with a grimace.

Macklin narrowed his eyes at the boy's parents. "How can you do this to your son?"

"I didn't make society sick, okay?" The woman waved her finger reproachfully at Macklin. "I don't know who the fuck you are, but I'll tell you this—if the pervs get off looking at my kid's picture, I'd rather they do that than go and rape someone, you know?"

"You're doing it for the money. You don't care about anything else," Macklin replied.

"Hey, the kid knows what he's doing. I asked him if he wanted to be in the movies and he said he did." The father cocked his head toward the set and yelled to his son out of the corner of his mouth. "Right, Jimmy?"

"Sure, Dad," the boy mumbled, absorbed in his toy cars again.

"So the kid helps Mom and Dad bring home the bacon." Saputo grinned. "I call that wholesome family unity."

"You're scum," Macklin hissed.

"And you're on borrowed time." Saputo motioned to Tice. "Take this man to the dungeon."

Macklin shot a sideways glance at Tice. "He's a little heavy on the melodrama, don't you think?"

Tice shoved Macklin ahead to the next set, which was designed to look like a medieval torture chamber. Macklin arched his eyebrows in surprise. A makeshift wooden rack rested beside a backdrop painted to look like it was made of stone. Cuffed chains dangled from the wall. Macklin saw a mace, the weapon consisting of a spiked iron ball and chain, and a branding iron lying on the floor.

"You guys have got to be kidding," Macklin remarked with a cynical grin.

Tice whipped the wrench out of his pocket and slapped Macklin viciously across the face with it. As Macklin fell to the floor, the warehouse swirling around him in a painful blur, he realized they weren't.

"I thought Mr. Jury was a fat Asian midget." Jackie Laylor scratched her cleavage and fingered the cursor controls on her computer terminal, the story on the screen reflecting off her sunglasses.

She didn't like computers. She remembered her mother telling her that sitting too close to the TV would make her uterus shrivel up and her father's warning that invisible rays coming off the screen would make her blind. A computer was just a TV with a keyboard to her. So she wore sunglasses to protect her eyes. And while other writers put the keyboard on their lap, she kept hers on the desk, far away from her uterus.

Jessica Mordente stood behind Laylor, looking over her shoulder as the city editor scanned Mordente's lengthy Mr. Jury article. She was certain Laylor had scratched her cleavage to draw attention to those big breasts, as if to say to Mordente, "I've got it and you don't, baby."

"Jackie, forget that description of Mr. Jury," Mordente said wearily. "The kid at the 7-Eleven or whatever is lying."

"What are you now, Jessie? Psychic?" Laylor sighed, scrolling through the story, the lighted characters rapidly passing across the screen. "Look, I can't print this."

"What do you mean? What's wrong?" Mordente tried to keep her voice even, keep her anger in check. She had spent the last two hours cleaning up her rough draft and inserting Shaw's vague remarks. She wanted the story to make the Sunday Metro section, maybe even the front page. "It's great stuff. We're telling the city who their mysterious vigilante is."

"We are, huh?" Laylor stored the article with few quick keystrokes. The eighty-five column inches blinked off the screen. She took off her sunglasses and rubbed her tired, bloodshot brown eyes. "This story is no story."

Mordente stepped back, stunned and outraged. "I don't follow. I've tracked down Mr. Jury, exposed him, and you're telling me there is no story."

Laylor sighed. "You got the last part right. There may be a story later, but not now. What you've got here, if we were irresponsible enough to publish it, is the grounds for a multimillion-dollar libel suit. Brett Macklin would own the *Los Angeles Times* after he got through with us."

"Brett Macklin is Mr. Jury. It's all there. His father was killed by the Bounty Hunters gang and"—Mordente snapped her fingers—"bang, they were all killed by Mr. Jury."

"Coincidence, Jessie," Laylor responded. "C'mon, you're a better reporter than that. You have no facts, just a lot of iffy circumstantial evidence."

"Okay, here's a fact. Two detectives are assigned to the Mr. Jury case. One disappears and the other, surprise of surprises, is Sergeant Ronald Shaw, Macklin's oldest friend."

"So? Maybe putting Shaw on the case wasn't the wisest decision the LAPD ever made, but it still doesn't prove anything." Laylor shrugged. "You're reaching."

"Jackie! Don't you see?" Mordente yelled. "Can't you smell it? This guy Macklin has blood on his hands. One cop realized that and arrested Macklin for murder. Don't you find it odd that Macklin was released the next day?"

"He was innocent—how's that for an explanation?"

Mordente went on, undaunted. "Then the arresting officer disappears. Now someone plants a bomb in Macklin's car and kills his girlfriend. Mystery, coincidence, and crime sure seem attracted to Macklin."

"You said it. Maybe he's just had his share of rotten luck. Maybe he is a shaky character. That doesn't make him Mr. Jury." The city editor rose from her seat, noticing for the first time that their argument had caught the attention of the newsroom staff. A half dozen heads were turned in their direction. "Face it, there isn't anything to the story yet. If you can dig up something more, something solid, I'll run with it. Not yet."

"This man can't be the innocent bystander he says he is!"

"He sure can, Jessie," she replied evenly, quietly, hoping Mordente would follow her cue and settle down. "Until someone proves otherwise."

"I have! The story is there," Mordente roared. "Or have you been sitting behind a desk too long to know a story when it bites you in the ass?"

Laylor stiffened. Anyone who hadn't been watching them before certainly was now. "I'm going to write that remark off as exhaustion. I've been working you real hard. That had better be why you've suddenly reverted to a cub reporter with dreams of front-page, banner headlines, because I'm giving you three days off and you had better come back the reliable reporter you used to be."

Mordente's face reddened with anger and, as she felt the stares of her coworkers, a trace of embarrassment as well. "Jackie, listen to me. I'm convinced Brett Macklin, alias Mr. Jury, walked into the bank robbery yesterday afternoon. If we run with the story, that will pressure the police into comparing the bullets in the bank robbers' bodies with those from Mr. Jury's other victims."

"Don't make me get any harsher, Jessie. The answer is no."

"I'm working an FBI source now," Mordente said sharply. "If Macklin is in the photos the bank camera took, then we've got Mr. Jury."

Laylor walked away. "No."

Mordente wanted to scream furiously at the top of her lungs. Instead, her body seemed to tremble for a moment before she willed herself to turn away and walk back to her desk. She picked up the phone and dialed.

"Hello, Chet? This is Jessie." She tapped her pencil against the VDT screen. "Why don't we get together for dinner? Yeah, Sunday is fine for me. See you then."

The mental disarray of returning consciousness was becoming a familiar state to Brett Macklin. Before his father's murder, his only experience with unconsciousness had been a fast ball to the head in high school. Nowadays it seemed like everyone was trying to pitch something against his head. The whirling kaleidoscope of sensory perceptions, like a blurry television picture that defies adjustment, didn't make Macklin as insecure as it used to. He no longer grasped for solid bits of perception, but rather waited for the storm to abate.

After a few minutes, things inside his head began to settle and Macklin tried to blink open his eyes, which felt weighed down with cement blocks. Mucus gave his throat a sticky, acidic feel, and swallowing burned. His heartbeat pounded in his head and his appendages tingled as if they were asleep.

Macklin focused his eyes on the rafters on the ceiling above him and realized he was lying flat on his back. His arms were stretched out behind him. He tried to lower them to his sides and felt a bolt of pain race through his body.

What the fuck?

Macklin peered down at his feet and saw his ankles were tied with rope. He guessed the rest. He was on the rack, ropes tied around his wrists and ankles, pulling them taut. Macklin knew all it would take was a crank or two on the pulleys at his feet and behind his head and *rip!*—his guts would slop onto the floor like a plate of spaghetti absently knocked off the dinner table. Macklin closed his eyes and tried to think.

This is one film Macky boy won't be able to stomach. Stomach—HA-HA-HA-HA-HA! teased a devilish voice inside him. *Hey, Macky, Gene Shalit says you'll bust a gut laughing at this madcap comedy—HA-HA-HA-HA!*

I'm going to get out of this, Macklin told himself.

"How are you doing, Mr. Smith?" Macklin heard Wesley Saputo say, smelling the nicotine breath before Saputo appeared over him. "Are you ready to become a star?"

"You're a real tough guy, Saputo, a real specimen of manhood. You tie me down and then slither around molesting defenseless children," Macklin said. "You're some kind of stud, all right. Next you're gonna start fucking corpses."

Saputo's face flushed with anger. "As an actor, Mr. Macklin, you'll need to stretch a bit for this role." Saputo leaned forward and turned the crank clockwise.

The pain clawed its way up Macklin's throat as a scream. He gritted his teeth and forced it back.

"Relax, Macklin, you won't have long to wait." Saputo walked away. "Your screen debut is imminent."

Macklin lay panting, his body drenched with sweat, the pain ebbing into an intense ache. He closed his eyes and enjoyed the painkilling, cool darkness. Time slipped past him until he heard a voice.

"What are you doing, mister?" a meek voice inquired.

He turned his head and saw the little girl bashfully standing a safe two feet away. Macklin blinked his eyes clear, not knowing how long he had been blacked out. The girl had chocolate cake smeared around her face.

"Come here, honey," Macklin whispered gently.

She stepped back. Macklin realized his tactic was all wrong. Everyone was probably talking sweetly and quietly to her, gaining her reluctant trust and then doing her harm.

"What's your name?" Macklin asked in his normal voice.

"Erica Tandy. I'm ten."

"Really? Is it your birthday today?" Macklin wanted to order her to untie his bonds, but his rational side realized the necessity of moving slowly. Painfully slowly.

"No." She stepped toward him. "They're making me pretend."

"Where's your mom and dad?"

She shrugged. "I want to go home."

Macklin felt her sadness and wanted to reach out and comfort her. He imagined Cory, his daughter, the loss and fear she would feel if she were in Erica's place. "I do, too. If you come here and help me untie these ropes, we can leave here. Would you like that?"

"Uh-huh," she mumbled.

"Come here." He jerked his head back, motioning her. So took a step forward.

"*Erica!*" Saputo yelled from behind the set. Erica froze. "Beautiful? Come here!"

Erica shot Macklin one frightened glance and then dashed back behind the wall to the dining room set. Macklin dropped his head and closed his eyes. *Damn!*

CHAPTER ELEVEN

The Cadillac exploded again and again in Macklin's mind. It was a relentless pounding that rocked his body and sent shock waves of pain rolling through him.

Macklin squeezed his eyes shut, willing away the torturous images. A giant tombstone loomed up in his psyche. Six names were carved into it.

JD Macklin. Melody. Saul. Moe. Cheshire. Mort.

There was no way back now. There had been an irrevocable, jarring turn in the course of Macklin's life, and the bodies of his loved ones lined the curve.

Dad, Melody, Saul, Moe, Cheshire… Mort.

The only name missing was his own.

"Help me, mister," Macklin heard Erica whimper. He flashed open his eyes and saw her standing beside him again, naked, tears rolling down her puffy cheeks.

"Erica," Macklin whispered, "I want you to turn that handle behind me counterclockwise. Do you know what that means?"

She nodded.

"Okay, go ahead. Do it slowly." She reached out to the handle and pushed it down. Immediately, Macklin felt the muscles in his arms recoiling painfully. "A little more, Erica."

She pulled the crank around to an upright position. That gave Macklin enough slack to sit up. He felt a hot flush burn his skin as blood surged through his body, revitalizing his traumatized limbs. Macklin quickly began to untie the knots around his wrists.

"Where's Erica?" Saputo yelled from behind the set. Macklin saw Erica tremble. Erica wasn't going to go back to that set. Which meant, Macklin knew, that Saputo would come looking for her. Macklin freed one wrist and struggled with the rope on the other.

"Damn it! Who let her wander away?" Saputo growled. "Earl, go find her. She's got to get back here. We've still got to do the come shot."

Macklin leaned forward and frantically pulled on the rope around his ankles, trying to loosen it enough to get free. Erica whimpered.

"Shhhhh," Macklin hissed at her. He heard heavy footsteps approaching.

Macklin freed one ankle. The footsteps were close, a yard or two away.

"Run!" Macklin whispered to Erica and fell back on the rack, extending his arms as if he were bound. With his left hand, he felt around for the mace.

Erica froze.

"Run, Erica!" Macklin's hand found the mace. He hid his hand behind the pulley as Earl, one of Saputo's gorillas, emerged to Macklin's right.

"Hey, kid, get away from him!" Earl roared. With both hands he pushed Erica aside. She shrieked and fell to the floor, scrambling away like a frightened animal.

Earl laughed, watching her bare rear end disappear behind the wall. "The little runt," he mumbled, turning his head and looking down at Macklin. In the instant it took Earl to comprehend the meaning of Macklin's loosened bonds, Macklin swung the mace, the thorny iron ball whipping into Earl's startled face.

The mace audibly smacked into Earl's skull, the spikes plunging deep into his eyeball, temple, and cheek. Earl screamed and blindly stumbled back, the mace stuck in his head, blood gushing out of his face. Macklin yanked the rope off his ankle, leaped off the rack, and pulled the gun out of Earl's shoulder holster.

Macklin shoved the gun barrel into Earl's fleshy stomach and squeezed the trigger. The blast of the .38 shook the warehouse. Earl burst apart like a piñata, splashing blood against the dungeon wall.

"Get the kids out of the way. Lock 'em in the van," Macklin heard Saputo shout. Macklin scrambled through a maze of sets toward the opposite end of the warehouse.

Saputo called out after him. "Forget it, Macklin! There are no windows and no other doors. There's only one way out of here for you, asshole!"

Macklin crouched behind the last set and peered around the edge. He saw a stack of tires against the wall to his left, by the breaker box. Ahead and to his right were the film and the painting supplies he had seen when he came in. He glanced at the multiple arms of electrical cord that stretched out from the junction box on the slick cement floor. Scanning the ceiling, he saw only sprinkler heads. Not a single skylight. Saputo was right. He was trapped.

Macklin sprinted across the open floor toward the paint supplies, hoping there might be something there that could help him escape. The sound of a footfall behind him made him jerk around midstep. He saw a man and muzzle flash when the floor suddenly slipped out from under him, the gun's report cracking in his ear. As he hit the floor on his right shoulder, he sensed the bullet streaking above his head and realized he had tripped over the junction box.

Macklin bolted upright and fired. The slug slammed into the gunman's chest and kicked him back into a set wall. The line of sets tumbled down like a row of dominoes.

Macklin scrambled to his feet and, glancing over his shoulder, saw paint thinner spilling out of a jug that had apparently been pierced by the gunman's bullet.

There is a way out, Macklin thought. Quickly, Macklin searched through the gunman's bloody clothes, turning out the pockets. *C'mon, let it be there…* The gunman shook spasmodically as death tightened its grip on him. Macklin looked into the gunman's open, blank eyes and felt the pack of matches in the man's inside jacket pocket. *Bingo*!

"There he is!" the father cried out, appearing around the edge of the fallen sets, waving his finger at Macklin.

Macklin struck a match and lit the matchbook. Saputo and Franken, brandishing snub-nosed revolvers, and two of Saputo's crewmen emerged behind Macklin, who tossed the flaming matchbook into the stream of paint thinner and dived away.

"Hit the deck!" Saputo screamed, throwing himself forward.

The fire chased the fluid back into the jug. The jug exploded, splattering flame out in all directions.

Macklin crawled toward the opposite wall. The blaze spread in an instant, feeding on the nearby packs of film.

Glancing back, Macklin saw the flames climb the wall, licking the ceiling and prompting the sprinklers to life. Macklin tipped over the stack of tires and threw himself on them just as the water rained down.

Macklin aimed his gun at the junction box on the watery floor and saw Saputo and his men rise to their feet.

Saputo grinned at Macklin and pointed his gun at him. "You're mine, Macklin," he yelled over the roaring blaze and cool shower.

Macklin fired, splitting open the junction box and exposing it to the water. He heard the whiplike snap of electric current. The movie lights fluttered.

Saputo's eyes flashed open wide in an instant of terror and surprise. His body twitched and convulsed, hundreds of volts riding through him and bouncing him up and down like a human pogo stick.

Macklin, insulated by the tires, stared transfixed as Saputo and his men jerked obscenely across the floor in a last dance of death. He reached up to the breaker box and switched off the electricity. The warehouse, lit by the flickering of the dying flames, smelled like ammonia and spoiled meat.

He stood up and ran along the wall to the van. The mother's corpse lay twisted in a puddle beside the movie camera, her red tongue lolling out of her open mouth. Macklin stepped over her body and splashed through the water to the van. He put his gun into his waistband and pounded a fist against the side of the van.

"Are you okay in there?" he shouted, hoping the van's tires had kept them safe from the electric current.

"Uh-huh," Erica and Jimmy mumbled in unison from inside the van.

"Stay put. Help is on the way." Macklin, soaking wet, flung open the warehouse door.

Tice stood outside in the alleyway in front of him, a laconic grin on his face and Macklin's .357 Magnum in his hand.

"Help is here," Tice whispered. Macklin saw Tice's finger tighten on the trigger and braced himself for the bullet that would rip through his stomach. Macklin winced, the handgun's deafening report ringing out twice in his ears. Macklin stiffened. And felt nothing.

He tentatively opened his eyes and saw Tice sprawled on the ground, blood frothing out of a ragged crater in his head. Chunks of blood-soaked gray-beige brain matter and jagged slivers of bone dripped onto the pavement. Macklin took in a deep breath and looked up and down the street, confused. There was no one in sight.

Then he heard the sound of someone gagging in the alley beside the warehouse across the street. Macklin sprinted to the other side of the street and moved cautiously into the alley.

He stopped short, stunned. Mort leaned over the side of the trash bin, vomiting into the street.

"Mort, you're alive!" Macklin said with astonishment.

"I sure as hell don't feel like it," Mort groaned, holding the gun limply in his right hand. Mort steadied himself with his left hand and lifted a leg over the rim. Macklin wrapped his arms around Mort's waist and helped him out.

"You saved my life, Mort. Thanks."

"No problem. Anytime." Mort heaved for breath, dizzy, the sour taste of vomit in his mouth and nose.

"Take it easy." Macklin put his arm around Mort and held him tightly. He noticed the matted hair and dried blood on the side of Mort's head. "What happened to you?"

Mort swallowed and glanced up. The white oval moon shone down on him and he could see the side of the warehouse he had been atop. The pieces fell together for him.

"That asshole I shot must've sidelined me with a crowbar or something, I dunno." Mort shivered. "I guess he tossed me off the building. That garbage bin must be the only thing that saved me from being a nasty smudge on the pavement. The way my head and stomach feel, I think I would rather have died. Damn concussion."

Mort stiffened. Bile shot up his throat, spurting out and onto the ground in one quick convulsion. "Fuck…"

Macklin could hear the sound of police sirens drawing near. "Are you okay? Can you walk?" Mort nodded. "Yeah, let's go."

As Macklin led Mort to his car, he realized his anger would never die. It wasn't the Bounty Hunters gang or Wesley Saputo or Crocker Orlock. They were just germs, part of a bigger disease that was growing and infecting the vital organs of society. He hadn't stopped it when he avenged his father's death. And, Macklin knew, it wouldn't stop if Orlock's operation was crushed, either.

No more of my friends will die. I won't let the disease spread. The voice inside Macklin that cried for retribution was now his own.

Mr. Jury and Brett Macklin were one.

CHAPTER TWELVE

"Mister Jury is dead."

Mayor Jed Stocker solemnly faced the two dozen reporters in the press room and reveled in the absolute attention his statement engendered.

Stocker stood crisp and clean in a dark blue pinstriped suit under the city's seal, doing his best to exude leadership and stature. This was the first time he had ever shut the reporters up, and on a slow news day like Saturday, Stocker was sure this press conference would dominate the local media, just as he had planned.

Jessica Mordente's perplexed expression didn't escape Stocker's notice. First of all, as his pick as the best-looking of the LA press corps, he was always looking at her. Second, that was the reaction he had intended to invoke. She was, no surprise to him, the first to break the stunned silence.

"Who is he?" she asked.

Stocker shrugged. "We don't know. He was found with a bullet in his head outside a Culver City warehouse."

"How do you know it's Mr. Jury?" Mordente, Stocker thought, had the look of a shell-shocked soldier.

"A good guess." Stocker grinned. "He was carrying a .357 Magnum that ballistics testing has conclusively tied to the Mr. Jury killings." He leaned forward against the wooden podium. "Police investigation thus far suggests that Mr. Jury was on the trail of a gang of child pornographers who used the warehouse to film motion pictures that featured kidnapped young children."

Stocker cleared his throat. "These children were sexually assaulted and murdered. Mr. Jury killed the gang involved and rescued two children, one of whom was Erica Tandy, the ten-year-old girl who disappeared yesterday while playing at a Van Nuys park."

"What happened to Mr. Jury?" Al Zimmer, a reporter with the *Herald Examiner*, slurped up the saliva dribbling out the corner of his mouth. Zimmer's chin was always wet with the spittle forced between his lips by the ever-present wad of chewing gum.

"We aren't sure." Stocker sighed. "He was fatally wounded in the head by someone outside. Perhaps one of the gang escaped. We don't know."

"What do the children say?" A toupee-topped TV reporter cried out from the back of the room.

"They are severely traumatized, as you can well imagine. Erica is under a doctor's supervision and remembers nothing at this time." Stocker shifted his weight uncomfortably. "The other child, a young boy, has a long history as a victim of sexual molestation. Sergeant Clive Barer of our Sexually Exploited Child Unit is handling the investigation."

Mordente frowned, narrowing her eyes. "Who was Mr. Jury?" she asked again, noticeably dissatisfied with what she was hearing.

"We don't know."

"Of course you don't," Mordente mumbled angrily, and folded her arms under her chest.

"We have tried everything—dental charts, fingerprints, the works," Stocker argued. "Still we come up blank. This man lived and died an enigma." Stocker hurriedly shuffled together the papers on the podium. "That's all for now. We'll let you know as soon as more information becomes available."

The mayor walked away, dodging a volley of questions, and slipped out a side door and into a narrow gray corridor. Shaw leaned against the wall, his hands in the pockets of his jeans.

"Did Mordente buy it?" Shaw asked.

Stocker smiled, clapping his hand on Shaw's shoulder. "Our worries are over. The dogs have been thrown off the scent."

Brett Macklin lay in the bathtub, his knees bent out of the water and his head propped up by an inflated plastic pillow stuck to the tile wall. Steamy water dribbled out of the spigot in a weak and steady stream, keeping the bath water hot and soothing.

He absently stroked the rim of a chilly wineglass, half-filled with Chablis, that rested on the lint-dotted red bath mat and listened to Stevie Nicks crooning gently from the bedroom.

His muscles were relaxed for the first time in days. Tension floated out of him and the world began to seem less black, less ominous, to him. Droplets of perspiration dotted his face.

His watch, on the floor beside the glass, beeped once, letting him know it was noon and his bath would be short-lived.

As if on the cue, the phone, which Macklin had brought into the bathroom and set on the toilet seat, rang shrilly, shattering his calm. Sitting up, he reached out for it and extended his legs in the hot water. The tortured muscles, so brutally stretched by the rack, said ahhhhhhhhhhhhhh to him.

"Hello," Macklin drawled sleepily.

"It's me," Shaw replied briskly. "The press conference went smoothly. Mr. Jury is dead, at least as far as the press is concerned."

"Good," Macklin said. "What about Orlock?"

"We've turned up reels of kiddie porn and hundreds of mailing lists at the warehouse," he replied. "His kiddie-porn operation is over and we're moving in on dozens of his friends. Christ, Mack, some of the names on his mailing list would shock you."

"So you have Orlock behind bars, right?"

A heavy silence fell for a moment between them.

"Ronny, how can he still be a free man?" Macklin barked.

"The ties to Orlock are still tenuous," Shaw replied, "obscured by layers of dummy corporations and other crap. His lawyers are holding us at bay, at least for now, fielding our questions and keeping Orlock out of it."

"I don't like this, Ron, not one damn bit."

"I know. Neither do I," Shaw said, pausing for a few seconds before speaking again. "I've contacted Judge Fitz and he's reviewing all the evidence we've got. He should have a decision by tomorrow morning. And Orlock is scared. I think he will run. Either way, this will break tomorrow."

"How are you coming on the equipment I asked you for last night?"

"We're getting it together, but it's not easy." Shaw sounded tired. "I'll probably be able to drop it off at your hangar sometime this evening."

"All right." Macklin turned the spigot knobs with his feet, shutting off the water. "Thanks, Ron."

"Don't thank me, Mack, thank the mayor." Shaw hung up, and Macklin put the receiver back on the cradle. The doorbell chimed downstairs.

Macklin groaned. It never rains, it just storms. The doorbell chimed again.

"Coming!" Macklin yelled. He pulled out the stopper with his foot, letting the water drain out, stood up dripping, and reached for his ybathrobe.

"Hold on!" He scampered out of the bathroom and down the stairs to the front door, beads of sweat rolling down his face, his damp body clinging to the robe.

Wiping the sweat out of his eye, Macklin opened the door. Jessica Mordente stood on the porch. He noticed now, in the sunlight, the dark-skinned sensuality and sharp features he hadn't seen a few nights earlier. Her loose-fitting white blouse, trim khaki pants, and matching low-heeled boots accentuated her slender build.

"Oh, I'm sorry," she said, eyeing Macklin from head to toe. She, too, liked what she saw. "I didn't mean to disturb you."

Macklin shrugged. *So Mr. Jury is dead, huh? Somebody forgot to tell her.* "What do you want?"

"To apologize," she ventured softly. Macklin raised an eyebrow, relieved but wary. "I was trying to find Mr. Jury. I investigated the whole thing very hard, very seriously. My strident style isn't always the most diplomatic. The police found him today, dead." She shrugged apologetically. "I'm sorry if I treated you rudely, Mr. Macklin."

Macklin smiled, not sure whether he believed her. "It's okay. I didn't exactly give you the VIP treatment, either." Her eyes drew him in. Words spilled out of him before he knew it. "Look ... ah ... I was just getting dressed. Why don't you come in for a moment, have a cup of coffee, we'll start off fresh."

Her eyes lit up. "I'd like that."

Macklin moved aside. *Shit, what am I getting myself into?* "Come in, then. Make yourself at home while I get ready." She walked past him and he closed the door.

"Have you ever been up in a helicopter?" he asked.

"No," she replied.

"Tell you what, then." Macklin led Mordente into the living room. "Why don't you go into the kitchen, rummage around, throw some things into the basket above the frig, and we'll go on a helicopter ride around the city."

She laughed. "Sounds great to me."

"Then it's a date." Macklin patted her on the back and dashed up the stairs. She watched him go, and her smile faded. Half of her was excited. The other half was scared shitless.

They flew north over the beaches, following the Pacific Coast Highway, and then veered eastward over the wooded Palisades. The asphalt of Sunset Boulevard wound snakelike through the hills, forming the northern boundary of Brentwood, the upper-middle-class neighborhood flanked on the south by San Vicente Boulevard.

Macklin glanced at Mordente and pointed out the stately houses that lined San Vicente.

"Those are houses that want to grow up and be mansions," he observed. "And look at that median strip. It's better landscaped than most of those homes."

She nodded, grinning. She noticed that a steady stream of joggers, in their designer warm-up suits and slashed sweatshirts and satin shorts, were scurrying up and down the grassy median. The joggers, to Mordente, seemed less interested in losing pounds and staying fit than in picking up bedmates.

"I can't believe how much you can see from up here," Mordente yelled into the mouthpiece of her headset.

Macklin winced, her voice booming in his ears. "You don't have to yell," he said softly, hoping to set an example. "I can hear you just fine."

She grimaced guiltily. "Sorry, it's just that I've never worn a spacesuit like this before."

Macklin nodded. "I know. You get used to the fireproof jumpsuits and all the paraphernalia after a while. Think of this as the *Starship Enterprise* on a strange new mission, and the getup is easier to bear."

Mordente tossed back her head and laughed. "Actually, with these seat belts and the cozy backseat, I feel like I'm in a flying Buick LeSabre. All this needs is a hood ornament and a rearview mirror with a garter on it or something."

"Sounds like you ride around in some classy cars, lady," Macklin joked, bringing the helicopter down low across the sprawling Veterans Administration graveyard, the tombstones like neat rows of pebbles below them. He pulled the helicopter up again, over the UCLA dormitories, and then down over the track field.

"I spent hours down there." He pointed to the track. "That ground is soaked with my sweat."

"And I bet all the students think the bad smell in the air is from the smog."

Macklin chuckled dryly. "Cute. Anyway, I got into UCLA on a track scholarship. I thought I would be an Olympic athlete or something."

"What happened?"

He steered the helicopter slightly southward to a cluster of short gray buildings just shy of the mazelike structure of the medical center. "I got lost down there amidst the corridors of the engineering schools. Ended up at Hughes Aircraft boring myself to death."

"How did you escape?" she asked. *Questions,* Macklin thought, *come very easy for her.*

Macklin tapped the glass in front of him. "This baby. I decided I'd rather fly the aircraft than draw them all day."

He purposely made the turn northward sharp so Mordente was nearly passing over the ground sideways. Straightening the helicopter, Macklin turned to her and half smiled. "Airsick yet?"

"Nope." She grinned.

Macklin shook his head in mock disbelief. "Damn. That's the turn that gets them every time."

The trees that shrouded the elegant Bel-Air homes of the stars and millionaires from the tour buses and casual passersby offered no protection from curious eyes in the sky. The homes were revealed in all their resplendent excess to Macklin and Mordente.

She whistled long. "If people only knew..."

"There would be an armed revolt," Macklin said, "starting with the poverty-stricken masses of Watts and sweeping through the rent-gouged apartment dwellers of the west side and Hollywood. The folks down there would have to dig moats around their castles."

"Castles is right," Mordente murmured, her face pressed to the glass, staring down in wonder at the vast acreage, the glimmering blue swimming pools, and the massive homes reminiscent of the seventeenth-century estates that dot the England countryside.

"There are some modern wonders, too." Macklin nodded toward a stark white structure with jutting lines and tall panes of glass.

"And I always thought Space Mountain was at Disneyland," she remarked sarcastically, sipping from the beer she had kept between her knees. Mordente tipped the beer toward a home coming up on their right. "Whose place is that?"

Macklin glanced over and felt his heartbeat pick up its pace. "That's Crocker Orlock's estate. You can tell by the heart-shaped swimming pool."

Mordente looked down at it as Macklin circled the estate. Three limousines were parked on the circular driveway, which surrounded a stone fountain. Pillars of white water shot high into the air.

"That's quite a spread." Mordente nodded in appreciation at Orlock's large Georgian home with its Greek-style columns in the front. "It looks like an Athens tract home, you know what I mean?"

Macklin smiled.

"Have you ever seen his boat?" she asked.

"Nope. What's it like?"

"The *Queen Mary*."

They laughed, Macklin making a southward pass over the famed "HOLLYWOOD" sign and heading westward above the office buildings and condominium towers of the Wilshire Corridor.

"Ready to head back?"

Mordente shrugged. "Whatever you say, Captain."

"I say let's pick up two steaks and let me make us some dinner. How does that sound to the crew?"

She chuckled. "The crew will postpone the mutiny. For now."

CHAPTER THIRTEEN

"I didn't know men knew how to cook," she said, her eyes half closed, the gentle effect of the wine. Sitting close to Macklin on his couch, she wasn't sure if the warmth she felt was from the wine, the crackling fire, or him. Perhaps it was an enticing combination.

"They don't." He grinned. "The steak was real—everything else was Stouffer's." He felt childishly nervous, his heart fluttering like that of a teenage boy who was afraid his newfound deep voice would crack and reveal his uneasiness.

She looked into his eyes and laughed, the sound tickling him. It made him happy, and it made him guilty. Only three days had passed since Cheshire's death, and already he wanted another woman.

He held the gaze despite himself and she slipped her arm around him, sliding snugly against his side.

"I can't," he whispered, starting to rise. She grasped him tightly, holding him down.

"You can't what?" she replied softly. "All I did was put my arm around you."

Macklin chuckled self-consciously.

She grinned back at him and removed her arm from his shoulder. "Look, that was a stupid thing for me to say. I know you're feeling confused right now. So am I."

They stared into each other's eyes silently. Macklin needed to feel close to someone now. He needed someone to accept him as a loving human being and not as Mr. Jury. Her eyes offered a sanctuary from the world of violence he lived in.

She tentatively brushed his cheek with her fingers and leaned toward him uncertainly. Macklin tensed, repulsed and drawn to her at the same time. Her lips touched his with such tenderness that he couldn't stop himself from wrapping his arm around her and drawing her close.

His arm felt strong and assured to her, though the pounding heart she felt against her side hinted at his trepidation.

Macklin's kisses were light and uneasy, barely touching her lips. His conflicting emotions and the strength of his desire were dizzying. He was frightened. She understood, parting her lips slowly. But Macklin could sense the hunger in her breaths, in her gentle shivers. The sensuality of her response stoked his desire into an uncontrollable firestorm. His hand dropped to her breast, stroking it through her shirt. She made a luscious, soft sound and caressed his thigh, letting her hand drift tantalizingly close to his stiffening penis. He raised his hand slightly and undid the buttons of her shirt.

Mordente moaned, spreading her legs and leaning back against the couch. Her breasts tumbled out the wide V of her open blouse, the nipples aroused into hard points. Macklin dropped his head and, with deliberate slowness, kissed and sucked and licked his way down her chest, moving off the couch and leaning over her. She writhed, running her fingers through his hair, massaging his scalp. He molded his lips around the stem of her right nipple, teasing it with his moist tongue. She dragged her fingernails across his back, parting her legs wide and pushing herself against the bulge of his erection. They ground to a quickening rhythm.

Macklin slid one hand down her flat stomach to her belt, carefully unbuckling it. She felt his hot breath on her cleavage as he moved to her left nipple, already excited by his sucking of her other breast.

She pulled his shirt out of his pants and slipped her hands under the tight waistband and over his buttocks, soft and smooth to the touch. Macklin's erection pressed uncomfortably against his jeans.

Leaning back, Macklin yanked down her pants, and she opened his, slipping down his briefs and wrapping her hand tightly around his penis. She looked into his eyes and smiled, pulling him to her. "Let me take *you* on a ride..."

Noises that invaded Macklin's sleep always seemed ten times louder than they did when he was awake. That didn't change Sunday morning. When the phone rang, it sounded like a fire alarm going off next to his ear.

He grabbed for it angrily, nearly knocking the whole thing on the floor, where it would undoubtedly have crashed down like a two-ton boulder.

"Yes?" he whispered with aggravation, looking over his bare shoulder at Mordente, who lay on her left side with her naked back to him. His fingers traced the thin white lines left on her back by the straps of her bathing suit.

"It's me," Mort said. "The stuff is here and I've checked it out. It's fine. What the hell do you plan to do with it?"

Macklin picked up his watch on the nightstand and glanced at the time. Nine o'clock.

"I'll tell you when I get there, around two," Macklin mumbled, gently lifting up the sheet and admiring Mordente's firm buttocks and slim, crossed legs. "How are you feeling?"

"Better than you'd think," Mort laughed. "But I look like Quasimodo's uglier half-brother."

"Bye." Macklin set the phone down gently and slid close to Mordente, pressing himself against her back and slipping one hand between her legs.

She stirred, uncrossing her legs. Macklin nuzzled her neck and let his fingers explore her.

"Good morning," she said, her eyes still closed.

"Good morning," he echoed. "How are you?"

"Fine." She grinned. "And getting better." Macklin rolled over on top of her and gave her a deep kiss.

"But," she said, holding his face in her hands, "I've got work to do today, a freelance story that must go to New York by Express Mail tomorrow morning."

Macklin kissed her again, stroking her between her legs with his forefinger.

"Maybe," she moaned, "it could wait for an hour or so."

⚜ ⚜ ⚜

The moment Macklin walked into the hangar, he could tell something was wrong. Mort was in the office sitting on Macklin's desk, holding the phone close to his ear, his brow furrowed.

"Brett, it's Shaw," Mort said, putting his hand over the mouthpiece. A large white bandage covered the side of his head. "All the equipment is in the chopper."

Macklin nodded and took the receiver from him. "Bad news?" he asked Shaw.

"Yep, I think Orlock skipped out on us this morning," Shaw said. "I'm trying to get a search warrant to go through the house, but it will take time. It's Sunday and all the judges are on the golf course."

"Shit, where is he?" He couldn't stand the idea of Orlock slipping through his fingers.

"That's a dumb question," Shaw snapped. "How the hell do I know? His lawyers say he's here but unavailable. I think it's bullshit and I can't get the law on my side to force its hand. The cogs of the legal machine move slowly on weekends."

The legal machine always works slowly, Macklin thought, *if it even works at all.* "Who is Orlock's lawyer?"

"Jules Baldwin, a young Century City type, the kind who works seven days a week," Shaw said.

Macklin glanced at Mort. There might be a way to find Orlock after all.

"Orlock can't be far. Look, Ronny, don't you worry about it. I'll find out where he is." He gripped the receiver tightly. "You just get me the go-ahead from Harlan Fitz."

Shaw sighed. "I already did."

Jules Baldwin knew his wife didn't like the stainless steel–modern look of his new law office, the glass-walled corner of the fifth floor of a Century City tower. He didn't give a shit whether she liked it or not. The decor was one way of keeping the pain in the ass out of the office. He loved his work far more than he'd ever love his wife.

It was a $300-an-hour decorator, a woman he described to friends as "extremely fuckable," and a late-night rerun of *UFO* that had given him the inspiration for the office's sci-fi style. The hanging prints were all new-wave splashes of color framed in silver against a white wall. The plants were potted in silver vases beside silver-wrought hi-tech chairs that Captain Kirk would be quite comfortable sitting in.

Baldwin sat in just such a chair, hunched over an ink-scrawled yellow legal pad that lay amidst a smattering of papers on his glass desk. Behind him was a window that afforded him a sweeping view of the Century Plaza Hotel.

He'd stare out the window at the hotel and console himself by thinking that though he didn't have a view like the other partners, he had Andrea for a secretary.

His mind had begun to wander to Friday's lunchtime dictation, which Andrea took between his legs, when the white phone rang and interrupted his pleasant memories.

"Jules Baldwin," he said, his New York upbringing turning "Baldwin" into "Bowldwin" as he spoke.

"Yeah, this is the garage," the caller drawled. "There's been an accident down here with your car."

Baldwin's eyebrows shot up and the color drained from his face. Images of his BMW 320i as a crumpled mass of twisted metal flashed in front of his eyes. "M-My car?" It came out "cah." "My car? Shit, I'll be right down."

He slammed down the receiver and dashed out of his office.

Macklin, downstairs in the garage beside the bank of elevators, hung up the pay phone with a smile and waved to Mort, who sat behind the wheel of Macklin's idling Impala.

Macklin pressed his back to the wall beside the elevator door and waited. A second later, the doors parted and Baldwin rushed out. Macklin stuck out his leg.

Baldwin cried out, falling face first onto the cement. Macklin was on him in an instant, sitting on Baldwin's back and pinning back the lawyer's arms. Baldwin, his cheek to the cool cement, screamed out in terror as the Impala shot forward out of the shadows and closed in on him.

"NOOOOOOOO!" Baldwin cried shrilly. The Impala screeched to a stop two feet short of his head.

Baldwin panted, fear dampening his face with sweat.

"Where's Orlock?" Macklin demanded, twisting Baldwin's arm.

"Who's Orlock?" Baldwin's yelled, the sound of the engine in his ears, the exhaust filling his nostrils. "I don't know anyone named Orlock."

The Impala jerked forward. Baldwin screamed and squeezed his eyes closed as the front end of the car passed over his head.

He opened his eyes and stared into the tread of the left front tire, now inches from his face.

The engine growled above him.

"Tell me where Orlock is or they'll be wiping you up with a mop," Macklin hissed.

"On his boat. He's on his fucking boat, okay?" Baldwin exclaimed. "He's going to Costa Rica."

"Why?"

Baldwin was silent.

"Two seconds, scum, and you're dogshit on my tire."

The engine revved hungrily. "Okay, okay, he's gonna pull a Robert Vasco," Baldwin said, his voice cracking. "All his money is safe in Swiss banks, so he's running. He wants to be out of the country before the cops are able to get past me to him. He's going to disappear into South America and die a wealthy man."

"Not if I can help it." Macklin stood up, pulling Baldwin up with him. The lawyer's head smashed against the underside of the car. Baldwin let out a sharp, guttural cry of pain. Macklin lowered him a few inches and then suddenly yanked him up again. Baldwin's head hit the car with a metallic thud.

Macklin released Baldwin, leaving the dazed, limp lawyer shaking on the ground, and got into his car on the passenger side. Mort slipped the gear into reverse and sped backward out of the garage.

As unconsciousness closed in on Baldwin, he thanked God his car was all right after all.

CHAPTER FOURTEEN

Brett Macklin's helicopter streaked westward, chasing the setting sun across the Pacific's blue, frothy swells in search of Orlock's yacht, the *Profiteer.*

While Macklin peered out the window, scanning the ocean, Mort guided the chopper south of Catalina Island, which loomed several miles to their right against a purple sky.

"Brett, pretty soon it's going to be too dark," Mort said.

Macklin kept his eyes on the water skirting past them. "He's not going to slither away, Mort. We're going to find him."

"Maybe Baldwin lied. Maybe this is a wild-goose chase."

"No, I can feel it. Orlock's out there."

"Where out there?" Mort groaned to himself.

Macklin heard him but made no comment. *Orlock won't escape,* Macklin thought. *This time Orlock* will *pay for his crimes.*

Macklin's eyes narrowed on a white dot in the distance. *Yes, it has to be.* He nudged Mort and pointed. "That's him."

"How can you be sure?"

Macklin slipped on the leather gloves in his lap. "I'm sure," he said, picking up a rifle from the floor.

He slid open the window and stared down the rifle's sight, following the one-hundred-foot yacht's wide wake to the stern, where he could see the word *Profiteer* behind a wet bike secured to the diving platform.

"All right, Mort, it's showtime," Macklin said with a grim smile. He strapped on a wide brown harness that had three carabiners, looped metal clasps, dangling from it.

Macklin had ordered the equipment from Shaw in case the law couldn't get near Orlock and Macklin would have to seek justice himself. The equipment was for an assault on Orlock's mansion. But, Macklin realized, the open sea was much better. No witnesses. No danger of being identified. No police to intrude.

"It's going to be tricky, Brett," Mort said. "He's going about twenty-five knots."

Macklin picked up the rifle again, sticking the barrel out the window and sighting the upper deck, close to the wheelhouse. "Then we'll just have to slow 'em down."

He squeezed the trigger.

The tear-gas canister burst out of the rifle and whistled down to the yacht, missing its target and hitting the launch crane. The smoking canister clattered to the deck floor and shrouded the yacht's stern in thick, eye-stinging fog.

"Damn," Macklin hissed, taking aim on the wheelhouse again. "Get me closer, Mort, and keep her steady."

A man emerged from the wheelhouse, firing a machine gun at the helicopter. Mort veered away, the machine gun a flickering spark on the *Profiteer*'s deck.

"No!" Macklin scolded Mort. "Stay on her ass."

Mort, realizing the futility of arguing, reluctantly brought the helicopter to bear on the yacht again. Macklin adjusted his aim, centering the sights on the turtleneck-clad gunman.

Macklin fired, the canister slamming the gunman through the wheelhouse window. A second later, billows of tear gas rose from the wheelhouse and the yacht slowed.

"Okay, let's get on top of them," Macklin said, dropping his rifle on the floor and opening the door. A burst of cold wind rushed into the helicopter, chilling their skin.

"Brett, are you sure you want to do this?" Mort asked.

Macklin ignored him, yelling over the whir of the chopper blades and the rush of sea air. "Bring her down as close as you dare over the stern, then get up and keep your eyes open."

Mort nodded. "Be careful, Brett."

Macklin smiled. "I will." He slipped a .44 Magnum automatic in his harness, pulled a gas mask over his head, and dropped one end of a nylon rope out the window. The rope spilled out, dangling seventy-five feet below the chopper and disappearing in the gas cloud on the *Profiteer*'s stern.

He snapped a carabiner to the rope, which ran through the metal loop on down between his legs. Holding the rope tightly, Macklin backed out of the helicopter, pausing with his body hunched outward and his feet planted firmly against the doorframe.

"You're crazy, Brett," Mort bellowed.

Macklin, straddling the rope, winked and pushed off. He slid down the rope quickly. He enjoyed the illusion of being stationary, the ocean raising the boat up to him, offering Orlock on a one-hundred-foot, narrow platter.

The rope suddenly ran out, slipping through his fingers. Macklin dropped through ten feet of thin air into the tear-gas cloud. Without warning, he crashed onto the hardwood deck.

Macklin lay stunned, curled up on the deck, pain buzzing in his legs, fireworks bursting in his eyes. *So this is what it's like to be a raindrop.* The sound of bullets clamoring for him brought him to his senses. He tumbled like a bread roller along the floor, the bullets cutting a trail across the wood inches from his body.

He bolted to his feet and yanked out his .44 Magnum automatic in one motion, catching sight of a figure staggering in the greenish haze near the cabin directly ahead. Macklin squeezed the trigger, the Magnum spitting slugs through the smoke. The bullets hammered into the figure, skipping him across the floor like a hand-tossed stone skimming the surface of the water.

Macklin dashed to the cabin wall and pressed himself against it. His heart throbbed in his throat and he felt slightly queasy. A ticklish feeling pinned him to the wall for fifteen seconds. Fear. *C'mon, Ace Commando, you can't chicken out now.*

Taking a deep breath, he slid to his left toward the cabin door. He hesitantly reached out for the latch and pulled it open. No gunfire exploded through the doorway. *That means nothing,* Macklin thought. *Whoever is inside might just be waiting to see the whites of my eyes.*

Pivoting on his right foot, he spun in a crouch facing the open door, his gun ready. He saw a lavish living room, complete with piano, wet bar, plush couches, and dark wood bookcases lined with volumes. A stuffed swordfish was mounted, midjerk, on the wall above the bar. Pictures of Tinseltown pirates, from Errol Flynn to Robert Shaw, hung around the cabin.

Macklin entered the cabin slowly, moving toward the low door directly in front of him. He stepped down the two steps leading to it cautiously and thought about how much he hated closed doors and what they might hide. The abrasive sound of the chopper circling overhead was reassuring. At least he wasn't alone.

Pressing his shoulder to the door, he twisted the handle and burst into the dark passageway. He froze, listening for a sign of lurking danger. His face was hot in the gas mask, his warm breath trapped inside.

He crept slowly forward, waiting for someone to leap out of an adjoining room. An explosion behind him shook the passageway. A single split second of understanding, long enough for Macklin to realize a gun had been fired, preceded the two bullets. They pounded into his back, shoving him forward onto the floor. Flat on his stomach, his consciousness swirling and his body numb, he desperately tried to suck in breath as darkness closed in on him.

Mort buzzed above the yacht, worried. He hadn't seen any sign of Macklin for several minutes. That wasn't good. The tear gas had dissipated, and he could see the launch crane swinging out over the water, a single figure in the motorboat. It had to be Orlock.

Damn. Mort flashed on the front-mounted three-million-candle-power searchlight Stocker had stolen from an LAPD Air Support Unit allocation. A bright beam of light sliced the darkness and concentrated on the speedboat slapping the surface. A man in a yellow life vest cowered in the light, unclasping the launch ties.

Orlock—it had to be Orlock. Mort switched on the loudspeaker.

"You're not going anywhere, Orlock," Mort's voice boomed down from the sky. Orlock settled behind the wheel and twisted the key, the outboard motor sputtering to life.

"Damn it," Mort said to himself in frustration. "Where's Brett?"

The launch sped away from the yacht, cutting a sharp swath in the water.

"Orlock is escaping in the launch," Mort barked into the mike, following the boat with the searchlight.

Macklin lay motionless in the passageway, Mort's words vaguely registering in his throbbing head. He felt the floor shudder under the weight of approaching footsteps. Macklin steadied his breathing, willing his head to clear.

The footsteps stopped. A hand gripped Macklin's shoulder and turned him over. Macklin pumped three shells into the man's gut. Blood burst out the man's back, splattering the walls.

The gunman staggered back, blood bubbling from his stomach, his face drawn into an expression of confused surprise. His half-closed eyes asked, How?

"Flak jacket, asshole," Macklin hissed, driving his foot into the man's bloody midsection. The man's face bloated and his stomach imploded with a squish, swallowing Macklin's foot.

The man toppled backward and Macklin heard the wet slurp of his foot being released. The body landed with a dull splash in the puddle of blood.

Macklin sat up slowly, his back rigid with pain from the impact of bullets into the flak jacket concealed under his jumpsuit.

Reaching out to the wall for support, Macklin was able to pull himself into a standing position. He stepped around the gunman's corpse and forced himself to move quickly back up the steps, through the main cabin, and out onto the deck.

Yanking off his gas mask, Macklin turned to his right and saw his helicopter hovering above him, its searchlight trained on a motorboat racing through the night toward Catalina.

"Are you all right?" Mort blared from the helicopter.

Macklin waved and then pointed frantically in the direction of the speeding launch. *Go after him!* After a second or two of hovering, Mort got the message and veered away in pursuit of Orlock.

Orlock mustn't make it to Catalina and contact the authorities, Macklin thought, suddenly remembering the wet bike he had spied in his rifle sights earlier.

Macklin leaned over the stern and saw the wet bike, an ocean-faring version of a motorcycle, secured to the fantail. Glancing over his shoulder as he leaped onto the platform, he could see the launch swerving as the helicopter snaked in and out of Orlock's path.

I hope Mort can slow him down, Macklin thought, untying the wet bike. If Orlock made it to the island, Macklin knew the authorities would place Orlock in protective custody. Orlock would relax safely in the taxpayers' care while sympathetic publicity casting him as a victim raged in the media and muted the city's chances of putting Orlock behind bars on kiddie-porn charges.

Macklin's back screamed with pain as he bent down and lifted the wet bike, bracing his legs to take most of the weight. What if Orlock saw the call letters on the chopper? The thought teased Macklin as he lowered the wet bike onto the water and straddled it. Orlock could end up remaining free while Macklin faced a lifetime in prison for murder.

The wet bike jerked forward and skipped across the swells toward the launch, which sped in a curving path under the bright searchlight of the low-flying helicopter.

That's it, Mort, pin him down. Macklin twisted the throttle, urging the wet bike forward. Cool mist splashed his face and his hair.

The helicopter swooped down on Orlock, who frantically twisted the wheel and brought the launch around, crossing Macklin's path. Orlock noticed his pursuer for the first time. Macklin could see Orlock's wild, enraged face in the white light, his teeth gritted and his eyes wide.

Macklin closed in on Orlock's boat, his wet bike bouncing violently in the choppy water kicked up by the spinning helicopter blades and the converging wakes from the circuitous path cut by Orlock's outboard motor. A loud mechanical grind, the cacophony of engines, grated against Macklin's ears.

Macklin's one chance to stop Orlock came in an instant. Orlock swerved to avoid the chopper and momentarily came alongside the wet bike. Macklin threw himself into the boat. The Magnum slipped out of Macklin's harness into the ocean as he bashed painfully against the edge of the boat and tumbled inside.

Orlock abandoned the wheel and pounced on Macklin. The boat spun out of control. Orlock fell forward onto Macklin and they rolled toward the stern. Macklin, dazed and disoriented, felt Orlock's chilly hands squeeze his neck, cutting off his air.

Lifting Macklin by the neck, Orlock draped him over the back of the boat beside the growling outboard and forced his head down to the water. Macklin reached out, scratching and pulling at Orlock's face. But it was no good. The cold water rushed up Macklin's nostrils as Orlock pushed his head under. Macklin's head pounded, deprived of air, and he could feel the deadly motion of the rotor blades buzzing an inch from his left ear.

Macklin grabbed the boat with his right hand and pressed the palm of his left hand under Orlock's chin, trying to push him back. Time was working against Macklin. The lack of air was weakening him, and Orlock was edging Macklin's head to the rotor, now so close Macklin could feel the blade skimming past his ear.

Frantic, his chest swelled with agony, Macklin slapped the outboard with his left hand. He felt the rotor blade slice at strands of his hair. His fingers fell on the gear shift and he yanked it down.

The boat jolted into reverse, the momentum jerking Macklin forward. Macklin used the split-second advantage, ramming his knee into Orlock's groin. The momentum, combined with the blow, knocked Orlock off balance.

Orlock tumbled over Macklin and splashed into the water beside the back-circling boat. Macklin pulled himself up, heaving, each breath a razor-sharp dagger plunged down his throat. Water streamed down Macklin's icy blue face.

Looking back, Macklin saw Orlock bobbing in turbulent waters, and he flipped the gear shift up. The boat kicked forward and Macklin scrambled to the wheel.

He pushed the throttle lever forward and gunned the boat, bringing it around in a wide circle and bearing down on Orlock, who bobbed like a buoy ahead.

"No!" Orlock screamed, trying to dive, the vest keeping him afloat.

Macklin kept coming, seeing only the murdered children and Orlock's grand estate.

Make them pay!

The launch ripped through Orlock, tearing his body apart in a crimson splash of water.

EPILOGUE

Jessica Mordente felt edgy and uncomfortable when she emerged from Cock'n Bull, an English-style buffet fronting the west edge of the Sunset Strip. The feeling had begun when Chet picked her up at her apartment and continued unabated through their empty dinner conversation and her forced light-hearted repartee.

Navarro came up behind her, chewing on a toothpick, and put his arm around her shoulder. "What happened to the old Jessica Mordente?"

"Why? What does she have that I don't?" she asked, walking with Navarro away from the restaurant. She shouldn't be mad at him, she knew. After all, she had been the one to ask him out on Friday and he'd been affable all evening. But with each moment spent with him, her uneasiness intensified.

"An appetite, for one," He removed his arm and shoved his hands into his pockets. "You used to eat everything in there except the table. Tonight you barely were able to stomach your crumpet."

Mordente shrugged. "I dunno, I just wasn't hungry. I've been working pretty hard and snacking all day." She knew that wasn't it, though. It was that sense of impending doom that had been hanging over her like a dark storm cloud.

"And item two," he continued, stopping beside his sleek, white Pontiac Fiero. "I usually have to dodge ten zillion questions from you. That would irritate most sane people, but not me. I like that about you, that mix of a sharklike predatory instinct coupled with a dash of good-natured inquisitiveness. It's fun in a masochistic sort of way."

He flashed a playful grin at her. "Now you're a sissy. I don't get it."

"C'mon, Chet, take it easy on me," she sighed. "I'm sorry. You've tried very hard and it's been a pleasant evening. I guess you're right. I'm not myself tonight."

Navarro unlocked the car and opened the door. "Maybe this will bring you back to your senses." He reached behind the seat and pulled out a manila envelope, then turned and held it out to her.

"Here's one of the photographs taken by the bank camera," he said, looking at her sternly. "This is strictly off the record, understand? You can look at it, but that's it."

Mordente nodded expressionlessly and took the envelope.

"To be honest," he continued, "we see no reason to go after the guy, you know?"

She lifted the flap and pulled out the photo.

"Not a bad picture, huh?" he asked.

"Crystal clear," she muttered, her throat dry. Brett Macklin's piercing gaze was unmistakable.

THE END
Brett Macklin will return in
PAYBACK

PAYBACK

BY LEE GOLDBERG

This novel is a work of fiction. Names, characters, places, and incidents either are the product of the author's imagination or are used fictitiously. Any resemblance to actual events or places or persons, living or dead, is entirely coincidental.

Originally published in paperback as *.357 Vigilante #3: White Wash* under the pen name "Ian Ludlow" by Pinnacle Books, October 1985

Special thanks to Jerone Ten Berge for the cover art and Eileen Chetti for proofreading.

To Bill, my (sometimes) better half, and to Karen E. Bender, who makes me whole.

PROLOGUE

Sunday, May 27

Sergeant Ronald Shaw always thought his own death would catch him by surprise, leaving him only a split second to contemplate his doom. He never thought it would be like this.

The black homicide detective lay flat on his back, his legs straight and his arms flush against his sides, as stiff as the wood that imprisoned him. The air was hot and heavy, making him think of the musty wool blanket his mother used to drag out of the attic and put on his bed in the wintertime. He was thinking a lot about the past now, mostly of sunlight and open spaces.

The worst part had been the pain, which sat in the hollow of his empty stomach and seeped, milky and sour, into every vein and capillary of his body. But he gradually accepted it and it stopped being an adversary and became a companion. The enormity of his loneliness was worse than the pain.

His eyes were open wide now, fixed on the tiny shaft of light that fell through the narrow metal pipe and dripped fresh air on his face. It was his only connection to the outside world, a world separated from him by the coffin walls and six feet of dirt.

Shaw had no idea how long he had been buried here nor how much time he had left until it no longer mattered. Sometime ago—he didn't know when—he had come to accept his death, even welcome it. His only fear now, in those rare moments of lucidity between his forceful memories of the past and chilly unconsciousness, was that Brett Macklin would make the fatal mistake of trying to save him.

CHAPTER ONE

Friday, May 18, 10:45 p.m.

We're in deep shit.

That's what twenty-year-old Dennis Vercammen thought, sitting snug and thoroughly buzzed in the white leather backseat of his Daddy's custom-made 1981 Eldorado convertible, his arm around Gloria Pensky and his hand cupping her gelatinous left breast. Sandra Muirdoe sat in front of him, shooting worried glances at Reeves Rabkin, who was driving and stomping the gas pedal in a desperate attempt to stop the sputtering engine from dying.

The white convertible glowed like neon in a neighborhood where everything looked black. The beaten gray buildings blurred into the shadows and the streetlights cast a yellowish haze over the roadway that dissipated before reaching the sidewalks.

The car made one last, spasmodic lurch and everyone in the car realized what Dennis already knew.

"We're in deep shit," Sandra muttered.

Reeves glanced over his shoulder at Dennis with wide eyes that said *this can't be real.*

Dennis nodded and looked past Reeves into the shadows. He saw three black youths, with their rigid faces and furious eyes, move off the curb and glide towards the car.

"C'mon, Reeves, start the car. This isn't funny," Gloria whined, noticing the three blacks. Dennis felt her heart pounding in his palm and gave her breast a squeeze.

Reeves noticed Gloria and Dennis looking past him and turned in the direction of their gazes.

"Fuck." Reeves eyed the three guys heading towards them. He glanced back at Dennis. "Stay cool and let me handle this."

Dennis shrugged, his head bobbing on his rubbery neck. Drinking made his head feel like someone had ripped open his skull and scooped out the heavier parts of his brain. That was why he let Reeves drive and that was why he gladly accepted Reeves' offer to deal with this. After all, it was Reeves' idea to go to that goddamn frat party at USC and his fucking shortcut to the freeway that got them stuck in this hellhole. So Reeves damn well better handle this.

Dennis could tell the three blacks weren't goodwill ambassadors coming to welcome them into the neighborhood. They were too poor to look hip and too hip to look poor. One guy, perhaps no more than fifteen years old, wearing jeans, blue canvas tennis shoes, and a ratty, black leather jacket, stopped at the front of the car and started twisting the hood ornament absently, his eyes licking Sandra's body like it was a Popsicle.

Sandra sank uneasily down in her seat under the teenager's stare. Another guy, with pockmarked cheeks and deep-set, thin eyes, wearing a gray sleeveless sweatshirt that let his muscular arms sway unhindered, strutted around the passenger side and stood next to Sandra.

"Hey, shouldn't you guys be out there break-dancing or something?" Sandra's voiced cracked. "I'd sure like to see you dudes do a quick moonwalk right back where you came from."

The third man laughed, adjusted his reflective sunglasses, and came up beside Reeves. Dennis noticed the deferential way the other two blacks looked at the third man and assumed he was the leader.

"We've had some engine trouble," Reeves said evenly in a neutral, matter-of-fact tone that was utterly emotionless. Dennis immediately thought of Mr. Spock. "Is there a gas station nearby we can push the car to?"

The guy in the sunglasses ignored Reeves and faced Dennis. "Look, Benny, that asshole is grabbin' the bitch's tit."

"Dennis, let go of Gloria's tits," Reeves said in that same flat tone without looking back. Dennis didn't respond. He didn't feel like he was there; it seemed like he was watching it all on TV.

Suddenly the pockmarked man next to Sandra thrust his hand into her blouse, grabbing one of her breasts. She shrieked and grabbed his wrist, trying to pull his hand out.

Benny laughed, his hand deep in Sandra's blouse. "I got me some tit, too, Luthor." He twisted her breast until she cried out. "Ain't bad, neither."

"We don't want any trouble, guys," Reeves said. "We just want to get our car fixed and get out of here, okay?" Dennis expected Reeves to paralyze Luthor with a Vulcan neck pinch.

"Trouble?" Luthor crooned. "What trouble?"

The teenager in front of the car twisted the hood ornament roughly until it snapped off in his hand with an audible metallic crack. Reeves glared at him. Dennis wasn't too thrilled, either. His dad had dished out $20,000 to a Jewish man with buck teeth to fix up the car, to cut off the roof and add a wheel well to the trunk. The flow of cash from Dad into Dennis' pockets might dwindle severely if the car was damaged. And to Reeves, that meant there would be less cash to leech off Dennis, which meant less booze, less coke, and less pussy in Reeves' future.

In short, things were getting serious.

"That's just about enough, boys," Reeves hissed, his face twisted into a snarl. Dennis was surprised. He had never heard Reeves talk that way. Reeves dropped the Mr. Spock bit and was now doing his best Charles Bronson.

"Really?" Luthor asked in a singsong voice.

"You heard me, bro," Reeves said. "Why don't you boys just take a walk."

"Dipshit here is getting mad," Luthor said, glancing at his friends. "He wants us to take a walk. My, my, what should we do?"

The teenager in front of the car whirled, hurling the hood ornament at the windshield. Gloria screamed and everyone in the car dove down as the windshield crackled. Reeves slammed the car door open into Luthor's gut and spilled clumsily out of the car.

Luther recovered quickly. Before Reeves could stand, Luthor jammed two fingers into Reeves' nose and yanked him up. Reeves squealed, blood streaming out of his nostrils and down the back of Luthor's hand. Reeves looked into his reflection in Luthor's sunglasses.

"You think you got balls, huh?" Luthor grunted, suddenly grabbing Reeves' crotch with his free hand and crunching the testicles between his fingers. Reeves screamed, squirming in Luthor's hands. "Don't ya, prickless?"

Luthor laughed. "Hey, Benny, ream this asshole's woman so she knows what she's been missin'."

"No!" Sandra yelled.

Benny lifted her effortlessly out of the car and dumped her, kicking and writhing, on the ground at his feet. "Get ready to gargle some manhood, cunt. You're gonna get a third world tonsillectomy."

"Hey, fellas—," Dennis began. Benny interrupted him with a sobering backhand slap across the face that sent Dennis sprawling onto Gloria.

"Faggot," Benny cackled at Dennis, who lay dazed in Gloria's lap. Then a loud blast rang in Dennis' ear and Benny's head burst apart in an explosion of red froth and gray bits.

Dennis watched in stunned horror as Benny's headless torso stumbled towards him and then toppled over the edge of the car, blooding gushing out of his neck and splashing onto the white seats. Dennis knew his dad would never let him borrow the car again.

Dennis looked past Benny's gurgling body and saw a man in a red leather jumpsuit emerge from the darkness across the street, a band of black makeup over his eyes. A new-wave Superman, Dennis thought.

Luthor released Reeves and dashed away into the street, the black teenager running at his side. Reeves crumpled into a heap. The man in red turned towards the fleeing blacks, calmly raised his gun, and fired once. The bullet tore into Luthor's back, lifting him up off his feet and tossing him forward. The teenager flinched and kept running.

The gun bucked again in the stranger's hand. The teenager yelped with pain, spun, and fell backwards onto the ground.

The man spit and walked past the car without even looking at Dennis or his friends. Reeves reached up, grabbed the car door, and pulled himself to his feet, his eyes on the man walking towards Luthor, who lay motionless in the street.

The man glanced at Luthor's blood-soaked corpse and then stepped over to the groaning teenager, crushing Luthor's shattered sunglasses under his heel. He stopped at the boy's feet and stared down at him. The boy clutched his left leg, blood spraying between his fingers like a small sprinkler.

"I-I'm hurtin' bad." The boy trembled.

The man grimaced. "Fucking nigger." He aimed the gun at the boy's stomach and pulled the trigger. Three bullets pounded into the boy in rapid succession, skipping his body across the asphalt.

The man shuffled up to the mangled body, fired one more shot into it, and then walked towards the car, his gun hanging limply at his side.

Reeves curled his lips as if to speak, but he couldn't summon his voice. Sandra whimpered on the ground, thankful yet afraid, careful not to look at the man as he passed. Gloria sat straight up in her seat, staring expressionlessly forward. Dennis watched the man slip back into the night.

"Who are you?" Dennis yelled impulsively.

The man whipped around and Dennis shrunk back, half expecting to taste a bullet. The man flashed a cynical grin and pinned Dennis under an icy gaze.

"Mr. Jury."

The sleek, fin-tailed, black '59 Cadillac Brett Macklin was so carefully polishing in his garage had almost ended up sticking ass backwards out the roof of a seedy Hollywood eatery.

The mean-grilled street shark had suddenly become prized, and woefully misunderstood, Americana. People would gut the cars like fish, junking the powerful V-8, 325-horsepower, 390-cubic-inch engine that gave the '59 Cadillac it's bite, slop a few coats of glossy paint on the chassis, and turn it into a bubbling Jacuzzi or mount it on some burger joint.

No one seemed to see the injustice in it, except Brett Macklin. The 1959 Cadillac wasn't made to hang above a restaurant door, it's twin bullet taillights blinking like a Christmas tree ornament. It was the last American car with balls, with aggressive styling that said *fuck you* and stole the road. Nowadays, Macklin lamented, American-made cars were microscopic bits of tin that farted along roads dominated by boxy foreign cars with high price tags and engines that fit in the glove compartment.

In the three weeks since he outbid a pear-shaped Greek man who wanted to put the car on his West Hollywood falafel hut, Macklin had done nothing but work day and night restoring and modifying it. The exhausting labor kept his mind off the anguish smoldering in his chest.

On a chilly morning less than a month ago, his girlfriend, Cheshire, got into his '59 Cadillac and twisted on the ignition, triggering a bomb that blew her and the car to smithereens in the driveway of his Venice home. The bomb had been meant for him, planted by a gang of psychopathic pedophiles the impotent justice system had failed to punish. Macklin hunted down the killers, as he had the murderers who set his father aflame a year before, and made them pay for their crimes.

Now he was alone again. And angrier than ever before. While restoring the car, he restored himself. Both the car and Macklin were now sophisticated killing machines. Using money and supplies covertly appropriated by Los Angeles mayor Jed Stocker, Macklin drew on his years as a helicopter designer for Hughes Aircraft and his education in aeronautical engineering to turn the Cadillac into a tank equipped for the urban battlefield.

Macklin was actually bringing the Cadillac back to its spiritual roots. The chassis of the 1959 Cadillac was inspired by the World War II Lockheed P-38 Lightning Fighter plane, and now his new, restored "Batmobile" was just as lethal.

First, Macklin made the car nearly impregnable to gunfire. He replaced the fuel lines with steel tubing, armored the 221-inch chassis with metal plates, fitted the sloping, teardrop-shaped cab with bulletproof glass, and equipped the car with self-sealing whitewall tires.

Macklin hid a set of strong halogen lamps, designed to blind nighttime pursuers with a burning flash of white light, behind the rocket-like rear grill beneath the sharp fins. But the teeth of the 1959 Cadillac's defensive power lay cloaked behind its menacing front chrome work. Two air-cooled .50-caliber machine guns, capable of firing bullets three times as heavy and three times as destructive as .44 Magnum shells, could burst out spitting hot lead from the centermost of the quadruple headlights.

Macklin stepped back, admiring the car's gleaming black finish, and reached for his can of Michelob on the garage workbench. Sitting in the stuffy garage throughout the humid evening, Macklin felt like a battered Kentucky Fried Chicken in a pressure cooker. His white, 1984 Olympics T-shirt clung to the damp skin between his shoulder blades and against his sternum.

His Levi's cutoffs itched his small buttocks firmed by years of jogging. The T-shirt was his passing nod to his teenage dream of being an Olympic-class runner. The dream died but was strong enough to get him through UCLA on a track scholarship.

The remaining three gulps' worth of beer was lukewarm, a pleasant reminder of how long and how deeply he had been immersed in his work. He wanted to finish the car in time to drive himself and Shaw to the campaign fund-raiser Sunday for black state assemblyman Cecil Parks, an old friend of theirs running as the Democratic candidate for U.S. senator.

Humming the Michelob jingle, Macklin strode to the rear of the car, squatted, and pulled a folded sticker from his back pocket. He removed the brown backing and carefully affixed the sticker to the gleaming chrome bumper.

It read: "PROTECTED BY SMITH AND WESSON."

"You vicious, sadistic bastard!"

Startled, Macklin jerked his head up and saw Jessica Mordente, a reporter for the *Los Angeles Times*, standing in the doorway leading to his laundry room. She wore faded blue jeans and a pink oxford shirt. Her olivine green eyes were wide and glassy, rage tightening her face and forcing the veins and tendons in her neck to bulge against her flushed skin.

"You're Mr. Jury," she shouted, making quick stabs towards him with her finger, "and I'm going to expose you!"

CHAPTER TWO

Macklin rose slowly, an eyebrow cocked, and regarded her with wary curiosity.

"Mr. Jury is dead," he said.

"A lie," she shot back. "A trick to throw the press off the trail. That corpse wasn't the vigilante. You are."

She whipped the manila envelope out from under her arm and waved it at him. "I got this photo from a source at the FBI. They don't care who you are. They think you're a hero. I've kept it a secret because I thought maybe they were right."

She tore open the envelope, pulled out the photograph, and thrust it at him. "This is a picture of you taken by a security camera. That's you gunning down a couple of bank robbers last month."

Macklin felt a shiver of apprehension crawl down his back. He took the picture and held it with both hands. There he was, in crisp black and white, his .357 Magnum flashing.

"Your murder spree is over, Macklin," she said vindictively.

He fell back against the car and let go of the picture, letting it float gently to the floor. In a strange way, he felt relieved. He wouldn't have to kill anymore. But unmasking would mean publicity. The horror that had killed his father and Cheshire, that had turned him into a vigilante and destroyed so much of his life, would now inflict the final injustice—the destruction of Cory, his eight-year-old daughter, and Brooke, his ex-wife. Sergeant Ronald Shaw, who strenuously objected to Macklin's vigilante justice but was tied to him nonetheless by years of friendship, would be prosecuted as a willing accomplice. So would Mort Suderson, the ex-LAPD helicopter pilot Macklin had hired to work for his charter airline company.

"Don't think about killing me," Mordente said with undisguised disgust. "I've already made arrangements for this picture to be circulated if I suddenly vanish."

Macklin shrugged. "You win, I'm Mr. Jury. Now what?"

"I expose you."

"Then why not just do it? Why come here first?"

Mordente bent over and picked up the photo. "I wanted to see your face. I wanted to know why you became a killer."

"A street gang ambushed my father, doused him with gasoline, and set him on fire. The law let them go free. I couldn't stand by and let those savages roam the streets and do to others what they did to my father."

Macklin looked into Mordente's eyes. He didn't expect any compassion from her and wasn't getting any. Her eyes were as cold as before. He simply wanted her to understand what he had only just begun to realize—that what he was doing on the streets was worth sacrificing himself and, yes, perhaps those he loved for.

"You killed others, too," she said.

"Psychos. They raped and killed children and filmed it for profit. I stopped them. It was the right thing to do."

"I was beginning to believe that, too," she shot back, her lower lip trembling with rage. "I really wanted to believe that. But tonight you went too far. You murdered a fifteen-year-old kid. A child. I let you go and you murdered a kid and reveled in the bloodshed."

Macklin shook his head, his brow wrinkled with confusion. "What?"

"I had that picture of you three weeks ago," she continued, talking to herself now, looking at him without seeing him. "If I had acted on it then, maybe three people would be alive tonight.

But I can make damn sure you don't kill anyone else. Tomorrow I write the story that puts you away."

"I didn't kill anyone tonight," Macklin said. Her head snapped up and she glared at him through narrow eyes. "I've been here, waxing my car."

"Christ, Macklin, when does the lying stop, huh?"

"Look, I have nothing to gain by lying now," Macklin said, keeping his voice steady. "I'm telling you I've been here all night."

Mordente ignored his protest and turned her back to him. "You're finished, Macklin."

"So you're going to leave now and write your article," Macklin said. "Tie me up and hang me out to dry."

"You got it," she said.

"Tell me, Jessie, how are you going to explain the last three weeks?"

She slowly turned around to face him again.

"How are you going to write your way out of knowing the truth and keeping it quiet for so long?" Macklin continued. "How are you going to describe the night we made love?"

"You're inhuman," she hissed.

Macklin shrugged. "I'm innocent of the killing tonight. Give me seventy-two hours and I'll prove it."

"No," she said, her eyes narrow and furious. "You'll run."

"Where could I go?" he replied. "If you write your story, you will stop me. But you will also crush my family. For their sake, not mine, give me a chance to prove my innocence. Three days, that's all I ask. If I don't find the impostor, I'll turn myself in to you and tell all." He paused. "Almost all. I won't say a word about our ever meeting before and that you've known the truth for three weeks. Your exposé will appear ethically and journalistically sound, and you might still have a career afterwards."

"All right," she muttered through tight lips. "Seventy-two hours." Her voice rose sharply into a shout that slapped him. "A second more and I'll destroy you, Brett Macklin, I promise you that." She turned and stormed into the house.

He listened to her stomping though the house, and then, a moment later, he heard his front door slam shut.

Macklin slumped against his car and sighed. He had three days to save his life. Who was the impostor? Was he just a vigilante or was there more to it? Where could he find him? The only place he could think to begin his search was where it all began—the dark alleys and grimy, forgotten streets of South Central Los Angeles. The urban jungle.

The crack of splintering wood broke into Macklin's thoughts. He whipped his head around and saw the back door of the garage burst open and slap against the wall. A police officer, his legs spread out and his gun braced in both hands, stood framed in the doorway.

Macklin shifted his gaze and saw another officer, in his crisp blue suit and hat, standing where Mordente had stood just a few minutes ago. The muzzle of the officer's gun was right in front of Macklin's face.

"You so much as twitch, Macklin," said the cop behind him, "and we'll give you a couple extra assholes."

It was after midnight when Macklin pulled open the glass door and stepped into the darkened hallway of the superior court, the two cops behind him with their guns out.

Their footfalls echoed eerily through the empty, gray-tile corridors as they walked in measured steps towards the last courtroom door. The tall oak door was about a half inch ajar when they approached to it. Pushing it open slowly, Macklin saw the room was lit only by the moon glow spilling in through the windows and a tiny reading lamp on the judge's bench.

Ex–superior court judge Harlan Fitz sat behind the bench. He wore a white polo shirt with a red sweater tied around his neck by its sleeves. When Macklin entered, Fitz leaned forward on his elbows, his hands supporting his head and flattening his puffy cheeks, which rolled up against his eyes and gave them an Asian slant.

Los Angeles mayor Jed Stocker stood in the center of the courtroom with a gun trained on Macklin. The mayor wore a crooked sneer and a gray three-piece suit, the vest unbuttoned and his tie loosened at the collar.

Shaw sat in the jury box, his legs crossed and resting on the wooden partition. The sleeves of his shirt were rolled up past his elbows, and his brown corduroy jacket was draped carelessly over the arm of the chair next to him. He acknowledged Macklin's presence with a quick, subdued glance. Macklin had grown up with Shaw and knew the glance meant that Shaw was trying to separate himself from Macklin. Not a good sign.

"Isn't this a bit melodramatic?" Macklin strode casually into the courtroom towards Stocker. The cops stood stoically in the doorway looking to Stocker for their next move.

"Just shut the fuck up, Macklin," Stocker barked. The mayor waved his gun at the cops and said, "I'll take it from here, boys." The cops nodded affirmatively and closed the door.

"Are those two monkeys really cops?" Macklin asked, jerking a thumb over his shoulder.

"My cops, Macklin." Stocker met Macklin's gaze and held the gun steady. "They know who runs the city, they know who to listen to, and they know when not to ask questions." Stocker, Macklin mused, had never stopped being chief of police.

Macklin glanced past Stocker to Fitz. The judge wearily beckoned Macklin forward with a subtle, backwards toss of his head.

"If you'll listen to me for a second," Macklin began, "I can save us a lot of time. I—"

"No, Macklin, it's you who needs to listen," Stocker broke in, shaking his gun for emphasis. "You've lost control. You've become a psycho . . . a liability."

"I didn't kill anyone tonight, folks." Macklin cautiously sat on the edge of the prosecutor's table, careful not to spook Stocker, and rested his hands on his knees. "I don't even know what happened."

"We didn't say anything about killings," Fitz said in an accusatory tone.

Macklin dropped his eyes. He wasn't ready to tell them about Mordente yet. "I heard about them an hour ago. I can't say from whom right now. All I know is that three guys were killed and Mr. Jury is the prime suspect."

"Three black gang members were roughing up a couple of white kids who accidentally violated their turf," Stocker explained with a patronizing tone. "A guy toting a .357 stepped out of nowhere and gunned down the gang members."

"You think I did it," Macklin stated.

Stocker nodded. Shaw sat passively.

"What about you, Ronny—do you think I did it?"

Shaw shrugged. "I'm not sure."

"Then why the hell is this brainless creep pointing a gun at me?" Macklin yelled, looking directly at Stocker.

"You're out of control," Stocker hissed at him, "and that makes you a dangerous man."

"There are some extenuating circumstances," Shaw said. "The mayor left out the sadistic part. The killer went up the boy, called him a fucking nigger, and pumped three more bullets into him."

Macklin nodded.

"Everything he did up until that point sounds like your usual style," Shaw said, "except for that. Maybe you've just grown to like killing."

Macklin shook his head disbelievingly. "You're crazy."

"Our mental capabilities aren't in question here," Fitz said. "Yours are. What happened tonight was a massacre. We can't let that happen again."

"Your problem, gentlemen, isn't with me. There's a sicko running around out there. He's the one that has to be stopped. We have to find out who he is and why he is killing people." Macklin stood up, crossing Stocker's path. "C'mon, look at this rationally for a moment. I was the one who insisted Judge Fitz become involved, remember? I'm the one who asked for a judicial review of my actions."

Macklin walked up to the jury bench and faced Shaw. "Mr. Jury was dead, Ronny. Why the hell would I resurrect him?"

"Yeah, and what about the death car you've been building in your garage?" Stocker said, a snide smile etching a crooked line across his face. "Is that a recreational vehicle or what?"

Macklin whirled around. "Before you shit through your mouth again, just remember you're the one who forced me into becoming Mr. Jury and you're not about to let me stop."

"It didn't take a helluva lot of force, Mack," Shaw said. "And you can stop anytime you want. Let's not kid each other. You want to be Mr. Jury. I realized that a long time ago. So don't act so goddamn self-righteous."

Macklin sighed wearily. "We're just going around in circles. I didn't kill them. Granted, it was the sort of situation I might have stepped into and cleaned up, but I certainly wouldn't slaughter a defenseless kid."

He turned back to Shaw. "And I wouldn't call him a fucking nigger. We all know I'm not a racist. Besides, if I had become a blood-crazed lunatic, I don't think I'd be here now arguing with you."

"Unless you were afraid we'd stop you from having your grisly fun," Stocker said.

"Stocker, I'd shine the toe of my shoe with your scrotum right now if I didn't think that would support your stupid allegations."

"That's enough," Fitz declared. "Put that gun away, Stocker."

Stocker hesitated, glaring at Macklin.

"Now," Fitz said again.

Stocker reluctantly slid the gun into his waistband.

"I think Macklin deserves the benefit of the doubt," Fitz said.

At least someone believes me, Macklin thought.

Shaw chuckled derisively. "I can't believe what I'm hearing. You're all ignoring the implications of this. Can't you see what this vigilante lunacy has finally come to? If Mack didn't do it tonight, someone else did. Other people may jump on the meat wagon, too. The Mr. Jury we created has become the justification psychos need to butcher people."

"Don't dump those bodies on my doorstep. Don't blame me for the actions of crackpots and psychos," Macklin said. "They don't need any justification for their actions. They could use Mr. Jury or Jesus—it makes no difference."

"Where do you draw the line between good murder and bad murder? You're both killing people," Shaw responded.

"That's like asking what's the difference between Hitler's Nazis and the soldiers who hit the beaches at Normandy, for Christ's sake," Macklin said. "In this country we have a system of law, we don't have a system of justice. Violent crime is running rampant in this city, and I'm doing something about it. Every day that these murderers roam the streets, your family and mine are in danger. I've never killed an innocent person."

"Yet," Shaw said.

"That's all irrelevant right now, gentlemen," Fitz said solemnly. "We've got a sadistic killer on our hands calling himself Mr. Jury."

"And while we're in here sitting on our asses, he's still on the streets." Macklin approached the judge's bench, feeling Stocker's insolent glare against his back. "I'd like to do something about it."

Fitz didn't hesitate. "Get him."

CHAPTER THREE

Saturday, May 19, 11:53 a.m.

The single-story, white, wood-frame house sat on a granite point overlooking the shimmering blue lake. The aluminum, triangular roof reflected the sun's rays, beaming down from a cloudless sky, into Jessica Mordente's eyes as her car bounced along the fifty yards of unpaved roadway leading to the house.

A tall guard tower flanked each side of the cyclone gate in front of her, the only opening in the two parallel, electrified fences that circled the tree-lined mile around the private lake. A single man, a rifle slung over his shoulder, stood like a life-size plastic GI Joe doll in each of the two thirty-foot-tall stations. In the gap between the fences, expressionless men in brown fatigues walked at a marchlike clip and, like the dogs at their sides, seemed to snarl instead of breathe. The guards probably lifted their legs to pee, too, she thought.

The gate in front of her parted just wide enough to let one of the guards pass through. She slowed her Mazda RX-7 to a stop and rolled down her window.

The guard had a long snout and a butch salt-and-pepper crew cut. He licked his lips with his pink tongue as he rounded the front of her car. She wondered if she'd have to offer him a doggie treat to get him to speak. She'd rather ask him to roll over and play dead and just let her drive through.

"My name's Jessica Mordente," she said, all smiles. "I have an appointment to interview Anton Damon."

The guard grunted, which was a more literate response than Mordente had expected, and walked leisurely to the gate again. He picked up a military-issue walkie-talkie and spoke into it. She saw him nod at the men in the guard tower.

The gate swept open towards her with an electric whine. She drove forward. The guard immediately raised his hand, palm out, and she stopped. She watched as a fourth guard emerged from behind one of the towers and walked to her car with the snout-faced man.

"We have to search your car," the snout-faced man said.

Mordente had expected it, but that didn't make her any happier about it. She rose from the car, her purse slung over her shoulder. "Sure. While you're poking around in there, could you empty the ashtrays and vacuum a bit, too?"

The guard gave no indication that he had even heard her. "Your purse," he said.

She took off her purse and handed it to him. He unzipped it and dumped the contents out on her hood. Mordente lunged for two canisters of lipstick and a couple of tampons before they could roll off the sloping hood. When she straightened up, she saw that both guards had their guns out.

Mordente carefully set the lipstick and tampons on the hood and stepped back. "Take it easy, boys, I'm not going to gloss your lips and shove tampons down your throats."

The guards faced her motionlessly for a long moment and then holstered their guns. While the snout-faced man examined her microcassette recorder, wallet, creased reporter's notebook, and assorted crap, the other leaned into the passenger side of her car and clawed and sniffed around the interior. He tossed out a half-empty can of Pepsi Free and an Egg McMuffin canister.

Mordente sighed and turned her back to them, deciding she'd rather give the compound the once-over while they searched her car. The house was white with green trim and had a rustic, woodsy look about it that suggested it was built by hand by some dedicated woodsman fifty years ago. *Then again,* she thought, *there are a lot of prefabricated tract homes that have the same woodsy look.*

Take away the mongrel guards and the electric fences, and the grounds could be a summer camp or a cozy lakeside resort where families could relax and get away from the crush of urban life in smog-shrouded Los Angeles, which was down the mountain and sixty-five miles northwest. It seemed wrong that such a warm place was home for such a cold organization. This was White Wash Group territory, no dark-skinned individuals allowed.

"Hey," the guard snapped. She turned and saw him holding a small metal detector. He jerked the detector to motion her towards him. Mordente shuffled to his side and he ran the metal detector over her body. At least he didn't try a strip search, she thought.

"All right, you can drive through," the guard said, clicking off the detector. "Slowly," he drawled.

Mordente shrugged and took her purse from him. To her surprise, everything had been neatly put away in her purse, tampons and all. She wondered if he had sharpened her pencils, too. Mordente got into her car and drove through the gate.

As she wound around to the front of the house, Damon emerged and stood on the porch, right beside the short American flag that jutted in a jaunty salute from one of the green posts. Damon's wide hips and thin legs were held tight in a pair of blue Genera jeans, the front pockets bulging with what looked like marbles or something. His short-sleeve, cream-colored shirt had epaulets on the shoulders and was unbuttoned, following the loose strands of gray hair from his sun-pinkened chest to the diminutive asterisk-like navel in the center of his bloated belly. Twelve years of prison life had plumped him up like a Ball Park frank.

Mordente reached into her purse and clicked on the recorder. She pulled the purse strap over her shoulder, rose from the car, and immediately exuded her brand of reporter friendliness, not unlike the forced buoyancy of an airline stewardess. She was all smiles as she met him on the porch, which was covered with a fine layer of brittle pine needles.

"Expecting a war to break out?" Mordente asked, shaking his outstretched hand. His squeeze was tentative but firm, and he met her question with an amused smile. She noticed his teeth were bone white and perfectly straight. She was also uncomfortably aware of his eyes on her sweat-moistened cleavage, slightly exposed by the open collar of her white, short-sleeve blouse, and resisted the urge to cover herself with her hand.

"Depends on what you mean. Am I on the defensive from direct frontal assaults like the one you just mounted or from an armed offensive against those gates?" He grinned affably and shrugged as he stepped off the porch to her side. "I'd have to say both."

He slid his arm around her shoulder and led her around the house towards the lake. His arm felt like a heavy, damp hose draped around her neck. She knew he was sneaking sideways glances down the opening of her shirt.

"As you know, there are many people who are violently opposed to my earned freedom," he said. "The guards make me feel secure."

"But isn't all this weaponry a blatant violation of your parole?" she asked incredulously. The guards pacing along the sandy shore gave the two a wide berth as Damon led her to a small dock stretching out into the lake.

"I am merely a guest here," Damon said. The sparkle in his eyes was reminiscent of the fiery young Damon, the charismatic man who brought the white supremacists he led to national attention during the middle-class upheaval of the late sixties and early seventies. "The lake belongs to Justin Threllkiss and the guards are in his employ."

It figures, she thought, pausing to take off her white leather pumps before trudging across the sand. She knew Threllkiss;

most LA reporters did. The eighty-three-year-old industrialist and archconservative was always good for a headline-grabbing quote or two about the inferiority of Jews, homosexuals, Mexicans, women, and, most of all, blacks. Threllkiss' gnarled, squat body, pale freckled skin, and thick, tortoiseshell glasses made him appear to all the world like a harmless eccentric made senile by time and conservative by wealth. Articles about him were given the same serious consideration readers gave Broom-Hilda and the Wizard of ID.

Mordente was wary of his infirmed, elderly persona. Threllkiss' multinational oil, construction, and chemical corporations were among the world's largest, and he was still very much in control, directing them all while he scooted around his private Palm Springs golf course in a customized cart larger than some midsize sedans.

He had groomed his son to take over, but he was killed a decade ago in a helicopter crash. Now all Threllkiss had under his thumb was his grandson, a nervous twenty-three-year-old with a taste for PCP, Marilyn Chambers movies, and Hollywood parties thrown by local Republicans.

So the White Wash became Threllkiss' paternal interest. Threllkiss was the financial heart that pumped life into the White Wash, even when most thought the cult was dead and buried.

"You, of course, are the only one who knows I'm here," Damon said, leading her onto the dock. "I trust you have stuck to the agreement my lawyers reached with your editors."

"Of course," she said. "Your location is still a secret."

"Good," he said. "You know how nasty those civil rights activists can get."

The dock's wooden planks groaned under the weight of their footsteps. A twelve-foot-long aluminum barge rocked on the lake's tiny swells, bouncing against the side of the dock. Four foam-rubber boat pillows covered in colored plastic had been tossed haphazardly on the boat's three benches amidst a clutter of fishing tackle.

Mordente shrugged. "They think you volunteered for the bone-marrow transplant with the Jewish child as a blatant parole ploy," she said. "And no one has forgotten the Kallahan slaughter that put you behind bars in the first place."

Damon held the palms of his hands out in front of him and gave her a Santa Clausian guffaw comprised of three quick *ho-ho-hos*. "Now, that's a loaded remark full of leading questions and ill-advised charges. I'll tackle that once we're out on the lake." Damon stepped into the boat and sat on a pillow next to the dirty white outboard motor. She heard the air sigh from the pillow beneath him.

"Out on the lake?" she asked.

He grinned mischievously. "This is a fishing expedition, isn't it?"

"Cute." She smirked.

His grin didn't waver. "Nothing relaxes me more than still-fishing on a sunny afternoon. You'll enjoy it."

Damon reached his hand out to her. She ignored it and got into the boat on her own, settling down on the center bench. Damon untied the boat and yanked on the cord. The engine roared and churned the water. He looked past Mordente to the open lake and switched the engine from neutral into forward gear.

The boat sliced into the water with a sudden jolt, the bow rearing up. Mordente grasped the rim of the boat to steady herself. The rush of clean mountain air was exhilarating after weeks of being trapped in the sweltering heat of Los Angeles by a sludge layer of car exhaust and industrial filth. Suddenly, this assignment wasn't so miserable after all.

"I know a spot on the lake, an underwater hole, where the trout like to hide," Damon yelled over the grind of the engine. Mordente nodded mutely. Big deal. She had never fished in her life. As far as she was concerned, that was Mrs. Paul's job.

Damon killed the engine and let the boat glide on its forward momentum as he dumped a cement-filled coffee can attached to a rope over the side. He clapped his hands together.

"Now we're all set." Damon lifted up a fishing pole and plucked a five-inch-long night crawler from a jar on the floor. It wiggled between his thumb and forefinger. "You know, when I was in prison I used to dream about fishing, the solitude of it and the freedom, the thrill of feeling the rat-a-tat-tat of a fish on the line."

Mordente pulled the tape recorder out of her purse and set it on the bench beside her as she watched Damon thread the hook through the head of the night crawler. Yellowish goo spurted out of the worm where he inserted the hook.

Damon pointed to a light band around a portion of the worm. "You can cut a worm anywhere but here, separate it into a dozen pieces and it will live as dozen new worms. But break this band, and the worm dies. This is band is the creature's bond with life."

He pinched the worm apart just below the band and tossed the remainder back in the jar. The hooked worm squirmed, the hook running up the center of its body.

"My dreams weren't enough to fill the emptiness of prison life," he continued. Judging by his paunch, Mordente figured exercise wasn't enough, either. "I realized I had to start life anew, I had to go back in time and rebuild my wayward life. I dedicated myself to becoming reborn in mind and born again in spirit through Jesus Christ."

He handed her the pole. She took it and let the hook tap the surface of the water. She could see the worm wiggling in the water.

"Hit the switch on the reel to release the line and let it drop until it goes slack, then reel it up three times," Damon said, baiting his hook.

She pressed the switch with her thumb. The hook dropped into the water, and line spilled out of the reel. Looking over her shoulder, she could see a guard on the nearest shore spying on them with binoculars.

His own line baited, Damon faced the water and let his line fall over the side of the boat. When his line curled slack, he reeled it up until it was taut.

Damon sighed, pulled a handful of peanuts from his bulging pocket, and popped two, shell and all, into his mouth.

"So, Ms. Mordente," he said, crunching on his peanuts, "I suppose you'd like me to talk about those people I dismembered."

CHAPTER FOUR

He didn't look like the same Anton Damon who had butchered Dr. Martin Kallahan, his wife, Emma, and their nineteen-year-old daughter, Angela, on that muggy afternoon in 1968. He didn't look like the man who chopped them into pieces with an ax and scattered their remains over a dry riverbed.

Kallahan was the first black University of California chancellor, a man who encouraged the sort of minority achievement the White Wash abhorred. Damon took it upon himself to correct that.

The nation was captivated by his sensational murder trial. It was a Damon tour de force. He sat in the courtroom like a bird of prey perched on a sharp ledge, with his legs drawn against his chest, his head resting on his knees, and his intense eyes trained on the judge. Damon's outbursts were sudden and vicious, unpredictable. He would hiss insults at witnesses, launch into passionate speeches about racial inferiority, and, as he did twice, leap on the defense table and try to piss on the judge.

The Anton Damon that was forever emblazoned in Jessica Mordente's mind was the defiant, sweat-dampened face that stared back at her from the cover of *Newsweek* magazine, the eyes that dared you to read the stark white type in the banner headline across his chest:

GUILTY!

This Anton Damon munching peanuts in the boat seemed like a different person. Gone was the intensity, the violence, the hate that oozed from every pore.

"I'm not the same man," said Damon. It was as if he had read Mordente's mind.

"You aren't? What's different?" Mordente asked. "While in prison, you wrote *Supremacy*, and the doctrine preached in those pages differs little from the doctrine of your White Wash days. You still seem to believe that inferior human beings, mainly blacks, gays, and Jews, are unjustly obtaining positions of social power over superior whites in order to destroy white civilization. You still believe they must be stopped."

"I don't advocate violence. Once I did. I've learned the value of human life," Damon replied, shoving another handful of peanuts into his mouth. His chewing sounded like someone stomping on gravel. "Most importantly, I've found Jesus and redemption through him. I'm a new person." He crammed two fingers into his mouth and searched for a sliver of peanut shell that jabbed his cheek. Mordente tried to remember if those were the same two fingers that had impaled the night crawler on the hook.

"And what about the Kallahans? You did murder them."

He flicked the shell particle into the lake and wiped his mouth across the back of his wrist. "All men have sinned and fallen short of the glory of God." Damon sighed. "I have sinned more than most. But the only sin that is not forgiven is the sin of blasphemy against the Holy Spirit. Any other sin, including murder, including the vile mass murders for which I do repent, can be forgiven and is forgiven."

Without warning, a thunderous bellow erupted from Damon's throat and he yanked his pole back towards him. Mordente jerked with surprise and nearly dropped her pole into the lake. Damon began reeling quickly. The reel buzzed electrically, like a swarm of bees, as it dragged in the thirty-five feet of ten-pound test line. Mordente sat still, her gaze fixed on the expression on Damon's face. She recognized his expression now as the same crazed one she'd seen on the cover of *Newsweek*.

"Come on, come on," Damon urged, his eyes aglow, his face flushed.

She heard a splash and shifted her eyes to the water. A fish danced on its tail fin along the top of the water, trying to break free. Damon brought the line in steadily.

"It's a two-footer, look at that, a two-footer," Damon boasted. He reached for the net with his right hand and thrust it into the air under the fish. Capturing it in his net, Damon brought the fish into the boat.

"Damn, it's a two-footer all right." Damon said. "A beautiful rainbow. I'll let you take it back, Ms. Mordente. They're good eating."

Mordente felt the interview slipping away. Luckily, the agreement his lawyers had struck with her publisher was for two separate interviews. She knew now she'd need them. "You still believe blacks are inferior, don't you?"

"My beliefs are irrelevant in the light of God's indisputable truths." Damon pulled a long knife out of his shoe-box-size plastic tackle box with one hand and picked the fish up by the gills with the other. The fish convulsed madly in the air between Mordente and Damon. "Blacks, it has been proven, are genetic mutations weakening the human species. The trend toward racial integration does not bode well for the future strength of Christian society."

Damon jammed the knife into the fish's belly and sliced up towards the gills. Blood spilled out of the fish's gut and painted Damon's arm in dozens of creeping crimson stripes.

Mordente swallowed, her throat dry. The fish was still alive, squirming and splashing it's blood on Damon's shirt in tiny specks.

"You have to bleed them," Damon said, regarding the fish and giving it a disgusted scowl, "or they rot." He dropped the knife, yanked out the fish's organs, and tossed them over his shoulder into the water.

"We, as Christians battling the forces of Satan, are severely outnumbered by the forces of disbelievers." Damon opened the Styrofoam ice box and dropped the fish onto the block of blue ice. He stared at it a moment. Mordente could see the fish's gills were still trying to suck in some water.

"Stupid things. You tear out their guts and yet they still aren't smart enough to know when they are dead." Damon looked up at her. "Oh yes, anyway, if you use simple mathematics and combine the number of Jews, Muslims, Buddhists, Hindus—not to mention the pagan cultures of the American Indian and African tribesman—you can see that the minions of Satan far outnumber the followers of the Lord."

Damon splashed lake water on his hands and washed the blood off his arm. "However," he continued, "Jesus says fear not, little flock, for He is our good shepherd and the ravenous wolves will be powerless to render any harm to those of us who recognize Him as our Lord, our savior, and our commander in the never-ending battle against those who would turn the cross upside down."

"Doesn't Jesus also say love your enemy?" Mordente asked.

"But I do, Ms. Mordente." Damon, eager to get his line back in the water, quickly stuck another worm on his hook. "I love them so very, very much. That's why I don't want to see them harmed by misplacement in society. To make someone live in a way contrary to their nature is the greatest injustice you can inflict." Damon was about to drop his line in the water when he froze, intently watching Mordente's pole.

"What weighed most in the parole board's mind was not your history as a model prisoner or your renewed devotion to religion. It was, they say, your willingness to volunteer for an extremely dangerous bone-marrow transplant to save the life of a Jewish girl," Mordente said. "Why? You must admit it seems contrary to your doctrine."

"I brought a lot of pain and misery to society. The least I could do was undertake one unselfish act that might help an innocent child." Damon nodded towards Mordente's pole. She followed his gaze. The end of her pole bobbed madly towards the water.

"I think you've caught something." He grinned.

Damon entered the house as Mordente's RX-7 bounced back along the roadway towards the gate. Two fish were on ice in the Styrofoam cooler on her passenger seat. He figured the suffocatingly dense heat in the car would melt the ice by the time she was down the hill. Soon the car would smell like a trawler, the fishy stench clinging to her body like a lustful drunk.

"How did you rationalize giving your marrow to a Jew?" asked the stocky man at the dining room table, removing a set of headphones from his ears and setting them on the listening device in front of him.

Damon shrugged indifferently. "One step back, two steps forward."

Saturday evening, 11:37 p.m.

His hard-on strained against his red leather jumpsuit towards the jiggling ass that bounced up the stairs in front of him. The stairwell had the acrid stench of urine, the wails of hungry babies echoed down the halls, and the wallpaper was peeling off in ragged sheets that exposed the cockroaches scurrying along the decaying wooden framework.

The black whore in front of him was oblivious to it. The tiresome responsibilities of the business at hand and a life spent in this familiar terrain shut out the environment. Her world for the next fifteen minutes would be the loser in the bullshit outfit behind her.

She had met him only a couple of minutes ago, outside of her apartment building.

"What you s'posed to be? Huh? Halloween ain't happenin' yet, honey," she had told him when he approached her on the street, the $20 bill balled up in his hand like a wad of used Kleenex. "Sado" was written all over this wimp, dressed up like some kind of funky Batman, utility belt and all. She figured she was in for a slap or two and then a quick, meager ejaculation. Five minutes, tops.

Behind her now, the sound of him lustily dragging in the air was like the ragged noise a dull saw blade makes against wood.

His eyes, jade oracles in a raccoonish dark band of makeup, took in her body. Her buttock-hugging, black polyester minidress accented the garters that held her red lace stockings over her rippling thighs. The dress was cut low down her sway back, clear to the dark mole that rested atop the curve to her jaunty rear. She had black pumps with three-inch heels that thrust her butt up so high he figured a satellite could fly right up her ass. *Or*—he grinned to himself—*my powerful love rocket.* She'd like that.

The merchandise, though, the stuff he paid the $20 for, was up front. And he got another look at that as she turned from the stairwell and walked back towards him along the hall. Her gargantuan breasts hung low and unrestrained, swaying lazily from side to side with each step.

When he emerged in the hallway, she had already disappeared into the room, leaving the door open behind her.

He unzipped his jumpsuit as he walked and unclipped one of the plastic pouches on his belt. When he entered the room, she stood facing him, her back to the bed, which was a sunken mattress on a rusted spring frame. The water-stained acoustic tiles on the ceiling were yielding to gravity and threatened to drop at any moment. The double-sashed window was propped open with a brick.

She looked at the pale flesh revealed in the wide V of his open jumpsuit. If it hadn't been for her wealth of anatomical knowledge and the two nearly indiscernible dots of sickly red on either side of his torso, she would never have known it was a chest. She lowered her eyes and saw the red leather cone jutting between his legs. At least, she thought, there was something vaguely manly about this guy.

"You got the biggest cock I ever saw," she intoned. The words sounded as decayed as the room. "I can't wait to feel it inside me."

He closed the door softly behind him and swaggered over to her. *Five minutes, tops,* she told herself. He put his hands on her shoulders, his penis pressing against her stomach, and peeled her dress down, letting it drop in a heap at her feet. Her breasts were two drooping sandbags hanging from her shoulders.

His eyes followed her breasts to the rolls of her waist, then down to the tuft of pubic hair fluffing out of her crotchless underwear.

The man pulled down his jumpsuit so that it cupped his testicles and then slammed the palms of his hands against her saucer-size nipples, making her tumble backwards onto the bed. As her body hit the solid mattress, he watched her breasts bounce and then sag to her sides.

"Nigger," he hissed.

She stared up at him. One of those slave masters, she thought, fear tickling her between the shoulder blades. They were always the worst.

He dropped on top of her and jammed himself into her, delighting in the way her body buckled defensively. His thrusts began immediately, hard and fast, his breathing locomotive.

She expected him to come in an instant. He didn't. His body twisted and squirmed with each thrust. She raked his back with her fingers, going through the motions of faking pleasure, surprised at the tremendous perspiration that already soaked his skin.

He was pleasurably aware of the frenzy he was working himself up to. His penis was a spear, plunging deep into the heart of this wretched species, conquering and subjugating them. Each thrust gave him more power, each thrust struck deeper and deeper into their heathen soul. His manhood, his strength, his overpowering physicality, would beat them all.

No one had ever pounded her like this. No one had ever been so totally consumed. It hurt bad, and her eyes were closed tightly against the pain, her body rocking against his thrusts. She was afraid to stop him, better to wait for the inevitable end and have Horace, her pimp, beat the shit out of him later.

His reward was growing. The once distant sensation was now running down his back and into his pelvis, expanding. He plunged further and further into that subhuman soul, harder and harder. A blinding, beautiful white light burst in his head and covered his body in its soothing glow. He gritted his teeth and stiffened as the light ebbed. His eyes fluttered open.

He looked down at the whore. Her teeth were clenched, her chin high, and the tendons in her neck tensed. She looked down her face and into his eyes. She thought she was staring into a corpse. His colorless lips curved into a coldly maniacal grin as he reached back to his belt with one hand. She followed the hand and saw the glint of clean steel.

"No!" she whispered huskily.

Jerking back his pelvis, he pulled his penis out of her. And jammed the knife in.

CHAPTER FIVE

Sunday, May 20, 5:03 a.m.

The air was still. The smoky brown haze that hung over the city glowed as the sun crept reluctantly into the sky. The mechanical hum of Brett Macklin's Cadillac was the only sound on the street. The buildings loomed lifeless and dull three stories high on either side of him. A drunk disappeared down an alley like a rodent scurrying into the crevice between two boulders.

Brett Macklin watched the sun burn through the night the same way he had watched the day bleed into darkness twelve hours before. The passage of time, which he spent driving endlessly through the maze of South Central Los Angeles streets, had changed nothing for him.

The impostor was still out there somewhere.

Macklin eased the car to a stop at the curb and stared at the asphalt on the street. Three red splashes. The errant drops of red from some unseen painter's giant brush. Here was where the impostor had emerged from the darkness to take three lives and plunge Macklin's life into an abyss. Macklin was no closer to finding the son of a bitch than he was twelve hours ago.

Only a handful of hours, he knew, remained before Mordente exposed him—and Cory and Brooke were destroyed.

He tapped the dashboard nervously with his right hand. Cory and Brooke, he thought. He saw it as it once was, in his Venice house, when they were a family, before the arguing, before the coldness, before they left and Macklin was alone.

Macklin pressed on the gas, screeched across the street in a sharp U-turn, and headed north. He wanted to see them once more, before Monday, before they hated him too much to ever see him again.

Sunday, May 20, 8:12 a.m.

The mattress was a blood-soaked sponge under the black prostitute's splayed body. Shaw approached the bed slowly, feeling the three Winchell's donuts he'd eaten an hour before churning in his stomach. Her body reflected her assailant's murderous frenzy. A net of deep, jagged slashes crisscrossed her torso, and her thighs were totally obscured by grotesque lumps of clotted blood, matted pubic hair, and torn flesh.

"Her name's Anita." Vice Sergeant Sage Mitchell, clad in his favorite checkered polyester sport coat, took a deep drag on his Marlboro and exhaled the smoke through his nostrils. "I've picked her up dozens of times for whorin' and dealin' along this block."

Shaw glanced at her face. Her eyes were stark white ovals wide with terror. "Didn't anyone hear anything?"

Mitchell shrugged. "Sure they did."

"No one called the police?"

Mitchell chortled. "C'mon, Shaw, be serious."

Shaw ground his teeth and scratched his brow nervously. He felt an irrational urge to reach out and strangle Mitchell and didn't quite know why. The man was just going through the motions of his job, and that's all he expected Shaw to do, no more and no less. After all, both of them knew Anita's murder would never be solved. Why waste any effort?

Shaw understood that, he really did. Anita was anonymous, part of the flotsam swirling in the stormy undercurrents of the streets. Occasionally, some of the flotsam washed up on blood-soaked mattresses in fleabag hotels, in rusted garbage bins in forgotten alleys, or crumpled in heaps amidst the weeds in a vacant lot.

Shaw hated the role he had to play whenever he faced a corpse like Anita's. It made him feel like a glorified garbage man, making sure bodies get zipped into bags and hauled away before they become smelly and bothersome. The taxpayers didn't give a damn who made the mess as long as it got cleaned up. The thing that made Shaw angry was that Mitchell accepted it all so naturally.

"Did anyone see the guy she came in with?" Shaw asked.

"Yeah, some kinky asshole in a red jumpsuit."

A shiver rippled down Shaw's back. "Red jumpsuit?"

"Yeah, and he had this black shit, makeup or something, across his eyes," Mitchell said. "A real wacko, by the sound of it."

Shaw's heart pounded in his chest. The same man who killed those black youths had butchered this black prostitute. It couldn't be a copycat killing because the police hadn't released to the press that the Mr. Jury who shot the black youths wore a red jumpsuit.

Fear, tinged with guilt, colored Shaw's thoughts. He had been too hard on his friend Brett Macklin.

"Watch me, Daddy. Watch me," Cory yelled as she stood shivering wet on the edge of the diving board. "I'm gonna dive now. Watch me."

"I'm watching," replied Brett Macklin, shifting the Sunday *Los Angeles Times*, two pounds of unread newsprint, from his sweat-dampened bare legs to the ground between his chaise lounge and Brooke's.

Cory smiled and took a deep breath. "Okay, I'm gonna go!" She bent over tentatively, stretched out her arms, and then tumbled into the water in a nearly fetal position.

Within a second she burst up through the surface, shaking her head and spitting water. "How'd I do, Daddy?"

Macklin grinned. "Just great, honey. Next time try to be straighter, like an arrow." He glanced to his left at Brooke, his ex-wife, her face alight with an amused smile. Sitting so close to her, he could smell the coconut oil that made her copper skin, amply revealed by her skimpy white bikini, so slick and shiny. Sweat beaded on her sharp cheekbones and above her full, scarlet lips. Macklin felt the old desire percolating. Brooke's allure hadn't waned. Macklin had caught several men around the pool sneaking furtive glances at her.

"She sure loves to see you, Brett," Brooke remarked. "Just look at how charged she gets." She regarded him solemnly. He sat shirtless in his swimsuit, watching with bloodshot, tired eyes as Cory climbed out of the pool. "You used to see her every weekend. Now months can go by. She thinks it's something she's doing wrong."

"I'm going to dive again, Daddy," Cory said, marching to the end of the diving board.

Macklin smiled and nodded. "Go ahead, we're watching."

"You've been a real bastard," Brooke hissed out of the side of her smile. "You've changed."

Brooke was right.

Macklin had been afraid to see his daughter, afraid the violence that seemed to stalk him would get her. It was a different kind of fear that brought him here today. Last night, during his fruitless search through the grimy underside of Los Angeles for the phony Mr. Jury, he realized that only a handful of hours remained before Mordente exposed him—and Cory and Brooke were destroyed.

All he could think about last night was seeing them once more, tranquil and happy, before the end... before they hated him too much to ever see him again.

This morning he simply showed up, unannounced, at their apartment. Cory was overjoyed, jumping into Macklin's arms. He gave her a tight hug that nearly brought tears to his eyes. Brooke made pancakes and eggs. Macklin didn't realize how hungry he was until he started eating, eventually horsing down eleven pancakes, six eggs, and three glasses of orange juice before they trudged down to the pool.

"Are you going to disappear again and break her heart?" Brooke said, regarding Macklin carefully. His chest was hard and covered with droplets of sweat. "Because if you are, Brett, leave right now."

Macklin swallowed, his throat dry, conflicting compulsions waging war inside him. He wanted to grab them both in his arms and run away someplace. He wanted to tell them about his vigilantism before the *Los Angeles Times* could. He wanted to hide, melt into the air and become invisible. He wanted to tell Brooke he still loved her. He wanted to scream with frustration until his lungs burst. He wanted to bring back his father and start over.

He wanted to be happy again.

"It's been a rough time for me," Macklin said, sorry he had come this morning. Now he realized it would just make things worse. "Dad's murder was a big shock. I had barely gotten over that when Cheshire was killed. My world keeps doing somersaults. I'm not ready to bring Cory and you back into that world yet. Until I can settle things down, both of you will have to be patient with me."

"Here I go!" Cory yelled, vaulting off the diving board. Her straight little body sliced smoothly into the water.

Brooke sighed. "Want to do me a favor?"

"What?"

"You try explaining that to her."

Macklin left Brooke and Cory at five thirty feeling worse than he had the night before. Seeing them made the doom he faced even more frightening.

He hadn't been able to explain anything to Cory and ended up making vague promises to see her soon. Macklin could feel Brooke's scornful gaze burning into his back as he left the apartment. She had every right to be pissed. But once she knew what he had been doing the last few months, Macklin was sure she would be thankful he had stayed out of their lives.

Macklin had wanted to spend his last evening as a free man with them but couldn't handle the oppressive guilt he felt every time he looked at their faces. He fought the urge to once again aimlessly roam the streets in a ridiculous search for the phony Mr. Jury. Tonight, he decided, he wanted to spend his time with friends. There were two tickets to senatorial hopeful Cecil Parks' fund-raising dinner in Macklin's glove compartment, and he was going to use them.

7:00 p.m.

The New Horizons hotel, which everyone called simply "the Arrow," had given Los Angeles the stunning architectural landmark the downtown high-rise district desperately needed. It rose, gleaming, from the shadows of the downtown skyscrapers as Macklin drove towards it.

The hotel looked like two giant staircases back to back, a pyramid with two graduated faces. Interesting, but hardly striking. What set the hotel apart was the arrow of cement, steel, and glass that shot out of the twenty-fifth floor. Though quite solid, the five-story shaft that peaked with a four-level black triangle had a sense of motion to it. To Macklin, it looked like the arrow was soaring towards the stars.

A bright neon glow spilled out into the night from the lobby's covered entranceway. Macklin eased his shiny Cadillac to a stop at the front door. A broad-shouldered black man with a gray mustache wearing a red top hat and tails opened Macklin's door, smiled warmly, and held out his hand for the key.

"I haven't seen a car like this in twenty years," the doorman said enviously. "It's stunning, sir. A damn shame they don't make them like this anymore."

Macklin grinned and emerged from the car in a simple black tuxedo with a ruffleless shirt. The doorman's eyes were taking in the car with honest appreciation.

"It's a beautiful dinosaur, all right," Macklin said, slipping his keys and a crisp $20 bill into the doorman's chubby palm. "Take good care of her for me."

"I will, sir." The doorman nodded reverently, gesturing away an approaching teenage carhop wearing an ill-fitting white suit. "It will be waiting for you right here."

As Macklin walked towards the lobby, he looked back as the smiling doorman slowly lowered himself into the driver's seat and firmly grasped the wheel. The lights above Macklin were so bright that he couldn't see anything in the blackness of the street beyond his car.

Macklin tried to shrug away the itchy irritations of the suit against his sunburned shoulders as the lobby doors slid open with a whisper and he strolled into the cool, air-conditioned lobby. He faced a clear wall behind which three glass elevators ascended and descended along the center of the hotel to the restaurant, bar, observation deck, and ballroom housed in the arrowhead twenty-five stories up.

One of the elevator doors parted and Macklin saw a familiar face.

"Holy shit, you wore a tux!" boomed Kirk Jeffries in a voice almost as loud as his clothing. "Knowing you, I thought you'd show up in a fucking T-shirt and jeans."

Jeffries wore a bright blue, crushed-velvet tuxedo with black trim, three four-inch cigars wrapped in cellophane sticking out of his pocket. Blue-trimmed white ruffles spilled out of the opening of his jacket, which barely contained the bulk of his belly.

Macklin felt a broad grin stretch across his face and his chest swell with warmth. He was glad he came.

Jeffries limped out of the elevator and grabbed him in a hearty bear hug.

The pollster clapped him solidly on the back. "It's good to see you."

Macklin pulled back and regarded his friend. "How's your arm and leg?"

Jeffries waved a hand in front of Macklin's face. "Shit, the doctor finally got a welder, a blowtorch, some steel, and put them back together just fine."

"Have you been able to get Cecil's campaign back on track?" Macklin asked. He knew Jeffries well enough not to be fooled by his sloppy manner. Jeffries was a wizard at manipulating poll and survey results to a candidate's benefit. Once Jeffries had segmentized the populace, he could hone a candidate's delivery and bring in the right votes.

Jeffries slipped his arm around Macklin's shoulder and led him to the bank of elevators. "Cecil's campaign has been like a paid vacation. He got hold of me just in time. I'll make him senator just like I made him the first black student body president back when all of us were at UCLA."

Macklin could tell by the heavy weight on his shoulder that Jeffries' leg was a bigger handicap than he let on. The elevator doors in the middle parted and they stepped into the bullet-shaped glass capsule. The elevator lifted with a jolt and quickly rose through the roof of the lobby, offering Macklin a sweeping view of Los Angeles, a vast grid of sparkling lights spread out below him.

A glass elevator whooshed past them, startling Jeffries and Macklin. "Christ, they come close," Macklin said. He looked down and saw that the elevator had stopped at a floor below them.

"This middle elevator is an express straight to the top. It doesn't stop at any of the hotel floors," Jeffries said, answering Macklin's unspoken question.

Macklin could now follow the trail of lights flowing on the Santa Monica Freeway clear to the ocean. He saw the glittering Century City towers to his far left and the tiny dots of lights from the homes that clung to the sharp faces of the Hollywood Hills to his right.

They were suddenly enveloped in blackness as the elevator pierced the arrowhead. The doors slid open at level one, the ballroom.

Macklin ambled slowly out of the elevator, his eyes wide. The window-lined ballroom was filled with hundreds of people sitting at round, white-clothed tables with flower arrangements in the center. There was a stage, a dais, and a long white table lined with well-known movie stars and politicians. The clatter of silverware and the low rumble of conversation were inviting. Hanging in the center of the room was a gigantic crystal chandelier that was dwarfed and made insignificant by the beauty and vastness of the twinkling night sky that surrounded everyone.

"Incredible," Macklin muttered. "It's like we're gods sitting on a cloud."

Jeffries chortled. "What a bunch of horseshit. You'd make a lousy poet, my friend."

They weaved between the tables towards the front of the room. Macklin spotted Ronny Shaw and his girlfriend, Sunshine, at the table he was being led to. Beyond them, he noticed Mayor Stocker among the celebrities at the table on the stage. He felt the warm feeling that he had been nurturing evaporate. He cursed himself for being so caught up in running away from his fear that he had ignored the fact that they would be here. It was as bad as staying with Cory and Brooke tonight would have been. These people were stark reminders that he couldn't run away from tomorrow's fate.

As Jeffries and Macklin neared the table, Cecil Parks excused himself from a cluster of men he was mingling with and came over to greet them. Jeffries went on to join Shaw and Sunshine.

"Brett!" Parks grinned, giving Macklin a firm handshake with one hand and clapping him on the shoulder with the other. "It's good to see you."

Parks' greatest asset had always been his bright, turquoise eyes, which radiated friendliness. They were beaming warmly now. He wore a tuxedo seemingly identical to Macklin's and had the same trim jogger's build. Macklin hadn't seen Parks in more than a year. They used to jog together until his hectic political life ate up all his time.

"You still jogging twice a week, Cecil?"

Parks shrugged. "No time, Brett. I do all my running nowadays at banquets and speeches, in interviews and commercials, on fliers and talk shows."

Macklin grinned. "It's the shits, isn't it?"

"Yeah, but I want to be senator," Parks said. "Jogging with you and complaining about high defense appropriations, tax credits for schools that racially discriminate, the decay of the social security system, and covert government activities in Central America only makes me lose my breath quicker and doesn't change any of it. I want to show that one person can count."

Macklin held up his hands in mock defense. "Okay, okay, you got my vote, Cecil, you can stop your speech now."

They laughed gently until Parks' chuckles waned. "Uh-oh, that oil man married to the movie star with the big tits is looking my way. I'd better go over and schmooze with him. He donated big to my campaign." Parks slapped Macklin's shoulder again. "Hey, Brett, let's not be strangers, okay? I miss those talks we had when we jogged together."

"You have my number," Macklin said, forcing a smile onto his face to hide the despair he feared would creep onto it if he didn't. There would be no more early morning jogs together. Jessica Mordente would see to that tomorrow.

Parks walked towards the oil magnate, and a flash from a camera caught Macklin in its glare and temporarily blinded him. The burning light, though, illuminated something in Macklin's mind that he had overlooked.

He had just ruined Cecil Parks' career.

A shiver coursed through Macklin's body as he realized the implications of his presence in the ballroom. He had been seen with Parks in a friendly embrace, perhaps even photographed together with him. When the news broke that Macklin was Mr. Jury, the ensuing scandal would destroy Parks, too.

Macklin glanced at Shaw, Sunshine, and Jeffries, then at Parks chatting with the fleshy Arab. All he wanted to do now was go, escape into the night until this nightmare was over. Without bothering to stop by the table, he turned and left.

CHAPTER SIX

Sunday, 9:47 p.m.

Bruce Springsteen was singing about Cadillac Ranch on the tape deck as Macklin steered the Batmobile off the southbound Harbor Freeway and into the turbulent neighborhood where his father, an LAPD beat cop, was ambushed and set aflame by a street gang.

The urban, middle-class neighborhoods Macklin spent his life in were always changing, forever young. The people who lived there wore their neighborhoods like bright white, starched dress shirts. Occasionally the shirts got stained, but they could always be washed clean.

These streets were different. People here wore their neighborhoods like dirty work shirts. Decay encircled the buildings like vines.

Macklin's Cadillac glided almost invisibly down the streets, a black breeze moving silently in the dark night.

He had driven here almost unconsciously and didn't know where he was going until now. His eyes traced the contours of the sidewalk gray buildings, read the spray-paint scribbles on the walls, looked into the angry and weary faces, and he wondered how a world so far outside his own could affect his life so much.

In Macklin's middle-class world, this neighborhood could be avoided for a lifetime. It was severed from everyday experience and existed only in the abstract. Never did the two worlds have to meet.

Not true for Brett Macklin. This neighborhood had seeped through some crack in the barrier and was now spilling like a waterfall into his life. It had suddenly swept him up, and now he couldn't escape its treacherous currents.

Macklin turned the car around a corner. He saw the hamburger-shaped restaurant down the block and the revolving, blinking sign that read "BURGER BOB'S" atop the sesame-seed-bun roof.

The river that had swept Macklin up more than a year ago surged forward and carried him over a precipice.

Burger Bob, his broad belly wrapped in an apron and his balding head capped with a cook's cauliflower-top hat, looked like the Pillsbury Dough Boy smoking a cigar.

With the cigar stub clenched in the corner of his mouth, Burger Bob scrawled down the order the two jittery black guys on the other side of the counter had given him.

"What'll ya have on your burgers?" he asked, looking up from his notepad and down the barrel of a Saturday night special. He felt his heart drop like a boulder into his foot.

"All the cash in the register." The black guy in the oil-stained undershirt grinned, waving his gun towards the register for emphasis. "And hold the mayo."

The black guy next to him screeched with laughter, his mouth open wide as if he expected to catch a baseball with it. His missing lower front teeth suggested he might have tried once. Burger Bob didn't notice. Burger Bob's eyes were on the gun shaking in Big Mouth's hand.

There was no one else in the restaurant. The last time Burger Bob was held up, some short guy eating a cheeseburger and fries tried to be a hero and ended up swallowing two bullets for dessert. The *Los Angeles Times* spread the news over the top of the Metro section, and business slowed for three months.

"Move, fatso, or your brains are gonna be sizzling all over that grill behind you," the guy spoke again.

Burger Bob hesitated, fear cementing him to the floor. Suddenly, the gun bucked in Big Mouth's hand, shaking the restaurant with a tremendous roar. Burger Bob screamed and jumped two feet back, his buttocks slamming into the grill. His hat fell onto the floor. The bullet had scorched a hole through the center of the hat.

"Bufus don't tell a man nothin' twice, asshole," Big Mouth said. "You want to inhale the next bullet? Get us the cash."

"To go." Bufus grinned.

Burger Bob saw a flash of red behind Big Mouth, and everything became a slow-motion nightmare. A blast thundered in Burger Bob's ear, and then Big Mouth was flying over the counter, his arms reaching out for him, his eyes wide and white. Burger Bob flung himself sideways, felt Big Mouth sail past him, and then heard the dull thud as the black man collided into the wall and dropped onto the grill.

As Burger Bob rose, the dream state dissipated and the world returned to normal speed. Big Mouth lay crumpled facedown on the grill, tiny curls of smoke rising from his body as he sizzled like raw hamburger in his own blood. The gun slipped from Big Mouth's lifeless fingers and clattered to the floor.

"You're a real comic genius, nigger."

Burger Bob turned to see who had spoken and saw a man in a red jumpsuit standing behind Bufus, who stood as still as a statue, his eyes to the floor.

"Drop the gun," the stranger said, his .357 Magnum held steady in his right hand.

Bufus dropped his Saturday night special, which landed heavily on his foot. He forced back an agonized wail, his face wrinkling in pain.

The stranger laughed with sputtering dry heaves akin to gagging. Bufus wasn't laughing. He was wincing. "That was funny," the stranger said. "A joker like you should appreciate that." He walked around to face Bufus and grinned. "We're gonna have some more laughs, aren't we Bufus?"

The stranger jammed his gun into Bufus' groin. Bufus doubled over, a guttural cry of pain escaping from his throat. The stranger pushed the gun into his testicles. "Move back and lie down on the table," the stranger said, forcing Bufus back by digging his gun into him.

Bufus hit the table with his buttocks and then laid flat on his back atop it, knocking a napkin container and a salt shaker to the floor.

"Close your eyes and open your mouth wide," the stranger hissed, his gun still pressed into Bufus' groin. "You so much as breathe funny and I'll decorate the wall with your balls."

The stranger turned his head toward Burger Bob. "Bring me a ladle of French fry oil."

"Please, mister—," Bufus pleaded. The stranger jabbed his gun into his testicles, choking back Bufus' words.

"Keep quiet, nigger."

Burger Bob, a ladle of boiling oil in one hand and Big Mouth's gun held unsteadily in the other, shuffled nervously up to the stranger.

"Thanks, friend," the stranger said, taking the ladle from Burger Bob and flashing an amiable smile. "Now please step aside where it's safe."

The stranger looked down at Bufus, who jerked as though an electrical current was running through him. He tipped the ladle over Bufus' gaping mouth. "Eat hot death, nigger."

"Hold it!"

A drop of boiling grease dropped onto Bufus' cheek as the stranger turned to face the voice. A tuxedo-clad Brett Macklin stood poised in the doorway, his .357 Magnum trained on the man in red. Heavy, sludge brown smoke billowed out of the kitchen, blanketing the room in the thick odor of charred meat.

To Burger Bob, it was beginning to look like a grisly costume party.

The stranger's lips curled into a smile. "Hey, it's okay, I'm Mr. Jury." He kept the tipped ladle poised over Bufus' mouth.

Bufus whimpered, tears streaming from his closed eyes and trickling onto the table.

"No, it's not okay," Macklin hissed, stepping into the center of the dining room. "And you're not Mr. Jury."

He could see the stranger's face tighten and his makeup-shrouded eyes narrow on Macklin's .357 Magnum. Macklin saw the stranger's eyebrows arch in realization and noticed him nodding his head slightly.

Then Macklin sensed a motion behind him. Before he could turn, an explosion of pain burst in his head and he felt himself tumbling forward into a swirling, murky gray cloud.

His eyes were open, but it was like looking at the world through wax paper. Macklin was aware of Burger Bob standing over him, holding Big Mouth's gun by the barrel. Burger Bob had smacked him a good one with the butt of the gun.

Macklin could barely make out the outline of the phony Mr. Jury as he poured the hot oil into Bufus' mouth. The black man thrashed wildly, his back slapping against the table becoming an incessant, agonizing beat that echoed in Macklin's head. Macklin willed his limbs to move, but they wouldn't obey him. He felt as though he was paralyzed from the neck down.

"Thanks, Mr. Jury," he heard Burger Bob say. "Those black animals have been terrorizing me for years."

A man's shadow fell over Macklin and, through the foggy haze of semiconsciousness, he saw the phony Mr. Jury point his gun at him.

"It's all right," the gunman said. "Us white people have to stick together. It's the White Wash way."

"It's the American way," Burger Bob replied.

Inky blackness dropped like a curtain over Macklin's eyes and he felt himself plunging into a bottomless abyss. He saw some light ahead and suddenly he felt himself fall into through the ice of a frozen lake, the chilly water enveloping him.

Macklin coughed and his eyes sputtered open. Burger Bob stood over him, holding a pitcher of water. He splashed some more water on Macklin, who sputtered and held his hands up in surrender.

Burger Bob held a hand out to Macklin. He grabbed Burger Bob's outstretched hand and pulled himself up to a standing position. The restaurant felt like boat on stormy seas. The floor seemed to roll on unseen swells.

"Get out of here, you dumbfuck." Burger Bob handed Macklin his .357 Magnum and jerked his head towards the door. Macklin massaged the back of his head and glanced at Bufus. The black man's limp arms and legs dangled off the edges of the table like the corners of a large, wrinkled tablecloth. Steam escaped from his wide mouth and clouded his open, dead eyes.

"Get out of here," Burger Bob insisted, poking Macklin in the stomach with the barrel of Big Mouth's Saturday night special. Macklin acquiesced, his stomach churning with nausea. He turned slowly and dragged himself weakly to the door.

"What the hell were you doing, anyway?" Burger Bob shouted at him. "Mr. Jury is a godsend!"

Midnight

"It was that gun, and the way he said it." The caller's panicky voice was shrill and irritating. "We've got trouble."

Anton Damon sighed and absently arranged the peanuts on the table in front of him into two large *W*s. "You think he may have been the real Mr. Jury."

"Yeah," the caller replied. "I mean, you shoulda heard the way he said 'You're not Mr. Jury.' He knew, man, he really knew."

"That does complicate things," Damon said. "It means Mr. Jury was never killed. It means that people, perhaps even the police, have mounted an organized effort to cover for him and we have endangered that."

"So what do we do?"

"Nothing," Damon said flatly. "Absolutely nothing. We sit tight for now and see what happens. Mr. Jury's unexpected resurrection may help our cause."

"And if it doesn't, what then?"

"We find him and kill him."

CHAPTER SEVEN

Monday, May 21, 8:30 a.m.

Brett Macklin was awake, but he didn't want to move. This, he knew, was his day of reckoning. He wanted to lie in bed forever.

The sheets were twisted into heavy ropes that were coiled around his perspiring, naked body. The side of his head was nuzzled comfortably in a warm pocket formed by his pillow. He could see sunlight spilling in through the window curtains, which were billowed by gentle puffs of lukewarm morning air.

Every time he began to move, someone pounded a wooden stake into his skull. Macklin had Burger Bob to thank for that. The pain was a tangible reminder of his dismal failure during the confrontation with the phony Mr. Jury.

Macklin cursed himself for not killing the sadistic madman when he had the chance. After Macklin left the restaurant, he called Shaw to warn him about the two murders and learned about the death of the black prostitute. The phony Mr. Jury, Macklin discovered, was even sicker than he had imagined.

But now there was nothing Macklin could do about that. Tomorrow, he would be in jail, his life destroyed. Macklin rolled over onto his back and took a deep breath. The circulation returned to his paralyzed arms and legs, making them feel like sacks filled with scurrying ants.

As the paralysis waned, Macklin untangled himself from the sheets and sat up.

His sinuses were clogged up and his eyes burned. He combed a hand through his slumber-matted brown hair, coughed, and stood up. The wooden stake drove deeper into his skull and he could feel his heart pulsing behind his forehead.

Macklin stepped into a pair of jogging shorts on the floor and pulled them up around his waist before he left the bedroom. Holding the handrail, Macklin trudged down the stairs to the front door, opened it, and brought in the morning *Los Angeles Times*. This, he assumed, was his last morning of freedom, and he wanted to spend it in the routine, pleasant way he always had.

He flipped through the sections of the paper as he shuffled into the kitchen. Jessica Mordente's interview with Anton Damon covered the front of the Metro section. Macklin dumped the paper onto his butcher-block table, opened the refrigerator, and pulled out a carton of orange juice and half a cantaloupe. He took a spoon out of a drawer and brought his breakfast to the table.

Taking a big gulp of juice from the carton, he began reading Mordente's story. He hadn't read her work before and he thought he might as well see if he was going to be exposed by a good writer. Macklin found himself paying less and less attention to the writing and more and more to Damon himself. Damon's racist views hadn't changed, though his low-key delivery was a sharp contrast to his outspoken pre-prison days. Macklin remembered when Damon came to UCLA and caused a riot by rallying the students to urinate on the administration building to protest the increased minority enrollment.

Damon was no longer the counterculture radical. Macklin thought Damon came off now like a right-wing, conservative politician. Although Damon danced around the issue of whether or not he was still the leader of the White Wash, it seemed clear he was working hard to give the group some mainstream legitimacy.

It's like the Hells Angels trying to convince people they're really the Mickey Mouse Club, Macklin thought.

He found the new, politically aware Damon a far greater threat than the revolutionary youth he once was. Damon, according the article, had even hired a media consultant to further hone his mainstream image.

Macklin turned the page and felt anxiety grab his guts and squeeze them. Mr. JURY KILLS TWO BLACKS IN SADISTIC BLOODBATH, the headline screamed, followed by a subhead reading LOCAL LEADERS FEAR RACE WAR BREWING.

His morning routine was shattered. Reality leaped from the page and slapped him in the face. The phony Mr. Jury had struck again. By tomorrow, he knew, Mordente would expose him as Mr. Jury and the sadistic killer would remain free. Macklin brought the paper close to his face with trembling hands and scanned the story.

> "He said he would protect innocent people from black lawlessness," said Robert Roberts, owner and operator of Burger Bob's restaurant. "He said us white people have to stick together."

Several random quotes from people on the street praised the phony Mr. Jury and supported his remarks about blacks. Community leaders, the article said, feared that Mr. Jury's racist views, because of the vigilante's popular appeal and media attention, could heighten racial tension and spark a race war.

Macklin reread Burger Bob's quote again and again. There was something missing.

He said us white people have to stick together.

He lowered the paper, feeling a hot flush sweep over his body. A raspy voice whispered to Macklin through hazy memories.

It's all right. Us white people have to stick together. It's the White Wash way.

The phony Mr. Jury worked for Anton Damon. Macklin grimaced. It was diabolical but brilliant. Damon didn't really have to gain public trust to get people to listen to his racist doctrine. He'd let Mr. Jury, someone the public already supported, someone the public saw as a hero, do it for him. The phony Mr. Jury, Macklin realized, was a White Wash power play paving the way for the emergence of Anton Damon as a right-wing political force.

He bolted from his seat, grabbed the phone receiver off the wall, and punched out Jessica Mordente's home phone number with his index finger. He had to make her understand.

The phone rang twice.

"Hello?" Mordente snapped.

Macklin's hand tightened on the receiver. "This is Brett Macklin. I made you a promise and I'm ready to honor it."

"What you made was a stalling tactic so you could indulge yourself in one last kill," Mordente yelled, her voice quivering as she held back her tears of fury.

"Listen to me, I—"

"People end up dying when I listen to you," she broke in. "You're inhuman, Macklin, a monster."

"It's Anton Damon, Jessie, he's the one behind all this. The phony Mr. Jury is Damon's stooge," Macklin said. "Don't you see? Mr. Jury is already part of the public's collective cognition as a good guy, a positive force. Damon is using that to propagate his racist drivel. He's going to get a lot of people killed."

"Fuck off, Macklin. Save it for your trial," Mordente barked.

Macklin exhaled slowly. She wasn't going to listen. There was no use trying to convince her. *Face it,* Macklin told himself, *it's over for you. There's nothing you can say to her to stop it.* "Okay, Jessie, how do you want to play this? I can come over to your place. I could be there in Brentwood in fifteen minutes."

"No way, Macklin. You're not getting me alone," she said. "Meet me downtown at the *Los Angeles Times* office. We can talk in the newsroom. Then I'm calling the cops." She hung up.

Macklin rapped the receiver against the wall like a hammer. There was nothing he could do. It was over. He felt none of the sadness he had felt before, only anger. He would be behind bars, and his family shamed, all for nothing. The phony Mr. Jury's murders would be attributed to him and eclipse any arguments he might make to justify his vigilante work. Worst of all, Damon's psychopath would still be free.

Taking a deep breath, Macklin called Los Angeles mayor Jed Stocker on his private line at his office. Stocker was always in the office by three a.m., thumbing through the morning papers and watching *Good Morning America.*

"I thought I should warn you," Macklin said, "a reporter is going to—"

"Forget it, Macklin," Stocker interrupted. "Mordente won't write her story."

Macklin was stunned. "What?"

"I put a couple voice-activated bugs in your house a few months ago," Stocker said. "Unfortunately, I didn't get around to listening to the tapes from Friday until last night."

"You rotten son of a bitch," Macklin hissed. "Who the hell do you think you are?"

"You can shove your fucking indignation up your goddamn ass, Macklin. I'm saving us all," Stocker shot back. "My people are on their way to take care of Mordente right now."

A chill of fear brought goose bumps to Macklin's skin. "You're going to have her killed," Macklin stated.

"Yeah, that's right, Macklin," Stocker said cockily. "That's the way it has to be."

"My God, Stocker, are you crazy? You can't just go out and kill someone!" Macklin shouted into the phone.

Stocker chuckled derisively. "What the hell do you think you've been doing, Macklin? You don't think what you do is killing?"

"That's different, Stocker. Those people were murderers," Macklin barked. "Mordente committed no crime. She's the public we're supposed to be protecting!"

"Damn it, wake up, Macklin! Mordente will ruin us all. The scandal she'll create will plunge this city into anarchy." Stocker said. "She must be sacrificed for the greater good of this city."

"No," Macklin insisted. "You've got to stop it."

"It's too late," Stocker said. The line went dead.

9:15 a.m.

"Could I please see your license and registration?" asked the police officer. The traffic on the Santa Monica Freeway surging eastward was a blur behind him.

Jessica Mordente frowned, stretched across the car to her glove compartment, and saw that another police officer was standing on the passenger side. *The fuckers. Of all the goddamn mornings to get on my case…* She rummaged around the cassette tapes, maps, and notebooks for her registration papers and snuck a glance up at the cop. He looked like a clone of the guy on the driver's side. Both hid their eyes behind reflective sunglasses and wore crisp, pressed blue uniforms.

Fascist assholes, Mordente thought. *If I don't hurry, Macklin is going to get to the* Times *before I do.*

Mordente sat up in her seat and handed her registration to the cop on the driver's side and then pulled her tattered driver's license from her purse and gave that to him, too. He gave both papers a cursory glance.

"Please step out of the car, Ms. Mordente."

Mordente narrowed her eyes, perplexed. "Why? What have I done wrong?"

"Just step out, please."

Mordente heard the officer on the passenger side unclip the strap over his gun. Her heart fluttered. *What is going on here?* She opened the door and stepped out. She felt the officer's strong hand grasp her arm and guide her towards his black-and-white four-door Plymouth. As he led her to the rear of the police car, she read the emblem on the door: "TO PROTECT AND TO SERVE."

"Hey, you guys aren't the highway patrol," Mordente said. "You're LAPD."

He reached around her and opened the backseat door. "Get in, Ms Mordente."

"You haven't told me what I've done wrong," she protested. "Am I under arrest or what?" She looked at his name tag. It read "VICTOR DEESE." "You had better start doing some talking, Officer Deese."

Deese shared a glance across the roof of the police car with his Partner. Without warning, he twisted Mordente's arm painfully behind her back and rammed her face-forward against the open door. Before she had a chance to struggle, she felt the cold steel of a handcuff close tightly around her wrist. Deese yanked back her other arm and cuffed it.

Mordente spun around, enraged, her arms restrained behind her back. "What kind of bullshit is this? If you two think you can get away with this harassment, you're wrong."

"Get in that car before I push you in," Deese said between clenched teeth.

He meant it. Mordente reluctantly ducked into the backseat. Deese slammed the door closed and then slipped in behind the steering wheel. His partner sat down beside him. They were separated from Mordente by steel grillwork. Deese eased the car into the flow of traffic. The cop on the passenger side leaned against the door and looked at her. His name was Ron Laird.

"This isn't an arrest, is it?" Mordente asked coolly.

Laird grinned and shook his head from side to side.

"What is it?" she asked.

"A murder," Laird replied.

CHAPTER EIGHT

Monday, May 21, 9:22 a.m.

This time he wore a white cotton jumpsuit that read "MARINA DEL REY TOWERS" in curly script over his breast pocket. A pair of dark black sunglasses shrouded his eyes and accentuated the paleness of his face. He stood in the center of the yellow-painted, black-scuffed service elevator as it groaned upwards towards Aaron Tate's penthouse. No wood grain and muzak for the hired help, no sirree.

In his left hand, he held a stack of neatly folded clothes chest high in front of him to hide the silenced .357 Magnum. He imagined it was still hot from the slugs it spit into the nigger laundry man in the basement. He'd made him strip so the jumpsuit wouldn't get dirty and then shot off his balls.

The elevator jolted to a stop, the doors squealing rustily as they slid open, revealing a floor covered in white wood planks to resemble the patio of a country home.

He stepped out. The doors closed behind him and he noticed a second elevator to the right of the service one. He faced forward again. The double doors to Tate's penthouse looked like the front door to a home, complete with ornate brass doorknocker, lighted doorbell, and patio doormat. Potted plants flanked either side of the door, and a planter box filled with bright flowers rested below the draped, bay window to the left of the door.

The nigger drug peddler had certainly made some money. He wasn't impressed. He had seen a lot of expensive extravagance in his life. He pressed his finger against the doorbell. He heard a muted chime from somewhere beyond the door. A dark form passed behind the drapes and he heard heavy footsteps approach the door.

The door swung open and a tall, bald, cold-eyed black man, wearing black satin sweats and a white tank top that was about to tear against the strain of his chest, filled his vision.

"I've got something for vou."

"I'll take it," the black man said tonelessly.

The magnum popped once and the black man stumbled back, his eyes wide, as if he had just swallowed something down his windpipe. Red burst across his white tank top. He dropped into a sitting position on the white shag carpet, wavered for a moment, then toppled flat on his back with a thud.

He dropped the laundry and closed the door behind him softly. Behind the black's body was a white Steinway piano in front of a picture window that offered a breathtaking view of the frothy Pacific swells. All of Tate's furniture was white. All the pictures were framed in white.

White as the coke Tate sells, he thought. *White as the man whose gonna kill him.*

He moved towards the hallway to his left.

"Hey," someone said behind him.

He whirled, squeezing off two shots into the bathrobe-clad woman who emerged from the kitchen. The first bullet slammed into her shoulder and spun her around. The second burst through her chest and splattered the wall with her heart.

He turned back to the hallway. Ahead of him was the door leading to the helipad stairwell. To his right was Tate's office door. He pushed it open. A long, uncluttered mahogany desk and another picture window faced him, and the walls were lined with bookcases.

Tate was to his left, riding his white Exercycle, his eyes staring out the window at imaginary bike trails. He was trying to work off the ten-pound roll around his middle that poked out underneath his white satin jogging jacket and hung over the waist of his matching pants. His jacket was unzipped to his midsection, exposing a damp, rounded chest decorated with about seven gold chains.

"Who the fuck are you?" Tate huffed, trying to hide his surprise with anger.

"Mr. Jury."

Tate noticed the silenced Magnum for the first time and froze on his Exercycle. "What have you come to take, huh? Money? Drugs? What?"

He grinned. "Your life, nigger."

9:30 a.m.

The torrent of cars on the Santa Monica Freeway below Macklin's helicopter flowed towards the cluster of skyscrapers mired in the greenish haze to the east. To him, the downtown buildings looked like a tangle of tall weeds in a muddy landscape.

"Mordente has already left her place," Shaw's voice crackled from the headset speakers. "She must be on the road."

Ahead, Macklin could see the cars slowing and blurring into a solid black line of stalled traffic beginning at the distant Crenshaw exit. Traffic inched eastward at a crawl.

"Were you able to find out what squad car Stocker's monkeys are driving?" Macklin's heard his own amplified voice echoing in his ears.

"Yeah," Shaw replied. "Deese and Laird are in car fifty-four."

"All right, where are you now?"

"I'm making the transition from the southbound 405 to the eastbound Santa Monica Freeway."

"Ten-four, over and out." Macklin heard the whisper of static signaling the end of the transmission.

After discovering Stocker's plans, Macklin called Shaw, gave him a quick explanation, and sent him to the reporter's house. Then, wearing only his jogging shorts and sneakers, Macklin hurried to the Santa Monica Airport, slipped a Kevlar vest over his naked torso, grabbed an Ingram and a handful of clips, and took to the skies to search for Mordente.

The helicopter rumbled across the sky. Macklin peered down at the freeway, searching for the white top with the black number 54 painted on it. On the shoulder he saw a parked sports car. He brought the helicopter down and made a low pass over it.

He saw a red Mazda RX-7. Grimacing, Macklin circled above Mordente's car. "Ronny, I've found her car. It's been abandoned about a mile west of the Robertson Boulevard exit. I'm going to continue east, searching the freeway."

"Roger," Shaw responded. "I can see you ahead."

Macklin made one final pass over Mordente's car and saw Shaw's beige Ford sedan roaring down the shoulder, a red light flashing on its roof. He turned the helicopter away and veered into a parallel course following the freeway. From his vantage point, the city looked like a collection of cardboard buildings and toy cars laid out on a child's dirty bedroom floor.

"I'm coming up behind the car now," Shaw said. "It looks empty."

Scanning the freeway ahead of him, Macklin spotted a black-and-white patrol car shooting free of the congested traffic and gliding down the La Cienega Boulevard exit.

The helicopter bore down in a tight, right arc and streaked southward over the patrol car. Macklin smiled with grim satisfaction. He'd found car 54.

"Forget her car," Macklin shouted into the mike. "They're heading south on La Cienega Boulevard."

"Take it easy, Mack," Shaw advised, "don't spook them. I'll take the Roberson exit and haul my ass to La Cienega."

The long boulevard began as a steep slide off the glittering Sunset Strip into the homosexual colony bisected by Santa Monica Boulevard. Then La Cienega seeped into the city like an infection, decaying the area around as it ate its way through to LAX. It turned the flesh of the city absolutely rancid at the rise to Baldwin Hills.

Macklin watched the patrol car pick up speed as La Cienega widened and became a six-lane quasi-freeway to scale the dreary, sunbaked hills that looked like a lunar landscape covered with dead dune grass. Hundreds of rusty oil pumps bobbed on the foothills and sucked the land dry for Chevron and Getty. Cyclone fences ringed with barbed wire chopped the hundreds of acres into jagged, puzzle-piece chunks of gangrenous land licked by the asphalt tongue of La Cienega Boulevard.

The patrol car turned right onto Stocker Street and into the secluded wasteland. A swirling cloud of dirt billowed out behind the car as it veered off the road and into the vast oil fields.

The sour odor, a rotten smell reminiscent of natural gas and hot tar, blew through the open windows in the front seat and into Jessica Mordente's face. The police car sped over the gravel in a winding, upwards trail between rusted oil pumps, piles of trash, and corroded piping.

Her head throbbed from the heat, the smell, and the fear. Deese and Laird had been silent since the freeway, though Laird kept looking back at her with a sickly smile on his face. That left her to her thoughts, none of which were very uplifting. She had always thought the police and Macklin were tied together somehow. She never thought they'd do his killing for him.

Mordente knew her chances of escape were slim, but she resolved to give them a fight. Killing her wouldn't be easy.

The car stopped beside a lone oil pump on a tall slope. It's rhythmic, screeching grind was eerily reminiscent of a heartbeat, as if the land were alive. A torn and soiled mattress, it's stuffing spilling out, was crumpled against the pump in a patch of dead weeds littered with crinkled beer cans, Burger King bags, and an empty package of Trojan condoms. Mordente peered out the window at the surrounding area. The slope they were on was sheltered by a circle of foothills covered with nodding oil pumps.

They were utterly alone.

Deese wearily pushed open his door and stepped out. "Yeah, this will do just fine."

He yanked open the back door, grabbed Mordente around the neck with his left hand, and pulled her towards the door. "Get out, you damn cunt."

Mordente stood up from inside the car, met Deese's eyes, and then rammed her knee into his groin with every ounce of strength she could muster.

Deese grunted and doubled over. Mordente pushed past him and dived over the edge of the slope, tumbling head over heels onto the loose rocks and dirt. She rolled uncontrollably down the steep face, her hands cuffed behind her back, her eyes closed tight.

Mordente could feel the gravel tearing at her skin and could hear the explosive crack of gunfire above her. Finally, when it seemed like her tumbling would never end, she crashed through a tangle of barbed brush. She lay there dazed on her back for a moment, the world spinning. When the sense of motion subsided, she rolled over on her left and saw Deese and Laird standing on the crest, firing their guns at her. Slugs chewed into the loose dirt around the brush.

Then Deese held his gun up in the air and, half sliding and half running, charged sideways down the hill towards her.

Mordente looked to her right and saw only the rise of another foothill. The face of the slope was steep and afforded no cover. If she tried to scale it, they could pick her off with ease.

A current of gravel, kicked out from under Deese's feet, spilled against Mordente. She whipped her head around and saw that he was only twenty yards away, a victorious grin on his face. She heard a chopping sound echoing between the hills and saw Deese's smile wane.

Suddenly a helicopter burst over the crest behind Deese. Laird whirled around. The landing skid smashed through his face and sent his body toppling towards them. Deese forgot about Mordente and scrambled towards the brush. The helicopter streaked down the hillside and closed in on him like a hawk.

He dived into the brush, rolled, and came up in a crouch, firing two shots at the helicopter, which roared over him, banked, and climbed the face of the hill to Mordente's right. It stopped, hovering high in the air, its rotors thwacking, and turned around in place to face Deese.

"Drop your gun and raise your hands," a voice boomed from the helicopter.

Mordente stared at the helicopter incredulously through the tangle of dry foliage. *Macklin?* Her confusion now was as strong as her fear.

Mordente sensed a motion to her left and turned just as Laird's headless, blood-splattered body crashed into her. Stark terror grabbed her and she let out a piercing scream that momentarily distracted Deese. He suddenly remembered his prey and pivoted towards her, aiming his gun at her.

She saw Deese shudder, a splash of red blossoming on his chest. His gun arm faltered. He raised it again and his body jerked, a tuft of hair flying off his head like a golfer's divot. Deese, his face blank, slumped forward as if in prayer.

Shifting her gaze from Deese's crumpled body to the helicopter, she saw the muzzle of a silenced Ingram poking out the window. Macklin retracted the Ingram and brought the helicopter down, chopping up the air and whipping up the loose dirt in a giant brown cloud. Mordente pushed Laird's body away and crawled out of the brush.

She felt a two strong hands grab her by the shoulders and pull her up. When she looked up, she saw the concerned expression on Sergeant Ronald Shaw's familiar face.

"Everything's all right now, Ms. Mordente," he said, turning her around and unlocking her handcuff's with Deese's keys. He jerked his head towards the clearing between the two foothills. "Let's get in the copter."

Mordente, not knowing what else to do, ran in a crouch alongside Shaw to the helicopter. Shaw opened the back door, and she climbed in. Macklin lifted the helicopter into the air as soon as Shaw was inside. Shaw and Mordente slipped their headsets on simultaneously.

"Mack," Shaw said sternly, "get us over to Marina Del Rey Towers as fast as you can."

"This stunt doesn't change a thing," Mordente broke in.

"Jessie," Macklin said calmly, "I just saved your life. Doesn't that tell you anything?"

"Yeah, it tells me you remembered at the last minute that if I die that story is published anyway," she shouted, residual fear cracking her voice. Both Macklin and Shaw winced as her voice boomed in their ears. "What did you think killing me would accomplish, Macklin? And why use two crooked cops?"

Macklin sighed with frustration and decided it was best to ignore her for the moment. "Ronny, why are we going to the Towers?"

"I got a call. There's been a hit on Aaron Tate, the black mobster behind 80 percent of the drug traffic in this city," Shaw said.

"Is he dead?" Mordente asked quickly, suddenly the reporter. Macklin grinned to himself, certain now that she was all right.

Shaw peered out the window at the hint of blue water in the distance. "Not yet."

CHAPTER NINE

Monday, May 21, 10:23 a.m.

Macklin's helicopter streaked over Chace Harbor, where the frothy swells were cluttered with all manner of pleasure craft, and across the rooftops of dozens of stylish condominium and apartment complexes.

Looming up in front of Macklin were the four, staple-shaped Marina Del Rey towers, facing each other and forming an imposing, eighteen-story steel cloverleaf without the rounded edges. A shimmering blue swimming pool and lush green putting green filled the center space between the towers.

"It's the tower on your left," Shaw instructed.

The helicopter veered towards the building and closed on it in a slow, gentle descent. Mordente hastily finished wiping the blood off her arms and face with alcohol-soaked gauze pads from Macklin's first aid kit.

A pale young police officer who looked like he was just out of high school appeared on the roof as the helicopter touched down. He had a perplexed, lost expression on his face. Macklin pushed open his door and jumped out, faintly aware of how strange he must look in his Kevlar vest and jogging shorts. Why, he wondered, had Shaw insisted they come here?

Shaw and Mordente dashed past him. The reporter shot an icy glare at Macklin and stayed close to Shaw's side. Her hair was mussed, her face was lined with scratches, and her blouse and slacks were specked with dirt and blood. Yet she hardly showed the trauma. Her stance was firm, and her face reflected a strong anger and determination. Her whole body radiated strength. Macklin regarded her with genuine admiration. She was quite a woman.

Macklin remained at the helicopter and watched while the officer animatedly explained something to Shaw, who waved Macklin over with his arm.

"C'mon, Mack," Shaw yelled over the sounds of the whirring chopper blades. Macklin reluctantly sprinted to the doorway to the stairs leading into the building. Their footsteps clattered down the stairwell to the penthouse.

"Tate was found ten minutes ago by one of his aides," Shaw explained as he turned and started down the second flight of stairs. "The aide called the paramedics and the police. Unfortunately there's nothing any of us can do."

"What do you mean?" Mordente asked impatiently.

Shaw pushed open the door that led to a hallway carpeted with thick, white shag. The walls were covered in dark wood. Two medics paced in the hallway in front of a pair of open double doors and turned abruptly when Shaw, Macklin, and Mordente appeared in the hallway. Behind them, in the living room, Macklin could see two bodies crumpled on the floor and splashes of blood on the walls.

"Hey, don't be mad at us, we're just following the law here," one medic said, raising his hands defensively in front of his chest and nodding his head toward the door to his right.

"They don't pay us enough to deal with that shit," the other one said, dispensing with a defensive posture altogether.

Macklin and Mordente followed Shaw past the medics and right through the double doors. Mordente involuntarily grabbed Macklin's wrist in terrified surprise and froze in the doorway.

Aaron Tate, clad in a white satin jogging suit, lay on his back atop his long mahogany desk. His arms were slit open lengthwise and bound to his sides by steel wires that wound around his body and joined at a lump of gray clay on his chest.

Blood flowed out of Tate's fleshy arms in thick streams that dripped onto the floor and formed a huge, expanding stain in the white carpet around his desk. His eyes were open wide and he was shivering.

"That lump of clay on his chest is contact explosive," Shaw whispered. Mordente, realizing she was grasping Macklin's arm, jerked her hand away as if electrocuted. "It's a mixture of clay and nitroglycerin. If he moves too much, or if someone tries to remove those wires, he'll blow up."

"He's shaking," Mordente muttered, staring at Tate.

"I think that's the idea," Macklin realized. "It's from the blood loss. He's going into shock."

"The bomb squad probably won't get here in time to dismantle the bomb before he bleeds to death," Shaw said. "That is, if his convulsions don't blow him up first."

"What are we doing here?" Mordente asked.

Shaw didn't answer.

"Stay in the hall and get the medics to stand clear of the room," Shaw told the officer.

"You got it, Sergeant," the officer said, stepping away eagerly.

Shaw glanced nervously at Macklin, then at Tate. The detective motioned Macklin to follow him and then strode confidently into the room. "Tate," he ventured.

Tate looked at Shaw with two horrified eyes. "Please help me, Shaw, I'll do anything," he said in a weak, drowsy voice. "I'll give you names, dates, places. Just get me out of here."

Shaw bit his lower lip nervously and stopped a foot short of the desk. Macklin came up cautiously beside him.

"Who did this to you, Tate?" Shaw asked carefully.

Tate swallowed, his shivering increasing. Macklin glanced back at Mordente and saw that she now stood only a few feet behind them, just clear of the creeping bloodstain.

"Mr. Jury," Tate sputtered.

Shaw sighed, looked back at Mordente, and then to Tate again. "This man standing beside me, is he the one who did this to you?"

"No," Tate muttered.

"Are you certain?" Shaw insisted.

"Yes," Tate replied, wincing. "I'm not going make it, am I, Shaw? Am I?" Macklin watched as a wave of violent muscle contractions crept up Tate's legs.

Macklin tapped Shaw in the side with the back of his hand. Shaw watched, transfixed in grisly fascination, as Tate's body shook.

"C'mon, Ronny, let's go." Macklin grabbed Shaw by the arm and led him away slowly. Mordente had back-stepped through the doorway into the hall.

"Where are you going? Huh?" Tate yelled. "Help me, damn it, help me!" His stomach rose and fell with his anxious breathing. Convulsions wracked his body. "Don't go!"

Macklin pushed Shaw through the doorway into the hall just as Tate burst apart in a whirlwind of blood and flame.

A powerful fist of scorching air punched Macklin in the back and flung him against the wall outside the room. He flew into it like an insect splattering against a car windshield. The air rushed out of his lungs, and he slid dizzily to the floor, chunks of spongy flesh, cheesy adipose, and thick droplets of blood raining down on him.

Lying sprawled out and dazed on the floor, the world spinning around him, he was unsure if the blood on him was Tate's or his own.

Mordente, flat on the floor beside Macklin, was the first person to stand. She braced herself on the wall and rose shakily to her feet, nearly stumbling on a mangled Exercycle wheel. The windy sound of hungry flames filled her ears. The medics, at the far end of the hallway, were beginning to stand up. She peered around the charred doorframe into Tate's office.

The carpet where Tate's desk had been was aflame, tongues of fire snapping at the ceiling and flicking out the shattered window into the blue sky. Torn flaps of flesh were plastered to the blood-smeared and fire-blackened bookcases around the room.

"Give me a hand," Shaw said, his voice distracting her from the carnage.

She turned and saw Shaw wrapping Macklin's right arm around his shoulder. Swallowing back the bile rising in her throat, she grabbed Macklin's other arm, and together she and Shaw lifted him to his feet.

"Are you all right?" Shaw asked Macklin, whose head swayed weakly from side to side.

"Yeah," Macklin sputtered. "Give me a second to catch my breath." He stood in front of Tate's doorway and stared into the office decorated in gore. Damon's Mr. Jury had to be stopped.

"Do you think you can fly your copter?" Shaw released Macklin's arm and was glad to see his friend could stand on his own.

"Yeah." Macklin nodded, glancing away from the room and at Mordente. She didn't look like she agreed with his answer. "Help me up the stairs," he told her.

"Hurry up. I want you out of here before this place is crawling with authorities," Shaw urged them. "I'll touch base with you later."

Macklin nodded and they struggled to the stairwell, the door closing behind them just as the bomb squad appeared at the opposite end of the hall.

Hot water pounded from the Shower Massage into the sore muscles between Brett Macklin's shoulder blades. Dried blood washed off his skin and swirled around the drain, reminding him of the murder scene from *Psycho.* A hand suddenly pulled back the shower curtain, and Macklin jumped back, nearly losing his balance on the slick enamel of his bathtub.

"Take it easy," Jessica Mordente said softly, lifting her slim, naked leg over the bathtub rim. Macklin closed his eyes, relieved, and exhaled slowly. He had expected Norman Bates to slash him up with a knife.

When he opened his eyes, Mordente stood bare in front of him. Water sprayed off his shoulders in a fine mist that coated her breasts with tiny beads. Her eyes met his and he felt her trembling fingers brush his chest.

She had already taken a shower. While she was doing that, Macklin had scoured the house, found all of Stocker's listening devices, dropped them on his garage workbench, and crushed them with his hammer. He was brewing a pot of fresh-ground coffee when she came downstairs. When Macklin had left her a few minutes later, she was curled up on the couch in his terrycloth robe and sipping a cup of hot coffee.

"Being alone, downstairs, all I could think about was all the bloodshed." Her voice was raspy and her shaky fingers traced circles around his nipples. "I need to be with someone."

Macklin understood how she felt. He had endured the same empty, floundering sensation when he first began his vigilance. Only for him, there was no one around to turn to. The fear, the disgust, and the uncertainty had just chewed away at him. He was past that now. Death was no longer a stranger to him.

Her hands slid across his flat stomach and down to his buttocks. She gently kneaded the firm flesh and drew him closer until he could feel her warm breath on his face. He held her by the shoulders and kissed her lips, feeling her pliant body melt against his.

He pulled back and let his hands slip from her shoulders to the smooth swell of her breasts. While kissing her, he lightly stroked her nipples with the palms of his hands. Her excited nipples hardened, poking into his palms. Her head fell back against the tile and her breathing became ragged.

"Suck them, please," she urged him in a dreamy, far off voice. Macklin lowered his head, tenderly cupping her breasts and flicking his tongue across one of her pointed nipples. Then he encircled it with his lips, sucking and rolling his tongue across the soft areola. The shower's hard stream massaged his neck, the hot water cascading in sheets down his arched back and soothing his aching muscles.

She moaned, her back pressed to the cold tile, her hands tightening on his shoulders. He placed his right hand between her legs and let his fingers slip deeply into the softness.

Mordente's legs began to shake, and she slid moaning down the tile into a sitting position with her knees bent in front of her. The pulsing water drilled the tile above her head. Macklin stood and felt the hot water punching his sore back again and the luscious warmth of Mordente's mouth around his stiffening penis.

She sucked and licked him with abandon, holding his erection with one hand and milking his testicles with the other. Macklin heard himself groaning pleasurably and was aware of his hips instinctively jerking back and forth. The tingling pressure of his excitement was becoming too much.

Macklin, breathing hard, gently pulled himself away from her and unclasped the Shower Massage from the wall. He adjusted the dial to soft massage, spread her legs, and held the head over her auburn pubic hair. Jets of water splashed between her legs in rhythmic pulses. She writhed, dragging her fingernails across the tile and clenching her teeth.

"Now, Brett, now," she managed to mumble, tossing her head and lifting her hips closer to the shower head. Macklin dropped the shower head, pulled Mordente towards him, and thrust his throbbing penis into her, both of them crying out with ecstasy as he began thrusting.

They were lost in their own passions, and the horrors they had witnessed today no longer existed. Their bodies slapped together, their pleasurable, breathy moans resonating off the tile walls and intensifying as their excitement grew unbearable.

The dwindling rays of the afternoon sun melted into the blue-gray shadows of approaching nightfall. Macklin, propped up against his headboard, stared out his bedroom window at the changing contrast of the trees set against the sky. Usually, he didn't notice the subtle transformation of light to dark. He didn't miss it. There was an emptiness about it that chilled him.

Jessica Mordente nuzzled closer to him, shifting her head from his chest to the warm space between his neck and shoulder. He felt her lips lightly caress his neck. He had told her everything, sharing with her every detail of his life since his father's death. Then they made love again with a hypnotic slowness that built to a frenetic climax that left them sweaty and languid in each other's arms.

"Does it scare you?" she whispered. It was the first time she had spoken since Macklin had told his story.

"What?"

"The thin line that separates you from the fake Mr. Jury."

Macklin said nothing.

"You don't think you two are much alike, do you?" she asked softly, her breath warming his neck.

"I don't have as much hate."

"C'mon, Brett, sure you do."

Neither of them said anything for several long moments. Macklin felt warm and snug under the sheets. The sun had disappeared and the bedroom was dark. His skin was sticky with sweat where Mordente was pressed against him. Her body was like a smoldering fire.

"I don't kill because I like it and I don't kill because I disagree with someone's skin color, religious beliefs, or political bent," Macklin said.

"You kill because you think you're right. You kill to protect someone or to uphold the law. But by the very act of killing, you're making a mockery of the law you force others to abide by with their lives," she said. "So far, the people you've killed probably deserved it. But what about tomorrow or the next day, or the day after that?"

Macklin sighed. "I have to have faith in myself. I have to hope that I'll know if I've slipped over the edge into the kind of madness that's driving him. I know, I know. He thinks he's making things right, too. But *I am*. That's the difference."

"It's all how you look at it, Brett."

"How do you look at it?"

"I don't know," she replied, her voice shaky.

Macklin squeezed her tightly against him. Her smooth body felt good and solid against him. He found the feel of her body close against his fortifying and comforting.

"I'm sorry, Brett," she whispered. "I came very close to ruining a good man."

"There's nothing for you to apologize for, Jessie. You were doing what you thought was right."

"A part of me knew it couldn't be true," she said. "But I would have destroyed you anyway."

"It's over now." Macklin buried his lips in her hair.

"No, it isn't." She sat up, leaning forward on her elbows, and gazed into Macklin's eyes. "There's still a killer out there. You aren't going to rest until you get him, are you?"

Macklin nodded.

"I want to help you," she said firmly. He knew he couldn't talk her out of it. He wasn't sure he wanted to.

"When's your next interview with Anton Damon?

"Thursday."

Macklin leaned forward, brushing his lips against hers. "Bring me with you as your photographer."

"Okay," she replied huskily, slipping her hand under the sheets and down his thigh, "on one condition …"

CHAPTER TEN

Tuesday, May 22, 11:30 a.m.

"There is no tangible connection between me and your vigilante," said Anton Damon, tilting back until his chair tapped the interrogation room wall, "besides a similar view of the world, Sergeant Shaw."

The black detective unbuttoned his collar and loosened his tie. He could feel perspiration rolling down his back. It was 102 degrees outside and, Shaw mused, 125 inside.

"C'mon, Damon, let's cut the shit." Shaw leaned against the wall facing Damon, who sat at the end of the table beside his attorney, Steve Gregson. Shaw figured that Gregson would gladly trade his Century City office and Mercedes convertible for a thatched hut on a Malibu beach and a surfboard with a cellular phone. Gregson's sandy blond hair, seamless tan, and bright blue eyes made Frankie Avalon tunes ring in Shaw's ears. "The phony Mr. Jury is White Wash and those illiterate reprobates can't piss unless you help them aim."

"Mr. Damon, being a parolee doesn't mean you've forsaken your constitutional rights." Gregson sneered at Shaw. "You don't have to answer these ridiculous, pointed questions."

Damon shrugged. "Relax, Steve. Let Sergeant Shaw here flex his muscles. It's amusing." The White Wash leader cocked an eyebrow. "What makes you think this isn't the real Mr. Jury?"

"The real Mr. Jury is dead," Shaw replied. "And while he was alive, he didn't hunt down blacks for sport. This man does, and calls it the White Wash way. Your way."

"Shaw, you aren't thinking," Damon said, giving Shaw a reproachful glare and waving a scolding finger at him. "Mr. Jury is a vigilante who protects people from violent crime. I've yet to meet a black who hasn't committed a crime and wasn't a potential killer. It's only natural that blacks dominate the list of criminals Mr. Jury has ... ah ... restrained."

"Oh, you are amazing." Shaw approached Damon, looking down at the White Wash leader with disgust. "You sit there, glib as hell, talking about potential killers as if you're the pope. You butchered three human beings."

"I wouldn't call them that," Damon smirked.

Shaw whipped Damon across the face with the back of his hand, the slap of flesh cracking like lightning in the tiny room. Gregson bolted out of his seat but was halted by Damon's upraised hand.

Damon, still smirking, a red mark on his cheek where Shaw had struck him, stared into the detective's furious eyes. A uniformed police officer yanked open the interrogation room door. Shaw stepped back, combing one hand through his hair and waving the officer away with the other.

"Like I said, Shaw, I've yet to meet a black man who wasn't a criminal," Damon huffed. "I believe he just broke the law, Steve."

Gregson grinned. "Damn right he did, and I'm going to file a formal complaint."

Shaw's back was to them. He couldn't believe he had let Damon get to him. The racist bastard had won this round. Shaw could barely contain the urge to wring Damon's neck until it crunched between his fingers.

"Sergeant Shaw," Gregson chided, "I demand you either charge Mr. Damon or release him immediately."

Shaw turned around slowly, his anger waning into weary frustration. Sometimes, the law made him feel as if he was hog-tied. "Damon isn't going anywhere. We're keeping him in custody until we can investigate his parole violations."

"What violations?" Gregson yelled.

"Associating with known felons, for starters." Shaw pulled a sheaf of papers folded lengthwise from his inside jacket pocket and dropped them on the table. "All these people are sharing quarters with him at the Threllkiss retreat."

Gregson stacked the scattered papers neatly and placed them into his thin leather briefcase and snapped it shut. "You'll be out of here in twenty-four hours, Mr. Damon, I promise you that."

Damon made a steeple with his fingers and smiled at Shaw. "No problem, Steve. Take your time—I'm in no hurry."

12:45 p.m.

Mayor Jed Stocker rarely left the movie star's house in a good mood. Now in his three-piece suit and carrying his tennis clothes in a duffel bag and his racquet under his shoulder, Stocker strode around the ornate marble fountain in front of the manor and walked to his car. The experience of playing tennis with the big-name actor, who had a string of R-rated box-office successes that were critical disasters, always brought some troubling truths home for the mayor.

For one, the movie star always kicked the shit out of him on the court, so Stocker, who thought he was a pretty hot tennis player, left feeling like the beginner he actually was. And while Stocker ran all over the court trying to sustain volleys, the movie star casually bragged about the naked, buxom starlets he got to fuck for the cameras.

What bothered Stocker was that the movie star was actually paid to hump beautiful women. So while the movie star talked about lying on top of Catherine, Raquel, Jacqueline, Lynda, Bo, and the rest, Stocker was left to ponder his less-than-scintillating erotic encounters with his wife, Norma, and his occasional, furtive meetings with the shoe repair lady with the compact buns. Whenever Norma uttered her "I'm too bored to fuck" line, it was off to get those suede shoes fixed and his gonads fired up.

And then there was the final, sobering blow that visiting the movie star always dealt him. Stocker got into his Oldsmobile Cutlass Brougham, started the engine, and drove slowly around the fountain and past the movie star's sleek Maserati sports car. As much as Stocker would like a finer car, and as much as he could afford one, he knew the public would have a shit fit if he drove something classy. They'd think he was dishonest.

I'm a fucking leader—why don't they let me live like one? Where are the royal perks? Why can't I drive a nice car? Stocker drove through the gate and thought, like he did every Tuesday, how much he hated playing tennis with the movie star. He let the car coast down the narrow winding roads that hugged the tall stone walls and tall, densely packed trees that hid the Bel-Air mansions from the street.

Stocker was gliding around another curve when suddenly a black car burst into his path from a driveway on the left. He twisted the wheel and slammed the brake pedal to the floor. The Olds fishtailed to the left, the tires screeching as they gripped for a hold on the asphalt.

The Olds stopped across the road and rocked from side to side. Before Stocker could get his bearings, the driver's side door was yanked open and he felt rough hands grab him by the shirtfront and pull him out.

Brett Macklin spun Stocker around, slammed him forward against the hood, and yanked the mayor's right arm up behind his back.

"What the fuck do you think you're doing, Macklin?" Stocker yelled, his cheek flat against the car's hood. He could hear the engine humming underneath it.

Macklin pulled up on the arm until Stocker cried out. "We're finished, Stocker. I don't ever want to hear from you again."

"Fuck you, Macklin—you need me."

"You're mistaken," Macklin said softly.

"You're pushing it, Macklin," Stocker blustered, his anger tinged with desperation. "If you value your daughter's future and your health, you'll let go of me right now. Otherwise, I'll expose you and let my men deal with you."

"Deese and Laird are dead." Macklin twisted Stocker's arm up towards his neck until he heard the mayor's sharp scream of pain and felt the arm tear free of its socket.

"You're on the wrong side now, Stocker. You better stay away from me and watch yourself," Macklin said, leaning close to Stocker's ear, "or Mr. Jury might just come gunning for you."

Macklin walked back to his Cadillac and left Stocker whimpering on the car, the mayor's arm hanging limply at a grotesque angle behind his back.

11:00 p.m.

"Attorneys for onetime White Wash leader and convicted murderer Anton Damon allege that his detention for parole violations is police harassment..."

Macklin sat in the darkness of his living room, his face lit by the glow from the television screen. The silver-haired anchorman, dressed in a red jacket with the station logo on the breast pocket, related Gregson's complaints in a dull, detached monotone and then switched to a taped interview with Gregson on the deck of his Malibu beach house.

"Sergeant Shaw, I should mention, is a black. My client believes that Sergeant Shaw is simply trying to sanction him for his using his right to free speech provided by the constitution," Gregson said. High afternoon waves crashed against the sand and crawled up the beach behind him. *"He didn't bring Mr. Damon in for alleged parole violations or his alleged connection with the Mr. Jury killings. No, he is hassling Mr. Damon because of what Mr. Damon believes."*

Macklin sighed and pressed the remote control in his lap to change the channel. Shaw's face, with a microphone thrust in front of it, filled the screen.

"Mr. Jury is dead. This man's MO is entirely different. He is just using the Mr. Jury name as a justification for his actions. He is killing only blacks, and we have reason to believe that he is a member of the White Wash cult, which we all know was founded by Anton Damon."

The camera focused on an Asian woman, the station logo dangling from her necklace into her cleavage. *"How do you respond to Damon's claim that this is just thinly disguised police harassment?"*

"I don't," Shaw said.

Macklin's phone rang, distracting him from the television. He clicked the set off and lumbered into the kitchen, where the phone rang insistently. Snapping the receiver off the wall with one hand, Macklin opened the refrigerator with the other and looked for something good to eat. "Hello?"

"It's me," Shaw said, his voice dripping with fatigue.

"I just saw you on TV." The refrigerator was full of balls of aluminum foil. He didn't feel like finding out what aged food they contained. Macklin closed the refrigerator and sat down at the kitchen table.

"Yeah, I come off looking like shit," Shaw replied. "Damon will be out tomorrow. Have you talked to Stocker?"

"Yes. I convinced him to stay out of our way."

"How did you manage that?"

"I charmed him with my disarming personality," Macklin said. "So did you get anything out of Damon?"

"A formal complaint that will probably get me booted from this case," Shaw said.

"What happened?"

"I hit the son of a bitch."

"Hooray, hooray. I don't supposed that loosened him up?"

"I could have shoved bamboo under his fingernails and he still wouldn't have lost that self-satisfied smirk. But I know he's behind it—I can feel it in my gut. It's sitting there rotting like food that won't digest," Shaw said. "This killer could be anyone in his organization. We've asked for a list of White Wash members, but Damon's lawyers, naturally, will have to hear it from the Supreme Court before they will give it to us."

"What evidence do we have?"

"We've got a lot of nothing. We've got four wildly different descriptions out of those kids. We're trying to meld them, along with your description, into one composite, but who knows if it will even vaguely resemble him. We've also got two strands of hair, which may or may not be from his head, some pubic hair, some of his skin from under the prostitute's finger nails, and a teaspoon of semen. A couple of detectives are running down the plastique, but I don't think it will take us anywhere."

Macklin tapped the table with his fingers. He felt helpless.

"All I can do is put more patrol cars on the street and wait," Shaw said, filling the momentary silence. "Damon and his killer have to make a mistake soon."

"Yeah," Macklin sighed, "but how many people will die first?"

CHAPTER ELEVEN

Wednesday, May 23, 10:15 a.m.

Sergeant Ronald Shaw sat with his feet up on his desk and looked across the empty squad room at Wes Craven standing beside the door. He wondered if anyone ever suggested to Wes Craven that he should rent the space on his forehead for billboards. Craven was already as stoic as a signpost, and Shaw figured the guy must have about two inches of extra skull between his eyes and the errant, dry strands of blazing red hair that lay on his head like dune grass.

Shaw would even be the first to scrawl a message across Craven's face. It would read: "SANDBLAST MY MOUTH OUT WITH AJAX." The mint Craven was sucking made the squad room smell like the cube of ice blue disinfectant found in urinals. Shaw had heard that Craven, who leaned against the wall in his three-piece, Bond St. tailored suit, was obsessed with fresh breath. Craven probably picked up that habit, Shaw assumed, from spending so many hours leaning close to Justin Threllkiss and getting his orders.

The old coot and his decaying dentures must smell like steaming dog shit, Shaw thought, sitting with his crossed legs propped on the edge of his steel, battleship gray desk.

Craven, of course, was waiting for Anton Damon.

The squad room door beside Craven opened and the man immediately straightened to attention, like a soldier expecting General MacArthur to come bounding in.

Lieutenant Bohan Lieu grinned at Craven as he entered the room. "At ease, Craven."

Craven fell back against the wall and looked straight ahead through the slats of the blinds at the Sumitomo Bank building that bordered Little Tokyo outside.

Lieu was beginning to look like a Hershey's kiss wrapped in a seersucker suit and bow tie, Shaw thought, smiling back at his superior, who had sparkling, playful eyes framed with fleshy eyelids above and tiny bags below. Lieu always had a bag of Sugar Babies on him or stashed in his desk and liked to walk with his hands in his pockets. Shaw respected him and, more important, he liked him. There were too many assholes Shaw could respect but not many he could call a friend.

"I hear Mr. Personality has been around here all night," Lieu said, pausing beside Shaw's desk.

"Yep, Threllkiss sent him down here about midnight just in case we decided, as we often do, to release prisoners at two a.m." Shaw swung his feet off his desk and stood up. "Can I steal a cup of coffee from your office?"

"Sure," Lieu said, leading the way to office, which was a glass-partitioned corner of the squad room. "I wanted to chat with you anyway."

Shaw groaned inside. "Chat" was Lieu's buzzword for trouble. He made a beeline for Lieu's Mr. Coffee, found a Dodgers mug lying facedown on a napkin, took a chance that it was clean, and filled it up. When he turned around, Lieu was sitting behind his immaculately clean desk, unbending a paper clip. Now Shaw was certain he was in trouble.

"Why is it, Ronny, that every time I take a day off to have a cavity filled there's trouble?" Lieu asked rhetorically. Shaw took a seat in front of the desk. "I just found out you took a swing at Damon."

Shaw nodded.

"That's going to cause us both a lot of aggravation."

"I know." Shaw sipped his coffee. "It was a stupid, reflexive thing to do. I can't say I'm sorry I did it, though. The guy is scum."

"Saying the guy is scum isn't going to clear you with the board," Lieu said. "It was bad timing, too, Ronny. It hasn't been that long since the Tomas Cruz thing."

"Are you pulling me off the vigilante killings case?" Shaw asked.

"Nope, but you won't ever question Damon again, and there might be some strict, official repercussions later. There's also the possibility of a lawsuit."

The squad room door opened and Anton Damon, smiling, was escorted in by Steve Gregson and two uniformed officers. Craven popped a fresh mint into his mouth and moved to Damon's side.

"Maybe not," Shaw said, setting his coffee cup down on Lieu's desk. "He's not wearing a neck brace."

Shaw and Lieu walked into the squad room.

"Mr. Damon is leaving now, gentlemen," Gregson said, handing Lieu a slip of paper. "I'll bring you all into court for this outrage."

"If you will come with me, Mr. Damon, I have a limousine waiting at the loading dock," Craven said curtly.

"Thank you," Damon said smugly, shooting a taunting grin at Shaw. "Good-bye, Sergeant. Good luck with your investigation. I'm sure you will reap what you sow."

With that, Damon, Craven, and Gregson left the room. Lieu nodded. "I can see why you socked him."

Anton Damon opened the limousine's refrigerator and made himself a screwdriver while Wes Craven adjusted the color TV and inserted a videotape of last night's newscasts into the portable VCR.

Damon watched the newscasts silently for two or three minutes, sipping his drink, as the limousine hummed east towards the San Bernardino Freeway. Craven sat beside the TV across from Damon, watching the White Wash leader's face for reactions. Craven saw nothing.

"You can turn it off, Wes." Damon said.

Craven pushed off the color TV switch with his thumb.

"What does Mr. Threllkiss think?" Damon asked.

Craven shrugged. "It's publicity, he said. He'd like it if I stayed on with you for a while."

Damon nodded. "I think Sergeant Shaw knows who the real Mr. Jury is."

"Why?"

"A hunch, a look in his eye, the way he talks about him. It also makes good sense. I think the real Mr. Jury is an LAPD puppet."

"What do you have in mind?"

Damon swallowed the remainder of his screwdriver and shook his glass, jingling the ice. "If we get Shaw, we'll get Mr. Jury."

"What if you're wrong? What if Shaw and Mr. Jury aren't connected?"

Damon shrugged, leaning forward to make himself another drink. "So? One less nigger cop."

Thursday, May 24, noon

The Los Angeles Times Building looked like the unfortunate victim of an architectural Dr. Frankenstein. The clock-topped cement tower of the once-proud art deco building had been grafted onto a block-long cube of brown-tinted glass. The windowy addition was kept nice, shiny, and impenetrable, while the chalky remains of its violated host were left to collect grime.

Macklin weaved the car through the First Street traffic, giving the Los Angeles Times Building a passing glance as it disappeared to his right and the civic center blurred to his left. He moved into the left lane. At the stoplight, he looked out the passenger window at Joseph's Men's Wear, "The Store for Mr. Short," and noticed that the store proudly displayed multicolored Sam the Eagle and Olympic stars-in-motion neckties in the window.

The tie for the elegant gentleman, Macklin thought. The detectives in Parker Center across the street probably bought them by the dozen.

He turned left on San Pedro, where First Street melted into Little Tokyo, and made an immediate right into a blue-painted steel parking structure. A thin Chicano with a Bela Lugosi hairdo held an MJB can out to Macklin for the 25-cent entrance fee. Macklin dropped the quarter in and then drove the Cadillac up the winding ramp to the top of the structure.

He parked his car on the dividing line between two empty spaces and got out, slinging his friend Mort's camera gear around his shoulder. Mort was in Hawaii and wouldn't miss it. Macklin hurried down the urine-stained stairwell to the street and walked briskly past a gaunt Asian man selling sushi on paper plates wrapped in crinkled Saran wrap.

Macklin sprinted across the street, the cameras bouncing against his side, and was striding up First Street when he saw Jessica Mordente standing on the next corner at the edge of the old Times building. *Hey, Lois, it's me, Clark Kent!*

There was a wry smile on her face Macklin couldn't decipher but found attractive anyway. Her hands were thrust deep into the pockets of her pleated silk slacks. Her arms were slightly crooked at the elbows, bunching back the flaps of her matching jacket, revealing a loose-fitting blouse that caught the slight breeze and fluttered. Lois Lane never looked this good.

Macklin dashed across the street on a green light, cutting across oncoming traffic. Horns blared angrily in his wake.

"Do I look like a hotshot news photographer?" Macklin asked.

Mordente frowned, pinning a tattered press ID to his dirty white Paramount Studios sweatshirt. "You look like a tourist, but you'll pass."

She put her hand on the small of his back and led him to her Mazda, double-parked a few feet away. Mordente opened the hatchback and motioned Macklin to remove his camera equipment.

"It's a two-hour drive to Damon's place, so you may as well stow your stuff back here," she said. Macklin dropped the cameras in a clump beside a scruffy shoulder bag covered with outdated press-pass stickers and pins. He pulled on the strap with one hand. It felt as if the bag was stuffed with bricks.

"What is this thing?" he asked.

"The rest of your cunning disguise. I borrowed it from a photog friend of mine. It's got a bunch of lenses and crap in it. He thinks I'm shooting my sister's wedding," she said, slamming shut the hatch and walking around to the driver's side door. "Get in. There's a six-pack of beer and couple BLTs in the icebox behind your seat."

"Great, I'm starving."

Macklin opened the door and dropped himself into the contoured bucket seat. Mordente shifted and the car shot forward with a lurch. *She's a little tenser than she looked,* Macklin thought. He twisted in his seat, put the icebox on his lap, and opened it.

The fishy stench sprung out into Macklin's face like a jack-in-the-box. "My God, Jessie, how long have you been storing Flipper's carcass in here?"

Mordente shrugged. "Do you want to complain or do you want to eat?"

His growling stomach answered that question. He rummaged through it while she steered right onto Third Street and onto the southbound Harbor Freeway. He removed two cold

Heinekens from amid the ice, took two of the four BLTs out of a Ziploc bag, and helped himself to a bunch of seedless grapes in a plastic bag.

"What can I get you?" he asked.

"Just put a sandwich on my lap," she said. "I'm great at eating and driving. You can wedge the beer between my seat and the gearbox. Gimme a napkin, too—they're in the glove compartment."

Macklin tossed a sandwich in her lap, popped open a beer, and crammed it into the tight space beside her seat cushion. The napkins, which had been rolled up and stuffed into the glove box, fluffed out into Macklin's lap when he opened the compartment. A glare from Mordente stifled his grin, and he gave her a napkin.

They ate in silence. Macklin's sandwich tasted like rotten tuna fish, and his grapes were so fishy they could have been plump salmon eggs. And even though he spent five minutes wiping the rim of his beer can with a napkin, it still tasted like he was drinking the water out of a goldfish bowl. His hunger overcame his distaste, and he ended up eating the other two BLTs and swallowing half of another beer during the ride up to Threllkiss' lakeside retreat.

"Great breakfast, Jessie," he said as they turned off the winding road that rimmed the steep hillside and onto a gravel trail. Ahead, he could see the vague outline of the fence lining Anton Damon's compound and a streak of blue water through the pine trees to his right.

"Let's hope that sadist you saw at Burger Bob's isn't at Damon's place," she said, "or that may have been our last meal."

CHAPTER TWELVE

It smelled like someone's old grandmother lived inside Justin Threllkiss' lakeside home. There were plenty of Uzis, dark sunglasses, sweat-soaked khaki shirts, mud-caked Jeeps, and even a small, dragonfly-like helicopter, but not a single grandmother in sight.

Brett Macklin paused in the doorway and let Jessica Mordente enter the house ahead of him. *She Lone Ranger,* he thought, *me Tonto.* The guy who opened the door for them had a thick, short neck and a fleshy, insolent face with red circles under his deep-set eyes.

"Howdy, I'm Brett," Macklin said, flashing a toothy grin and thrusting his hand out at Flesh Face. He thought a little Mr. Good Ole Boy might do him some good. "Nice, friendly place you folks got here."

Flesh Face ignored him. Macklin shrugged and followed Mordente into the living room. Anton Damon stood in front of the stone hearth in an Izod polo shirt and jeans, holding a strawberry daiquiri in a frosted glass.

"Welcome, Ms. Mordente, welcome," Damon said, waving his free hand expansively. Two facing couches and a coffee table separated Damon from Macklin and Mordente. Rising from the couch to Macklin's right was a red-haired man with a pale forehead that seemed to glow. "This is my associate, Mr. Craven."

The man with the glossy forehead bobbed his head as his way of saying hello.

"I'd like you to meet my photographer," Mordente said.

Macklin reached around Mordente and pumped Damon's hand enthusiastically. "Brett Macklin's the name. It's a real pleasure, Mr. Damon."

Damon beamed. "Thank you. Where would you like me to stand?"

Macklin dropped the heavy pack on the hardwood floor beside a small stack of freshly cut wood near the hearth. "Right there is fine. You just talk with Ms. Mordente and I'll get you natural. 'Posed' is a dirty word with me, Mr. Damon."

"All right," Damon said. "Wes, why don't you bring our guests something cold to drink." He smiled at Mordente and Macklin. "Wouldn't you both like that?

Mordente opened her mouth to speak when Macklin suddenly cut in.

"Yes, sirree, we certainly would!" Macklin chirped, pushing up his sleeves and crouching beside his pack, rummaging through his gear.

Damon nodded at Craven, sending Threllkiss' emissary off to make some fresh daiquiris.

Mordente sat down on the couch that faced the window looking out over the lake. Damon was to her left. She set a tape recorder on the glass coffee table beside a bowl of roasted peanuts.

"Last time we talked about your future. This time I'd like to talk about your past." She scooted into the couch corner and angled herself towards Damon.

While Damon talked, Macklin scrambled around the room taking pictures. He didn't know what the hell he was doing. All his moves were picked up from watching reruns of *Lou Grant* and Cheryl Tieg commercials. But he listened to Damon and kept his eye on the guard movements outside, thereby getting a feel for both Damon and his operation.

Macklin paused every so often to take a drink of his daiquiri. Craven may not ooze charisma, but he sure as hell knew how to make a fantastic strawberry daiquiri. It was the first one he'd ever had that didn't taste like a 7-Eleven slurpee.

"... my past is so detached from me. It's like trying to remember the scenes and plot of a movie you saw somewhere once years ago," Damon concluded, an hour later. "It's hard for me to connect with the man I used to be. Jesus is standing between him and me, blocking the view."

"So have you been back to the dry riverbed where you killed the Kallahans?" Mordente asked. Damon was looking weary—she wasn't. She would probably never run out of questions and had managed to expose some nerves. Macklin, though, had gone through four rolls of film and didn't know whether a single shot had turned out.

"Yeah, yeah I have," Damon said, holding his glass out to Craven, who had sat across from Mordente through the whole interview and hadn't said a word. But his presence was felt. He reeked of Ty-D-Bol. "Can I have another, Wes?"

It was Damon's third. Macklin had helped himself to two. Mordente was still sipping her melted strawberry ice and rum. Craven had nursed a Dixie cup of water. Maybe he was watching his weight, Macklin mused. Maybe Craven would splurge and have a saltine for dinner. Craven went past him into the kitchen.

"Anyway, I went out there. I was disappointed," Damon said. "I don't know what I expected to find, a memorial perhaps, an engraved stone or plaque. I thought maybe somebody would have done something to mark the spot. It was an epicenter of a great movement, of a great controversy. Blood was spilled there, lives were changed there, and consciousness was raised there. Its historic significance has been overlooked." Damon sighed and shrugged. "They're building a new canal or aqueduct or something there."

"Yes, but what did you feel?" Mordente said.

Damon rubbed the side of his nose with his index finger. "I don't know. Sadness. Anger. Wistfulness. Separation. I saw a social movement lingering above the soil like wisps of evaporating dew. I saw an angry young man that I didn't recognize anymore wave a shiny clean ax and grin at me. I saw the Kallahans in the blend of dark shadows cast by the trees."

He shrugged again and Macklin snapped a photo.

"Then I walked away," Damon said, "and bought a double cheeseburger and a chocolate shake at this great Fosters Freeze I know in the valley. God, it was still as good as I remembered it."

"Okay, let's move on to something else," Mordente said.

"Sure," Damon said.

Craven returned with new daiquiris for everyone.

"Why don't you move by the window," Macklin suggested out of boredom. Besides, he wanted an excuse to watch the guards along the shore. "We'll change background and lighting a bit, you know? Maybe I'll win a Pulitzer or something, huh?"

Damon obliged, strolling over to the window. Macklin leaned against the back of the couch, twisted the camera lengthwise, and held the trigger for a few shots.

"What are your feelings regarding Mr. Jury?" Mordente asked.

"I wondered when you'd get around to that." Damon grinned, walking past Macklin and sitting on the couch beside Mordente. "Now you're going to get brutal."

Mordente smiled.

"I think it's unfortunate that people are dying," Damon said.

Cagey bastard, Macklin thought.

"Do you also think it's unfortunate that he's getting a lot of publicity and that his beliefs are similar to your own?"

Damon laughed. Craven crinkled his Dixie cup and tossed it towards the fireplace. He missed. It bounced onto Macklin's shoe and he threw it in as he got up and sat down next to Craven.

"I don't know what his beliefs are, Ms. Mordente, and I have no feelings on the publicity he's getting. It doesn't concern me," Damon said.

"But he says what he's doing is the White Wash way. Certainly what he does is a reflection on your movement, and you haven't denounced him publicly," Mordente countered.

"For one, he may be a White Wash member, but that doesn't mean we endorse him or that he reflects our concerns. I have not made any public statement regarding his actions because, for one, I don't want to establish any sort of connection between the two of us, negative or positive. Mr. Jury is Mr. Jury and Anton Damon is Anton Damon. Let's leave it that way."

"The police, by questioning you, have already made the negative connection you speak of."

Damon's smile had slowly disappeared. His lips were tight in grim resolution. "You're right in a way. But, I believe theWhite Wash–Mr. Jury issue was overshadowed by the outrageous, unwarranted behavior of Sergeant Shaw. The issue wasn't Mr. Jury. It was the free expression of ideas. Shaw was acting out a personal vendetta aimed at silencing me. He's a Negro, you know."

Mordente nodded.

"Shaw and the Negro people are afraid of me," Damon said, jabbing himself in the chest with his thumb. "They shouldn't be. I only want to make life better for them. I want them to settle into their proper, God-ordained places. Attaining happiness will be painful for some of them, but happiness always has a cost, doesn't it?"

Macklin took a picture. The tiny click shuddered like a cannon blast in the suddenly silent room.

"That'll be a dandy picture." Macklin grinned.

As the gate swung closed behind them, Macklin reclined the bucket seat in Mordente's car and exhaled slowly.

"What a frightening bastard," he said.

She nodded. "Do you think he's behind the killer?"

"I'm certain," he replied, closing his eyes.

"What now?"

"You got me. I'm gonna sleep on it."

"Before you start your hibernation, let me ask you one question."

"Go ahead."

"How did the pictures turn out?"

Macklin opened one eye. "Fine. All of 'em are masterpieces. Why?"

"Because my name's going on them—that's why. How do you think I convinced the *Times* not to send a photographer?"

"How will you explain that to Damon?"

"By then, it may not matter."

Damon remained at the couch, staring at the place where Jessica Mordente had sat, thinking how much he would like to make love to her. She looked like a loud one.

Craven appeared from the kitchen. "I just talked with Mr. Threllkiss about your proposal."

"And?"

"He agrees."

"Good." Damon nodded and then yelled. "Dalander!"

Flesh Face lumbered into the room. He was in Laguna shorts with a towel around his neck and he carried a bottle of Coppertone number 4 and the latest *Soldier of Fortune* magazine in his hand. He had been on his way out to catch a few rays.

"I want you and our Mr. Jury to grab Sergeant Shaw tonight and bring him here," Damon said. "Use restraint. Don't rough him up any more than you have to."

"Right," Dalander said.

CHAPTER THIRTEEN

Friday, May 25, 3:32 a.m.

"He's with a white woman," Dalander whispered, astonished, as he and the killer crept into Shaw's darkened bedroom. Since Dalander was rarely able to convince a woman to voluntarily sleep with him, he didn't see how a black man possibly could. And a white woman, at that.

A table fan whirred on the dresser across from the bed, and sheets were bunched up around the couple's ankles. Shaw and Sunshine wore only bikini underwear, and their bodies were slick with sweat.

Sunshine, who slept on the left side of the bed, lay curled against Shaw's back, her arms wrapped around him and her hands resting on his stomach. They looked snug and peaceful.

"Nigger bastard," said the man in the red leather jumpsuit, gliding around Shaw's side of the bed. He grabbed Shaw by the neck with his left hand and yanked him up. Shaw's eyes flashed open and the killer punched him in the face with a right cross, knocking the detective out cold.

Dalander pulled Shaw off the bed by the legs and smiled when Shaw's head thudded against the floor. Sunshine rolled over groggily and opened her eyes. Only a terrified gasp escaped her lips before the killer scrambled onto the bed and straddled her half-naked body.

"Keep still. We just saved your life, bitch." He crushed her cheeks in his left hand and coaxed her up into a sitting position.

She could see Shaw's motionless body sprawled on the floor at Dalander's feet. "You should be fucking your own kind. You're lucky we aren't cutting off your tits and turning them into couch cushions."

She closed her eyes, her chest heaving, and tried to choke back her fear.

"That's better," he said. His breath was sour. "Listen. Nigger here has three days to live. Mr. Jury can save his life by showing up, unarmed, at the Hollywood sign at midnight Saturday or Sunday. No show, and the nigger gets chopped up into puppy chow. Got it?"

"I don't know who Mr. Jury is," she sputtered, her words muffled by his grip on her cheeks.

He slammed her head back hard against the backboard. "Shut up, bitch. You better meet him, then, huh?" Tightening his grip, he nodded her head affirmatively. "Good." With his free hand, he covered her right breast and mashed it flat. "You're a real babe. Maybe you'd like me to come back some night and show you what a real man is like, huh?" Laughing, he forced her to nod her head again. "You'd like to suck my awesome cunt sword, huh?" Again, he jerked her head up and down. Releasing her head, he let his hand drop and then drove his fist into her stomach.

Sunshine jerked forward, her mouth gaping open, as the air rushed out of her lungs. The killer grinned at her, sat up from the bed, and back-handed her across the face with a loud thwack. Sunshine slammed back against the headboard then fell face forward on the bed.

"Sweet dreams," Dalander said to her and began dragging Shaw by the legs through the doorway like captured game.

The killer lingered by the bed, staring down at Sunshine. He leaned forward and rolled her over onto her back. Her skin was flushed and she moaned softly, dazed and weak. He knew she couldn't wait. He knew she was ready for him.

He slowly unzipped his jumpsuit. "Stuff the cop into the trunk. I'll be out in a few minutes."

⚜ ⚜ ⚜

8:47 a.m.

Someone tentatively rapped a fist against Brett Macklin's door. The near-silent thud jostled him a little, but he remained asleep on his back, Jessica Mordente lying on her side to his left.

Again there was a knock at the door, harder this time. Macklin's eyelids fluttered.

Knock, knock, knock.

He licked his dry lips, swallowed, and opened his eyes slowly.

Knock, knock, knock.

Downstairs, someone wanted his attention. Macklin exhaled slowly and slid his legs out from under the covers and set his feet on the floor.

Knock, knock, knock.

Careful not to wake Mordente, Macklin eased the rest of his body out of bed. More knocking. He remembered he hadn't fixed the doorbell yet. A terry-cloth robe lay draped on the towel rack in the bathroom. He put it on, tying it as he hurried down the steps to the door. His eyes stung and his hair felt tangled.

He slipped the bolt and turned the cold doorknob, pulling the door open towards him and taking a step back into the entry hall.

Sunshine stood on his porch in a pink bathrobe and slippers. A bluish welt colored her cheek. Her body seemed lifeless and driven by some supernatural force, like one of the walking dead in a George Romero movie.

The shock of seeing her hit him in the chest like a tossed brick.

"Sunshine, what are you doing here?" Macklin asked, taking her cold hand and guiding her inside. He didn't see her car in the street behind her. Could she have walked six blocks like that?

"They've got Ronny," she mumbled.

He closed the door and saw Jessica Mordente standing at the top of the stairs clutching his maroon wool robe tight around herself.

"Who, Sunshine? Who's got Ronny?" Macklin asked.

Sunshine sat on the bottom step, her back to Mordente. "You're Mr. Jury, aren't you?"

It was a statement, not a question. Macklin glanced up at Mordente, couldn't read her face, then looked back down at Sunshine.

He nodded.

Sunshine sniffled and wiped her nose on her sleeve. "They came in middle of the night. Two men, one in a red jumpsuit. They took Ronny and said he has three days to live. If you don't give yourself up to them at the Hollywood sign at midnight Saturday or Sunday they'll kill him."

Macklin's heart thumped furiously, like machine-gun fire in his chest. Anger and disgust bubbled acidly in his throat. Mordente eased down the stairs, sat beside Sunshine, and tentatively placed a reassuring arm around her shoulder.

"Did you call the police?" Macklin asked hoarsely.

Sunshine shook her head no. "This is outside the law. It's part of whatever you and Ronny have been doing."

"Are you all right?" He squatted in front of her and wiped a tear from her cheek.

She shook her head no again.

"One of 'em," she began, but her voice cracked and she started sobbing, her body heaving and tears streaming down her face. Mordente pulled her close.

"Th-the one in red," she choked out in a weak voice. "He raped me."

Macklin stood up slowly, clenching his teeth in grim resolve. Sunshine fell against Mordente and shuddered with deep, woeful sobs. Mordente looked up at him with teary eyes and held Sunshine tightly against her.

"I'll get him back," Macklin said, his hands knotting into fists. "And I'll make those bastards pay."

Noon

Brett Macklin's Cadillac charged down the gravel road towards the White Wash compound gate like a vicious Doberman, it's engine growling, it's shiny grillwork gleaming like bared, moist fangs.

The guards in the towers that flanked the entranceway began firing at Macklin before his car was even in range. He turned up the stereo. Wagner's "Ride of the Valkyries" boomed from the car's four interior speakers.

The bullets skipped off the Cadillac like hailstones as he closed in on the gate. He wore Levi's, a gray sweatshirt, a Kevlar vest, and .44 Magnum automatic in a shoulder holster. An Ingram lay on the passenger seat.

A guard planted himself in the center of the roadway behind the gate, spread his legs to brace himself, and fired his machine gun at Macklin's approaching car. Macklin pressed the accelerator flat against the floorboards.

The Cadillac burst through the gate, splintering it into a hundred jagged chunks, and plowed into the guard, tossing his body into the air. The body rolled up Macklin's hood, glanced off the windshield, and tumbled into the car's wake.

Macklin leaned forward, squinting through the blood-splashed windshield, and saw a dozen guards spill out of the house and scramble towards him. One of them tossed a grenade. Macklin wrenched the wheel and felt the ground heave under the right side of the car, the explosion spitting dirt into the air. Another grenade erupted in front of him. A wave of dirt splattered against his windshield.

Spinning the car in a donut shape, Macklin pushed in the lighter and faced the guards again. The twin .50-caliber machine guns emerged from the front of his car spitting slugs. The guards were cut down in one short, staccato burst. Their bodies were chewed up into fertilizer under the car's tires as Macklin blazed a trail to Damon's front door.

Grabbing the Ingram, Macklin threw open the driver's door and fell out of the car in a crouch, facing the demolished gate and firing.

Three approaching guards did a jerky death dance as a breeze of bullets blew against them. "Ride of the Valkyries" blared from the car and echoed on the lake. An invasion led by Francis Ford Coppola seemed imminent. A bullet pinged off the driver's side window behind Macklin's head. He spun, dropped to his side, and rolled, firing at the porch as bullets chipped at the ground where he had been.

Macklin saw Dalander framed in the doorway and squeezed the trigger. A slug carved out Dalander's Adam's apple and painted the front door with it. Flesh Face stiffened and fell forward. Macklin almost yelled "Timber!" and scrambled across the porch to the door. He kicked it open and flattened his back to the wall. Someone inside sprayed the porch with bullets, pumping several fresh holes into Dalander's corpse. The gunfire stopped and he heard the clattering of footsteps.

He abruptly pivoted low and fired into the doorway. There was no one. He had riddled the staircase with bullets. Macklin crept into the entry hall and peered to his left into the living room where he had photographed Damon yesterday. He cautiously stepped in, his finger tensed on the Ingram's trigger, the .44 Magnum automatic comfortably snug under his left arm.

Macklin sensed a motion to his right and ducked down as a beam of flame streaked across the living room towards his head. It singed his hair as it flashed over his head, bursting through the window behind him and igniting the curtains. Macklin patted down his hair and squatted behind the couch, ready to spring. Anton Damon, he knew, stood in kitchen doorway with three tanks of napalm on his back and a flame-throwing nozzle in his hands.

He heard Damon's wild laugh. "You shouldn't have fucked with me, Mr. Jury."

A burst of fire splashed against the couch, setting it aflame. Macklin tossed himself forward into the entry hall. Damon swept the room with flame, trying to torch him.

Macklin turned to face the archway he had just jumped through, heard Damon's approaching footsteps, and showered the fire-engulfed room with bullets. The Ingram jammed, empty. He threw the machine gun aside, whipped out his Magnum, and scrambled through the front door just as Damon appeared in the entry hall, scorching the ground where Macklin had stood.

An arm of crackling flame reached for Macklin, who flung himself off the porch, rolled across the hood of his car, and fell behind it. The fire skipped across the black hood.

Macklin peered over the hood at Damon. Flame lashed out and smashed into the car. Wisps of fire refracted off the armored steel and dissipated. Macklin hunched down, unsure of what to do. A footstep behind Macklin broke his thoughts. He whirled, firing. Two bullets rammed into Macklin's chest, knocking him breathlessly backward. The guard curled forward, the flurry of Macklin's .44 Magnum punches pounding into his stomach.

Macklin braced himself against the Cadillac's fender, tiny sparkles of light dancing in front of his eyes. The vest had stopped the bullets from piercing his skin but hadn't blunted the impact. His lungs were empty and his chest was a plate of pain. He crawled into the car and slammed the door shut.

Damon laughed and sprayed the car with fire. Macklin heard a familiar rumble and saw a helicopter rise over the house. The copter circled low over the compound, kicking up the dirt and whipping the black smoke from the burning house, and then hovered in front of the car.

Macklin straightened up in the driver's seat and stared up into Wes Craven's angry eyes. Macklin jerked the gearshift into reverse. The Cadillac wheels tore into the gravel and the car shot backward. Craven veered off and streaked away over the lake. The White Wash leader stood on the edge of the porch, chasing the car with flame. Macklin spun the wheel around and turned the car towards the porch, shifted into drive, and pressed the gas pedal flat.

Damon back-stepped and turned, saw the burning doorway behind him, and faced the oncoming car as it plowed into the porch, chewing through the planks. The porch crumbled and Damon was swallowed by a gaping hole of splintered, upended planks.

Macklin burst out of the car and climbed over the rubble to Damon, who lay bloody and twisted amidst the broken planks. Macklin grabbed the flamethrower's nozzle, put his finger on the trigger, and pressed it against Damon's mouth.

"Where's Shaw?" Macklin demanded.

Damon glared at him defiantly. "Fuck you, Macklin. Your nigger friend is going to die."

"That's not what I want to hear, Damon." Macklin grimaced. "You're going to have a very sore throat in about two seconds unless you start talking."

Damon laughed. "Kiss my ass, Macklin."

Macklin swung the nozzle away from Damon's face, aimed it at the White Wash leader's feet, and squeezed the trigger. Damon wailed in agony, his feet aflame.

"Talk," Macklin yelled over Damon's screams, planting his foot on Damon's chest so he couldn't rise.

"Shaw is buried alive—I don't know where!" he screeched. "Put out the fire!"

Macklin held the nozzle over Damon's face. "Who knows where, Damon?"

"Our Mr. Jury!" Damon cried, the fire creeping up his legs.

"Where is he?"

"A-At the Arrow," Damon wet his pants and his voice began to wither. The fire licked at Damon's belt buckle and the tanks on his back. Macklin removed his foot from Damon's chest and stepped away.

"Who is he, Damon?"

Damon raised his flaming hand over his face and stared at it in grisly fascination. "I'm dead."

Macklin dropped the nozzle and scrambled back to the car. He jumped in, slammed the door closed, and ducked under the dashboard.

The tanks ignited and Damon exploded in a fireball that burst through the flaming walls of the house and brought it crashing down on Macklin's car with a volcanic roar. The house collapsed with a fiery sigh into a towering pile of burning wood. The few surviving guards fled down the gravel road, flames licking at their heels.

A grinding sound caught their attention. They turned back and stared at the fire. Something rumbled at its core. Macklin's Cadillac blasted through the mountain of flame in a shower of cinders. The guards jumped into the brush along the roadway as the black, smoking specter tore past them, the engine growling furiously.

CHAPTER FOURTEEN

Friday, May 25, 7:45 p.m.

The doorman at the New Horizons Hotel stood aghast, his mouth gaping in shock, as Macklin's charred Cadillac rolled to a stop at the lobby doors. Macklin emerged wearing a tuxedo that nicely hid the bulge of his .44 Magnum automatic under his shoulder.

"My God, sir, what happened to your beautiful car?" the doorman asked, genuinely concerned.

Macklin dropped the keys into the doorman's open hand. "Acid rain," he mumbled, striding into the lobby and onto the express elevator to the Arrow.

A young couple, giggling and affectionate, shared the elevator with him. The couple kissed and nibbled at one another while the elevator shot upwards. Macklin peered out at the glittering Los Angeles skyline and noticed the rush of the other two glass elevators that flanked his as they passed during his ascent.

The couple nuzzled their way out of the elevator when it hit the restaurant level, and Macklin rode up alone past the observation deck and office level and finally to the ballroom that topped the structure.

The doors slid open and Macklin slipped into the ballroom. The bustle of activity added a tangible charge that crackled through the room. Dinner was being served, and waiters scurried between the tables delivering prime rib to the Southern California democrats who paid $100 a plate to fete Cecil Parks.

The Arrow symbolized progress, and it was no accident that Jeffries had many of the Parks events staged here.

Macklin wound through the tables, searching faces. Somewhere was a killer waiting to strike. In the front of the room, Parks sat at a long, white-draped table chatting with powerful area democrats. Kirk Jeffries, seated at the end of the table, spotted Macklin and shot a surprised glance at him. Macklin wandered slowly up to his friend.

"I don't want to sound unfriendly, Brett, old chum, but what the hell are you doing here?" Jeffries asked in hushed tones. He narrowed his eyes on Macklin's hair. "And why does your hair look burned?"

"Someone is going to make an attempt on Cecil's life tonight," Macklin whispered, hunching over and resting his hand on Jeffries' shoulder.

"What!" Jeffries exclaimed. Several heads turned along the table. Parks didn't notice. Jeffries smiled awkwardly and glanced up at Macklin. "How do you know?"

"Just trust me. We have to get Cecil out of here."

"We can't," Jeffries protested. "He still has to make his speech. These people paid a hundred dollars to see their candidate."

"They are going to see a corpse if we don't get him out of here."

"We'll call the police." Jeffries began to rise. Macklin held Jeffries down by the shoulder with a little friendly pressure.

"No," Macklin said, looking out over the crowd in front of them. "They can't be involved. Ronny's life depends on it."

"Christ, Brett, what is it with you two? Violence stalks you around," he said. "Am I gonna get blown to bits every time I see you?"

The elevator on the left opened, and a waiter emerged carrying a tray of empty wineglasses. Macklin squinted at him and straightened up, pulling the .44 Magnum from under his jacket.

"Don't move, scumbag!" Macklin shouted across the ballroom.

The waiter simultaneously dropped the glasses with a crash and blasted off a shot at Macklin with a .357 Magnum. The bullet burst a vase of flowers to Macklin's left and someone screamed. Macklin aimed and panic erupted in the room. People, clamoring and running about, obscured his line of fire. Cursing, Macklin dashed through the crowd, his gun held high. Jeffries sat still at the table in stunned disbelief as pandemonium swept the room.

The elevator opened behind the killer and people spilled out. He scrambled through them into the elevator. Macklin burst through the frantic dinner crowd just as the elevator doors were closing in front of the killer. The far right elevator door opened.

"Get out!" Macklin yelled, barreling through the departing elevator crowd like a linebacker. He hammered the "down" button with his fist, braced his back against the cold glass to his left, and felt the elevator drop. It fell through the dark overhang of the Arrow into the twinkling night sky.

Macklin saw the flash erupt on his right and flattened himself against the door. The glass to his right shattered. The cool night wind blew into the elevator. The killer's elevator, which had stopped at one of the upper hotel floors, now disappeared as Macklin's dropped below it.

A bell clanged and Macklin's elevator stopped. The doors parted and a elderly couple wearing cowboy hats began to step in.

Macklin shoved the man in the chest with his elbow and braced himself for a shot at the killer's descending elevator. "Stand clear!" he said to them and jammed his foot between the doors to keep it from closing and the elevator from descending.

The killer's elevator dropped into line and Macklin fired. The glass face of the other elevator crumbled and he saw the killer stumble. Perhaps a hit. The other elevator descended past him. He removed his foot and the doors slid closed. His elevator dropped. Macklin clasped a railing and hung out of the hole left by the shattered window.

Wind whipped his face. Aiming down at the killer's elevator two floors below, he squeezed the trigger. The bullets cast sparks as they glanced off the elevator's top. Macklin couldn't get a clear shot at him.

The killer's elevator stopped and Macklin closed on it. Macklin squared off for another shot. The killer fired first, the slug tearing the fabric from Macklin's left shoulder and spinning him. Macklin was about to squeeze off a shot when the express elevator, full of people, whizzed upwards between the two elevators, which were now descending at an equal rate.

Macklin fired the moment the express elevator was past. The bullet kicked the killer back into the railing, draping him over it like a damp towel. He was about to shoot again when the killer's elevator stopped and Macklin's continued downward to the lobby.

He holstered his .44 Magnum and dashed out of the elevator a moment later when it stopped in the lobby. He didn't want to be arrested for murder. As Macklin strode out of the lobby towards his car, he heard a woman's shrill scream and knew the killer's elevator had come to rest.

Saturday, May 26, 11:47 a.m.

"I don't think you killed enough people yesterday," Mordente said between clenched teeth and paced back and forth across Macklin's kitchen. "Maybe the raging forest fire you left behind you can bring the body count up a bit."

Macklin sat on the countertop in jeans and a sweatshirt, sipping a cup of coffee from a brown ceramic mug that Corinne had made him. It said "DAD" on it in childish scrawl.

"Go to hell, Jessie."

Mordente froze, arched her eyebrows, and let her arms dangle limply at her sides. "What did you say?"

"You heard me," Macklin said. "And stop yelling. Sunshine is finally asleep upstairs. Or have you forgotten that those White Wash sadists raped her and kidnapped her boyfriend?"

"Fuck you, Brett. What you did yesterday was unnecessary slaughter. There were other ways to handle the situation."

"No, there wasn't," Macklin said. "Damon had to be stopped."

"Yeah, but are you any better off than before? You killed two dozen people, left a fire burning out of control, and shot up the New Horizons Hotel. We still don't know where Shaw is, and that psycho may still be on the loose. The cops didn't find his body."

Mordente pulled a chair out from the kitchen table and sat down wearily. "Bravo, Mr. Jury, bravo." She clapped her hands.

"You know, I'm getting damn sick and tired of these confrontations with you. Make up your mind about me, Jessie, and try to stick to it for a day or so, okay?

"How can I make up my mind? With you, I'm not dealing with one person—I'm dealing with two. There's the caring father, the sensitive man, and then there's the merciless vigilante who takes lives without remorse. And you want me to deal with that?"

"I've got the same problem," Macklin said. "Part of you wants to love me—the other wants to hang me. Let me tell you something, Jessie: the only difference between you and me is that you carry a notepad and I carry a gun."

Her head fell and she wiped imaginary dirt from the table. "I'm not sure I can live with what you are." She looked up at him. "I'm not sure you can, either."

"Neither one of us can deal with this right now," Macklin said, slipping off the counter and standing in front of her. "My closest friend is buried alive somewhere, slowly dying if he isn't dead already. I've got to find him."

"What about the psycho?"

"Maybe some of his White Wash friends carried his corpse away," Macklin said, "and maybe he's alive. It doesn't matter right now. Cecil Parks is under heavy guard, and now my only concern is finding my friend."

"So where are we going to start?" she asked, the attacking tone ebbing from her voice and letting fatigue creep in.

Macklin sighed and slid into the chair beside her. "I don't know."

CHAPTER FIFTEEN

Sunday, May 27, 2:47 p.m.

Brett Macklin's stomach ached with tension, as it had since Saturday morning. Over and over again he racked his brain searching for an answer to Shaw's whereabouts. He lay on the living room couch with his head propped on an armrest and a half-empty beer can balanced on his chest.

If Shaw was buried anywhere near Damon's stronghold, he was dead now. The surrounding lands were scorched by hungry flames that had already devoured hundreds of acres. Ruling out the compound, that left the entire state of California as a possible burial ground.

All of Macklin's musings, he knew, could be useless. Shaw, in all likelihood, had been killed shortly after his abduction. They never intended him to live—that was for sure.

Macklin sat up, stretched, and swallowed the rest of his beer. The house felt larger than it was because of its emptiness. Mordente had taken Sunshine to a rape victim counseling center, where Shaw's girlfriend would spend the next few days under their care. So now, after having two guests, the house seemed huge and hollow. It had felt that way only twice before, when his marriage collapsed and when Cheshire was murdered.

Perhaps Damon had lied. Perhaps he did know where Shaw was hidden. Macklin paced in front of the couch, crushing the beer can in his hand. *If I were Anton Damon, where would I bury Shaw?* he thought. *I wouldn't bury him. I'd kill him.*

Macklin shook his head. *Don't think like that, Macky boy. Have some hope. Now, where would you bury Shaw? In the cop's own front yard.*

No, Macklin had already checked that.

He tossed the beer can into the fireplace and pulled the folded, smeared clipping of Mordente's interview with Damon out of his back pocket and reread it for the twentieth time. Nothing.

Sighing, Macklin shuffled into the kitchen, opened the refrigerator, and scrounged around for something to eat as he thought about what Damon had said during the second interview. Macklin always munched down food when he felt the pressure of nervous tension. Finding an apple, he pulled it out and bit into it. The apple snapped with freshness. He yanked a Dixie cup from the dispenser over the sink and turned on the faucet to get a drink. He had already had too many beers.

He filled the tiny cup and let it overflow, staring at the water spilling out of the faucet. The water felt cool on his hands. A tingle of apprehension traveled up his spine. The bottom of the paper cup ripped and the water splashed on the porcelain sink.

Macklin knew where Shaw was.

Leaving the faucet running, Macklin grabbed the phone off the hook and hurriedly dialed Mordente's number at the *Times*.

"Jessie," Macklin said, "Shaw's buried in the dry riverbed where the Kallahans were killed."

"How do you know?"

"I just know," Macklin snapped. "Tell me how to get there." She quickly rattled off the directions to the canal construction area.

"All right," he said, "I'm on my way. Meet me at the construction site with food, water, and some first aid supplies."

"Do you really think he's still alive, Brett?" she asked cautiously.

"I don't know," Macklin said. "I don't know if I can take losing another person I care about."

He hung up the phone, grabbed his .44 Magnum automatic from the kitchen table, and dashed into the garage, where he loaded a shovel and pickax into the Cadillac and drove off.

The construction site was a barren swath cut into a gentle expanse of flat land dotted with gnarly trees and knee-high weeds. Macklin drove slowly past the dirt-caked bulldozers and tractors, the white construction office trailer, and the scattered stacks of lumber, piping, and iron bars. To his surprise, he didn't see any security guards.

He parked his car at the edge of the unfinished canal and got out. The unearthed dirt was rich, healthy brown and lay in tiny mounds along the edge of the wide, deep gorge carved out of the soil where a river once ran. The sides of the canal were flat, blunt drops of about thirty feet and were reinforced with cement pillars with wooden planks stretched between them.

A few yards away, a huge cement pipe with a six-foot-wide mouth poked out of the dirt and pointed into the canal. Macklin's eyes followed the pipe and saw that it climbed the side of a hill and disappeared, probably into the canal system that he knew lay beyond it.

Macklin walked beside the canal towards the massive pipe, scanning the land, not sure what he was looking for. Shaw could be anywhere here, and he had no idea where to begin looking. He was certain Shaw was here. It fit in with Damon's twisted sense of this place. The White Wash leader wanted a monument to his bloodshed here, and burying Shaw here must have seemed to Damon like a good first step.

Something about the stack of scrap wood and garbage to Macklin right caught his eye. He didn't know what, but he wasn't going to argue with instinct. Macklin walked to it and looked into the pile.

The gold wristwatch on a black-skinned arm glinted at him from the center of the pile. Macklin quickly dug through the scraps, tossing aside empty bags of cement mix and planks of wood to get to the body underneath.

He saw the bloodstained sky blue uniform and slowed his efforts. Lifting a triangular sheet of soiled plywood, he looked into the dead eyes of the black security guard.

Macklin heard the gunshot before he felt it. *Dumb fuck forgot to wear his vest,* he thought to himself in the split second before the white-hot slug tore into the flesh under the right side of his rib cage. The impact lifted Macklin off his feet and tossed him backwards onto the hard soil.

Bile bubbled up his throat, and his mind was spinning, a kaleidoscope of pain and confusion, but he was aware of a person standing over his paralyzed body. He forced open his eyes and stared up the barrel of a .357 Magnum at the killer, clad in his red leather jumpsuit, a streak of black makeup over his eyes. *The impostor is still alive!*

Perspiration dotted the killer's face and Macklin knew the man was in pain. Macklin had shot him at least once at the Arrow. The impostor idly tossed Macklin's .44 Magnum away.

"Now we're both carrying lead," the man wheezed. "I could've killed you just now, you know."

Insistent waves of nausea, coupled with minor spasms in his stomach, urged Macklin to vomit. He willed it back and felt the searing pain in his side intensify twofold. Sensation, though, was beginning to return to his immovable limbs.

"You've got something to see before you die," the killer said, walking around Macklin and wrapping his free arm in a pincer grip around Macklin's neck. He dragged Macklin by the neck, painting a crimson trail in the dirt.

Each bump in the dirt sent daggers of pain cutting through Macklin's body. The warm blood seeping out of Macklin's wound felt oddly comforting as it coated the skin over his trembling stomach muscles.

The killer released Macklin beside a network of metal piping and stepped over to a large valve jutting from the pipe work three feet away.

Wincing, Macklin propped himself up into a half-standing position against the pipes. A tremendous bolt of agony made him buckle. The killer leaned against the valve and trained his gun on Macklin.

Macklin saw the blood soaking through the leather jumpsuit over the killer's right shoulder and lower left side and felt a little better about his situation. The only edge the killer had on him was the gun and, judging from the wild look in his eyes and his nervous shaking, perhaps PCP pumping in his veins.

The killer motioned to the canal with a jerk of his gun. "Your nigger friend is down there." He grinned.

Macklin glanced down at the canal, then back at the killer, who began to giggle.

"Watch this, Mr. Jury. You're gonna like it," he said, twisting the valve wheel with his free hand.

Macklin watched helplessly as an incredible, ground-shaking rush of water spilled out of the massive pipe twenty yards away and raged down the canal, washing away the support planks and eating away at the loose dirt.

Shaw was dead.

"Being bloated and green is better than being a nigger." The killer smirked. "I just did your buddy a favor."

Macklin flung himself at the killer, grabbing for the gun. The killer shrieked and drove his fist into Macklin's wound. Macklin screamed and fell away, hitting the ground and rolling onto his back, squirming with pain.

"Shitface, ass-sucking, nigger-loving son of a bitch," the killer whispered hoarsely and jabbed the gun barrel at Macklin's damp forehead. "Death to your kind."

Macklin heard the explosion of a gunshot to his right. The bullet slammed into the killer's chest and stood him straight up, his mouth gaping open and his eyes wide. The eyes stared down at Macklin, and he leveled his gun at Macklin's face again.

Another gunshot rang out. The killer's forehead split open and blood dribbled out in a thick, globby stream. Macklin propped himself up on his elbows and watched the killer fall to his knees. A huff of sour air hissed out of the killer's mouth like escaping helium from a balloon, and then he toppled face forward and slapped into the dirt beside Macklin.

Gravel crunched behind Macklin and Jessica Mordente appeared beside him, his .44 Magnum held firmly in her hand. They looked at each other and he saw a familiar cold emptiness in her eyes. He had seen it before, what seemed like a long time ago, in his own eyes. Now she, too, was a vigilante.

She kicked the killer over on his back with her foot and stared down at him with disgust.

"It's Justin Threllkiss," she muttered.

"Threllkiss?" Macklin said, glancing at the bloody face. "Threllkiss is an old man."

She nodded weakly. "This is his grandson, Justin Threllkiss III, his only living heir."

Macklin frowned and tried to stand. Mordente shoved the gun into the waistband of her slacks and helped Macklin to his feet.

"Can you stand?" she asked.

Macklin nodded and looked over his shoulder at the water rushing down the canal. He had failed. Another loved one was claimed by the disease. Leaning against the pipes, he examined his wound for the first time. It looked as though the bullet had passed right through him.

"What about Shaw?" She stood at the canal's edge, looking down at the torrent of water. Her voice was flat and emotionless.

Macklin hobbled to the valve. "He's down there." Together, Macklin and Mordente turned the valve and shut off the flow of water. It was a hopeless gesture, but somehow it seemed like the right thing to do. The water thinned out and they could see the ravaged soil peeking through.

"You need to see a doctor, Brett. You're bleeding awfully bad."

Macklin slipped his arm around her shoulder. "Yeah, let's go."

Slowly, they made their way to Macklin's car. He fell against the hood, breathing heavily, his face flushed and wet from the exertion and pain.

"I'll follow your car out of here," he said.

"You can't drive—you can barely stand," she protested. "You're liable to pass out on the road."

"We've got no choice," he said hoarsely, his throat dry and feeling raw. "We can't leave a car here. We can't be connected with this."

Mordente knew he was right. "Okay, I'll go to my car and be back here in a sec."

He felt as if he was on fire, the flames from his bullet wound scorching the rest of his skin. Macklin crawled into his car and sagged in the driver's seat. Drowsiness fogged his eyes. Macklin blinked hard and twisted the ignition. The engine grumbled to life.

Mordente's Mazda RX-7 pulled out in front of him and Macklin jerked the gear into drive and followed her down the tree-lined dirt roadway. He held on to the wheel tightly and gritted against the pain each jostling bump of the roadway caused.

They had driven less than half a mile when Macklin saw Mordente's brake lights flash on and her car stop. Mordente got out and walked back to Macklin's car. He rolled down the window.

"The road is washed out," she said, grimacing. "We're going to have to walk from here."

"Shit," Macklin groaned, throwing open the door. He got out and stomped past Mordente and into the trees. Anger, he discovered, blunted the pain. The water had settled into a huge pond where the current had washed out the roadway. She fell into step beside him. Silently, they walked around the water-torn roadway and the followed the watery landscape.

She reached her left arm across his back and held him firmly under the left shoulder. Macklin smiled at her and put his right arm around her shoulder, using her for support. He felt as if they were the last two people on earth, and he wouldn't have been surprised if the ground suddenly opened under their feet and swallowed them up.

Mordente slowed.

"What's the matter?" Macklin asked, concerned but thankful for the rest.

"Listen," she whispered.

Macklin concentrated. At first he noticed only the stillness of the valley and the trickle of water in the muddy dirt beside them. Then he noticed the thumping. It sounded distant and muted, like someone punching a pillow.

The sound was ahead of them and across the muddy divide. Mordente and Macklin, without discussing it, plodded through the mud and water downstream towards the sound.

The closer they got, the more distinct the pounding became. It was frantic and insistent. Macklin squinted into the trees and bushes ahead but saw nothing. His curiosity made him forget the pain just a bit. It was still there, but it wasn't immobilizing him.

Mordente stumbled and Macklin pressed ahead a few feet, looking back to make sure she was okay. He rounded an outcropping of brush and then stopped, frozen with surprise.

"What is it, Brett?" Mordente said, coming up behind him.

Macklin begin to smile. A plywood casket with a narrow pipe jutting out of it stood upright in the mud like a signpost, water spilling out of its seams.

"Ronny," Macklin shouted. "Are you all right?"

"Just get me out of here," Shaw replied weakly.

Macklin scrambled to the casket, his pain overwhelmed by his relief that his friend was alive. He and Mordente pried the plywood with their fingers while Shaw kicked and pushed at it from inside. They heard the screech of nails being forced from their holes and yanked the plywood face loose.

Shaw, bruised and soaking wet, fell stiffly forward into their outstretched arms. They gently held him up in a standing position. His eyes were closed and his chest heaved as he hungrily breathed in the air.

"How the hell did you survive that?" Macklin asked incredulously. Mordente was looking at Shaw as if he was a ghost.

Shaw blinked open his eyes and stretched his parched lips into a smile. "How?" He chuckled dryly and held up the index finger of his right hand. "I just jammed this in the pipe."

"The water must have washed away the loose dirt, the casket rose to the surface, and the current carried it away," Mordente explained. "Someone must be on our side. You should have drowned."

"I almost did." Shaw pulled away from them and tried standing on his own. His legs were wobbly, so he wrapped his arm around Mordente's shoulder to steady himself. "But I held my breath, something happened, I stopped moving, and suddenly the water seeped out of my little box."

Macklin, the forgotten pain from his gunshot wound suddenly reasserting itself, also slipped his arm around her shoulder. With Shaw and Macklin hanging on either side of her, Mordente put her arms across their backs and led them away.

"Is it over?" Shaw asked, looking over at his injured friend.

"Yeah," Macklin said. "It's over."

EPILOGUE

The rays of the noonday sun beamed down from a cloudless sky on the lush green grass that blanketed the golf course. A fountain in the center of a pond near the ninth hole sprayed white water high into the air against a backdrop of shrubless, rocky hills. Palm trees ringed the course and provided a natural division between the healthy landscape and the barren desert beyond it.

A single, metallic red golf cart that looked like a cartoonist's caricature of a Rolls-Royce scooted down one of the tiny slopes and stopped beside a sand trap. The rake trails could still be seen in the smooth sand, not a grain of which spilled onto the putting green or the surrounding grass.

The squat, freckle-skinned old man in yellow slacks and a red long-sleeve shirt emerged from the cart and waddled up to the golf ball lying on the rim of the putting green, uphill from the hole. He adjusted his tortoiseshell glasses, firmly grasped his putter, and hunched over the ball. Staring at the ball, he saw it shake.

He straightened up and saw a plain white golf cart bouncing along the grass towards him. The man leaned on his golf club and watched the cart approach.

The cart glided to a stop with an electric whine beside his customized model. The driver wore a wrinkled flannel suit, and his large brow was crinkled with emotion.

"I know who killed your grandson," Wes Craven said. Justin Threllkiss frowned. "Who?

"Brett Macklin, a Los Angeles charter airline pilot. He's also Mr. Jury."

Craven thought he saw Threllkiss nod, or perhaps it was just the old man's palsy shake. Threllkiss hunched over the ball, then glanced at the hole, then down at the ball again.

Threllkiss tapped the ball gently with his putter. The ball rolled slowly down the green, circled the hole once, then fell in with a clunk.

"Brett Macklin will come to know tremendous suffering," Justin Threllkiss said, "and then he will die."

THE END
Brett Macklin will return in
GUILTY

GUILTY

BY LEE GOLDBERG

This novel is a work of fiction. Names, characters, places, and incidents either are the product of the author's imagination or are used fictitiously. Any resemblance to actual events or places or persons, living or dead, is entirely coincidental.

Originally entitled *.357 Vigilante #4: Killstorm* and written under the pen name "Ian Ludlow."

Special thanks to Jerone Ten Berge for the cover art and Eileen Chettifor proofreading.

PROLOGUE

Los Angeles
Sunday, June 9, 2:45 p.m.

The pigeon did a Charlie Chaplin waddle and dropped dead on the man's shiny black shoe. The man kicked it away, startling a few of the other birds around his park bench into flight.

He reached into the pocket of his Brooks Brothers jacket for another Alka-Seltzer, tore open the wrapper, and began breaking the tablet into tiny pieces. A lazy Sunday in the park spent feeding the birds. He had forgotten how nice it could feel.

He tossed the Alka-Seltzer bits to the birds and dipped into his pocket for another tablet. Rays of sunlight filtered through the smog and ricocheted off the man-made lake into the reflective lenses of his aviators. Sweat glistened on his blunt, wide brow, and his skin itched under his gray pin-striped suit. He examined the palms of his hands, powdered white from the antacid, and ignored the two birds rattling on the pavement. He didn't ignore the bag lady.

The old woman was approaching from his left and pushing a rusted grocery cart that looked like it had been dredged up from the bottom of the ocean. The wire cage was bulging with brown bags overstuffed with newspapers, ratty clothes, and crushed aluminum cans. The woman was hunched over the cart, her leathery face staring into the bags as if she saw something there besides trash.

The woman parked her cart against the bench and sat down heavily beside the man. She smelled like a bucket full of old rainwater, and her face looked like a rotting apple.

"What are you up to?" the woman asked in a ragged breath nearly drowned by mucus.

"Killing time."

"That's my job." Her voice was smooth and soft this time, betraying youth. The man broke up another Alka-Seltzer in his hands and threw it to the tottering birds mirrored in his sunglasses.

"We have a job for you." He clapped his hands against each other to wipe off the powder and removed a manila envelope from the inside pocket of his jacket. He handed it to her without turning to look at her.

The woman set the envelope on her lap and opened the flap. Inside, she found six sheets of typewritten paper and six black-and-white photographs. A bird fluttered in the air, screeched, and dropped onto the bench between them.

She regarded the dead bird with a sideways glance and saw the Alka-Seltzer wrappers around the man's feet.

"Pigeons don't belch," the man said, watching the birds peck at the Alka-Seltzer bits. "Their stomachs just blow up."

She carefully slid the papers back into the envelope.

"My fee is a million dollars," she said.

"We've already wired the funds into the designated Swiss account."

"If you put a spring inside a piece of meat and toss it to a dog, he'll swallow it whole," she remarked casually, "and then scratch his stomach until he tears himself open."

The man smiled appreciatively.

She carefully sealed the clasp and slid the envelope between the slats of her shopping cart. "Why do you want me to kill a bunch of ordinary people?"

He rose to his feet with his back to her. "Brett Macklin is no ordinary man." He kicked a convulsing bird from his path and walked away.

Puerto Vallarta, Mexico
Monday, June 10, 3:37 p.m.

Mort Suderson would drink motor oil as long as they served it to him in a coconut. It was exotic touches like using coconut shells for glasses that made Puerto Vallarta so wonderful to him. He dog-paddled away from the hotel's palapa-covered poolside bar and merrily sipped away, oblivious to the chlorinated water spilling into his piña colada.

Swimming to the tile-rimmed island in the center of the pool, he paused, setting his coconut on the grass and squinting through the palm fronds at the emerald waters of Banderas Bay. *Sure beats the hell out of LA,* he thought, praising himself once again for coming down here to recuperate from his tongue surgery.

A white ferry, teeming with American tourists, chortled south towards the thatched huts and waterfalls on Yelapa, where yesterday a woman with sandbag knockers tried to sell Mort an iguana. He didn't buy the lizard, but he did eat five small tacos and had been backfiring more than his '76 Chevette ever since.

He looked away from the ferry, adjusted his Speedo briefs, and watched the waves steep and crash on the pebbled sands of Las Glorias Beach. The warm water crawled up the beach to a pile of horse droppings being sniffed by one of the mangy, wild dogs that had chased Mort off the beach that morning.

Mort took a sip of his piña colada and let his legs float up behind him. While his eyes panned over the women basking in chaise lounges around the pool, he kicked at the surface of the water, covering up the echoes of yesterday's tacos that emanated from his body.

His steady, traveling gaze moved unnoticed over oil-slicked backs and delicate buttocks, across sweat-dampened breasts and parched lips.

And then he felt her eyes on his back. Mort might have shrugged off the sensation, or reached back to swat off a nonexistent insect, or just ignored it. But he didn't.

He turned slowly, scanning the faces, and came to a jolting halt at a pair of radiant blue eyes—eyes that were staring straight into his. She was set against the bleached white of the Holiday Inn and seemed to move towards him, though she wasn't moving at all. She wore a black string bikini and sat on the pool's edge directly across from him, dangling her long, golden legs lazily in the water.

Grinning sheepishly, Mort picked up his drink and walked through the water towards her, contracting his pelvic muscles to jerk up his penis a little bit and give her something to dream about.

She watched him expressionlessly as he approached. She was dark, a Mediterranean, with cool eyes and sharp features, the kind of woman that used to scare him. They scared him because he wanted them but didn't think he could satisfy them.

That was before his operation. Now his tongue could work miracles. Now that woman could be his. He smoothed the beads of water off his chest to draw her eyes to it.

"Hey, *yo hablo* English?" Mort asked, doing his best Ricardo Montalban.

She regarded him for a long moment, during which his smile never wavered.

"Yes," she said wearily, closing her eyes and tilting her head back into the sun. Mort's gaze plummeted into her deep cleavage. He didn't need his pelvic contractions anymore.

"So you down here on your own?" Mort asked.

She sighed impatiently, unmoving. "Yes."

Many men would have quit there. Not him. Mort pulled himself up onto the deck beside her. "Ever seen *Kramer vs. Kramer*?"

"Yes," she said, raising her head and looking out at the bay.

"Most men are too busy being macho to admit this," he said, "but I cried during that movie—"

She stood up, the fluid motion interrupting him, and glided away with her back to him. Mort's open mouth narrowed into an angry grimace.

Frigid bitch, Mort thought. *She could have known absolute ecstasy.*

But he didn't turn away. He didn't slide back into the pool and paddle back to the bar. He was still watching her when she stopped, cast an aloof glance at him over her shoulder, and said, "Aren't you coming?"

Un-fucking-believable, absolutely un-fucking-believable.

It was every sex fantasy Mort ever had coming true—he sees a beautiful woman, their eyes meet, a few words are spoken, and then wham, they're in the sack, fucking each other silly.

Mort Suderson rested on his back, soaking the sheets with his sweat. She straddled him, moving herself gently up and down, her hands clutching his legs. He squeezed her breasts again to prove to himself that this was honest-to-God happening, that Mort Suderson was screwing perfection.

He always knew his life would be this way. He had faith. He kept believing. He didn't let the premature-ejaculation stuff or the impotence business get him down. No, he kept working at it. He got the right threads. He exuded the right attitude. He got the membrane snipped under his tongue.

He was granite, she was beautiful, and this was nearly heaven. They were burning the fucking sheets.

And now he would reward her.

"Lie down, baby," he moaned. "I'm gonna send you into outer space."

She lifted herself off of him and rolled onto her back beside him. Mort kissed her and let his hand glide between her warm, wet legs.

He stuck out his tongue at her. "See this?" he slobbered, pointing at his tongue with his index finger.

"Prepare yourself for the end-all, baby."

Mort pulled her by the hips to the end of the bed and stood on the floor, staring down at her. God, she was beautiful. She was smiling, but in a funny kind of way, like someone was whispering a joke to her that he couldn't hear. It didn't matter. He knew what her body was saying. Her eyes were closed, her stomach flat, her breasts firm and damp. He dropped to his knees, grinned, and spread her legs apart. He leaned forward and began probing and teasing her with his tongue.

Her body stiffened at his touch and she moaned, her legs closing around him. He took it as encouragement, flicking his tongue in rapid, light strokes. She rose into a sitting position, rested her hands on his head, and swayed pleasurably from side to side.

Her legs squeezed tighter, pinning his head in place. He sucked with increased ardor. Her fingers dug into his scalp. Mort put his hands on her thighs and gently tried to push them apart. He couldn't get air. She closed her legs even tighter, her breathing becoming ragged, a smile etching a crooked path across her face.

Mort squirmed, trying to stand, pounding his fists into her legs. She shuddered with ecstasy, gritted her teeth against the unbearable, joyous sensations, and jerked her pelvis sharply to one side. The snap of Mort's neck coincided with the thunderbolt of pleasure that left her trembling.

CHAPTER ONE

Los Angeles
Tuesday, June 11, 1:38 a.m.

The day had been the shits for Brett Macklin. His checks were bouncing at the bank and bills were clogging his mailbox. All the hours he had spent going through the books at his Blue Yonder Airways, his charter airline, didn't make things any better. In fact, they were getting steadily worse.

He was already a half hour late to pick up Jessica Mordente at the *Los Angeles Times* when his '59 Cadillac ran out of gas. Now, with $20 in his wallet, his savings account tapped, his girlfriend probably pissed, and night giving way to morning, he was stuck in the middle of downtown LA pumping his own goddamn gas.

The Chevron station was sandwiched between the dark, iron skeleton of an emerging high-rise and the Harbor Freeway off-ramp. The asphalt around the station was cracked and rippled, as if buckled by the tight squeeze. The streetlamp buzzed and flickered, the light being smothered by the surrounding darkness.

The porcine gas station attendant who was supposed to be washing Macklin's windshield was, instead, smearing the glass with the greasy shirt stretched over his stomach and ashes from his cigar. Macklin saw the name "Earl" embroidered on the man's bulging shirt pocket, smudged by oily fingerprints.

Macklin jerked his thumb at the big "NO SMOKING" sign over the gas pumps behind him. "Hey, Earl, can't you read your own sign? It's dangerous to smoke here."

Earl shrugged. "I like to live on the edge."

A white VW rabbit sputtered up on the other side of the pump island. A bespectacled teenager in corduroy shorts and a rugby shirt burst out of the car and dashed past them to the men's room.

Earl yelled, "The crapper's for customers only." But, it was wasted breath; the kid had already disappeared inside, leaving his VW shivering and choking.

"Shit, every whore and bum in town thinks that's their private crapper." Earl ambled over to Macklin and let his hand glide over the car, up over the teardrop-shaped cab and down along the sharp, arching fins. "Piss 'n' run, piss 'n' run. I gotta sell rubbers and dildos in there just so I can afford to clean up the place, you know?"

Earl leaned against the gas pump to Macklin's left, flicked his cigar, and stuck it between his plump lips. "Nice night, huh?"

"Oh yeah," Macklin groaned. "Nice night." He looked past Earl. The night trembled, like a movie when the film fails to catch on the projector's sprockets. The picture wasn't quite right. Macklin narrowed his eyes. A warm breeze blew scraps of paper across the deserted street like tumbleweeds. Then he saw the three blacks, illuminated in the lightning flash of the faulty streetlamp. One carried a bat, the others swung chains.

"A real nice night," Macklin muttered wearily.

He slowly turned to his right. Four more men peeled off from the darkness carrying crowbars and chains, led by a Michael Jackson clone. The gang leader wore reflective sunglasses, a white sequined glove, and a broad-shouldered red jacket Macklin guessed had been stolen off the doorman at the Westwood Marquis.

Earl followed Macklin's gaze and his eyes bulged with fear. "Th-The Bloodhawks," he stammered. The seven Bloodhawks formed a loose circle around the property.

Macklin kept pumping his gas.

Michael Jackson, bobbing to the beat of a private song, grinned and dismissed the station with his gloved hand. "Trash it," he said.

The three gang members behind Michael Jackson strolled up to the building, appraised it for a moment, and then smashed the windows out with their crowbars. The Bloodhawks spilled into the office. They bashed the shelves off the wall, whacked apart the candy machine, and tossed the desk into the street.

A black GI Joe wearing a beret and army fatigues strutted to the Sparkletts water cooler and swung his crowbar at the glass bottle. It exploded aqua blue, splashing the walls with water and glass.

At that moment, the teenager in shorts emerged from the bathroom. Before Macklin could react, GI Joe whirled, swinging at the teenager's head like it was another Sparkletts bottle. His skull broke like pottery and his body slapped against the wet wall, splattering it red.

"You're next, motherfucker." The Michael Jackson clone pointed a sequined finger at Macklin. "I've seen your fucking hearse before. You're the dogshit that's been coming onto our turf and kicking ass."

Macklin shrugged.

Michael Jackson whipped a switchblade from his back pocket and waved it in front of Macklin's impassive face. "Motherfucker, you're dead."

Macklin yanked the gas nozzle from his car and swung it in front Michael Jackson, spraying him with fuel. The man recoiled, spat, and charged blindly towards Macklin, who grabbed the cigar from Earl's mouth and tossed it at him.

Michael Jackson burst into flame. Shrieking with agony, he did a skittish moonwalk and tripped over his burning feet. He hit the ground rolling, screaming as he tried to smother the fire that consumed his body.

The gang members let out angry cries and ran at Macklin with their weapons raised. Macklin casually pulled the .357

Magnum from under his jacket and cocked it. Killing was becoming a reflex.

"Would anyone here like some .357 dental work?" he asked.

The men closing in on either side of him froze. The acrid stench of burned flesh filled the air. The only sound was the gang leader, crackling and bubbling.

"You can't kill us all," a gang member said defiantly.

Macklin shrugged. "Maybe it's my lucky day."

There was a long moment of indecision. Macklin could hear Earl's labored, anxious breaths.

"This isn't over, asshole," GI Joe hissed, holding his bloody crowbar out like a sword.

"It is for you." Macklin shot him. The bullet punched GI Joe in the chest and tossed him back onto the flaming corpse. GI Joe's crowbar clattered on the pavement.

Macklin sighed. "Who's next?"

The gang members looked at one another. They reached an unspoken agreement and suddenly scattered, leaving their two friends smoldering on the pavement.

Macklin holstered his gun, stuffed a crumpled $20 bill in Earl's breast pocket, and got into his car.

He started the engine and smiled through the open window at Earl's pale face.

"I like to live on the edge."

2:00 a.m.

"Being a vigilante is costing me a fortune," Brett Macklin said, his voice echoing off the bathroom walls. He sat on his toilet eating his double bacon chili cheeseburger and watching Jessica Mordente's naked body through the shower's frosted glass door.

"While I'm out on the streets, my airline business is going to hell. Things are even worse now that Mort, my only pilot, is down in Mexico." He slurped on his chocolate shake and set it on the toilet tank behind him. "Christ, do you know how much bullets cost?"

"So quit." Jessica scrubbed her shoulders with her Buf-Puf. "Go back to being a normal human being again." Steam spilled out of the shower stall and fogged the bathroom mirrors.

It's too late, Macky boy. It's a part of you now.

Macklin held the burger tightly in his hands and took a big bite. A glob of chili spurted out between the buns and dribbled down his shirt.

You can never go back, never...

Mordente pressed herself against the door and peered over the top at Macklin. "I didn't hear your clever retort."

He shrugged. His mouth was full.

She groaned melodramatically and turned away, letting the hot water beat against her chest. She luxuriated in the warm water, and Macklin, staring blankly at the floor, ate his Fatburger. The only sounds were the rushing water and the whirring fan.

"Have you heard of the Transformational Awareness Life Church?" she asked.

"That isn't the answer. I won't join." He swallowed his mouthful of food. "I don't want to become one of those EST-holes."

"I don't want you to join, and it isn't EST," she said. "I'm doing a story on them. It's one of those self-awareness, self-realization programs. A guy named Fraser Nebbins runs it. They have their own little community out in the desert."

"Yeah, so what's the story? There's dozens of weirdo groups like that in Los Angeles. They franchise them like McDonald's. I hear it's quite chic."

"The kids who join TALC go in but never come out."

"Uh-huh." Macklin finished the shake and dumped the paper cup amidst the pizza crust, Kleenex, and yogurt containers in the thin wicker basket beside the toilet.

"I'm joining them."

Macklin stared at her through the frosted glass. Her body was straight, and she was looking at him in an aloof, distant way.

"I want to find out exactly what's happening to those kids," she said.

"Yeah, that sounds great," he said. "But in practice it's pretty stupid. They are going to play around with your head. They're probably experts at it. You'll go in there as Ms. Gung-ho Journalist and come out as their publicity director."

"I know that, Brett," she said in a patronizing tone. "I'm taking precautions."

"There are other ways to tell the story. You don't need to go undercover."

"That's the way I want to do it."

The phone rang on the nightstand by the bed. Macklin glared at the phone as if that would shut it up. He glanced at Mordente, set his burger on the toilet tank, and reluctantly trudged out to the bedroom.

"Hello," he snapped.

"It's me," replied LAPD Sergeant Ronald Shaw, "the guy who should be home sleeping but is cleaning up your mess at the Chevron station instead."

The black homicide detective and Macklin had grown up together. It was Shaw, with Los Angeles mayor Jed Stocker's approval, who kept the LAPD from probing too deeply into Mr. Jury—the vigilante who had crushed a homicidal street gang, destroyed a ring of psychopathic pedophiles, and decimated a racist cult of deranged killers. The vigilante Brett Macklin had become.

Macklin turned and saw Mordente standing naked in front of the toilet, holding his hamburger with disdain over the toilet bowl.

"The attendant says the guys you toasted knew you," Shaw said.

She smiled at Macklin, dropped the burger in the toilet, and flushed it. Macklin grinned and turned his back to her.

"Yeah, they did."

"Shit, Mack, if the gangs know you're Mr. Jury, they're not going to rest until they've chopped you into little pieces," Shaw said. "You need protection."

Macklin glanced at his shoulder holster draped over a chair across the room. "Ronny, I've got all the protection I need."

"Give me a break, Mack. You aren't an invincible superhero. Tonight you were lucky. Tomorrow you may not be."

Macklin felt Mordente press her damp body against his back. She let her hands glide down his broad chest and over his flat stomach to his waist.

"It's time for you to give up this vigilante lunacy," Shaw said. "It's over. Move to another city or something and start again."

There were four dull pops as Mordente split open the buttons of his Levi's 501 jeans.

"Ronny, I've got to go." Her warm hands slipped under his bikini briefs. "Something just came up."

CHAPTER TWO

Wednesday, June 12, 8:30 a.m.

Their chests were heaving, their lungs clawing for air, as their bodies climbed the heights of their passion. Macklin felt the urgency in her hot breaths, in the trembling hands holding his neck.

Macklin sat at the bed's edge, his hands on Mordente's sides. She faced him, her eyes half-closed with pleasure, as she bobbed on his lap. The morning sun seeped through the shutters and sliced their sweaty bodies with beams of light.

He licked her lips with the tip of his tongue and brushed her erect nipples with his thumbs. She sucked in her stomach and involuntarily arched her back, offering her pleasure-hungry breasts to his hands.

"I can't hold out much longer," she gasped. "My hair will turn gray."

Macklin chuckled and kissed her, kneading her aching breasts. "Then I win."

She shook her head. "No way, damn it, you'll come first." She swallowed, trying to control her feverish breathing. "I can't afford to buy you dinner."

Her pelvic muscles squeezed tight around his penis. A bolt of pleasure shot up Macklin's spine. Her body rode him, pumping the pleasure in them both to an unbearable intensity. Macklin clutched her breasts and she saw his face become rigid.

"Having some problems?" she huffed, her face wrinkling as if she were about to sneeze.

Macklin shook his head and gritted his teeth, his upper lip quivering.

Their fingers dug into each other and a tremor rocked their bodies. Suddenly Mordente cried out, bouncing frantically and breathing in staccato bursts. Macklin stiffened, his face shaking, a low moan escaping from his lips. Their bodies shook with ecstasy, riding the orgasmic waves of pleasure.

Her movements gradually slowed and Macklin's body relaxed, a flush coloring his skin. She leaned forward and nuzzled her face against his neck.

"I think it's a draw," Macklin whispered, his eyes still closed.

Mordente laughed and hugged him tightly. She could feel his heart pounding against her. "So who buys dinner?"

The phone jangled.

"Shit." Macklin reached for it.

"It's me," Shaw said.

"Oh, for God's sake, Ronny, will you leave me alone?" Mordente laughed again and kissed his neck.

"I've got bad news, Mack."

Macklin kissed the top of her head. "Yeah, yeah, go on."

"Mort's been killed."

Every muscle in Macklin's body stiffened defensively. Mordente felt it and pulled back, staring into Macklin's cold eyes. For a second, she felt like she was the only person in the room.

"The Mexican police need you to come down and claim the body," Shaw said. "You're his only family."

"Tell me what happened." Macklin said in a monotone. Mordente slid off of him and sat on the bed, uncomfortably aware of her nakedness.

"I'm not sure. He was found in his hotel room with his neck broken," Shaw replied, pausing awkwardly for a moment before continuing to speak. "A cop named Ortiz will meet you at the airport. I'm sorry, Mack, I—"

"It's all right," Macklin interrupted. "I'll let you know if I find out anything."

"I'd go with you if I could."

"I know. I'll call you." Macklin slammed down the phone and pulled on his pants, which were lying in a clump beside the bed.

"What is it?" Mordente asked.

He picked up his chili-stained shirt and put it on. "Mort has been killed."

"Oh, Brett..." As she reached to touch him, he went to the closet.

He found a duffel bag and started shoving clothes into it. She watched him in silence and drew the sheets up over herself.

"Where are you going?"

"To Mexico. Someone's got to claim the body and someone has to find the killer." He dropped the duffel bag on the chair and strapped on his gun. "And make him pay."

He leaned over Mordente and gave her a light kiss on the lips. "Call my ex-wife. Tell her I can't take Cory to the movies tomorrow."

She nodded, put her hand behind his neck, and drew him to her lips again. He pulled back, looked into her moist eyes, and almost stayed.

He turned abruptly and walked out.

Noon

Brooke Macklin closed Isadora Van Rijn's portfolio and laid it gently on her desk. Van Rijn's paintings, depicted in the photographs in the portfolio, were among the most haunting works

Brooke had ever seen. Yet, she could barely keep her attention on them. Van Rijn herself was the most haunting thing Brooke had ever seen. Brooke's eyes kept drifting over the edge of the portfolio and locking on the slim, black-haired woman who had just breezed in and, in a voice that had the intimacy of a whisper and the jarring effect of a shout, asked if she could show the owner her work.

Ordinarily, Brooke would have stifled an incredulous laugh and shown the obnoxious stranger to the door. Instead, with trancelike submission, Brooke had taken it.

Van Rijn was browsing through Brooke's gallery, studying the paintings with her soft amber eyes.

The pull, which Brooke couldn't quite define, didn't wane as time passed. It only grew stronger.

Van Rijn's coal black hair was styled in a blunt bob cut that accented her cheekbones and gave her eyes a sharp, mean quality. She wore a black wool jacket over a baggy V-neck T-shirt. Brooke noticed the large, dark nipples poking against the white fabric as it brushed over the smooth swell of Van Rijn's unrestrained breasts. Her jacket had narrow lapels and hung past her hips. The sleeves were bunched up over her elbows, and her hands were buried in the pockets of her black leather pants.

"Your work is captivating, unusual," Brooke began. *And so are you.* She had trouble summoning her voice. Van Rijn cocked her head towards Brooke and smiled, a sort of half-amused expression that gave Brooke a chill and a charge at the same time. "How come I've never heard of you?"

Van Rijn shrugged. "I've kept to myself."

"Isadora, I'll be honest with you. People don't just walk in here out of nowhere and expect me to give them a show," Brooke said.

"I understand," Van Rijn said, approaching Brooke's desk. "I appreciate your time and patience."

Van Rijn reached for her portfolio.

Brooke put her hand over Van Rijn's. "Wait," she said, self-consciously removing her tingling hand. "That isn't what I meant. It's just that your work is so good, I can't believe you haven't been heard from before. I'd like to do a show with you."

The phone rang.

"Excuse me," Brooke said, swiveling her chair around so she faced the back of the store. "Cory? Could you get that?"

"Okay," replied a tiny voice in the back room.

"That's my daughter," Brooke explained, smiling. "She's teaching me and my staff how to use the computer I just bought."

"How old is she?" Van Rijn asked.

"Ten. And she's the only one who understands the damn thing."

Van Rijn laughed, a gentle sound that Brooke could feel tickling her sternum.

"Mom?" Cory walked out of the backroom and leaned against the doorjamb, crossing her arms under her chest. She had the stature of an adult and curious, intelligent eyes offset by a tiny pug nose crossed by a light sprinkle of freckles.

Brooke turned around and Cory continued: "It's Jessica. She wants to talk with you. She says it's important."

"Ask her if I can call her right back," Brooke said.

"Wait," Van Rijn interrupted. "I have to go now anyway. Is there another time I can see you?"

"How about this time tomorrow?"

"My days are complicated."

"Mom," Cory whined impatiently.

"Hold on," Brooke said sternly. She rolled her eyes at Isadora, as if to say, You know how it is… "Why don't we get together for dinner? I'll have some contracts drawn up and we can get to know each other."

"All right."

Brooke scrawled something on the back of a business card and handed it to Van Rijn. "This is my home address. Why don't you come by Friday evening, about eight?"

Van Rijn nodded shyly, said, “Thank you,” in a light, husky voice, turned, and walked out. Brooke sat in her chair for a long moment until Cory’s insistent “Mahhhhm” jarred her from her inaction and freed her from the lingering scent of Van Rijn’s subtle perfume.

Puerto Vallarta, Mexico, 3:00 p.m.

The palm trees were bent back against the hot, wet wind, their leaves fluttering. The frothing, bruised clouds crackled with quivering bolts of fire and crushed the morning’s blue sky in resonant quakes. The afternoon storm seemed alive, a creature daring Brett Macklin to step out of his Cessna and face its wrath.

Macklin emerged from the plane braced for the worst, clutching his jacket collar tight around his neck. But, to his surprise, it was sweltering outside, the humid air hugging his face like a steaming towel. The contrast between the amiable air and the furious sky made Macklin uneasy. He wasn’t quite sure how to react to it. He wasn’t quite sure how to react to anything anymore.

Except violence. Ever since his father was set aflame by a street gang, death stalked Macklin. It was there, lurking in the shadows, wherever Macklin turned.

It was here, too, in this strange land. It had taken Mort as it had JD Macklin and Cheshire Davis . . . as it would someday take him.

Violence had become the only constant in Brett Macklin’s life.

He pulled the hatch shut behind him and strode across the tarmac towards the small terminal building. Ahead and to his left, three passengers and two MexAir stewards filed up the mobile stairway into a 727.

The wind whipped Macklin's hair and the drizzle stung his face as he passed beside the plane. He imagined row after row of American tourists, wearing their ridiculous sombreros, waiting to be whisked back to their sedate world.

God, how he wished he could return to a time when violence to him was something that William Shatner did between commercials for Hamburger Helper and Fruit of the Loom. He had lived with the naive faith that he was safe from the savage dark side of humanity. He'd never thought about the fragile nature of his very existence; he'd wondered why nobody could make a frozen pizza that didn't taste like dry rot.

He glanced wistfully up into the cabin. A steward pulled a gun from inside his red blazer and motioned a stewardess down the aisle.

Macklin heard Fate giving him the Bronx cheer.

The other steward disappeared into the cockpit while a nervous stewardess began closing the plane's hatch. The familiar coldness washed over Brett Macklin and carried him forward. He dashed up the stairs like a flustered, rushed tourist.

"Wait, wait," he yelled, waving his duffel bag in the air, "don't go home without me!"

He came huffing into the plane and glanced apologetically to his right at the steward standing in the aisle. The man was breathing through his mouth, exposing his silver-capped incisors. Macklin couldn't see his gun, but he knew it was there by the expression on the stewardess's face. She stood behind the steward and looked like she might vomit.

"May I have your boarding pass, please?" asked the stewardess to Macklin's left. Behind her, the other steward stood in the cockpit doorway and, Macklin assumed, had a gun pointed at the woman's back.

"Sure," Macklin said, dropping his duffel bag and reaching into his jacket with his right hand.

In one quick motion, he yanked out his .357, shoved the stewardess aside, and shot the steward standing in the cockpit doorway. The slug burst open the steward's stomach, blasting out entrails and blood.

The seam between the passengers' world and Macklin's split open. They peeked in and recoiled in panic and revulsion. Some dived under their seats, others squirmed uncontrollably, a few just covered their ears and wailed. The cacophony of fear was lost in the deafening roar of gunfire.

Macklin spun into a crouch as the other steward's gun bucked. Macklin felt the searing trail of a bullet skimming over his head and pumped off two shots. The first bullet slammed into the steward's chest and spun him on his heels. The second bullet tore into his cheek, spraying the cabin with silver-capped teeth and bloody cartilage.

The blood-splashed stewardess in the aisle screamed, her horrified eyes locked on the convulsing, faceless corpse at her feet. Her scream became part of the echo of terror and gunfire that shuddered through the plane.

Macklin grimaced. Puerto Vallarta was just another battleground.

He stood up and twirled the gun around his finger so that he held it by the barrel. Avoiding the other stewardess's empty eyes, he bent over and snatched up his duffel bag. He let his gun arm hang limply against his side and calmly walked through the hatchway.

It was pouring rain. A lightning bolt flashed overhead and thunder rolled through the dark clouds. A half dozen soldiers scrambled out of the airport and aimed their rifles at him. One man, in a water-soaked khaki shirt and slacks, stood at the base of the stairway with his gun pointed at Macklin's gut. The man seemed oblivious to the drenching downpour.

Macklin slowly moved down the stairs and studied the man's face. It looked as though someone had run a steamroller over it a few times. The man's head was large, the skin puffy, the nose flat and wide.

The man regarded Macklin quizzically. "Are you Brett Macklin?"

Macklin nodded. Water streamed down his face, but he felt the death clinging to his skin, refusing to be washed away.

"We saw you leave your little plane and run into the jet." The man motioned to the .357 at Macklin's side. "You carry some interesting luggage, Mr. Macklin."

Macklin shrugged, offering the man the butt of his .357. "With this, I don't have to carry traveler's checks."

The man snorted, his lips twisted into a half-assed grin. He, too, had a couple of silver-capped teeth. Macklin hoped he'd never need a cavity filled in Mexico. The man holstered his gun and waved at the soldiers to lower their rifles.

"I'm Captain Jacob Ortiz of the Puerto Vallarta police." He took Macklin's .357, slipped it under his waistband, and led him towards the terminal. "I sincerely hope your stay will be short."

CHAPTER THREE

The downpour turned Puerto Vallarta's cobblestone streets into rivers of mud. The Chrysler sedan lumbered through like a barge.

Ortiz sat in the backseat beside Macklin, who squinted through the mud-smeared windshield at the thatched huts and chalky white buildings ahead.

"How long has the weather been like this?" Macklin asked. "It must be killing the tourist trade."

He felt the cold barrel of his .357 poke him in the side. Macklin glanced down at it in surprise and then up into Ortiz's impassive face.

"I guess you don't like small talk," Macklin said.

Ortiz nudged him with the gun. "Open your door."

Macklin pushed open the door. Muddy water splashed into the moving car. "If you wanted fresh air, you could have just asked me nicely."

"Jump out," Ortiz said.

Macklin sighed and looked glumly at the man. "You aren't Captain Ortiz."

"Brilliant deduction," the man said, "now jump."

Macklin hesitated. He knew it had been too good to be true. No one can step off a plane, kill a couple men two minutes later, and then expect to be politely escorted past customs into a waiting car without any hassles.

How could I be so goddamn stupid? I deserve *to be tossed out of a moving car.*

The man cocked the gun. "You either jump out or I blow you out."

"Shit," Macklin hissed, and tumbled out of the car. His body slammed into the cobblestone, knocking the breath out of him. He rolled off the embankment in a waterfall of sludge and dropped facefirst into a pool of mud.

He flopped over onto his back and lay there stunned for a moment, his eyes closed and face caked with mud. He could feel the coarse, dirty water riding over his skin like sandpaper. The raindrops felt like stones pummeling his body.

Welcome to Mexico, Macky boy.

He was starting to rise when a crushing weight on his neck forced him back down with a splash. His eyes flew open, and through the haze of rain, mud, and dizziness, he saw himself surrounded by trees. But no, they weren't trees, he realized—they were men. Macklin, barely able to breathe under the boot mashing his throat, to make out the dark human shape towering over him, grabbed the man's ankle and futilely tried to lift the boot off his throat. His lungs ached for air. Raindrops and dizziness clouded his vision. He couldn't get his arms to operate properly.

The men drew in close around him and simultaneously began kicking him. His body jerked between the men and he lost his grasp on the man's ankle. His arms fell like broken tree limbs to the ground. He was utterly helpless, a sack of flesh for them to stomp into bloody mush.

They're killing me...

His consciousness drowned in the inky blackness of agony.

Southern California
Wednesday, June 12 / Thursday, June 13

The old yellow school bus pulled off the eerily empty highway and bumped along through the black desert night on an unlit private road. Despite the jostling, of the two dozen people aboard, only Jessica Mordente and one teenage boy were awake. He was in the back, puking up his dinner into a plastic Ralph's grocery bag.

All Mordente could see out of her window was darkness. Her head was tilted against the glass, her cheek pressed to the cold, smooth surface. She could feel the vibration of the engine trembling in her larynx.

She'd lost track of time. How many hours ago was she wandering down Hollywood Boulevard, a lost look on her face? How long since they had found her, embraced her, cajoled her into coming to their white house on stilts that faced the beach?

She ate their dinner, drank their wine, soaked up their reassuring words. She filed onto the bus with the rest of the lonely people they had found, the people who had never heard of the TALC before but were ready to join it if it would just end their desperation.

How long until they arrived at the Talcon Colony? Hours? Days? No, she knew it couldn't be days. She knew where it was. It was in the desert somewhere … right? Mordente reminded herself that she was different from the others on the bus. She wasn't a lonely waif. She was a reporter.

Mordente tried to feel the immensity of the *Los Angeles Times*, the power of journalistic responsibility, lifting her up. It didn't work. The newsprint, the presses, and the green, luminescent letters on her VDT screen seemed far away.

Her eyes stung with fatigue, her butt ached from sitting so long, and her head felt heavy; they all were signals for her to let her body switch off. She knew she should be sleeping, but something kept her awake—curiosity, perhaps, and the desire not to give in to sleep as the others had. After all, she reminded herself again, she was different.

The bus turned, the motion swaying her body and lifting her cheek away from the glass. The gray wall of the Talcon Colony was revealed in the arc of the bus's headlights.

The driver honked twice. A simple iron gate, the only break in a sandblasted stone wall, swung open, and it became daylight in the desert. Dozens of hidden floodlights burst on atop the ten-foot stone wall and from their mountings in surrounding rocks and foliage.

An austere, pastel-colored hacienda with a faded, red-tile roof seemed to rise out of the night as the bus turned into the compound. Two unimaginative, barrack-style wings jutted from the main house. Mordente guessed they were built later, judging by the incongruence they created when matched with the hacienda.

The bus stopped with a lurch that made everyone on board jerk forward and wake up. Gears screeched, the engine coughed to death, and the doors folded back, letting the chilly desert suck the warmth out of the bus.

Mike, one of the TALC guys who had befriended Mordente on Hollywood Boulevard, popped into the aisle from one of the front seats. He looked about twenty-five and exuded so much energy, it looked to Mordente like a spotlight was on him. He was the sort of clean-cut type you find all over Provo, Utah, and wore a beige button-down oxford and a maroon sweater. His hands were half-buried in the pockets of his faded blue jeans, so his arms were crooked at the elbows, giving his upper body a sheepish, golly-gee-whiz hunch. His rubber-tipped, blue canvas tennis shoes added to the impression.

"Here we are, my new friends," he said, his smile unwavering. "You're with family now."

The Mike clones, who also worked for TALC, were sprinkled throughout the bus and clapped enthusiastically, stoking applause in their new charges.

"Total awareness and a new life"—he paused for effect—"begin now."

The brilliant white light that bathed the compound spilled through the bus doorway, casting a glow that reminded Mordente of the gaping entrance to the mother ship in *Close Encounters of the Third Kind*. Mike swept his right arm towards the door, bidding them all to step through the gateway to a better way of life. Mordente expected to hear a chorus of angels at any moment.

She hid her cynicism behind a mask of blank acceptance and shuffled out of the bus obediently with the others. She shielded her face with her arm against the painful glare from the klieg lights mounted on the sprawling hacienda's rooftop. If she squinted, she could make out two figures standing on the veranda across from the bus.

One wore a turban and sunglasses, apparently mistaking the klieg lights for the scorching desert sun. He was a few yards away but his body odor seeped out of his khaki shirt, which was unbuttoned to his belly. Mordente figured his shirt was gaping open because he was afraid he'd snag all that chest hair in the buttons. Or suffocate in his own BO.

The man beside him, Mordente assumed, had no nasal passages. He was also a lot more relaxed, casually dressed in a gray sweatshirt and faded blue jeans. Mordente squinted at Mr. Arab and Mr. Relaxed and wondered when the TALC leader, Fraser Nebbins, would make his grand appearance.

"Howdy," Mr. Relaxed said, plunging his hands into his pockets and shuffling forward to the veranda steps. "I'm Fraser Nebbins."

Mordente was caught completely off guard. Where was the full-size, glib prototype from which Mike and his legion of clones were born? Where was the smooth talker armored in three-piece Yves Saint Laurent who danced like John Travolta around press inquires? Where was the pomp, the show, the bullshit?

Nebbins stood in front of the line of street urchins like a general facing his troops. "I welcome you, my brothers and sisters, into our family." A smile rich in family warmth bloomed on his face. "Here you will have the peace and freedom to explore your inner selves and experience total awareness." He walked down the line of people, smiling at each of them, shaking hands, stroking hair. "These walls, and the brothers and sisters carrying firearms, aren't here to keep you in. They are here to keep the corruption and disease that's out there … out there."

Meek chuckles rippled through the line and Mordente felt her pulse quicken anxiously as Nebbins approached her.

"It isn't long before you forget life out there completely." He reached out his hand to Mordente's cheek and lightly stroked it. "Sleep well, everyone. Tomorrow you begin new lives."

Mordente lowered her head shyly and followed the others towards the rear of the hacienda. Nebbins crossed his arms under his chest, his eyes admiring the smooth curves of Mordente's slim body as she disappeared around the building's edge.

Achmed Sabib stepped quietly to Nebbins' side.

"She's stunning," Nebbins muttered.

Sabib absently scratched the hair on his chest. "Yes, she'll fetch us a good price."

Nebbins shared a grin with his friend. "Let's give her a test drive ourselves first, eh?"

They clapped their arms around each other and laughed quietly as they walked back into the hacienda, the floodlights clicking off behind them and submerging the colony in blackness once again.

Jessica Mordente knew what was happening to her. They were breaking her. And she didn't know how much longer she could hold on to her sanity.

The cell was pitch-black. The only light she saw was when she closed her eyes. Then it was the Fourth of July. The fireworks were dazzling, almost hypnotic, and she was afraid of it. When she opened her eyes, the colorful explosions of brilliant brightness disappeared. So she kept her eyes open and hungered for the light.

When she first entered the barracks (how long ago was that?), three men grabbed her and hit her until she was nearly unconscious. She was aware of them stripping off her clothes and jamming a needle in her arm.

Then everything was warm and she couldn't move. Her thoughts became disjointed, and everything she saw looked like reflections in a carnival Fun House mirror. They carried her down a cramped, dimly lit corridor that was hot with the smell of human sweat. They tossed her into a concrete cell. A single lightbulb entwined in cobwebs dangled from the ceiling. It had been on then. There was no window, no bed, no toilet. Just a hole in the center of the room.

The light went out before her head cleared. She crawled into a corner and curled up, shivering, staring into the blackness. She heard the ringing. It began softly at first and then became louder. It wouldn't go away. It just droned on and on, incessantly, drilling into her skull. She was sure that once it got inside, even if they turned off the sound, it would never go away.

She wasn't claustrophobic before, but now she could feel the unseen walls closing in on her in the darkness, pushing out the air, smothering her. Her breathing became deep and hungry, her lungs aching for air.

She closed her eyes against the fear and the brilliant whiteness returned, bathing her in an intense, soothing glow. A tingling sensation rode up her legs and traveled everywhere, across her chest, under her arms, over her lips. It felt like…

Her quivering hands rose to her face and she felt the hard insect bodies scurrying across her skin, into her hair, down her neck. She screamed hysterically and bounced herself madly off the cell walls until she collapsed, quivering, onto the floor and let the white light in her head claim her.

CHAPTER FOUR

Puerto Vallarta, Mexico
Thursday, June 13, 11:32 a.m.

"You should have listened to Karl Malden, Harv," Ivy Goldblatt said as they shuffled down the cobblestone road, adjusting her tube top every few steps. "We wouldn't be in this mess if we had American Express."

She punctuated her sentences by poking her husband in the shoulder with her index finger. It didn't bother him. Thirteen years of marriage to her had left tiny calluses all over his body. Other people, though, left conversations with Ivy looking like they'd been pistol-whipped.

"Shut up, Ivy." Harv shuffled along the embankment, his body hunched under the oppressive midmorning heat. "It doesn't make a goddamn difference what kind of checks we had. The goddamn bandito didn't ask me what was in the wallet before he lifted it, Ivy."

"Listen, mouth, where are you going to get a refund on Wanderin' Joe's traveler's checks here? Huh?"

"Yeah, and if you hadn't handed every goddamn peso we had to every goddamn street hoodlum selling phony jewelry, we could hail a fucking taxi."

His sunburned face felt like someone had used it for a pin cushion. The six coats of medicated Noxzema he had applied to his face that morning hadn't done a damn thing except make him smell funny. He was frustrated, uncomfortable, and tired and had to piss so bad he was afraid if he stopped moving his bladder would burst.

Some vacation.

"We should have taken the Love Boat cruise, Harv." Ivy poked him in the ribs and pulled up her tube top. "This is all your fault."

"That's it." Harv stopped, turned his back to the road, and started unbuckling his pants. "I'm gonna water the plants."

He unzipped his fly and fumbled with the flap in his underwear.

"Harv!" Ivy shrieked. "You can't do that. We're in a foreign country."

"Just watch the goddamn road or I'll whiz on you."

Harv sighed contentedly as he relieved himself off the edge of the embankment. He admired the nice, fine stream of urine spraying into the foliage and remembered those great high school piss contests. They used to see who could stand farthest from the toilet and still piss into it.

He always won. He was the undisputed Pissmaster.

Harv peered into the brush to see what he was drilling into. He was probably pounding some boulder into sand with his manly spray. But then he saw that it wasn't a rock he was hitting. It was a body.

"Holy shit." Harv's eyebrows climbed up his forehead. He let go of himself and stood very still, pissing into his shoe.

1:00 p.m.

The two attendants slid the stretcher carrying a bloodied, unconscious Brett Macklin into the white, '71 Cadillac ambulance and slammed the door shut.

Captain Jacob Ortiz combed his fingers through his shoulder-length brown hair and watched the ambulance shriek away down the street towards the hospital.

This Brett Macklin was one unlucky guy. And so, it seemed, were his friends—Ortiz had reread the autopsy report on Mort Suderson on his way over.

Although he couldn't prove it yet, Ortiz knew Macklin had thwarted the hijacking. All right, so the police hadn't been able to form a composite drawing from all the disparate descriptions they got from the passengers. But Macklin's plane had just landed and he would have been walking to the terminal at the time of the hijacking.

By the time Ortiz had showed up at the airport, the place was in pandemonium and Macklin was already gone. The man pretending to be Ortiz disappeared with Macklin before airport security realized they had been tricked.

Ortiz believed there was no connection between the hijacking and Macklin's abduction by the imposter. An unfortunate coincidence. In a way, he was glad Macklin was there. Macklin handled himself well. Too well. Christ, it was like Macklin was just swatting flies. Clearly, this was no ordinary man. And someone, a real pro, was going to a lot of trouble, risk, and expense to make life miserable for him.

But to what end? Why was Macklin still alive?

Ortiz loosened his red leather tie and opened his black-checked shirt at the collar. Ivy Goldblatt poked him in the chest, intruding into his thoughts, and once again he was listening to her drone.

"Okay, Mrs. Goldblatt," he interrupted. "I'll see if I can contact this guy, ah"—he looked at his notepad—"Karl Malden, for you about your traveler's checks."

"No, no," she said, stabbing him twice with her finger, "It's Wandering Joe. He's the one."

"All right, Wandering Joe, then." Ortiz put up his hands defensively to ward off any more blows. "I assure you, we won't leave you to roam the streets penniless."

"Thank you. You're very understanding considering we come from two different cultures," she said.

"We don't. I'm on loan from the LAPD," Ortiz said. "I'm the law enforcement version of an exchange student."

"You don't dress like a police officer," Ivy said with challenging eyes.

"I don't have to." Ortiz grinned. "They expect American cops to be different."

"But you're Mexican, aren't you?" Harv asked, studying his face.

"A Judeo-Mex-American." Ortiz grinned. He loved saying that to people.

Ivy Goldblatt paled. "You're Jewish?"

Ortiz nodded.

"Captain Ortiz?" an officer yelled behind him.

"Excuse me," Ortiz said to the Goldblatts and went to the car. "What is it, Mendoza?" he asked the officer in Spanish.

"They've located Sergeant Shaw," Mendoza replied. "They've got him on the phone at the station."

"Tell them to keep him on the line," Ortiz said. "I'm on my way."

Achmed Sabib, his arms folded under his chest, stared into Jessica Mordente's empty eyes. She stood, naked, just an inch away from him, her gaze trained on some distant dimension outside of Nebbins' wood-paneled study.

"She's gone," Sabib marveled, waving his hand in front of her expressionless face. She had been washed, her skin moisturized, her hair shampooed, and her teeth brushed.

"Oh, she's still here." Nebbins petted her shiny, fluffy hair and looked at Sabib over her tan shoulder. "Just enough of her, anyway, to pleasure us and our buyers. Think of her as a warm, giving robot."

Sabib slapped his palm between her legs. Mordente didn't react. "I could stuff a hot poker in her and she'd never notice."

Nebbins' lips stretched into a malefic grin. "That's the idea, isn't it?"

"Nobody wants an empty bag of flesh, Nebbins."

"Don't worry, Achmed." Nebbins walked around Mordente and clapped Sabib reassuringly on the shoulder. "She's still a fetus."

Nebbins stroked her cheek with the back of his hand. "My perfect program of deprivation, malnutrition, isolation, and drugs will make her unusually receptive to suggestion and manipulation without damaging her capacity for hard labor or sexual functioning." He strode to an overstuffed leather chair across the room and sat down, draping a leg over one of the armrests. "That's what makes my product the Mercedes of the mass-market slave trade."

"How are the others coming?"

"Three proved unmalleable and had to be killed," Nebbins said. "The others are developing nicely. We may be slightly overstocked with men, though."

"So we trim our inventory if necessary." Sabib pinched Mordente's lips.

Nebbins shrugged. "Some of them I'll allocate as specimens for research and development. I hate to be wasteful. This one, though, looks like she'll reap us many rewards."

Sabib studied her face and passionlessly fondled her breasts, examining them for workmanship. "So when can I begin reaping?"

"Patience, Achmed, patience." Nebbins grinned. "You can christen her on Sunday."

❦ ❦ ❦

Brett Macklin tumbled weightlessly through time and space, through the wispy clouds of memories real and memories imagined. The rhythmic, electronic bleeps of his electrocardiograph echoed from the furthest edges of his consciousness and scored his tormenting descent…

… he was in Mayor Jed Stocker's office. Shaw was there, too.

The mayor sat at his desk. "I told you about the problem in Chinatown because I want Mr. Jury to take care of it."

"Fuck off, Stocker," Macklin said. "I'm not doing anything for you."

"You will. You're still angry. You want to keep fighting."

Macklin glanced at Shaw. The black detective's eyes reflected an eerie, sad anger. Macklin turned, strode to the office door, and flung it open.

He was in a MexAir plane. Everything looked murky, thick, as if submerged in water. He jerked his head over his shoulder and looked through the doorway. Stocker's office was gone. All he saw was the Puerto Vallarta airport terminal behind him.

"May I have your boarding pass, please?" the stewardess beside him asked. She spoke like a record played far too slow. Macklin looked down the long, endless aisle. Brooke and Cory sat in every seat. They sat, he knew, in judgment. A ghastly image of himself stood in the aisle laughing, his pasty lips twisted in unrestrained disgust around swollen, bleeding gums and silver-capped teeth.

"May I have your boarding pass, please?" the stewardess repeated in that heavy half speed of dreams.

Macklin grinned cockily at his alter image and, in that same, drowsy slowness, said, "Sure."

He pulled out his .357, spun on his heel, and fired at the silver-toothed Macklin.

The stewardess droned endlessly over the painful reverberations of the gunshot. "May I have your boarding pass, please?"

Brooke and Cory joined the uninjured, silver-toothed image in sickly, malicious laughter. Macklin, confused, looked down at his chest. He was bleeding, gallons and gallons of blood, unreal, unthinkable, unbelievable streams of blood. The thick, frothing waves of red bubbled out of his body, splashed on the floor, and raged down the aisle.

"Who are you?" Brooke, Cory, and the silver-toothed Macklin screeched, their voices like chalk skidding across a blackboard. Macklin's blood lapped at their ankles. "Who are you?"

Macklin lifted his head from his wound and said, "The jury."

He dropped to his knees, the life spilling out of him.

"Who are you?" they wailed.

"The jury," Macklin yelled and fell forward. He grabbed at the air, uselessly reaching for something to stop his fall. He splashed face-first into a hot, bottomless pool of his own blood. He opened his mouth to cry for help. Blood rushed up his nostrils and filled his lungs, and he knew he was dead.

CHAPTER FIVE

Puerto Vallarta
Friday, June 14, 6:12 p.m.

The way Brett Macklin was feeling, he almost wished he actually was dead. He could feel the two hemispheres of his brain pulsing with a dull, swollen ache. His eyeballs floated in stinging oil, and the muscles in his body had been replaced with cement. So he just laid motionless in his bed, staring up at Jesus crucified on the wall above the iron headboard.

Macklin made no effort to contact anyone when he awoke, nor did he try to look at his watch, which wasn't on his wrist anyway. He was still getting used to the idea that he was alive, when the door to his room cracked opened and Captain Jacob Ortiz edged in.

"You're awake," Ortiz said, closing the door and disappearing again. The captain's sudden appearance prompted Macklin to focus his attention on his situation. Before he could do much thinking, the door opened again and Ortiz came in, accompanied by a doctor.

"How are you feeling?" Ortiz asked.

"I'll know in a minute," Macklin replied hoarsely as the doctor pulled back the bedsheets, exposing Macklin's wounds to them all.

His chest was bruised and his midsection was wrapped tightly in bandages. Bruises blotched the length of his legs.

"I'm better than I expected," Macklin said, raising his hands to his face, lightly brushing the swollen skin, and then over his head, which was covered with bandages.

The doctor smiled, listened to Macklin's heart with a stethoscope, said something to Ortiz in Spanish, and then left the two men alone.

"So?" Macklin asked. "What did he say?"

"He says you're lucky to be alive." Ortiz sat on the edge of Macklin's bed.

"How long have I been here?"

"Couple days," Ortiz replied. "You don't have any serious injuries, a few broken ribs and a lot of bruising, but the concussion and the trauma put you in a coma."

Macklin explored the inside of his mouth with his tongue. "What about my teeth? You didn't have to do anything to my teeth, did you?"

"Nope."

Macklin grinned. "Thank God. So who are you?"

Ortiz chuckled. "Aren't I the one who is supposed to ask the questions?"

"Yeah, but you won't get any answers unless I know who you are."

"I'm Captain Jacob Ortiz, Puerto Vallarta police."

"Great," Macklin said. "The last guy who told me that tossed me out of a moving car."

"That's what puzzles me, Mr. Macklin," Ortiz said. "Why would someone want to do that to you?"

Macklin would have shrugged if it wouldn't hurt like hell to do it. He just stared blankly at Ortiz instead.

"Why would someone want to kill your friend?" Ortiz continued. "Why would someone beat you and leave you to be pissed on?"

"Pissed on?"

"At first I thought you were one very unlucky man," Ortiz said. "But I was wrong, very wrong."

"What's this about being pissed on?"

"You're lucky I'm actually an LA cop, you're lucky to have a friend like Sergeant Shaw to pull strings for you, and you're lucky to be alive."

Macklin sat up slowly, gritting his teeth against the pain that squeezed his entire body with excruciating pressure.

"Someone pissed on me?"

Ortiz nodded. "Be glad. Otherwise, we might not have found you until there was nearly nothing left to find."

"I'm going to kill the motherfuckers who did this to me." Macklin turned his head to the bedside table. He saw the jug of water and the empty glass beside it. While Macklin was still deciding whether he wanted to try and get the water for himself, Ortiz stood up and poured Macklin a glass, holding it to Macklin's lips.

Macklin jerked his head away and took the glass from Ortiz's hand, spilling some of the water on himself in the process.

"Thanks," Macklin said, taking a sip.

"You're welcome." Ortiz sighed and sat down on the bed again.

"Tell me about Mort." Macklin swallowed all the water, leaned his head back against the wall, and closed his eyes.

"Suderson was found in his hotel room by a maid," Ortiz said. "We think a woman broke his neck while he was performing oral sex on her."

Macklin's eyes flew open. "What?"

"His face was soaked with vaginal discharge and there's evidence that extreme pressure was applied to either side of his head, " Ortiz said. "The position of his body when we found him clearly shows that he was on his knees at the time of his death. In addition, the traces of vaginal fluid we've found on the bedsheets and the carpet support the scenario."

Ortiz looked away so Macklin couldn't see the smile he could no longer hold back. "We don't think he was an accidental victim of unrestrained, overly enthusiastic orgasmic response. It was murder."

"A grotesquely appropriate way to kill him," Macklin observed. "Too appropriate."

Ortiz looked back at Macklin. "Who killed him?"

"You tell me," Macklin said. "I came down here to identify the body."

"And you almost became a corpse yourself." Ortiz stood up and paced. "C'mon, Mr. Macklin, let's not play games."

"Ortiz, I don't know anything. I'm more confused than you are."

Ortiz stopped and stared at Macklin as if the truth would suddenly appear in print on Macklin's forehead. "No, you aren't."

Macklin toyed with saying "yes, I am," but thought better of it. There was nothing to be gained by needling the man and everything to lose. He knew Ortiz could make life even less pleasant than it was now. *I did kill two men,* he thought, *and they could hold me forever on that. Or they could disclose to the press that I was the guy who did it.*

"What about the woman. Do you have any leads on her?" Macklin asked.

"A description from people at the pool where Suderson met her," Ortiz said. "Unfortunately, it's difficult to identify someone only from descriptions of her buttocks and breasts. Suderson, however, they all remembered."

Macklin couldn't help grinning. Mort never was very subtle, even in death.

"We've got passenger lists for all the outgoing flights since Suderson's murder, including the flight you ... ah ... disrupted," Ortiz said. "You're going to go through them and see if any name jogs your memory."

"Okay, go get them."

Ortiz was surprised. He thought Macklin would claim to be too weak, or in too much pain, to be helpful. Ortiz walked to the door, opened it a crack, and stuck his head into the corridor.

"Mendoza," he yelled, "bring me the lists."

Ortiz returned to Macklin's bed holding a sheaf of computer printouts and laid them on Macklin's lap. Macklin lifted the scroll and began scanning the names.

Alberts, Penelope ... Ames, Trisha ... Arness, Frances ... Banks, Helen ...

"This whole thing makes no sense at all to me," Ortiz said. "What did these unknown assailants gain by abducting you?"

... Bender, Karen . . Biagas, Loraine . Boucher, Laura ... Byrd, Betty ... Cabrera, Lucy ...

"They went to a lot of trouble and risk to do it, too," Ortiz continued. "But to what end?"

Carlson, Elisa ... Copeland, Dorothy ... Curran, Janice ...

"They didn't take your wallet or your watch," Ortiz said, "and they didn't beat you badly enough to kill you. They left you where you could presumably be found. I mean, they could easily have killed you if that's what they wanted."

Davenport, Katie ... Davidson, Burl ... Davis, Cheshire ...

Cheshire Davis.

Macklin felt a shiver course his spine. The killer, whoever she was, had a cruel, acidic sense of humor. Cheshire had been Macklin's lover. A gang of psychopathic pedophiles had tried to kill him by planting a bomb in his car. They'd killed Cheshire instead.

The killer chose the name knowing I'd see it, Macklin thought. *The killer is having fun with me. The killer is going to pay.*

"Why didn't the kidnappers kill you?" Ortiz continued. "All they succeeded in doing was putting you in the hospital for a few days."

Macklin looked up from the printout.

"What did you say?"

"I said, what were the guys after? All they managed to do was put you in bed for a while."

And keep me out of Los Angeles, away from ... away from Brooke, from Cory, from—

"Get me a phone," Macklin snapped.

"What?" Ortiz was startled.

"Get me a phone, damn it." Macklin tossed the printout at him. "I want to call my family."

"Cory is at a slumber party for the weekend," Brooke told Macklin over the phone. She was doing a poor job of hiding her exasperation. Mack had become so difficult lately. She could barely hear his barrage of questions because of static and the echo of her own voice on the line.

"With who?" he demanded.

"Her friends, Mack. Cory and a bunch of her friends are with the Hendersons at their cabin up at Big Bear Lake. Is that okay with you?"

"What are you doing?"

"None of your damn business, Mack," Brooke said, wincing as echoes of her words blared into her ear. "What the hell is the matter with you?"

"Nothing, Brooke, nothing at all," Macklin replied somberly. "I just wanted to know both of you were all right."

She stayed quiet for a moment, smiled at her dinner guest, and waited for the echoes to clear the line.

"We're all right, okay? Give the interrogation routine a rest."

"Be careful, Brooke, and keep a close eye on Cory," Macklin said. "You could be in some danger."

Oh God, she thought, *not this paranoid crap again.* Last time she'd let him nag her into leaving town. "No one's out to get us, Mack," she said.

"Don't be so sure," Macklin replied. "Mort's death wasn't an accident."

Brooke paused to consider her reply. Mort was probably killed by some tramp's enraged husband. Unfortunately, Brett had faced two other deaths in the last year or so, and a smart-ass reply wouldn't do much good. After all, anybody in his shoes would start to get a little unhinged.

"I'm sorry about Mort, I really am," Brooke said carefully. "But I haven't seen him in years and I never had much connection with the guy anyway. I doubt whoever wanted to hurt him would care about Cory and me."

"Brooke—"

"Look, Mack, I have to go," Brooke interrupted. "I have guests. Give Cory a call when she gets back Sunday night, okay?"

"Take care, Brooke."

"I will. Good-bye." Brooke hung up the phone and exhaled, sagging on her bar stool at the kitchen counter.

Brooke carried her empty glass to the table, where the dirty dinner plates sat unattended, and poured herself some more of the chilled wine, which was now lukewarm.

"That was my ex-husband, Brett." She filled her glass. "His father was murdered not long ago, and ever since then he's been behaving strangely."

She walked to the couch and cleared a space for herself among the dozens of hand-knit pillows.

"I just don't know how to deal with him anymore."

"Tell me about him." Isadora Van Rijn smiled warmly and put her arm around Brooke. "Maybe I can help."

CHAPTER SIX

"Where's the cat?" Laura asked, pushing open the cabin's screen door and stepping out onto the porch. She clasped her pink bathrobe tight around her neck against the cold night air and looked down at the hand-made clay cat dish, decorated with Garfield cartoons and glazed yellow. "She hasn't even touched her Tender Vittles. Rusty, have you seen the cat?"

"No," Rusty replied from inside the cabin, "and if I do I'm gonna clean the toilet bowl with it. Why don't you come back in here and watch Johnny Carson with me?"

She let the screen door slam behind her and stared into the wall of trees where the light cast from the porch melted into darkness. Crickets hummed and a gentle breeze wafted across the lake and ruffled through the tall trees.

"I'm going to go look for the cat."

"Lore-ahhhh," he drawled, "you don't want to be out there looking for the cat."

"Yes, I do." She stomped off the porch into the trees, her yellow thongs slapping against her heels with every step.

"For Christ's sake, Laura, have you forgotten about the escaped convict?" Rusty wailed. "Laura, did you hear me? Laura?"

She didn't hear him. She had already stormed angrily into the thicket, just glad she was going to be away from Rusty's Schlitz-y breath and clammy hands when Loni Anderson came on the Carson show. Loni and her trampy hair and cow teats always made him horny.

But her irritation soon cooled in the night air and she ran out of steam, stopping dead in her tracks. She stood still. The night closed in around her. She became aware of the crushing silence and the impenetrable darkness and realized she care didn't if Cuddles ate his Vittles or not.

She heard a crunch, the sound of leaves being crushed underfoot. Her head jerked instinctively towards the sound. It was behind her.

"Cuddles?" she ventured. Another crunch, then another. Something was moving towards her. She stayed planted to the ground, as immobile as the trees around her. "Cuddles?"

Suddenly there was a loud shriek. She stumbled backwards, startled, as a half dozen loons burst out of the brush screaming, wings fluttering, and flew off in every direction. She clutched her robe at the chest and felt her heart thumping excitedly. *Loons.* She sighed gratefully. *Just some loony loons.*

She was still looking at the trees where the birds took flight when she saw a familiar flash of blue terry cloth.

"Rusty, what the hell were—," she began, but then stopped. Her husband emerged from the trees, moving slowly towards her, his arms flush against his sides, his eyes staring past her, his jaw hanging open.

Then he stopped, just a few feet away from her, his lower lip twitching.

"Rusty, what's the matter with you?" she said, planting her hands firmly on her sides. "Why are you acting like a zombie or something?"

A sound, the beginnings of a word, growled in his throat, and then he tipped forward onto the ground. And she saw the ax buried deep in his back.

Laura's terrified scream melded with the killer's banshee cry of manic glee as he came running out of the trees like a pole vaulter, holding a pitchfork. Cuddles the cat was speared on the end.

She back-stepped into a run, clamoring wildly into the trees, yelling for help.

"Cuddles wants to seeee you," he cried after her, his pea coat flaring out like wings as he ran.

Laura scrambled through the brush, jerking her head around to see him gaining on her, his face alight with a wild, toothy grin. She screamed, stumbled, and went flailing into a tangle of bushes.

He loomed over her and held the pitchfork poised over her head. The cat's blood streaked down the three muddy prongs and dripped onto her pale, anxious face.

"Here," he hissed, "give Cuddles a kissy-poo."

The man wrinkled his face with disgust and brought all his weight down against the pitchfork... and a dozen fifth-grade girls squealed with gleeful terror and cowered in their sleeping bags, the glow from the TV set the only light in the Hendersons' dark living room.

"Their parents are going to kill me," Nina Henderson groaned in the kitchen, plucking the ten candles from her daughter Becky's birthday cake. "How could you let Becky talk you into renting *Bloodbath Daycamp for Girls*?"

Jake Henderson grinned at her from across the table, where he was dropping the paper plates and party favors into a Glad trash bag. "So what? It's her birthday—let her have a little fun."

"*Bloodbath Daycamp for Girls*," she repeated to herself as she put the cake in the refrigerator. Her husband set down his bag and tiptoed to the doorway and peeked into the living room.

The girls were all huddled around the set, their eyes wide, the light from the TV flickering like a campfire. His daughter Becky watched the movie while braiding Cory Macklin's long blond hair.

Nina Henderson flicked off the kitchen lights and pressed herself against her husband's back, wrapping her arms around his waist and patting his stomach.

"C'mon, Jake," she whispered into his ear, "let's leave them alone and go upstairs."

The phone in the kitchen rang shrilly, startling them both.

"Ignore it," she mumbled.

Jake shrugged apologetically, untangled himself from Nina, and went to the phone. "Hello?"

"Jake, this is Brett Macklin."

"Hey, how'ya doing?" Jake said. "I haven't heard from you in ages."

Who is it? Nina mouthed.

Brett Macklin, he mouthed in return.

Nina shot a confused look at Jake and then peered into the living room at Cory, who was frozen with the rest of the girls, their attention captured by something suspenseful on the screen.

"Want me to get Cory for you?" Jake said.

"No," Macklin said quickly, "that's all right. I just wanted to check in and see if everything is okay."

Jake scratched his forehead. "Ah, yeah, everything's fine, Brett. Why?"

"Just wondering," Macklin said. "Do me a favor, keep your eye on Cory, okay?"

Jake glanced at Nina, who was spying on the girls. "We've got our eye on her right now."

"Make sure she gets home all right," Macklin said, "and don't leave her alone."

"Sure," Jake said.

"Thanks." Macklin hung up.

Jake stared at the receiver. "He's nutso."

Brooke talked incessantly. It was the wine. It was the quiet of the apartment. It was the insistence of Isadora Van Rijn's eyes looking into her own.

"Your work is scary but it draws you in anyway," Brooke said, uncomfortably aware of the warmth of Isadora's arm around her. "That one with the faceless, naked woman sitting on top of the man, pinning his neck between her knees. It's as if she's strangling him with her femininity. It's unsettling as hell."

Isadora smiled and remained quiet, leaving Brooke to flounder in the pressuring silence.

"There's poetry to your violence, though." Brooke was trying to fill the room with words and force out the tension. She knew she was saying things thoughtlessly and wondered, for a second, if she sounded foolish. But the silence was more threatening. Her body was buzzing in a scary, thrilling way, and she wasn't sure if she liked it or not. "Your images are fraught with sexuality, death, and emotion. Where do you get them from?"

Isadora's other hand dropped gently onto Brooke's thigh. It choked the words rising in Brooke's throat, and she felt a hot flush ride over her. She met Isadora's gaze directly and gave in to what she knew she had been feeling all night. Isadora let her hand gently stroke the soft skin of Brooke's thigh and leaned slowly towards her.

Brooke knew she wouldn't stop her. She had been resisting these feelings for hours. *Go ahead,* Brooke thought, staring into Isadora's dark eyes. *I don't know what's going to happen, but I want to find out.*

She couldn't say these things to Isadora—she simply challenged her with her gaze. Isadora pressed her face close to Brooke's throat and let her hand slide up Brooke's flank.

Brooke felt Isadora's breath on her skin, warming it, making it tingle. She enjoyed a deliciously precarious feeling of hanging over a precipice, awaiting the inevitable fall into something wonderful.

Isadora sat up straight and took Brooke's wrists roughly in her hands. "Do you want the kiss?"

Brooke heard herself breathe out, "Yes."

"Then what I do for you, you will do for me."

Isadora pushed her down onto the pillows and kissed her deeply on the mouth. Brooke moved past thinking and let herself be led wherever Isadora was taking her. Isadora kissed her again, softer, with a tenderness Brooke didn't think was possible. Their lips barely touched, just enough to spark sensation. It made Brooke hungry for more. Her pelvis ground against Isadora and her breasts swelled.

The kissing stopped. Brooke heard herself panting. *Don't stop now…* She needed more from Isadora, wanted more. Then Brooke felt Isadora's moist tongue on her soft, sensitive neck. Isadora was drawing tiny circles on Brooke's neck with her tongue, barely touching the skin. It was an incredible feeling. Every time Isadora's tongue touched her skin, Brooke felt a pleasurable pulse between her legs. Brooke's chest rose and fell with increasing urgency. Isadora sensed Brooke's rising passion. She smoothed her hand over the delicate softness of Brooke's full, swelling breast. Brooke dug her nails into the couch cushions, stunned by the intensity of the pleasure she felt from Isadora's touch.

Isadora began to unbutton Brooke's blouse. Brooke longed for Isadora's gentle caress on her flushed, increasingly sensitive skin. She gasped when she felt Isadora's tongue brush the back of her neck. Her tongue glided over Brooke's neck, slid down the strong line of her sternum, and stopped at the rise of her quivering breasts. Brooke moaned weakly, her breasts aching for the withheld touch, and stared helplessly into Isadora's amber eyes. *Please…*

Isadora sat up, straddling Brooke's waist, and peeled open Brooke's blouse to reveal her breasts, starkly pale against the dark tan of the rest of her skin. Brooke had never felt so vulnerable or so lustful. It was wonderfully frightening.

Brooke could see Isadora's nipples pressing against her fuzzy white angora sweater and had to touch them. With trembling fingers, Brooke tentatively reached for Isadora's breasts, brushing the hard nipples and kneading the warm flesh. She could feel Isadora's heartbeat quickening.

Giving Isadora pleasure, arousing this perfect creature, heightened Brooke's excitement. She felt a giddy, transcendent sense of physical euphoria. She wanted Isadora to feel the desire she felt, to crave that ultimate release as badly as she did.

Isadora closed her eyes, flattened her hands on Brooke's belly, and leaned forward, pressing her face between Brooke's breasts. Brooke raked her fingers through Isadora's hair. Isadora gently licked Brooke's left breast and watched her soft, pink nipple grow dark and hard.

Brooke heard herself utter a sharp cry as Isadora's lip lightly brushed her nipple, dabbing it with her tongue. The excruciating pleasure was unbearable. She had never felt so wet, so wanton. Her thighs were soaked.

Brooke pushed Isadora's buttocks down and rubbed against the warmth between Isadora's legs. Brooke was utterly lost in her own pleasure. The rest of the world ceased to exist in the face of her overpowering lust.

Isadora sat up and unstrapped Brooke's belt buckle. Brooke lifted her hips and Isadora slid her jeans and panties over them and down her slim legs. She tossed the clothes to the floor and dipped between Brooke's firm thighs. The feel of Isadora's breath on her skin made her shiver. Her pelvis rose to meet Isadora's tongue.

Isadora explored Brooke slowly, finding the places where the moist skin was a raw nerve. Brooke cried out, a slave to the pleasure Isadora was giving her. Isadora teased and tormented, her tongue flicking, her lips squeezing, her fingers stroking. Each time Isadora's tongue touched her, exquisite jolts of pleasure shook Brooke's body until Isadora's touch didn't stop and the tension built, knotting her muscles in incredible ecstasy. Brooke writhed wildly as she peaked, her hips rising, grabbing for that orgasm.

Brooke huffed like a locomotive as she raced towards the brink… and then her body arched up, quivering, her face shaking, her mouth gaping open in a silent scream of joyous release. She was suspended for a long second, tears streaking from the corners of her eyes. Her body bucked violently once, twice, three times, and then she fell slowly to the cushions.

Brooke was laying there utterly spent, her body flushed and damp with sweat, when she heard Isadora's husky voice. "My turn."

CHAPTER SEVEN

Santa Monica
Saturday, June 15, 10:30 a.m.

"Look at yourself, Mack, you're walking like you have a ten-inch spike up your ass." Sergeant Ronald Shaw sat on a stool inside the Blue Yonder Airways hangar and watched Brett Macklin hobble away from the Cessna that had just taxied in. "You should have stayed in the hospital."

"Fuck you," Macklin said, dumping his duffel bag on the table behind the black detective. Shaw detected none of Macklin's good-natured ribbing in the remark. It was unadulterated animosity.

"Hey, buddy, before you start mouthing off, think about why you aren't rotting in a Mexican prison right now," Shaw said. "I want some cooperation from you, and I—"

"Save it, Ronny," Macklin interrupted. "I appreciate whatever you said to the Mexican authorities, but let's be honest, okay? You did it to save your ass, too. Stocker is scared shitless someone will find out I've killed for the LAPD."

Macklin dragged himself to his office. Without bothering to brush aside the dusty papers and files, Macklin carefully lowered himself onto the torn black vinyl sofa against the far wall. He closed his eyes and imagined the pain he felt as fluid, as a puddle, and visualized it evaporating into the air like the steam from a vaporizer.

Shaw sat on the edge of Macklin's desk and sighed. "You wouldn't be back unless you had something on the killer."

Macklin said nothing.

"What have you got, Mack? Tell me."

Shaw stared down at Macklin. Two long, silent minutes passed between them.

"It's my responsibility now, Mack."

"The Bitch killed Mort. The Bitch is after me."

"Mr. Jury."

"Yeah, Mr. Jury."

Shaw sighed. "I'm going to call Ortega. I'll find out what you know."

"Good. By then it will be over."

"You are such a goddamn hypocrite. What happened to your ridiculous creed? What happened to only killing when the law fails, when the guilty go free?"

"The law is irrelevant," Macklin said. "She'll kill you, my family, and whatever's left of my life." Macklin sat up slowly. "And then she'll slit my throat."

"That's hypothetical bullshit."

"I feel it."

"So sit beside Cory's bed with a shotgun in your lap and let me do my job."

Macklin stood up uneasily, grabbing Shaw's forearm to balance himself. "Don't push me, Ronny. I've got nothing left to lose. Get in my way, and I'll go to the press. Imagine what will happen when the city finds out the LAPD has an assassin on their payroll."

"You can't even stand up on your own," Shaw said. "How can you fight her like this?"

Macklin glared at his friend. "This began with me and it will end with me, one way or the other."

Shaw slid off the desk. "You are one stupid son of a bitch, Mack." He walked out the office door. "I hope you've got a coffin picked out."

⚜ ⚜ ⚜

12:30 p.m.

Surreal. That's what a handful of codeine made Brett Macklin's world—it made it tilt, it made the sunlight a different shade of bright, and it diffused pain into wisps of smoke that fleetingly breezed through his psyche.

The codeine gave him the illusion of health and strength he needed to find the downtown Los Angeles address "Cheshire Davis" listed as home when she came to Puerto Vallarta. That was the morsel of information Macklin brought back from Mexico with him.

He drove downtown expecting to find nothing but a vacant lot. He was almost right. The address was a decaying tenement. The windows on the bottom floor had been broken long ago. Rotted wood planks were nailed haphazardly over the windows. Many of the planks hung loose, barely held in place by a rusted nail or two. Graffiti over graffiti over graffiti painted the building in senseless scribbles.

People still lived in it, though.

He saw some underwear draped over a third-floor windowsill to dry in the sun. One floor below, a man in a tank top sat on the fire escape, nursing a beer and listening to Spanish music from a transistor radio.

Macklin got out of his '59 Cadillac and walked up to the door. It gaped open, inviting him into a hallway of soiled plaster walls and cracked tile floors. The heavy stench of urine, vomit, and booze was palpable; it was like walking through gel. As he pushed himself down the hallway, he could hear the life behind the walls. Starsky and Hutch argued with Huggy Bear. Babies cried. Laughter peaked and ebbed. Angry voices bounced off each other.

He came to the door: 107. Staring at the number, he realized how badly the codeine had fucked him up. *I forgot to go home,* he realized. *I forgot to get a gun.*

Too late now, shithead.

Macklin grasped the doorknob and debated whether to burst in or ease in. Since bursting in would hurt too much, easing in won by default. He slowly pushed open the door. The apartment was completely vacant. The floor was covered with dust. On the opposite wall directly across from him, Macklin saw a strip of computer paper hanging from the point of an exposed nail. Three words were written on it in dot-matrix, computer-generated type. Each letter was a different typestyle and size, as if she had taken each letter from a different newspaper headline. It said:

I'm not easy.

"Damn you." Macklin tore the paper off the wall and jammed it into his pocket. She was the puppet master, and he could feel her pulling his strings. And he hated it.

She's having a ball, Macky boy, and you can't do anything about it.

He could almost feel the strings being jerked on his arms and legs as he left the room and marched down the hallway. *Somehow,* he thought, *there has to be a way to cut myself free, to take some of the control away from her.*

Macklin was so wrapped up in his thoughts that he didn't see the five Bloodhawks until he was already outside. They stood grinning between him and his car. They carried chains and knives lazily at their sides.

He remembered their faces from the gas station.

The one nearest to Macklin sneered, wrinkling the scar that sliced the lunar landscape of his pockmarked left cheek and cut across his thin lips.

"See, motherfucker, it ain't over," Moonface said.

"Yeah," Macklin agreed wearily, yanking off one of the wood planks covering the cracked window to his left. He now had a bat... with four crooked, rusted nails poking out at the end. It didn't send the Bloodhawks scurrying away in fear.

"Fuckface is gonna take us all out with his nasty stick," crooned Moonface sarcastically, pointing his knife at Macklin and grinning at the guy beside him. "I might piss my pants I'm so scared, Rambo."

"Let's see how far we can jam it up fag boy's ass," Rambo replied, swinging his chain and shifting his weight from one to foot to the other.

The whole scene had such a dreamlike quality, thanks to the codeine, the heat, and the Spanish music, that Macklin half thought it wasn't happening. Maybe he was slowly dying in a Puerto Vallarta hospital, lost forever in the endless matinees at the Coma Theater. *What the hell,* Macklin thought, if this was his last dream, he might as well enjoy it.

"Stop talking and do something already," Macklin said. "You're boring me to death."

Moonface lunged, thrusting his knife towards Macklin's gut. Macklin sidestepped and clubbed Moonface's outstretched arm with his stick. The nails plunged deep into Moonface's bare arm. Moonface yelped like a wounded dog. It was a very satisfying sound.

Macklin wrenched the stick free and slammed him in the face with the nail-legs side. Moonface flew backwards, crashing into two of the gang members.

Rambo swung his chain at him. Macklin ducked, sidestepped, and brought the stick down on Rambo's back. The nails smacked into Rambo's flesh with a sickening, moist squish. A surprised, agonized cry escaped from Rambo's throat.

"Don't move. Your friend won't enjoy it," Macklin said to the others.

He held the stick embedded in Rambo's back and jerked it once. Rambo screamed, his arms and legs shaking.

"Think of this as a very short leash," Macklin hissed into Rambo's ear. "We're going for a walk."

He and Rambo shuffled towards the car.

Macklin guided the whimpering gang member with the stick and eyed the others warily as he moved into the street. The four men stood fuming on the sidewalk.

Moonface's smashed nose oozed blood down his face. Little droplets hung off his chin and dripped onto his chest. Moonface was clutching his bleeding arm and glaring furiously at Macklin, who edged towards the driver's side door of his black Cadillac.

Macklin jerked open the door. He let go of the stick, kicked Rambo hard in the butt, and hopped into the car, slamming the door shut and locking it. Rambo twitched facedown on the pavement.

Macklin was safe inside the hot, stuffy car. The windows were shatterproof and he had reinforced the chassis to withstand gunfire, flames, and small explosives.

The adrenaline of the fight had diminished the potency of the codeine, and pain squeezed Macklin's body. His deep, hungry breaths, from the anxiety and exertion, swelled his chest and pushed against his broken ribs. Tiny knives stabbed his sides.

He jammed his key into the ignition, twisted it, and pumped the gas. Nothing happened.

Moonface let out a raucous shriek and threw something at Macklin's windshield. It bounced off and rolled on his hood.

The distributor cap.

Moonface pressed his bloody visage against the windshield.

"Scumfucker's not going anywhere," Moonface said. "He's gonna eat his balls right here."

CHAPTER EIGHT

While Moonface and his buddies whipped the Cadillac with their chains, Macklin scrounged around the inside of his car looking for a weapon.

The oppressive heat inside the car was squeezing the sweat out of him, soaking his clothes and bandages in perspiration. The temperature in the car was building up. He knew he'd be pressure-fried if he didn't get out of there soon.

It's a damn funny situation, Macklin thought. *I'm inside a tank and yet, utterly defenseless.*

The two air-cooled, .50-caliber machine guns mounted under the front headlights couldn't do him much good now, unless Moonface obediently lined up his men in front of the car. Or maybe they would be kind enough to stare into his taillights so he could blind them with the halogen burst lamps.

Some tank.

If he survived this, Macklin promised himself he'd add some lethal, and highly illegal, modifications to this 221-inch Batmobile.

Macklin popped open the glove compartment and found some road maps, some .357 shells, a Bic lighter, a Bruce Springsteen tape, and a first aid kit.

Great, Macklin thought. *I'll flick my Bic at them, and while they stumble around blind, I'll hit them over the heads with the Springsteen tape and shove bullets down their throats.*

Moonface opened his fly and urinated on Macklin's car.

Christ, Macklin thought, *is there anyone who isn't pissing on me?*

He climbed over the seat and searched through the clutter that had accumulated on his backseat. Old cartons of food, yellowed newspapers, unreturned videocassettes, flight plans, hangers, small grocery bags, and other assorted garbage covered the seat and the floors.

Under the front seat he found an old, eel-skin shaving bag that he had lost months ago. It was his overnighter kit. He'd had one in his car ever since college. After all, he never knew when he might get lucky.

He unzipped it and found a disposable razor, travel toothbrush, sampler can of aerosol deodorant spray, shaving gel, toothpaste, and wintergreen Binaca breath spray.

Macklin squirted the Binaca in his mouth and tossed the kit on the passenger seat. The Binaca tasted good and gave him a little extra moisture on his dry throat.

"Watch out, faggot's gonna kiss us," said Groove, a purple-Mohawked scumking.

Macklin sat still for a moment and thought. A Bloodhawk jumped on the hood like a monkey. Moonface ran a finger down his bloody arm and wrote the word "FUCKER" in blood on the driver's side window.

Macklin had a plan. He scrambled around the car again, tossing papers aside as if still searching for something useful. In the process, he hid the Bic lighter in his left hand and twisted the flame control with his thumb to its highest setting.

Macklin took the deodorant in his right hand and reached for the door handle.

Moonface stepped back, grinning, fanning his hands towards himself to beckon Macklin. "C'mon out, motherfucker."

He burst out of the car, flicking his Bic lighter and holding it up to the deodorant can as he depressed the spray button.

A tongue of flame lashed out of the spray can and ignited Moonface's blood-soaked shirt. Moonface became a blazing effigy, his horrified screech swallowed by hungry fire.

"You shouldn't play with fire," Macklin scolded Moonface. The three terrified Bloodhawks scattered.

Macklin whirled, spraying white-hot death against the backs of two fleeing Bloodhawks. The fire crawled up the screaming men's backs and turned their heads into flaming wicks. They ran until they were formless lumps of sizzling blackness. The purple-Mohawked scumking escaped around the corner unscathed.

The man who had been listening to Spanish music on the tenement's second-floor fire escape was standing up and applauding.

Macklin stared down at the burning logs of flesh, dropped the deodorant can, and picked the distributor cap off the hood.

It was time to go home.

The dark, age-freckled skin was stretched tight over the eighty-three-year-old man's squat, gnarled frame. He leaned heavily on his pearl-handled cane and stared at Craven, his most trusted aide, through thick, tortoiseshell glasses.

The old man stood at the edge of the cliff and stared out at the sea. He owned every drop of it. He also owned every grain of sand within twenty-five miles of where he now stood. The gray skies and turbulent, heavy tides underscored the unbridled hate Craven saw burning in the old man's eyes.

"Tell me he's suffering," the old man wheezed. "Tell me he's bleeding to death inside."

The misty sea breeze blew into Craven's pale face and fanned his bright red hair. "Yeah, Macklin's hurting."

Vicious guard dogs prowled the property. One of them came up and licked the old man's age-spotted hand. Craven had a remote control in his pocket that, when activated, delivered an electric charge to the collar around each dog's neck. It was perfect for training and for keeping the dogs in line if they ever decided to turn on their masters.

The same collars worked just as effectively with some of Craven's lovers.

The old man turned towards Craven. "Do any of his family or friends still live?"

Craven nodded, staring into the old man's wise, scrutinizing eyes.

The old man faced the sea again. "Then he isn't suffering enough."

4:30 p.m.

Macklin's bedside phone was ringing, but he didn't want to move. The bed was nice and warm, his body was relaxed, and the pain from his wounds was a tolerable ache. His head rested in a snug hollow in the pillow, and the sheets smelled fresh and clean.

He could stay here forever.

But the phone wouldn't let him. Its shrill rings rudely yanked him by the ears, nagging him into motion.

Macklin angrily reached for the phone. The movement raised the sheets. Air rushed under the sheets and destroyed the delicate warmth he had generated during his sleep.

"This better be good," Macklin snapped, lying on his back. His broken ribs, irritated by the sudden movement, throbbed painfully awake.

"Is this Brett Macklin?" a man asked.

"Yeah." He closed his eyes. Maybe he could keep that restful, sleepy feeling from vanishing. Maybe the pain would go back into remission.

"My name is Marc Prine. I'm Jessica Mordente's lawyer."

All vestiges of sleep disappeared and Macklin sat up against the headboard. His ribs complained in sharp bolts of pain. He hadn't noticed Jessica's absence until now. He had been back in LA for only a few hours.

"What is it?"

"Jessica told me if she didn't call me four days after entering the Transformational Awareness Life Church I was to call you," Prine said. "I'm supposed to tell you that she's in trouble. She said you'd know what to do."

Macklin felt the familiar coldness, the rage, wash over him, submerging his emotions and invoking the killer inside him.

Yeah, he knew what to do. "What happens after I get her out?"

"Jessica made plans in case this happened. She selected a deprogrammer and gave her full legal authority in this matter. Take Jessica to her immediately. Her name is Raven Vanowen and she'll be expecting you." Prine gave Macklin Vanowen's Santa Monica address and the location of the TALC compound. "Jessica made me promise not to call the police. You aren't bound by that promise. You can call them. I suggest you do. If you go in there alone, you'll get killed. These people aren't playing games."

"Neither am I." Macklin hung up the phone and slid open the nightstand drawer. He pulled out his father's .357 Magnum and a handful of shells.

9:00 p.m.

Fraser Nebbins stood in front of the den's picture window, staring into the impenetrable desert night. The blackness had swallowed everything. All light, all shape, all motion, had been overcome by darkness. It made Fraser feel like the only life in the cosmos.

He liked the feeling.

That's why he'd moved to the desert. Here, he had a stronger sense of control over his destiny. Here, life was put into perspective. Here, screams were absorbed into the dry earth. Here, he could behead an uncooperative subordinate in broad daylight with impunity. Here, Fraser Nebbins was king.

Nebbins sighed, took a sip of sherry from the goblet cradled in his hands, and turned away from the window. Someone rapped insistently at the door.

"Come in," Nebbins said.

Jessica Mordente stood solemnly in the doorway in a gray T-shirt and sweats, the standard TALC uniform for new recruits. She looked healthy and aware, yet intellectually blank. Behind her, Achmed Sabib beamed enthusiastically, his face dominated by a leering grin. He gave her a slight push, and she obediently glided into the room.

Nebbins swallowed the remainder of his sherry and hit a tiny button on his desk. Two curtains moved across the picture window and collided in the center.

"You've done a remarkable job." Sabib closed the door and approached Mordente. "She's everything you promised she would be."

Nebbins bowed modestly. "I'm simply the best there is, Achmed."

Sabib snapped his fingers. Mordente's pliant body molded against his. She pinned his head in her hands and kissed him, probing his mouth with her tongue.

Nebbins laughed. "I see you've taken the liberty of teaching her a few commands."

Sabib freed himself from her hungry kisses. "I will take many more liberties with her tonight, and, as a token of my appreciation, you may enjoy her as well."

Nebbins smiled and settled into his leather armchair. Mordente's hands fervently groped Sabib's fleshy back.

"May I watch?" Nebbins asked.

"Of course." Sabib jammed his fingers between Mordente's buttocks and squeezed them in his hands. "You may want to raise your selling price once you see what she can do.

"Strip," Sabib ordered her, pushing her away from him.

Mordente peeled off her T-shirt, her unrestrained breasts bouncing free, flung the shirt aside, and quickly stepped out of her sweatpants. She stood before Sabib, naked and vulnerable.

"On your knees," Sabib pointed to the floor.

Mordente dropped to her knees, looking up at him with wet, puppy-dog eyes. Nebbins nodded approvingly. Sabib knew how to handle his women.

"Beg for it," Sabib yelled and winked at Nebbins.

"Fuck me, Master," she moaned, "please, please, take me."

"Master?" Nebbins grinned, arching an eyebrow. Sabib shrugged. "It has a nice ring to it."

Mordente fingered herself with one hand and fondled her breasts with the other. "I will do anything, just fuck me," she whimpered. "I can't live without you inside me. Fuck me now, Master, fuck me." Her eyes closed and her head lolled lazily on her shoulder. "I want you, oh God, how I want you."

Sabib folded his arms across his chest, winked conspiratorially at Nebbins, and gazed down at her reproachfully. "You must earn it."

"Anything, just fuck me," she cried.

He unbuckled his pants and unzipped his fly. "Blow me off."

A tremendous explosion rocked the compound, bathing the room in a flash of light. Nebbins scrambled out of his chair as another, unseen explosion erupted somewhere in the night. The house shook and the floor seemed to sway beneath the stunned, motionless Arab. Mordente, oblivious to the explosions, entwined herself around Sabib's legs and nuzzled his crotch.

Nebbins yanked out the top drawer of his desk and pulled out a Luger. Sabib was about to move when Mordente took him in her mouth. He braced his hands on her shoulders and smiled.

Another thunderous explosion quaked through the house, knocking paintings off the walls and toppling furniture. Outside, Nebbins could hear screams, the roar of an engine, and the clatter of gunfire.

Nebbins jerked his head towards Sabib, was about to suggest they get the hell out, but thought better of it. Sabib wasn't going anywhere. A light blazed through the curtains, illuminating Sabib and Mordente in an unearthly glow. Nebbins squinted through the curtains, trying to figure out what the light was coming from.

He back-stepped away from the window and aimed his Luger at it. The light was growing brighter. Closer. Nebbins heard the furious mechanical roar of it approaching. He fired into the curtains as if some giant monster hid behind them. The curtains billowed as the bullets tore through them.

He kept firing. A black shape hurled from hell tore through the window in a deafening explosion of glass, plaster, and ripped fabric. It splintered through Nebbins' desk and stopped just inches away from him. The settling debris filled the room with a smoky haze.

Sabib pushed Mordente away and confronted the fin-tailed 1959 Cadillac with an expression of astonished rage. Nebbins pumped bullet after bullet into the windshield, and the faceless driver behind it, until his gun jammed empty. The bullets didn't leave a scratch.

Brett Macklin, his .357 Magnum at his side, slowly emerged from the car and crippled Nebbins with a look of blistering hate. Then he saw Sabib, the Arab's penis jutting out obscenely between the Arab's legs. Mordente cowered at Sabib's feet.

"You will die for this," Sabib yelled, jabbing his finger towards Macklin. "I will suck the marrow from your bones."

"Suck on this." Macklin raised his .357 and fired.

The bullet blasted through Sabib's teeth and exploded out the back of his head. Sabib tottered, a glimmer of life still in his blood-splashed eyes. Nebbins scrambled fearfully away. Macklin fired again, bursting Sabib's belly open. The Arab crumpled to the floor and rolled onto his back, his erection sticking out of him like a harpoon.

Macklin whirled around to face Nebbins, but the TALC leader was gone. He lowered his gun and ran over to Mordente, who sat glassy eyed and empty.

"Jessie, you're safe now," Macklin said, jamming his gun in his pants and lifting her up. "I'm going to get you out of here."

He carried her to the car and positioned her in the front seat. Her face was blank. Macklin waved his hand in front of her eyes. Nothing.

"Jessie, what have they done to you?" he whispered sadly. The compound floodlights flashed on, shifting his attention away from Mordente. Glancing in the rearview mirror, he saw dozens of armed TALC guards running towards them through the rubble that littered the compound.

He strapped her in with a seat belt and closed the door.

"We're going home," Macklin said, jerking the car into reverse and pressing the gas pedal. The Cadillac shot out of the room, smashing into two of the TALC guards.

Macklin felt the car lurch as it rolled over the bodies. He flipped the car into forward gear, heard the wet grinding sound as the wheels ground into the flesh, and then sped towards the perimeter wall.

The compound was awash in light and pandemonium. The grounds were swarming with frantic guards. The kids Nebbins had turned into walking zombies marched aimlessly amidst it all.

Macklin weaved through the rubble, swerving to avoid hitting the mindless wanderers, and headed for one of openings he had blasted in the stone wall with dynamite. Bullets bombarded the car like hailstones.

He drove through the rupture, the car bouncing violently over the chunks of rubble from the wall. Once clear of the wall, the Cadillac roared across the dark desert landscape, the bright headlights slicing a path in the mess.

Macklin saw a set of headlights dancing in the rearview mirror. A jeep was pursuing them. He grinned and slowed, letting the jeep gain ground. As the jeep closed, Macklin edged the Cadillac to the right, towards the base of a slate mountain.

Fraser Nebbins stood in the jeep, washing Macklin's car with machine-gun fire.

"Asshole," Macklin hissed, flicking a tiny dashboard switch. Two powerful halogen lamps burst from concealment from beneath the Cadillac's rear grill in a flash of blinding white light.

The driver lost control. The jeep veered wildly to the right and smashed into the mountainside. A sharp thunderclap of flame blew the jeep apart and spit a fireball of twisted metal and jagged slate into the sky. The Cadillac raced away into the night.

Macklin rested his hand on Mordente's knee.

"It's over, Jessie." He searched her eyes for some kind of life, for anything. "I made them pay."

CHAPTER NINE

Midnight

Brett Macklin steered north along the Pacific Coast Highway while unseen, decaying forces exerted themselves all around him. To his right, the sun-baked, wind-whipped Santa Monica cliffside crumbled onto the asphalt. To his left, the ocean chewed away the beach. Above him, a wino pressed himself against the cyclone cage that enclosed one of the concrete pedestrian overpasses.

And somewhere, in the darkness, a killer lurked.

Jessica Mordente was asleep wrapped up in a blanket, her head slumped forward. Her chin bounced against her collarbone from the motion of the car. She reminded him of Cory and the way his daughter fell asleep in the car after a late movie. He gave her hand a gentle squeeze.

Macklin veered the car to the right, off the highway and up Chautauqua Boulevard, which wound up into the Palisades. The homes were set back from the upward-sloping boulevard and nestled among trees that rose and formed a lush, green canopy of intertwining branches above the roadway. Just before Chautauqua melded into the meandering course of Sunset Boulevard, Macklin turned left onto a driveway.

He listened to the sound of twigs and pebbles snapping under his tires as the car slowly approached Raven Vanowen's one-story home. She was still awake. Macklin saw a trail of smoke spiraling out of the brick chimney and light spilling out behind the shuttered living room windows. A sporty red Ferrari was parked in front of the house and gleamed under the glow cast by the porch light.

Macklin parked beside the Ferrari, got out, and walked around to the passenger side of his car. He opened the door and lifted Mordente out.

His ribs cried out in a scream of agony that echoed throughout his weary body. Gritting his teeth against the pain, he nudged the car door shut with his hip and carried Mordente to Vanowen's front door.

Vanowen must have heard Macklin drive up. She opened the door just before he reached it. Her blue eyes were covered by large round glasses and she had curly brown hair that spilled onto her shoulders. She looked snug and warm in her oversize wool sweater.

"Set her on the couch," Vanowen instructed, stepping aside and pointing to the two couches behind her. Macklin walked past her and gently laid Mordente down on the couch closest to the brick hearth, where dying flames crackled in the embers.

Vanowen brushed Macklin aside and leaned over Mordente. Macklin moved back and watched. Vanowen opened Mordente's eye lids and examined her pupils, then yanked off the blanket and scanned her naked body, looking for needle marks.

He turned away, trying to escape the reality of Mordente's inert body and lifeless eyes. *She's as good as dead,* he thought. *I was too late.*

The smell of dry wood permeated the house. The smoke that had been spilling out of the hearth for years had been soaked up by the walls or, more accurately, the books.

The house was a rustic library. Every inch of wall space was covered with books. The book-lined shelves reached up to the ceiling and overflowed with volumes. What the shelves couldn't hold was stacked up in discrete stacks in various corners and crannies of the room.

"You did the right thing by bringing her directly to me," Vanowen said. "I don't think it's too late to help her."

Macklin turned around and faced her. "You mean you can bring her back, break this damn spell or whatever it is?"

Vanowen smiled reassuringly and, placing her hand on Macklin's back, led him to the door. "It's not quite as easy as that. I'm afraid it will take a lot longer to cure her than it did to hurt her. She will never be completely the same."

Macklin opened the door. "When can I see her again?"

"Soon," Vanowen said. "I'll begin treating her tonight." He nodded and walked out. She closed the door behind him.

Vanowen sighed and put a fresh log in the fire. She heard Macklin's car drive away. The flames wrapped themselves around the wood. The dry bark snapped, spitting sparks against the black-charred brick.

She warmed herself by the fire for a few minutes and, when she turned, Mordente was sitting up on the couch.

Mordente's eyes were hypnotically locked on the dancing flames. Vanowen smiled.

"Hello, Jessica," Vanowen ventured softly. Mordente stared into the fireplace.

Vanowen sat down beside Mordente and put her arm around her shoulder. "Say hello, Jessica."

"Hello," Mordente whispered.

"My name is Raven." She kissed Mordente gently on the cheek. "I am your new master."

Sunday, June 16, 11:10 a.m.

Cory pressed the buzzer again and let her finger stay on it this time. She really leaned into it, putting her weight behind her index finger as if that would make the buzzer ring even louder.

If Mom was home, the buzzer should wake her. The buzzer could wake the dead.

"I thought you said you had a key," groaned Jake Henderson impatiently. There were four other girls, waiting to be dropped off at their homes, climbing all over his LTD Brougham, probably ruining the upholstery with greater severity with each passing second. Kids were worse for a car interior than rabid dogs.

"I do," Cory whined just as impatiently. She did have a key. She remembered showing the key chain, which she had made herself in school, to Isadora Van Rijn. How could she have lost it between her apartment and Mr. Henderson's car?

"Well, we can't stand here all day, Cory," Henderson said. "Let's go take the other girls home and come back."

"Wait," Cory protested. She didn't want to have to spend another minute with Mr. Henderson. He was such a goon. "Ms. Shih will let us in."

Cory pressed Ms. Shih's apartment buzzer. A young woman answered and Cory asked to be let in. The lobby door hummed and unlocked.

Henderson pulled it open.

"I can go in myself," Cory said. *He's* so *dumb.*

"I want to make sure your mom is home," Henderson said. He didn't really give a damn, but he remembered Brett Macklin's call. If Brooke wasn't home, maybe he could unload Cory on Ms. Shih.

Cory rolled her eyes in a theatrical show of frustration and led Henderson to the elevators. The doors slid open and they got in. Cory poked the third-floor button. "Kung Fu Fighting" played on the Muzak top forty.

"It smells like Grey Flannel cologne in here," Henderson said. "You ever notice that?"

Cory rolled her eyes again. Henderson sniffed some more and absently tapped his foot to the music. The elevator stopped and Cory marched to her apartment door.

"Where does Ms. Shih live?" Henderson asked.

"Next door," Cory replied.

"Can you stay with her if your Mom isn't home?"

"Don't ask me." Cory twisted the doorknob on her apartment door and walked in. She stopped, startled, a foot from the doorway.

Sunlight, hot and bright, streamed in through the windows and shone, like a spotlight, on the kitchen and dining room. The dinner dishes were still scattered over the table and the kitchen counters. Scraps of meat had rotted into sickly curls on the plates. The vegetables were black. A strange, furry slick floated on a curdled substance in a bowl. Two empty wineglasses were on the floor beside the couch.

"Mom?" Cory said.

Henderson's face wrinkled against the heavy, oppressive smell of decay as he stepped tentatively into the apartment. He was tempted to sprint back to the elevator for a refreshing sniff of Grey Flannel. Brooke Macklin was definitely the Slob Queen. *Dis-gus-ting.*

"Mom?" Cory headed towards the master bedroom. "Mom?" Henderson, a safe distance away from the dinner table, hiked up on his toes and leaned towards the dishes, examining the crud.

He glanced at the living room and noted the depression of the couch pillows. That's from bodies, he thought, *humping* bodies. He spotted the two wineglasses and smiled. Jake Henderson, PI, had the case solved. Brooke Macklin had a guy over for dinner. They started going at it and got so caught up in it they never stopped. Fucked all weekend.

That's why the decay of modern civilization was overtaking the kitchen.

The little kid was probably gonna walk in on the two of them going at it.

Henderson glanced down the hallway. He saw Cory Macklin standing in the doorway of the master bedroom. He quickly averted his eyes. *Yep, that's it, she's just interrupted "The Orgasm Marathon."* He jammed his hands into his pockets and waited.

It was awfully quiet. Not a voice. No we-were-just-fucking-and-I-was-gonna-come-but-you-walked-in panting. Nothing.

Henderson stole another look down the hallway. Cory was still standing in the doorway, her back to him.

"Hey, Brooke?" Henderson ventured. "I'm going to go now. It was a pleasure having your daughter for the weekend." He took a few steps towards the front door, but when Brooke didn't answer he stopped. "Brooke?"

Hearing nothing, Henderson hesitantly walked towards the bedroom. "Cory, is your mother here?"

Cory didn't answer. Cory didn't move.

"Is she asleep?" Henderson asked.

He came up behind Cory. The bed was neatly made and very empty.

"What going on here, Cory?" Henderson put his hands on her tiny shoulders and felt her shaking. He looked down at her feet and lost control of himself. Something warm rolled down his leg and soaked his pants. His stomach began to heave.

Brooke's decapitated head, grinning and staring up at them with dead eyes, was in the center of a white canvas. Her head was surrounded by chopped up limbs and organs arranged at odd angles. One arm was propped up on its elbow. The hand gave them The Finger. In the bottom right-hand corner of the canvas a name was scrawled in blood.

Picasso.

CHAPTER TEN

Sunday, June 16, 1:47 p.m.

Brett Macklin leaned against his kitchen counter and cradled the telephone receiver between his shoulder and his ear. He dialed his ex-wife's number and waited. Someone picked up the phone.

"Hello?" a male voice answered.

This had happened before. Macklin was used to it. The awkwardness had worn off.

"Hi," he replied, forcing a little extra buoyancy in his voice to show that he wasn't uncomfortable with the situation. He took the receiver in his hand. "I'd like to talk with Cory, if she's back, or Brooke."

"Hold on," the man said.

Macklin heard the phone being passed off to someone else, who took the receiver and said, "I was just about to call you."

Macklin's throat dried up in an instant. He knew what was coming next. He knew a nightmare was about to become reality. In the long second of silence on the line, Macklin heard his own heart thumping. "No," he said.

"Brooke," Shaw began, his voice cracking. Macklin heard his friend struggle to hold back his emotion and regain his voice. "Cory is okay—she's safe."

Shaw hesitated. "Brooke is dead."

Macklin tore the phone off the wall and hurled it at the kitchen window. It burst through the glass and shattered on the porch. Covering his face with his hands, he felt his body shaking.

The Bitch, the fucking cunt killer, had reached down his throat and yanked his guts out.

He slid to a sitting position on the cold tile floor. *The Bitch murdered Brooke.*

It was an unbearable atrocity. To Macklin, Brooke and Cory were sacrosanct. Mr. Jury, the violence, the misery, it was *never* supposed to touch *them*! They were symbols of the happiness he had sacrificed to his vigilance. They were the ideal that he was protecting.

But he had failed. The disease had spread. Brooke was dead.

It was a bad dream that had gone into reruns. Shaw looked out of Brooke's apartment window and watched his friend Brett Macklin run into the building. Shaw felt like Death's personal publicist. He was always calling people on Death's behalf.

I'm terribly sorry, Mr. Smith, but everyone you know and love has been slaughtered by a psychopathic, bloodthirsty maniac. Stop by the station when you get a chance, okay?

How many times had he called Brett Macklin and taken a life away from him?

There wasn't much more death could take from Macklin. First his father, burned alive. Then his lover, blown to bits. Then Mort, the punch line of an obscene and fatal joke.

And now Brooke, cut into pieces.

Shaw wanted to cry, but he was all cried out. His eyes stung and his head ached. He turned away from the window. Lab technicians were scooping the rotten food into evidence bags. Photographers were taking flash pictures of the couch. Weary detectives interviewed Henderson in the kitchen.

The medical examiner carried what was left of Brooke Macklin out of the bedroom. She was slung over his shoulder in a coroner's Glad bag.

Macklin burst into the room just as the coroner walked out. Before Shaw could get to him, Macklin dashed down the hallway to the master bedroom. He stopped cold at the doorway. The white, bloodstained canvas was still on the floor. Someone had drawn where the different appendages and organs had been and written identifications, like "head" or "big toe" or "lung," underneath them.

"Oh God," Macklin muttered hoarsely.

Shaw approached Macklin quietly.

"Did Cory find her?" Macklin turned around slowly.

Shaw nodded. Macklin's face seemed so cold. So evil. So inhuman.

"The woman did this," Shaw said. "She posed as an artist named Isadora Van Rijn."

"Where's Cory?" Macklin asked.

"Next door, at Ms. Shih's apartment," Shaw said. It was hard to even speak. "Stephanie McKimmon, a social worker, is with her."

"Is there somewhere you can take Cory?" Macklin said. "Someplace where she can get help and be safe?"

Shaw nodded.

"It's not safe with me," Macklin said, with an emptiness in his voice that made it sound machine made. "She's not safe with her father."

Macklin slid past Shaw and started to walk away. "Wait," Shaw said.

Macklin stopped.

"Aren't you going to see her?" Shaw asked.

Macklin turned. He started to say something and then cut himself short before the words came out. His gaze met Shaw's. He shook his head no and walked out.

Gallery West was closed on Sunday. Macklin stretched his shirt-sleeve over his fist and smashed his hand through the glass door. The alarm went off, a shrill clamoring that could be heard all over Westwood Village. He yanked up the door latch and let himself in.

He stormed straight to his ex-wife's desk and began pulling out the drawers, looking for anything that might lead him to Isadora Van Rijn.

The alarm drew a crowd to the Westwood Boulevard gallery from Mrs. Field's Cookies and Funtique, where a video display in the window showed continuous previews of *Molten River of Blood.* The people milled around outside the windows, munching their coco-mac cookies and watching Macklin search the desk.

Macklin found Van Rijn's portfolio in the bottom drawer. He sat back in Brooke's chair and studied the slides with horrified fascination.

There was a painting of a man with his head getting crushed between a woman's legs. There was a faceless man sitting in the backseat of a convertible, waving his hand, the top of his head missing. There was a towering Las Vegas hotel/casino, a hand clawing out for help from underneath its foundation. There was a bespectacled man with a guitar around his neck staring out an airplane window, the shadow of a tombstone falling across his face.

Dozens of paintings, each an enigmatic portrait of death. *Who the hell is this woman?* Macklin asked himself. *Why is she killing the people I love?*

Macklin slipped the portfolio under his arm and strode out of the gallery. He shoved past the people, got into his car, slid into the southbound traffic on Westwood Boulevard, turned right onto Wilshire, and headed towards the ocean.

The light switched to red at the Veteran Avenue intersection, and Macklin stopped. To his left was the giant tombstone that was the Federal Building and to his right, the thousands of gravestones that lined the grassy slopes of the Veterans Administration cemetery.

Macklin tried to sort out the confusing events of the last few days. None of it made sense. *Mort meets a woman in Puerto Vallarta and is killed. I go down, she flies up. I arrive and get beaten up. She uses the time to meet Brooke and kill her. I return to LA and then…*

Who is she? How does she know who I am? Why did she murder Mort and Brooke? Why doesn't she just kill me?

The Bitch wants you to suffer, Macky boy, she wants to watch you bleed.

The Bitch was making him bleed, all right. There were only three people left in his life—Shaw, Cory, and Jessica. Shaw could take care of himself and Cory was safe with him. Jessie was—

Vanowen!

Macklin stomped on the gas pedal. The Cadillac shot forward into the crossing traffic. Cars spun, screeched, and smashed into each other as the black specter roared untouched across their path.

I'm gonna kill the fucking BITCH!

Cory Macklin walked into Shaw's house like a mechanical doll powered by remote control. Her eyes were wide, lifeless orbs staring into nothingness.

Sunshine, Shaw's white, live-in girlfriend, was wiping away tears from her face and was still sniffling when she met Cory, Shaw, and McKimmon, the juvenile division social worker, in the entry hall. Sunshine embraced Cory and burst into tears again. Cory stared ahead impassively.

Shaw and McKimmon met each other's gaze. Cory was in shock and not even registering Sunshine's affection.

McKimmon brushed the blond hair out of her eyes and gently tugged at Sunshine. “Why don’t you let me take Cory to your bedroom. She needs some rest.”

Sunshine reluctantly pulled back and let McKimmon lead Cory away. “Oh God, Ronny, it’s so sad.”

Shaw wrapped his arms around Sunshine and held her tightly against him. “She’s tough, like her father. She’ll come through.”

She sniffled and buried her face against Shaw’s neck. “Will the killer come looking for her?”

“I don’t think so,” Shaw said. “But I’ll have an officer here at all times until we catch her.”

“Who is she? Why would she do this?” Sunshine sobbed. Shaw gently smoothed her long brown hair. His reply, the three pathetic words, clogged in his throat.

The Cadillac skidded on the gravel, fishtailing as it ground to a stop in front of Raven Vanowen’s house. Brett Macklin came out of the car in a crouch, his .357 Magnum in his hand.

He scrambled low to the house, braced himself flush against the wall, and slid with his back against it towards the door. Tentatively, he reached out to the doorknob and twisted it. The door was locked.

Macklin aimed at the doorknob and fired. The blast splintered the wood and cracked the latch. He slammed his foot against the door. It crashed open and he spun into a crouch, ready to fire.

All he saw were the bookcases. *Where’s the Bitch?*

He straightened up and moved cautiously through the doorway into the house. He caught a motion to his left. Macklin whipped around, bringing his gun to bear.

Jessica Mordente stood in the entry hall, her arms behind her back, regarding Macklin with curious eyes. She wore a pair of faded jeans and a sweatshirt.

Macklin relaxed, relief washing over him. The Bitch hadn't gotten her yet. She was alive. "Boy, am I glad to see you," he said. "Where's Vanowen?"

Mordente raised her right hand from behind her back. She held a gun.

"Jessie," Macklin began.

She fired. The white-hot slug tore into Macklin's left shoulder and slammed him back against the bookshelves. Macklin tumbled to the floor. The shelves collapsed and an avalanche of books pummeled him.

Mordente approached him, leveling the gun at his head. Macklin blinked to clear his eyes. "Don't, Jessie," he rasped.

He saw her finger tightening on the trigger and he rolled. She fired. A book fluttered into the air like a bird. Macklin crawled behind the couch and grasped a seat cushion to pull himself up.

"It's me," he yelled. He could feel his blood soaking into his shirt and streaming down his sleeve. "Don't make me shoot."

Mordente aimed. Macklin ducked the same instant the gun blasted. A slug ripped into the cushion and raised a snow of white stuffing.

Macklin popped up and fired. The bullet punched into her forearm. She absorbed the impact as if were just a person nudging her.

She narrowed her eyes and advanced on Macklin. He shuffled backwards, pointing his gun at her.

"Don't," he pleaded.

She didn't hear him. She aimed at his head. Macklin shot her twice, once in each leg. Mordente dropped to her knees, her gunshot going astray and slapping into a ceiling beam.

Tears of pain and sorrow rolled down Macklin's cheeks. He slumped against a bookcase, fighting the dizziness. His whole body felt warm from the blood oozing from his wound.

"Please, Jessie, put down your gun."

He watched her stand up. She seemed oblivious to the bullets in her legs and held her gun steady with both hands. She wasn't human anymore. She was a puppet.

Her finger gently squeezed the trigger.

"No!" Macklin screamed to himself as well as to her.

His .357 spat fire. Mordente shuddered. Her chest burst open, spurting blood and pink flesh. The blood-drenched gun dropped from her lifeless hands.

"Jessie," he cried.

She fell forward like a toppled toy soldier. Maniacal laughter wafted in from outside the house.

"I'm not easy, Macklin!"

He whirled around and saw Vanowen's red Ferrari tearing across the gravel. Macklin stared down at his lover, her body lying in an expanding pool of blood.

Jessie...

He had killed her. Just as he had killed Cheshire, Mort, and Brooke.

Now it was the Bitch's turn to die.

CHAPTER ELEVEN

Macklin's Cadillac skidded onto the street and rushed after Vanowen's speeding Ferrari as it charged down Chautauqua Drive.

A row of cars lined up in the left-hand turn lane. Vanowen sped around them, into oncoming traffic. A station wagon swerved out of her path and smashed into the line of waiting cars. Macklin floored it, tearing left across the highway in the Ferrari's smoky wake.

Vanowen weaved in and out of the southbound traffic. Macklin threaded through the traffic behind her. He blinked his eyes into focus. The warm blood from his gunshot wound was seeping down his stomach and soaking his waistband. His eyes blurred, and Macklin accidentally sideswiped a Toyota. The tiny car veered off the road and skidded safely across a parking lot.

Ahead, the Pacific Coast Highway split apart into Ocean Avenue and the eastbound Santa Monica Freeway. Vanowen roared under the Santa Monica Pier and up onto Ocean Avenue. The Ferrari vaulted into traffic with an ear-splitting left turn in front of the Holiday Inn.

A motor home skidded to a stop, smashing into a Nova and launching it into the air. The car burst through the Holiday Inn's cyclone fence and dropped thirty feet into the swimming pool below. People scattered in blind panic.

Vanowen screeched up Ocean Avenue, Macklin close behind. She made a sharp right-hand turn onto Broadway, straight into the face of oncoming traffic.

The cars on the one-way street veered crazily out of her path. One flew off the street and sailed through the plate-glass entrance to the Santa Monica Place mall. Tables, chow mein, people, shopping bags, potted plants, and Styrofoam shreds bounced off the walls. Another car spun out, coming to rest lengthwise across the street. One, two, then three cars smashed into it.

Macklin stayed with her. He wrenched the wheel around. The Cadillac skidded sideways across the asphalt before the tires grabbed hold. He shot up Broadway just as Vanowen's car, to Macklin's horror, turned left again onto what had once been Third Street.

The street was now a shopping center promenade, closed to traffic. The Ferrari barreled through the crowds of shoppers. Bodies rolled across her hood, glanced off her bumper, and flew into the air. People were screaming and scrambling out of her path in absolute terror.

Vanowen didn't avoid them. She aimed for them.

Macklin weaved madly in her wake, dodging the panicked shoppers and the twisted bodies writhing on the pavement. She crashed through the people like a bowling ball into pins. The Bitch was enjoying the carnage.

Twenty yards up, the Spanish-language cinema was spilling out moviegoers. She closed in on them like a shark.

Macklin leaned on his horn, trying to warn them. It was no use. She plowed through them in an explosion of blood, severed limbs, and tattered clothing. He wrenched his wheel to the right to avoid the fleeing crowd. The Cadillac blasted into the display window of a women's clothing store in a splash of glittering glass shards.

He came speeding out, dresses dragging from the edges of his car. Vanowen bounced onto Santa Monica Boulevard and charged to the left. The people crossing the street never had a chance to flee. She smashed into the wall of pedestrians, crushing them under her tires. Macklin couldn't follow her without running over them, too.

Macklin turned right and raced east on Santa Monica. Ahead, he could see three police cars, sirens wailing, speeding towards him. Vanowen was lost. He'd have to save himself now. He twisted the wheel right again and screeched down Fourth Street, made a sharp left onto Arizona, and then skidded into an alley on his left.

He steered the car into a Santa Monica municipal parking structure and spiraled up onto the fifth floor. No one was parked there. The car jerked to a stop facing the glimmering blue ocean. He could hear the police sirens wailing along the streets below him and sagged against the wheel. Unconsciousness was threatening to overtake him. A liquid sense of nausea and dizziness rode over him in waves.

He had to get help. Macklin opened the car door and weakly draped his leg out. He doubted he'd be able to stand. Grabbing the door for support, Macklin rose from the car. His legs were wobbly and the structure moved under his feet. Walls tilted in his eyes. Leaning on the car, he made his way to the railing overlooking Second Street.

Macklin slid along the rail to the stairwell. There was a pay phone on the wall. He fell back against the wall, found two dimes in his pocket, and slipped them into the phone. Squinting to clear his vision, he punched out Shaw's office number and prayed his friend was there.

Shaw answered. *Thank God.*

"I'm in a Santa Monica parking structure," Macklin sputtered. "I've been shot."

"Don't move," Shaw said.

"Don't worry," Macklin mumbled, sliding down the wall. "I won't."

6:00 p.m.

Patients were stacked like cordwood in the corridors of County-USC Medical Center. The hospital had just gotten its share of the sixty-five people injured in the wild Santa Monica car chase. Doctors and police, grieving families and concerned friends, story-hungry reporters and camera men, were all elbowing each other for space.

Brett Macklin was conveniently lost amid the chaos he had helped to create. Shaw wheeled his unconscious friend on a gurney down a maze of corridors and into the doctors' lounge.

Dr. Ralph "Cheeks" Beddicker stood in the center of the room, holding X-rays up to the ceiling light. "I'm risking my neck for you, Shaw."

"I know," Shaw said, glancing down at his unconscious friend. "Just give me the news, okay?"

Beddicker dropped the X-rays on a dinette table and sighed, patting his swelled stomach nervously. "He'll live. The bullet went clean through. It smacked his collarbone on the way out and took a hunk of flesh out with it. An itsy bit lower and it would have sliced open his subclavian artery and probably collapsed his lung."

"Can you fix him up?" Shaw asked.

Beddicker shrugged. "Sure, I'll just pump him full of antibiotics and sew him up."

"Great, can we do it now, right here?"

"This guy should be checked in," Beddicker said. "He's been shot, for Christ's sake. I already risked a lot just doing the X-rays. You don't expect me to just slap on something in the goddamn lounge, do you?"

Shaw nodded and locked the lounge door. "You owe me, Ralph."

"But this guy's gotta be tucked into a bed for a week or so," Beddicker protested. "His body is a fucking disaster area. You can't just run him through here."

"Just do it," Shaw said. "It's important."

"Shit, Ronny, what is this guy to you?"

Shaw pulled out a plastic chair and slumped into it. "A friend in a lot of trouble."

10:00 p.m.

Brett Macklin had to be stopped, Shaw thought as he drove away from Macklin's home, where he had left his semiconscious friend to sleep things off. Shaw knew it wouldn't be long before Macklin got himself killed. And, if today was any measure, maybe hundreds of others along with him.

If Macklin had called Shaw, told him about Vanowen, maybe she'd be behind bars and there wouldn't be anybody scrubbing the blood off the Santa Monica streets tonight.

But Macklin couldn't think rationally anymore.

Perhaps exposing the whole Mr. Jury lunacy was the only thing left to do. It could save lives, and it was a hell of a lot easier than coming up with more lies. He couldn't cover Macklin's trail, and the corpses that lined it, for much longer. The lies were getting weaker and harder to live with.

Shaw turned right on Rose Street and charged towards the ocean. *Macklin isn't thinking. He isn't in control. He isn't obeying any law but his own.*

He isn't Brett Macklin anymore. He's a killer.

I'm going to do my job. I'm going to stop them both. I'm going to end this.

Shaw turned left a few blocks shy of the trendy galleries and cafes of Main Street and wound through the narrow neighborhood streets, which were lined with tiny, boxy homes. Shaw neared his home and came to a grim realization. It was time to reclaim his self-respect. It was time to be a cop again, to enforce the laws Macklin had turned into a joke.

He eased the car to a stop in front of his darkened house and slowly emerged from the car. The ache in his joints reminded him how tired he really was. When he closed the door behind him, he saw a shadow dart into the shrubs surrounding the house.

His right hand reached under his jacket for the reassuring weight of his Smith and Wesson. Clutching his gun, he cautiously walked around his car and up the front walk of his house. His heart thumped and he felt an anxious tingle in his throat. Adrenaline fed his muscles and primed them for quick response. All it would take was the muffled *phump* of a silenced gunshot from one of those bushes and his brains would be fertilizing the lawn.

Stay cool. That's the edge. Be cool.

The crackly sound of dry leaves crunching underfoot came from the darkness to his left, beside the garage. He stopped, cocked his gun, and crept towards the sound. The woman was a professional. He had only one chance. Her first shot, he knew, wouldn't miss.

The chilly night air raised goose bumps on his flesh and heightened the uncomfortable tension he felt as he inched around the edge of the garage and into the black shadows.

He couldn't be seen from the street. She could slice his throat and no one would find him until the stench of his rotting corpse was picked up by the wind.

The bush beside him shook. He whirled. Something moved behind him. He turned again, spinning into a crouch and firing. He heard an agonized screech and saw the gun flash spark in a pair of eyes.

"Drop the gun," the woman said behind him.

Shaw heard the sharp click of a gun being cocked behind him. He hesitated.

"Drop it now."

He let the gun slip from his fingers and fall gently onto the grass. The Bitch had won.

"Turn around," she said.

Dogs barked up and down the street. He could hear the angry sounds of awakened neighbors. He turned slowly to face her and the bullets.

The policewoman stood with her legs spread, her LAPD-issue Smith and Wesson braced in both hands and held confidently in front of her. With her curly brown hair and freckled pale face, and her starched blue uniform, she looked ridiculously like a schoolgirl arriving for a costume party.

Shaw exhaled slowly, his shoulders sagging with relief.

She used one hand to pull a flashlight off her belt and shined it at him. "Sergeant Shaw?"

He winced into the light. He felt stupid.

"I'm Officer Barron. I was assigned to watch the house."

She lowered her gun and smiled sheepishly. "Are you okay?"

"Yeah." He looked over his shoulder. A lump of bloody fur twitched on the grass under the white light. A dead cat.

He closed his eyes and pinched the bridge of his nose. A fucking cat.

Monday, June 17, 7:00 a.m.

The house was completely still. The light from the morning sun spilled in through Brett Macklin's bedroom window—along with the last surviving member of the Bloodhawks gang.

Groove slipped into the shadowy room quietly, his eyes glued on Macklin, who slept braced against his backboard, a blanket bunched up over his legs. Macklin's left arm hung limply in a sling. Blood-soaked gauze wound around his chest and a rib brace hugged his midsection.

But Macklin wasn't hurting enough for Groove. When Groove was through, there wouldn't be anything left of Macklin to bandage.

Groove slid a satchel off his shoulder, his tiny eyes never leaving Macklin's impassive face. It was time to scrag this asshole for good. Twice Groove had seen Macklin. Twice Macklin had looked like easy prey. Twice Groove had watched his friends endure agonizing deaths.

He lifted a Molotov cocktail from the satchel and hefted it in his hand. The gasoline sloshed inside the Coke bottle. Groove grinned and ran his forearm across his sweaty brow.

Groove dug his hand into his pocket and pulled out a lighter. He flicked it. The light from the flame danced on the damp skin of Macklin's face. He touched the flame to the rag sticking out of the bottle and grinned again.

"Burn, you fucker," he hissed, tossing the Molotov cocktail. In that same instant, Macklin's eyes flashed open and he squeezed the trigger of the .357 he held under the blanket.

The bullet tore through the blanket and blasted apart the Molotov cocktail. It exploded in midair, igniting Macklin's blanket and splashing a wave of fire over Groove. The Bloodhawk fell screaming against the wall, his body melting into a ball of flame.

Macklin shook his head at Groove's flailing, fire-consumed body. "You never learn."

He casually tossed the burning blanket over him and pulled himself to his feet, his face knotted in pain. Macklin hobbled towards the door, glanced back once at the bedroom, now a chamber of pulsating fire, and then stumbled out, his singed legs smoking.

Wednesday, June 19, noon

Brett Macklin's name was chiseled in the marble tombstone. The fresh dirt underneath it was strewn with cut flowers. The grass surrounding the grave was flat and torn from the dozens of people who had stood mournfully an hour ago and listened to Father Harriman's standard eulogy.

He shifted his gaze from the distant tombstone, squinted up at the blazing afternoon sun and then down at his wristwatch. The crystal was cracked, but he could still see that only an hour had passed since the funeral, since he had crept behind this tree, lifted the binoculars to his bloodshot eyes, and watched his daughter, a hundred yards away, shake with sobs.

Not many men get to see their own funerals.

"This won't work, Mack," said a voice behind him. Macklin turned and saw Shaw approaching quietly, his hands buried deep in the pockets of his black slacks. Right on time. Macklin had called Shaw after escaping from the fire. Shaw made sure Groove's corpse was identified as Brett Macklin.

"If I'm dead, the Bitch will stop," Macklin said. "She'll let down her guard, get careless."

"She's sharp. She won't buy the ruse that you died in that fire." Shaw leaned against the tree and studied Macklin's face. "Even if this works, you aren't going to see Cory again, are you?"

Macklin shook his head. "Everyone I love dies. I want to spare my daughter. The money from our life insurance policies should guarantee her security."

Using the arm that had been in the sling, he put the tiny pair of folding binoculars in his pocket and walked away. The motion hurt bad. The pain was so strong, Macklin had a hard time remembering what life had been like without it. The pain wasn't only physical. His heart had been torn out and buried with the corpses of his loved ones. Mordente's body, jerking against the impact of his gunshots, danced in front of his eyes.

"What can you tell me about the Bitch?" Macklin asked.

Shaw shook his head. It had gone too far already. Giving Macklin any information now was like giving a lunatic a loaded gun.

"Nothing," Shaw said.

Macklin grabbed Shaw roughly by the shoulders, spun him around, slammed him forward against the tree, and jammed his .357 Magnum into Shaw's back. "I've lost everything now. My family. My friends. My daughter. My life. I want the Bitch who did this to me."

The jagged bark tore into Shaw's cheek. Tiny rivulets of blood dripped off his chin. "Go ahead, Mack. Pull the trigger. Go over the edge. You're no better than she is."

Macklin kept Shaw pinned against the tree, removed the detective's gun, and tossed it away. He searched him with his free hand, turning out the pockets and letting Shaw's badge, wallet, and assorted papers fall to the ground.

"C'mon, Mack, admit it. You don't think anymore. You just kill. You've lost yourself to the violence," Shaw said. "You're dead now. Walk away before your bloodlust kills more innocent people."

Macklin found the computer printout in Shaw's inside coat pocket. He shook it to unfold it.

"You ran my description of Vanowen and Cory's description of Van Rijn through Interpol," Macklin said, reading. "You got a match."

Macklin's eyes narrowed and he stepped back from Shaw, though he kept his gun trained on him.

"Demetria Davila," Macklin read slowly. "International assassin. Wanted for murders all over the world. Expert at disguise."

Shaw pushed himself away from the tree, picked up a Kleenex off the lawn, and wiped his bloodied cheek. Macklin eyed Shaw warily.

"She's a sadist. Big surprise," Macklin scanned the printout. "Delights in torture. Loves to kill. Murders are orgasms. Eighty-three gruesome killings have been tied to her. She's paid well. Governments are about the only ones who can afford her."

Macklin rolled up the printout and tossed it at Shaw. "She's a real Girl Scout."

"She's out of your league, Mack. You'll die and take innocent people with you," Shaw said. "I can't let you do that."

"Too bad," Macklin pistol-whipped Shaw across the face, knocking him to the ground, where he lay groaning in semiconsciousness. "You and Cory are all I have left. I'm doing this for you."

Macklin put the .357 under his waistband and walked away.

Macklin flew the chopper down the California coast to La Jolla and the heavily fortified cliffside compound belonging to the man who'd hired the Bitch.

There was only one man who had the money and the motive to curse him with Demetria Davila. After leaving Shaw, Macklin's subconscious had whispered the name to him with sickening clarity... Justin Threllkiss.

It was Threllkiss who'd covertly financed White Wash, a racist, white supremacist organization. It was White Wash that had convinced Threllkiss' coked-out, sadistic grandson to masquerade as Macklin and massacre blacks as a way to spark a race war. Macklin had destroyed White Wash—and the grandson with it.

But he'd left Threllkiss alive.

Threllkiss had to be the one.

But if Macklin was wrong, it was no loss. Threllkiss was racist scum who deserved to die, a loose end Macklin should have tied up long ago.

The security system at the Threllkiss compound had been built on the concept that if any threat ever came, it would be on foot or on wheels. Nobody expected an air assault.

Who would?

So the high walls, the razor wire, the security cameras, and everything else were rendered laughably pointless if the threat arrived in a helicopter.

And Macklin had arrived.

He buzzed the property, shooting two guards on the rooftop and three more that were walking the grounds, before he landed the chopper on the lawn. Macklin jumped out brandishing two Uzis, one in his right hand, the other slung by a strap over his left shoulder.

Three slavering guard dogs immediately charged towards him. He calmly took a remote control out of his pocket with his left hand and pressed its single button.

The dogs jerked spasmodically in midstride as their collars zapped them into submission.

Macklin knew about Craven's kinky love of electricity as a way to tame man and beast.

It wasn't hard for Macklin, before embarking on his assault, to discover the frequency of the dog collars and adjust his own garage door opener to match it. He didn't want to have to kill a dog... but he had no qualms about shooting the men on his list.

He released the button and the dogs whimpered away, perhaps assuming that Macklin was one of their masters by virtue of having the God-like power to zap the shit out of them.

A bullet tore into the grass at Macklin's feet. Another grazed his cheek. Macklin kept walking. He felt no fear. He felt no pain. Only hate. He pocketed the remote and gripped an Uzi in each hand.

He fired to his left at a guard crouched behind a bush. The guard's head burst like a piñata. He fired to his right. A guard screamed and tumbled out a second-floor window, splattering like a raindrop on the pavement below and splashing Macklin with warm blood.

He walked on. He was a man with nothing left to lose.

Craven ran out of the house with a shotgun. Macklin shot him in the leg, took the shotgun from him, and batted him across the face with it before tossing it into the bushes. Craven lay whimpering on the ground.

Macklin kicked open the back door and cleared his trail with blazing bullets. The scorching slugs propelled four guards along the shag carpet in a bloody living room ballet. Macklin squinted into the settling debris for any movement. Bullet holes had turned classic oil paintings into confetti. Priceless sculptures were reduced to piles of marble shards.

Macklin sloshed through the gore-soaked carpet and tracked blood, sweat, and brains across the marble entry hall and up the steps of the spiral staircase.

Bullets suddenly tore into the walls, handrails, and steps around him. Macklin quickly dropped down to a squat. His Uzis spat death. Three bodies tumbled down the stairs towards him. He flattened himself against the wall. The bodies rolled past, splattering a red carpet of welcome to the second floor.

He stalked down the hallway to a pair of tall oak doors. A guard whirled out of an adjoining doorway, brandishing a shotgun. Macklin fired his Uzis before the guard squeezed his trigger down. The lead spray spun the guard around. The guard's shotgun blasted wildly into the oak doors. The doors splintered open.

Justin Threllkiss stood in the dissipating cloud of wood shavings and smoke. Several hundred-dollar bills wafted in the air, propelled by the residual force of the shotgun blast. The rosewood desk beside Threllkiss was piled high with stacks of money.

Macklin moved slowly into the room, his Uzis trained on the freckle-skinned magnate. Threllkiss leaned shakily on his pearl-handled cane, his eyes wide behind his tortoiseshell glasses.

"All this"—Threllkiss motioned to pile of cash with his wavering cane—"and more is yours if you let me live."

Macklin shook his head. A hundred-dollar bill floated into the crystal chandelier above him. He walked up to the desk and stabbed at the stacks of money with the muzzle of his Uzi. Hundreds of hundred-dollar bills spilled onto the floor.

"You killed my family," Macklin said.

Threllkiss raised his cane and pointed it at Macklin. "And you killed mine."

A spear shot out of Threllkiss' cane. Macklin jerked out of the way as the spear sliced across his cheek and stabbed into the wall behind his head.

Macklin regained his balance and felt the blood dribbling down his cheek. The spear shaft quivered.

He wiped his cheek with the back of his hand and glanced down at it. Blood dripped between his fingers.

He looked up at Threllkiss.

"Almost," Macklin said. He bashed Threllkiss across the face with the back of his blood-smeared hand.

Threllkiss flew backwards into the pile of money. Thousands of dollars fluttered in the air. Macklin grabbed a handful of money and smothered Threllkiss with it.

The old man jerked and convulsed, trying to free himself from Macklin's suffocating grasp. Gritting his teeth, Macklin pressed down harder, crushing Threllkiss' face under the cold cash. Threllkiss thrashed, kicked, and grabbed, and Macklin felt none of it. His death hold wouldn't budge. The old man flopped like a fish.

Threllkiss' struggles gave way to the convulsing rattle of death. Macklin felt Threllkiss' life shuddering under him. The body jerked once, arched up, and then fell hard into the money.

Macklin released his hold, tossed aside the money in his hand, and stepped back. Threllkiss lay upon the cash, his eyes bulging and his mouth agape, crumbled hundred-dollar bills clogging his throat.

Justin Threllkiss was dead.

But in the blinding hate of revenge, Macklin had forgotten what mattered most—the Bitch was still alive.

Again, Macklin had failed. He had let Threllkiss die before getting something on the cunt who had killed Mort and Brooke, who had plowed over more than sixty innocent people.

Macklin backed out of the room and then dashed down the stairway, leaping over the corpses in his path. He emerged from the house and squinted into black smoke. On the lawn, several yards away, Macklin saw the way to find the Bitch.

Craven lay on the ground, his bloody leg twisted at a grotesque angle underneath him. The snarling dog snapped ferociously at Craven's face. In panic, Craven pressed his remote control. The electric charge coursed through the dog, jolting him, keeping him at bay. Barely.

Macklin came up beside the jerking, howling dog and pointed his Uzi at Craven. "Turn it off."

"He'll kill me!" Craven whined. Macklin squeezed the trigger. The slugs tore divots in the grass around Craven's head.

"Off," Macklin said.

Craven dropped the remote. Macklin crushed it under his boot. The dog lunged for Craven's throat. Craven bashed his fists against the dog's snout. The dog bellowed. Claws dug into Craven's chest. Craven screamed in terror and despair.

Macklin grabbed Sam's collar. The dog's moist fangs hung over Craven's ripe neck. Craven could feel the dog's hot breath on his skin. Sam strained against Macklin's hold, snarling viciously.

"Where's Davila?" Macklin demanded.

"I don't know," Craven whined, trying to slide away from the growling beast, from the wide, inhuman eyes, from the sharp, white fangs.

"You're Alpo." Macklin released the dog and it went for Craven, who screamed again, his arms flailing in a pathetic attempt to grab the dog's snout and keep the snapping jaws away from his neck.

Suddenly the dog reared back and hung suspended over Craven's face. Macklin again held Sam by the collar. Saliva dribbled from the dog's wet mouth onto Craven's wide forehead. Scratches oozed blood on Craven's face and between the tatters that remained of his clothes.

"Demetria Davila." Macklin said.

Craven shook with terror, his eyes locked on Sam's gaping mouth.

"She's going to kill your daughter," Craven huffed. Macklin's face tightened with rage.

The dog growled. Or maybe it was Macklin.

"No," Craven sputtered, reading Macklin's eyes.

Macklin let go of the dog's collar and sprinted back to the chopper. Behind him, Craven's guts flew like pillow stuffing.

CHAPTER TWELVE

"She's at your house. She's going to kill them all." Brett Macklin's words crackled over the radio in Sergeant Ronald Shaw's car.

Shaw called for backup. And, without looking, made a sudden U-turn across Lincoln Boulevard. Cars moving in both directions came to wild, screeching stops. His Plymouth tore down the street, the siren screaming.

He steered madly through the Venice streets, screeching around corners, jumping curbs, charging against oncoming traffic. Cars spun out all around him, clogging up the traffic in his destructive wake.

How could he have left them alone? How could he have been so stupid?

He skidded to a stop outside his house and burst out of his car, gun drawn. He aimed at his front door across the hood of his car. The engine rattled and the car felt hot. The house was still.

Somebody should have peered out the window. Someone should have come running out the front door. Officer Barron should have come out.

It felt bad. Real bad.

Shaw ran in a crouch from the cover of his car and cut a zigzagging path to his front door. He flattened his back against the wall and held his gun up high.

Across the street, Jess and Gladys Furnow pulled back their blinds and waved at Shaw. There was always something interesting happening at the Shaw house.

He took a deep breath and let his free hand drop to the doorknob. His hand twisted the knob open. The door creaked as it swung a few inches into the dark entry hall.

Shaw saw the Furnows looking curiously at him. Up the street, Dave McDonnell, a heavyset magazine editor, proudly waxed his black Porsche and, seeing Shaw, crinkled his face in confusion. If they only knew what evil thrived in their midst. Death, dark and sinister, was now their neighbor.

The detective held out his gun and spun into the door frame, ready to face Davila, in whatever guise. Instead, he faced a living room full of defenseless Levitz furniture.

And Officer Barron.

Her corpse lay sprawled like a lion-skin rug, head propped up on its chin, mouth taped open in a mock growl.

A fireplace poker sticking out of her back nailed her to the floor. Blood seeped into the cracks between the floor tiles.

The sadistic bitch was McKimmon.

Shaw swallowed back the bile and edged around the body. Barron was a fresh kill. Maybe Sunshine and Cory were alive. Maybe. His eyes searched the shadows for the slightest movement; his ears strained for the slightest sound.

Where the fuck is my backup?

He heard a glass break in the kitchen. In the silence of the house, the sound was like a sonic boom. Shaw inched his way across the living room toward the kitchen door. His shirt clung to his damp back and his jacket suddenly felt constricting.

The kitchen door parted a crack.

Inviting.

Shaw narrowed his eyes. His finger tightened on the trigger.

The broken glass, the open door. Bait to a trap.

But Shaw had no choice. He had to take action. The lives of Sunshine and Cory were at stake. The door loomed up, huge and menacing.

Behind it, he knew, hell waited.

He braced himself against the wall near the door hinge. Using his gun barrel, he eased open the door. The slowly widening crack revealed Cory, curled in a corner beside the kitchen table, her shocked eyes locked onto something across the room.

She's alive!

Shaw slowly slipped into the kitchen, his back hugging the door. Cory didn't seem to notice him. He followed her eyes to the opposite wall and straightened up.

Sunshine.

He stopped breathing. The room rolled under his feet and the door silently swung closed.

Sunshine was stabbed to the kitchen wall. Table knives. Forks. Steak knives. Skewers. Butcher knives. They all held her corpse in place.

Demetria Davila leaped out from behind the kitchen door, a gleaming butcher knife held over her head. Shaw spun and fired, blasting a hole in the wall where she had stood. She screamed with devilish glee, her eyes wild, her mouth wide in a delirious grin. He fired again as she buried her butcher knife deep in his chest. The errant slug blasted harmlessly into the ceiling.

Shaw fell backward, the shiny metal blurring in his eyes as she thrust again and again into his chest.

Demetria Davila stood up, her arms covered in Shaw's blood up to her elbows. She tossed back her head in a wild laugh. Cory gripped her face with her hands and screamed until she fainted, her t body falling to one side.

Davila planted her foot on Shaw's quivering stomach and yanked the butcher knife from his chest. It made a moist, sucking sound as it slid out of his convulsing body. Grinning, she stepped through the puddles of blood towards the child.

The house shuddered. Davila froze and heard the unmistakable rumble of helicopter blades churning the air. She dropped the knife, picked up Shaw's gun, and walked into the living room. Through the drapes of the living room window, she could see the dark outline of the chopper landing on the lawn. She smiled and fired. The slugs tore through the drapes and shattered the glass.

Brett Macklin dove out of the chopper, the bullets whizzing dangerously close to him. He rolled across the lawn, popped up in firing stance, and riddled the draped window with gunfire from his Uzi.

Macklin ran forward and leaped through the window. He landed, rolled, and came up in a crouch. Officer Barron stared lifelessly at him.

Outside, the wail of police sirens grew close.

"Killing is an art, Macklin," he heard Davila yell, "an art I've perfected."

He kicked the kitchen door open and burst inside. To his left, Sunshine's corpse stuck to the wall. Shaw twitched in blood at her feet. Macklin turned and saw Cory—covered in blood and crumpled in a heap.

Macklin rushed to her and gently turned her over. There were no wounds. The blood belonged to the others.

She was alive.

Davila was gone.

He left Cory for the police and ran back to his chopper. Neighbors were coming out of their houses. Police cars screeched around the corner. Macklin lifted the chopper into the air as the squad cars converged on Shaw's house.

From the sky, the neighborhood looked like a giant model. Everything was clear—nothing was hidden. Macklin peered down, searching for any sign of the murderous Bitch.

A few doors down from Shaw's house, Macklin saw Dave McDonnell lying facedown on his driveway, tread marks on his back. A mile ahead, Macklin could see McDonnell's black Porsche weaving between cars.

The Bitch.

Macklin dived for her speeding car. She turned sharply, careening into the maze of narrow streets that led to the famed

Venice canals. The network of seedy backwaters was all that was left of the tidal flats a turn-of-the-century developer tried to transform into Renaissance Italy.

Macklin could see squad cars closing off the streets in Davila's wake. She was trapped between the cops and the canals.

Or so he thought.

She burst through a picket fence and, to Macklin's sheer horror, charged for the family picnicking on the lawn. The family ran in all directions. He watched helplessly as she plowed over the family and then veered to strike a fleeing child. The kid bounced off her hood, sailed into the canal, and sunk into the morass of sewage.

The Porsche crashed through the fence again and skidded onto the street. Macklin stuck the barrel of his Uzi out the window. Bullets skitted on the asphalt around her car. She whipped around a corner and up onto a sidewalk. Macklin, in impotent rage, saw the carnage that was to come.

She cut a swath of blood through a crowd of beachgoers. Severed limbs spun into the air. The Porsche roared off the sidewalk and into the street. A huge Bekins moving truck suddenly pulled out of a side street. The truck grumbled into her path.

She veered sharply. The car spun. She regained control of the car and barreled across a vacant lot toward the narrow canal. Macklin charged over her, banked, and came around facing her as she picked up speed.

She was racing for the water.

She was going to jump it.

Macklin's eyes burned with fury. A victorious yell escaped from his lips as he bore down on the murderous Bitch.

The Porsche launched into the air above the canal. Macklin flew straight at her.

They smashed together head-on. The sky erupted with a monstrous thunderclap of flame. The helicopter and the Porsche meshed into a pulsating fire cloud that filled the sky and rained jagged, white-hot metal onto the grimy waters.

A helicopter blade spun through air and sliced into the side of the Bekins truck trailer. Trees and bushes along the bank erupted in flames. Windows shattered up and down the canal.

And amidst the steaming debris on the water, a blackened body floated facedown towards the shore.

EPILOGUE

December. Dawn.

The fog rolled in over the water and across the Pacific Coast Highway, slapping against the dry cliff like a wave and washing thickly over the Santa Monica high-rises.

Sergeant Ronald Shaw felt strange being outside. The world didn't seem the same. It probably never would.

He grasped the collar of his trench coat tight around his neck and looked out over the water into the hazy distance. An immense flock of squawking seagulls swirled over the frothy swells. He shivered in his jacket and scolded himself for not wearing heavier clothing.

The surf rode high on the beach, arms of water reaching out for the three or four joggers he saw traversing the shore. *Life goes on.* There were so many other people, so many who were living lives no different now from those they'd led six months ago. It was hard for him to believe.

God, how he wished he was one of them.

Shaw turned and strode down the pier, careful not to stray far from the security of the handrail. He wasn't used to walking yet, and lugging the heavy briefcase in his left hand was taking a lot out of him. Six months of confinement, hospital food, blank walls, and an endless stream of game shows were hard to shake off. So were the nightmares, the horrific, recurring images of Sunshine staring down at him with large, dead eyes.

But at least he had survived.

Shaw breathed deeply, relishing the cool bite in the air. The scent of rubbing alcohol was gloriously absent from the ocean mist. A lone merchant lifted the storm boards from the windows of his fish market and paid no attention to Shaw as he hobbled past. At the end of the pier, the single fisherman was just a misty, solitary shape.

"Hey, got a light?"

The voice startled Shaw. He turned, his heart thumping nervously. A stubble-faced wino grinned toothlessly at him, a cigarette stub hanging from the corner of his mouth.

"Don't smoke," Shaw mumbled, vaguely disappointed and, in an odd way, relieved.

The wino shrugged and shuffled off to bum a light off the fish merchant. Shaw sighed and walked on. His chest ached and his arms felt leaden.

The doctors said he'd be as good as new in a year. *Good as new.*

Shaw fell into a bench at the end of the pier. The fisherman hunched on the rail beside him and cast his line out to the warning buoys several yards out to sea. Waves whipped the pier's aging pilings. The heavy stench of fish hung in the air around the fisherman. Shaw glanced into the man's plastic bucket and saw two scrawny salmon flopping in a few cups of filthy seawater.

Shaw looked up into the fisherman's pale, scarred face and dark, brooding eyes and motioned to the bucket. "Is this good or bad luck?"

The fisherman glanced down at him and then his catch.

"Bad."

Shaw nodded. "Well, it's a nice morning, anyway."

The fisherman shrugged and gently reeled in his line. Shaw glanced over his shoulder and looked down the length of the pier. The wino urinated against the abandoned Sinbad dance hall. A woman in a dirty tank top and faded jeans roller-skated towards them, rolls of fat jiggling on her body as her wheels thudded between the planks.

Shaw faced the sea again. A trawler, anchored offshore, bounced on the water. He stared at it, strangely fascinated. Maybe he'd just do the same thing. Shaw shivered and buried his hands deep in his warm pockets.

The fisherman set down his pole and unscrewed the cap on a metal Thermos. Shaw smelled the tantalizing aroma of fresh, ground coffee, steaming hot. The fisherman seemed to sense this. His lips twisted into a thin smile.

He offered Shaw the plastic cup.

Shaw waved it away. "No, thanks, I—"

The fisherman ignored Shaw's protests and set it on the bench. "I'll drink from the Thermos." As if to prove his point, he took a sip. Shaw smiled and took the cup.

"Thanks."

The fisherman leaned against the wood railing and looked down at Shaw. "You feeling okay?"

Shaw nodded, savoring his sip of coffee. It was a far cry from the sewage the hospital served.

The fisherman nodded and took another sip. "I've been worried about you."

Shaw felt another shiver course through his body. But it wasn't the cold. He met the fisherman's hard gaze. The fisherman gave him a grim smile.

"Mack," Shaw said.

Brett Macklin nodded.

"My God, your face. It's completely different."

Macklin took a seat beside his old friend. "Most of it is steel, plastic, and superglue." He took a drink from his Thermos. The hot steam felt nice on his face. "I looked in the mirror and I saw a stranger. It's the way it should be."

Shaw used his foot to slide the briefcase over to Macklin. "This is from Mayor Stocker."

Macklin didn't look at it. "How much?"

"It's a hundred thousand dollars of the taxpayers' money," Shaw said. "He's buying your silence and the end of your vigilance in this city."

"Okay by me." He tipped the Thermos and swallowed the remainder of his coffee.

Shaw studied his old friend, looking for some sign of familiarity in the strange face. "Where will you go?"

Macklin stood and zipped up his Windbreaker. "Don't know. Wander, I guess." He squinted at the horizon. The rising sun was bleeding slowly into the clouds. "I've got a job to do."

Shaw sighed. "What do you want me to tell Cory when she gets out of the mental hospital?"

"Tell her the truth," Macklin said. "Tell her I'm dead."

He offered his hand to Shaw, who grasped it tightly for a long moment before shaking it. "Good-bye, Mack."

"Take care of yourself, Ronny." Macklin picked up the briefcase, smiled at his friend, and walked away.

Shaw listened to the waves break against the rocky breakwater and watched a lone seagull float gently on the crosswinds. Behind him, he could feel Brett Macklin quietly fading into the fog.

THE END

AFTERWORD

The creation of Brett Macklin—and "Ian Ludlow"—is explained in this essay, published as a "My Turn" column in Newsweek *magazine in 1985. Pinnacle Books went out of business before this novel—originally entitled* .357 Vigilante #4: Killstorm*—could be published. The fifth book,* Designated Hitler, *never got beyond the outline stage.*

HOT SEX, GORY VIOLENCE

How One Student Earns Course Credit and Pays Tuition

My name is Ian Ludlow. Well, not really. But that's the name on my four *.357 Vigilante* adventures that Pinnacle Books will publish this spring. Most of the time I'm Lee Goldberg, a mild-mannered UCLA senior majoring in mass communications and trying to spark a writing career at the same time. It's hard work. I haven't quite achieved a balance between my dual identities of college student and hack novelist.

The adventures of Mr. Jury, a vigilante into doing the LAPD's dirty work, are often created in the wee hours of the night, when I should be studying, meeting my freelance-article deadlines, or, better yet, sleeping. More often than not, my nocturnal writing spills over into my classes the next morning. Brutal fistfights, hot sexual encounters, and gory violence are frequently scrawled across my anthropology notes or written amid my professor's insights on Whorf's hypothesis. Students sitting next to me who glance at my lecture notes are shocked to see notations like "Don't move, scumbag, or I'll wallpaper the room with your brains."

I once wrote a pivotal rape scene during one of my legal-communications classes, and I'm sure the girl who sat next to me thought I was a psychopath. During the first half of the lecture, she kept looking with wide eyes from my notes to my face as if my nose were melting onto my binder or something. At the break she disappeared, and I didn't see her again the rest of the quarter. My professors, though, seem pleased to see me sitting in the back of the classroom writing furiously. I guess they think I'm hanging on their every word. They're wrong.

I've tried to lessen the strain between my conflicting identities by marrying the two. Through the English department, I'm getting academic credit for the books. That amazes my grandpa Cy, who can't believe there's a university crazy enough to reward me for writing "lots of filth." The truth is, it's writing and it's learning, and it's getting me somewhere. Just where, I'm not sure. My grandpa Cy thinks it's going to get me the realization I should join him in the furniture business.

I don't admit to many people that I'm writing books. It sounds so pompous, arrogant, and phony when you say that in Los Angeles. See, everybody in Los Angeles is writing a book or screenplay. Walk into any 7-Eleven, tell the clerk you're an agent or a producer, and he'll whip out a handwritten, 630-page epic he's been keeping under the register for a chance like this.

I do involve my closest friends in the secret world of Ian Ludlow. When I finished writing my first sex scene, I made six copies and passed them around for a critique. I felt like I was distributing pornography. "How do you compliment a sex scene?" a girl I know complained. "It's embarrassing." Another friend rewrote the scene so it sounded like a cross between a beating and extensive surgery.

Among my family and even my friends, I find myself constantly apologizing for what I'm doing. Maybe I wouldn't if I were writing a Larry McMurtry or John Updike book. But I know what this is. This is a black cover with a rugged hero in the forefront, shoving a massive gun into the reader's face. I feign disgust, mutter something about "a guy's got to break in somehow," and quickly change the subject.

But the truth is, it's fun. And since Ian Ludlow is the guy who will take the heat for it, I can let myself relax and enjoy it. I'm building on those childhood hours spent in front of my mom's ancient Smith Corona, banging out hokey tales about superspies and supervillains. My work is still hokey, except now someone is paying me for it. And paying me not badly, either. I can pay for a whole year of college from the advances for the four novels.

The opportunity came my way thanks to Lewis Perdue, a journalism professor who writes those bulky conspiracy thrillers and harbors dreams of being the next Robert Ludlum. I used to read his manuscripts and debate the merits of Lawrence Sanders and Ken Follett. Then, when Pinnacle asked him to do an "urban man's action-adventure series," he passed it on to me. Pretty soon I was buying books like *The Butcher*, *The Executioner*, *The Penetrator*, *The Destroyer*, and *The Terminator* by the armful and flipping through the latest issues of *Soldier of Fortune* and *Gung-Ho*. After a week or two of wading through this, I was ready to spill blood across my home computer screen.

There's a part of me that doesn't like what I'm doing. It lectures me while I'm making some bad guy eat hot lead. It tells me I should be writing a novel about relationships and feelings, about the problems my peers are facing. *I will,* I say to myself, *later. There's plenty of time.*

Made in the USA
Columbia, SC
16 December 2024

49275512R10322